Becoming Carlotta

Becoming Carlotta

A Biographical Novel

Brenda Murphy

BRICKTOP HILL BOOKS

2018

Bricktop Hill Books
PO Box 1016
Willimantic, CT 06226

Library of Congress Control Number: 2018912691

ISBN: 9780997366969

To George

Contents

Part 1

The Girl of the Golden West

Chapter 1

Nellie yanked the curtains open and stuck her head out the window, craning her neck to see the strip of sky between the two houses. It was bright blue. She couldn't help singing to herself as she tackled her Sunday chores. Then she got ready for church. She washed up, put on her freshly laundered white cotton shirtwaist and blue linen skirt, and took down her unruly hair. Eyeing it for a moment in the little mirror on the bedroom wall, she let out a quick sigh. Her sisters might envy her luxurious chestnut brown curls, but they didn't have to tame them.

"Nellie! Why are you just standing there? It's time to go," her mother said as she passed her room.

"Just five minutes, Mama!" she called after her.

She quickly wove her long hair into one braid and looped it up to the nape of her neck, tying a blue ribbon around it. Then, with the help of a hatpin, she set her little straw hat on top of her head at what she thought was a jaunty angle. Taking a quick look in the mirror, she decided it would have to do. She picked up her little bag and ran down the stairs.

Caroline Gotchett saw that her family walked to church together every Sunday, the three daughters and four sons still at home all decently dressed and well groomed. She might be divorced from their father, but that didn't mean the neighborhood would see them as anything but a respectable and united family. On this beautiful June day, they enjoyed their walk, and the younger boys had to be corrected a few times when they got a little rambunctious. Finally, Caroline made Oliver walk with her to separate him from Elonidas. During the service the two boys sat on either side of their mother, flanked by their big sisters, so they couldn't get up to much. Except for the sermon, the service didn't make the boys too restless. They enjoyed singing as much as the rest of the family, and they sang well.

After the service, Caroline lingered, talking with her neighbors while the boys ran around and the girls gossiped with their friends. Of all the places where she had lived since she and John Gotchett had come by wagon train from Missouri, Caroline liked Oakland best. The weather was perfect, to her way of thinking, and the town had the same pioneer spirit she had brought from the Midwest. All the people she knew had come with nothing to speak of and made lives for their families. In 1884, the wagon trains were becoming a dim memory. Everyone travelled by train now. The trip that had taken them weeks in 1857 now took three days. But many of her friends here remembered the early times. It was a bond they shared.

While she was talking with her friend Mary Swenson, Sophie Dahl came up to them with her brother Chris, a tall and husky man whom Caroline had met at his mother's funeral earlier in the week. Caroline had gathered that he was a farmer out in the San Joaquin Valley.

"I've been noticing that you have a fine big family, Mrs. Gotchett," he said. "Such lovely daughters."

Caroline reddened, a little embarrassed by the praise. "Well, this isn't all of them, Mr. Tharsing," she said, "I have another daughter who is married."

"Fred and I thought we would pay a little visit this afternoon if it's convenient," said Sophie, "and bring Chris to meet your family."

Caroline was little surprised. The Dahls were not in the habit of visiting her. "That would be very nice," she said. "Is your wife here as well, Mr. Tharsing?"

Chris looked at the ground. "My wife died a year ago," he said.

"I'm sorry to hear that," said Caroline. "It's hard to farm without a wife to help you. Do you have any children?"

"No," said Chris, looking at the little boys chasing each other around the churchyard. "It's one of the sorrows of my life that I haven't any little ones to bring up." His voice was gruff, with a Danish accent.

"Well, we look forward to seeing you in our home," said Caroline, as her boys came running up, now eager to get home to their Sunday dinner. "Why don't you come about two o'clock, and we can have our coffee and dessert together?"

"Why thank you, Mrs. Gotchett," said Sophie. "That would be lovely."

On the walk home, Caroline pondered Sophie's motives for bringing her brother to meet the family. It seemed likely that her daughters were the object in view. Chris looked to be in his mid-thirties, perhaps a good match for her Tena, who at twenty-five needed to find a husband soon. He was a little old for Alice at twenty-two, not to mention Nellie, who wouldn't be eighteen until October.

Nellie walked ahead with Alice, setting a quick pace. She was as eager as her little brothers to get home, but her goal was to get through dinner as soon as possible so she would be ready to go for a walk when Chapman came. Mel had started calling regularly on Sundays at the beginning of the summer, and their long walks together were the high point of her week. She loved spending time with him, exploring parts of the country she had never seen before, talking over their past week, listening to his big plans for the future once he was through law school. She was pretty sure he meant for those plans to include her. Last Sunday they had planned this week's excursion out to Lake Merritt, and he was coming right after dinner at one-thirty so they could get an early start. Alice had already promised to do her share of the dinner dishes so she could slip away.

When the girls were clearing the table and getting ready to bring in the dessert, Mrs. Gotchett told them to wait. They had guests coming at two o'clock, and they would have their dessert then. The girls looked at each other.

"Who, Mama?" asked Tena.

"Mr. and Mrs. Dahl are bringing her brother to visit. You know they lost their mother last week, so we should do what we can for them. I want everyone to be in the dining room at two o'clock."

Nellie looked up from the serving platter she was carrying. "But, Mama, Mr. Chapman is coming this afternoon. We have plans to take a walk."

Caroline pursed her lips and regarded her youngest daughter. "You and Melvin Chapman can walk anytime," she said. "Mr. Tharsing lives a long way out, nearly a hundred miles. We should entertain him as a family. Mr. Chapman can stay for the afternoon if he wants."

Nellie's cheeks flushed. She turned abruptly and walked out of the dining room, but she knew better than to make any more objections. Her mother must be planning for them to sing. She must want to impress this Mr. Tharsing. If she argued with her, she might just end up having to send Mel away.

When Mel arrived, exactly at one-thirty, she explained the situation. He wasn't nearly as disappointed about missing their walk as she had thought he would be. He settled in next to her on the couch in the parlor and talked with her about the events of the week until Tenie and Alice came in from the kitchen. Then they started a game of penny poker, seven-card stud, on the dining room table. Before long, Mel had all three of them giggling helplessly with his commentary on the game.

When the Dahls arrived with Chris Tharsing, they swept the cards away, pocketed their money, and went to the parlor to greet them. With a touch of pride, Caroline introduced her children in order. "This is Tena, Alice, Willie, Nellie, Freddie, Elonidas, and Oliver," she said, and they put out their hands in turn, the girls straightforwardly, the boys rather stiffly with a tinge of embarrassment. "And this is Mr. Chapman, a family friend," said Caroline.

Mel's clear blue eyes looked directly into Tharsing's, so dark brown that they were nearly black. Both of them were tall, although Tharsing was more thickly built. As they shook hands, Tharsing, gripping more tightly than was necessary, pulled Mel slightly off balance. "How do you do," he said.

Mel laughed. "I'm well, thank you. How are you? I understand you're visiting from Stanislaus County."

"Yes," said Tharsing. "My mother died last week, and I'm staying with my sister Sophie while my brother and I tend to her estate. I have a fruit farm in Tuolumne City, near Modesto. I'm a horticulturalist by profession, engaging in progressive and scientific farming."

"That sounds like interesting work," said Mel with a little smile.

"Yes, it is. What do you do?"

"Well, at the moment, I'm working in our family painting business while I study law. I'm going to spend next semester at the Law School and hope to be admitted to the bar at the end of the year."

Tharsing nodded. "It is a good thing you have the family business to fall back on. I hear it often takes more than once to pass the bar exam."

Mel looked at him. "I suppose you're right. I certainly have nothing against the painting business. It's kept our family going for a long time."

Sensing a little hostility in the air, Tena began questioning Tharsing about his farm and the landscape in that part of the state. Mel eased back on the sofa next to Nellie, listening. After a few minutes, Caroline opened the portieres that divided the parlor from the dining room and invited everyone to the table so the girls could serve the cake and coffee. The long table for twelve was rather a squeeze in the small room, but the family was used to the close quarters they shared with four boarders. The little boys ate silently, making a swift departure as soon as

Caroline said, "You may leave the table, boys." After another cup of coffee, the adults moved back into the parlor and the talk became more general and livelier, with everyone joining in. When an hour had gone by, Caroline said, "We should do something to entertain our guests, children. Willie, get your violin and we will sing something."

Caroline stood with her three daughters in front of the fireplace as Willie played some Swiss folk tunes, simple but elegant. The women, well-practiced in singing together, harmonized perfectly. Nellie, with her clear, strong soprano, was the best singer by far, but she was careful to blend with the others, and the result was truly beautiful. Mel, who had never heard her sing this formally, watched with shining eyes. Nellie smiled her broadest smile at him.

"That was very impressive, very impressive," boomed Tharsing. "You are a very talented family."

Caroline blushed a little. "We always have sung," she said. "I love the old songs, and it's important to me that my children know them too."

"It's a wonderful way to get through a long rainy night when you have eight or ten people sitting in the parlor," said Tena. "We have almost enough for a choir."

The party broke up soon after the singing, with Tharsing asking Caroline if he could call on them some evening.

"What was that all about, Mama?" asked Tena.

"I'm not sure I know," said Caroline. "But I think we gave them a nice afternoon."

After the others had gone, Mel lingered with Nellie in the parlor. "I'm sorry about our walk," said Nellie. "I feel that we've wasted the afternoon."

"Not at all," said Mel, looking into her dark brown eyes with admiration. I know something about you that I never knew before. I mean I knew you could sing, but not like this. You sound professional."

"I've had some lessons, on and off, and I sing in the choir. Lately I've been getting a lot of solos."

"You could go on the stage, Nellie. You really could. I'm not just saying this as a—friend. You really have something special."

Nellie looked up at him a little shyly. "You've guessed my secret dream," she said. "I've never told anyone because Mama would never allow one of her daughters to go on the stage, but I would love to study seriously with a real voice teacher in San Francisco and maybe sing professionally. But I'm afraid that singing in the choir is the closest I'll ever get to that."

Mel had an inspiration. "Yes, your mother is old-fashioned, but maybe we could ease her into the idea. There are theaters in San Francisco now that cater to families and have a mix of entertainment, including high class singing, even opera. Maybe we could take her to a show."

Nellie's eyes shone. "Oh, Mel! That would be wonderful, if we could ever get her to go."

"Tell you what, Nellie. I'll look into it and see what's possible. We can talk about it next Sunday."

Nellie's smile lit her whole face "Oh, thank you, Mel! I don't know what to say."

"Well, we'll see what happens." And Mel Chapman walked all the way from the Gotchetts' house on Sixteenth Street to the Chapman's on Eighteenth with a smile on his face.

Chapter 2

Chris Tharsing called on the Gotchetts on the following Tuesday evening and then again on Thursday. Caroline was at a loss to figure out what his intentions were. When he came, he asked if "the young ladies" were at home. He sat in the parlor talking with Tena, Alice, and Nellie until nine o'clock or so, and then took his leave. On Thursday, Caroline finally asked the girls, "Who is he coming to see?"

They looked at each other and giggled. "We have no idea, Mama," said Tena. "He doesn't really pay attention to any of us. He just sits there and talks about himself and his farm and his 'horticultural experiments.'"

On the following Sunday afternoon, Tharsing called again. He was very disappointed to hear that Nellie had gone out walking with Chapman. He spent a distracted hour having cake and coffee with Caroline, Tena, and Alice, and then took himself off, saying he had another call to pay.

"Do you think it could be Nellie he's after?" asked Alice.

"But she's much too young for him," said Tena. "There must be twenty years between them, and she isn't eighteen yet. She's too young to marry."

Caroline looked at them thoughtfully. "Well, I was just eighteen when I married. I made the wagon train journey out here from Missouri the next year when I was pregnant with Mary."

Neither of the girls said what was in their minds, that their mother was now a divorced woman in her forties with seven children at home to provide for. "That was back in the pioneer days, Mama," said Tena. "People marry later now."

"It's true," said Caroline. "And Nellie is a young seventeen. I fear I've spoiled her because she's my youngest daughter."

"I can't see Nellie as a farmer's wife, way out in the middle of nowhere," said Alice. "That's the last thing I see Nellie doing.

And Tharsing is too old for her. He seems far older than Mel Chapman, even though Mel is over thirty."

"Mel Chapman is taking far too long to amount to anything for my taste," said Caroline. "I guess we'll just have to wait and see what Tharsing has in mind."

Nellie laughed when Alice told her what they thought. "He couldn't be coming to see me," she said. "He's too old for me, and I'm not the least bit interested in him." On the following Tuesday, the sisters tried an experiment. Tena didn't come downstairs. Tharsing barely seemed to notice. After asking if she were well, he went on talking away to Alice and Nellie as usual. After half an hour or so, Alice excused herself, pleading a headache. Tharsing sat with Nellie for another hour, telling her every detail about his house and garden and saying several times how much they would profit from a woman's touch. It was all Nellie could do to keep a straight face, but she was polite to the end. She thanked him for coming and said she hoped they would see him again soon. He looked down at her and beamed.

After he left, she ran up the stairs and into the room she shared with Alice and Tena. "Well girls," she said, "I think it's me he's hunting. He all but laid out the floor plan of the house and handed me the garden trowel."

"Oh lord!" said Alice.

"What'll I do?" Nellie wailed comically.

"There's nothing to do but wait," said Tena. "At the rate he's going, I expect we'll know soon enough."

Tena was right. On Thursday, Tharsing came in the morning. When Alice answered the door, he asked to see Mrs. Gotchett. Caroline, who was in the middle of preparing midday dinner for her family of eight plus four boarders, was not happy about the interruption, but, with a suspicion of what might be coming, she wiped her hands, took off her apron, and composed herself before she walked into the parlor to see him.

Tharsing stood when she entered the room and took her hand. For a moment she feared that he was about to kiss it. "Good morning, Mr. Tharsing," she said. "This is a surprise."

"Forgive me for calling so early," he said. "I couldn't wait any longer to speak to you." She sat in one of the two stuffed chairs flanking the big window in the alcove. He sat down with an air of gravity in the other.

"What did you want to speak to me about?" she asked, trying to keep an even, neutral tone.

"I feel that I should speak to you before I ask for your daughter's hand."

Caroline looked at him directly. "Which daughter?" she asked.

He gave her an astonished look and blinked three times before he responded. "Why, Nellie, of course. I thought my interest in her was obvious."

A little smile escaped her control. "Fairly obvious," she said. "But Nellie is so young to marry. She's only seventeen. And forgive me, Mr. Tharsing, but you must be twenty years older than she is."

Tharsing stiffened a bit. "I'm thirty-six years old," he said. "I know it's a big age difference, Mrs. Gotchett, but that can be an advantage. I am a substantial man with a well-established farm. I can support your daughter and even afford her some comforts she doesn't have now. I have been married before, and I have been running my fruit farm for several years now. Nellie is young enough that I can teach her how things are done. My first wife was just eighteen when I married her."

"I was eighteen myself when I married," said Caroline. "But the life of a farm wife is so different from Nellie's upbringing. She's an excellent housekeeper, and she's a good plain cook, but she has no idea about everything else that's done on a farm. And you live so far away. Nellie has never spent any time on a farm or ever been away from her family. She really is young for her age."

"I've thought of that objection, Mrs. Gotchett, and I have a suggestion. Perhaps you and Nellie could come out to Modesto to visit. That would give you and her a chance to see where she would be living and what life is like on the fruit farm. I truly think she would like it. It is a beautiful place, so much more peaceful than the town. And, forgive me, but it smells a lot better."

Caroline nodded slowly. "I would be willing to do that," she said, "if Nellie is. This is my daughter's life in the end. I wouldn't insist on her marrying. My permission means nothing if she doesn't agree to the match."

Tharsing sat up straight, his broad smile showing a strong row of teeth under his mustache. "That's all I can ask, Mrs. Gotchett. May I speak to Nellie now?"

Caroline rose to her feet. "I'll get her," she said. "But remember that Nellie is a headstrong girl. She knows her mind. She is not going to marry anyone just on my say so. And I wouldn't I want her to. The wrong choice can lead to tragedy. I don't know how she feels about you, but you will have to persuade her to take this step on your own."

Tharsing nodded. While Caroline was gone, he paced up and down with his eyes on the rose-patterned carpet, his hands folded behind his back, planning his attack.

In ten minutes, Nellie appeared in the blue gingham dress she wore to do her morning work, her white collar hastily buttoned, her sleeves rolled down, and her flushed face showing that her mother had warned her of the interview to come.

Tharsing thought she made a charming picture. "Miss Nellie," he said, "I have something to ask you. I hope you will not be hasty in answering but will listen to what I have to say."

"Of course, Mr. Tharsing." She gestured to the stuffed chairs. "Please sit down."

When they were sitting side by side in the chairs, Tharsing turned to her, looking earnestly into her face. "Miss Nellie," he said, in a softer voice than she had heard him use, his Danish accent giving his words a slightly formal quality. "It can't come as a surprise to you that I admire you very much. I think you are a lovely girl, so accomplished and so charming. You would do me the greatest honor by agreeing to become my wife." As the flush on Nellie's cheek deepened and she opened her mouth to speak, he stopped her. "Please," he said. "I know there are many objections to our marriage, some of which your mother has already made. I am nearly twenty years older than you, and we have had so little time to get to know each other. But I have been married before, to a girl just your age. I can tell you that it is not age that matters in a marriage, but the respect that the partners have for one another. I would like to have the chance for you to get to know me better, so you can decide whether this is possible for you."

Nellie looked at him. Her head was in a whirl. This was really happening. She had just received a marriage proposal from Chris Tharsing. "I am so very grateful for your proposal Mr. Tharsing," she said, "but as far as I can see, we aren't suited for each other. We live two different lives. I'm a town girl. I couldn't go a hundred miles away from my family to live on a farm with no other people around."

He looked at her kindly. "I understand, Miss Nellie. You can't imagine life on a farm. That is why I invited your mother to bring you to Modesto for a visit to see what it is like. It will give us a chance to know each other better, and you can see what your life as my wife would be."

Nellie looked at him in surprise. "And my mother has agreed to this?"

"She has. She has been most encouraging. She would like to see the beautiful country near the Sierras and have a little holiday on my fruit farm. Assuming that you are willing. I will of course cover the expenses and arrange your trip from the railroad station in Modesto out to the farm."

"But it doesn't seem right, Mr. Tharsing. I really can't imagine that I could ever say yes to your proposal."

He took on a pleading look that she hadn't seen before. "Please give me this chance, Miss Nellie, and let me give your mother this little holiday. If you still feel that way at the end of your stay at the farm, no harm done. We will part friends."

For the first time that day, Nellie smiled at him in response, a warm and natural smile. "I'll talk to my mother, Mr. Tharsing, and let you know what we decide. It's very nice of you to invite us."

"I will call tomorrow evening if that is all right. I have to catch a train to Modesto on Saturday morning to make the trip home."

She nodded. "Yes, tomorrow evening will be fine." She stood up.

Tharsing rose and took both her hands in his. "Until tomorrow, then," he said.

Nellie found that her mother had given all the details of her conversation to her sisters. Alice gripped Nellie's arms excitedly as she came into the kitchen. "Are you going to go to the farm?" she asked.

"I don't know," Nellie said, looking at her mother. "What did you tell him, Mama?"

"I told him I would be willing to go, to give him the chance to show you what it's like out there, but only if you were."

"But what do you think, Mama?"

Caroline regarded her daughter soberly. "I think it's a good match, Nellie, except that he's so much older than you and you are young to marry. He is a substantial farmer, and fruit farming is not the kind that's hard on the farmer's wife. From what I've gathered, he seems to grow fancy table fruit. You would probably have to cook for a lot of people at harvest time, but not the rest of the year. I think we owe it to him to take the trip if you are going to consider his proposal seriously, but if not, we shouldn't go. Do you think you're ready to marry?"

Nellie blushed. "I hadn't thought of marrying so soon, no."

"Well, let's take the day to think before you give him your answer."

That evening, Mel Chapman paid a call. Caroline looked up in surprise when Alice brought him into the parlor, saying, "What brings you out on a Thursday evening, Mr. Chapman? Shouldn't you be studying your law books?"

Mel laughed. "Yes, I should be, Mrs. Gotchett, but I have something I promised to get for Nellie."

"What do you have for Nellie?" Nellie demanded, coming into the parlor on the heels of her sister.

Mel reached into the pocket of his jacket and pulled out three theater tickets. "As promised," he said. "I would like to invite you, Mrs. Gotchett, along with Miss Nellie to the new family amusement in San Francisco. It's called vaudeville. It has all sorts of wholesome entertainment, including some fine singers that I think you would enjoy."

Nellie looked startled and stood gazing at the tickets, saying nothing. With the events of the last few days, she had completely forgotten about the theater. Alice sat back in her chair to watch. Caroline eyed the tickets as if Mel held three snakes in his hand.

"It's nice of you to think of us, Mr. Chapman," she said, "but I don't know what possessed you. I couldn't go to a theater, and I wouldn't allow my daughter to go either."

Mel smiled, despite an increasing sense of unease. "Oh, it's not the regular theater, Mrs. Gotchett. There's nothing of questionable taste or anything, and the audience is made up of families, even small children. The women in the audience for the matinees outnumber the men. It's good wholesome fun."

"Well, perhaps it is, and it's very kind of you to offer, but Nellie and I will not be going."

"I'm sorry to hear that," he said. "I was hoping to give you a nice afternoon out."

"Well, I'm sorry too," said Caroline. "You really should ask before you buy tickets for something like that." She gathered up her knitting and left the parlor to the young people.

"Gee, I guess I bungled that," said Mel.

"Don't mention the theater to Mama," said Alice. "It's like a red flag to a bull. She still thinks it's the gold rush and the only women who go there are the ones of easy virtue on the prowl."

"We were hoping to ease her into it," said Nellie.

Alice laughed and raised an eyebrow. "I'll leave you two to hatch your next scheme. Good night, Mel."

"Good night, Alice," he said.

When she was gone, Nellie sat on the sofa and looked up at Mel. Tears began welling in her dark brown eyes.

Mel looked at her in dismay and sat down next to her. "It's not as bad as all that," he said, taking her hand.

"It's not the tickets," she said. "I have to tell you something, Mel. I've had a proposal from Chris Tharsing."

Mel gripped her hand tighter. "I knew that guy was up to some-thing," he said. "What did you tell him?"

"I told him no, but it's not over yet. He worked on my mother so that he's got her thinking it would be a good match, and he wants the two of us to go out there to his farm in Modesto for a visit, so we can 'get to know each other better' and I can see what it's like to live on a farm."

Mel expelled his breath in a soft whistle. "Modesto. That must be a hundred miles away. It's way east in the San Joaquin Valley. Are you going to go?"

"I don't know yet."

Mel laid his other hand on top of hers. "It's hard to think of," he said.

Nellie looked directly into his eyes. "I'd rather marry you, Mel."

"Oh, Nell," he said, "that's what I love about you. There's no playing it coy and hinting around. You come out and tell a fellow what you feel. I would marry you in a minute now if I could. I've been thinking a lot about it the last few weeks. But I'm in no position to ask you. I can hardly keep myself now, let alone a family. And ahead of me I still have law school and the Bar Exam and getting started in practice. It will be years before I have a steady income."

"I know, Mel, but I could wait for you. I'm only seventeen."

"I can't ask you to do that, Nellie. It wouldn't be fair as long as my dreams are just—dreams. I wouldn't exact a promise from you. Your mother would never approve anyway, and I guess I can't blame her." His grip on her hand tightened. "I guess you owe it to yourself to give this Tharsing a chance."

"But I can't even imagine it, Mel. Living on a farm a hundred miles from here. It sounds crazy. And I would have to give up my singing."

"I guess you'd better go and see, and then you'll know."

After he left Nellie, Mel walked slowly down Broadway toward a waterfront saloon where he could get a couple of cheap whiskeys. When he reached Thirteenth Street, there was a newsboy hawking the *Call* on the corner. He reached in his pocket and drew out the three tickets. "Here, kid," he said. "Go and see the show. I can't make it."

Chris Tharsing visited the Gotchett house that evening and professed himself delighted that Mrs. Gotchett and Miss Nellie would be able to come for a visit. They fixed the dates for the first two weeks in August, before the harvest so there would be plenty of time for socializing.

Chapter 3

It was a warm, dry morning in Oakland when Nellie and her mother left the boarding house in the hands of Tena and Alice and boarded the train for Modesto. The ride along the coast was pleasant, but after they changed trains at Niles and started eastward toward the San Joaquin Valley, the heat rose steadily. When they got out at Tracy to change again for Modesto, the sun beat down on the platform as the heat radiated up from the boards. Their city hats provided no real shade from the sun, and their traveling dresses felt heavy.

As the Modesto train plunged into the valley, Nellie settled into the heat and looked out the window at the intense green. The heat seemed to shimmer on the fields. Nellie had no idea what the different crops were, but her mother would from time to time exclaim, "look at that big beanfield, Nellie," or "I've never seen such a potato field." Nellie had never experienced such a combination of heat and the heavy scent of greenery except in the Conservatory in Golden Gate Park. As they approached Modesto, the crops gave way to orchards, field after field of little trees planted in rows with military precision. The scent of the almost ripe peaches and pears and plums drifted through the open windows as the train went by, and a heavy drowsiness fought Nellie's nervousness as they drew near to Modesto, where Chris Tharsing was waiting for them.

As the train pulled into the station, Nellie could see Tharsing get down from his wagon, a tall, solid figure in a Stetson "Boss of the Plains" hat. On the platform, he approached them with confidence, shaking hands and greeting them in a loud, hearty voice, picking up a carpet bag in each hand as he led the way toward the wagon. As they drove through the town of Modesto, Nellie could see that it wasn't much. Two unpaved main streets with a few side streets where there were little houses placed seemingly at random. Tharsing pointed with pride to a few bigger houses, which he referred to as mansions, as they drove out of town, saying they were owned by fine men whom he knew well.

They were soon out of town, driving toward the farm on a dusty, rutted road called Paradise. On either side were row upon row of little fruit trees, broken occasionally by houses and barns and small fields with other crops. Nellie's mother carried on an animated conversation with Tharsing about the different crops and the differences between raising fruit and other things. Nellie had no idea that she had accumulated so much knowledge of farming during her Indiana girlhood. Tharsing seemed to be impressed. To Nellie, all the fields except the orchards looked pretty much alike.

Nellie was relieved when they got to the farm and Tharsing led them toward the farmhouse, a good-sized structure that turned out to have four bedrooms and fairly large rooms downstairs. "The old farmer I leased the farm from has a big family," he said. "He hoped that his sons would take it over, but they didn't develop the love for farming, and they've all moved to the city."

Caroline was delighted as they settled in for their visit. The weather was very hot during the day, but at night a breeze came up, and the house was well ventilated, so it cooled off for sleeping. After sampling the first two days of cooking by Maria, the teenaged daughter of one of the hired men who came in during the day to keep house for Tharsing, she volunteered to take over the kitchen during their stay, telling Maria that it wasn't fair for her to have to cook for extra people. She seemed to take pleasure in returning to the ways of her Indiana girlhood, working in the kitchen garden, feeding the chickens and gathering eggs. Maria would do the housework in the morning and then disappear, only too glad of her semi-holiday.

Against the background of the farm, Chris Tharsing seemed a different person to Nellie than he had in the Gotchetts' parlor.

Dressed in an open shirt, high boots, and a broad-brimmed hat, he seemed far more at home than he had in his black broadcloth coat with his high collar and carefully knotted tie. Here his manner seemed confident, warm, expansive, in harmony with his surroundings, rather than blustering or domineering. On the first morning, when he took Nellie and Caroline on a long tour through the orchard, Nellie watched his face light up with enthusiasm as he explained this or that technique to her mother. "I'm not just a farmer," he would say proudly, "I'm a progressive orchardist. And I try to adapt all the new scientific thinking I can to growing fruit. We have quite a few experiments going on here." Later on, Caroline told Nellie that it wasn't just bluster. He knew what he was talking about. She couldn't follow all his explanations, but she could see the skill and knowledge with which he treated his crops.

In the evening, they sat in the parlor and talked for a while. At Chris's urging, Caroline and Nellie sang acapella, since there was no musical instrument available, and then they all joined in for "Home Sweet Home" and a few hymns they all knew. Chris's voice was a pleasant baritone, not especially strong, but true. Nellie like singing with him.

On the second day, Chris told Nellie to come out to the yard. Tied to a fence post was a small chestnut horse with a side saddle. "Do you ride?" Chris asked her.

"A little." Nellie's life in Oakland had afforded precious little chance to ride, but she had always liked horses.

"This is Sallie," he said. "She was bred as a saddle horse. I got her for my wife, but she didn't have much use for riding in her last year. I thought you might enjoy a ride." Once Chris had helped her into the saddle, she rode tentatively around the farmyard at a walk, as he gave her directions and encouragement. Sallie was gentle and obedient, and Nellie quickly grew in confidence.

"Good," said Chris. "You take well to the saddle. Tomorrow, we can go for a ride."

The next day was sunny and not too hot. Chris presented Nellie with a broad-brimmed straw hat. "You will want this in the sun," he said. She laughed but put it on. Her face was already sunburned from the day before. "Thank you," she said. "do I look like a farm girl?"

He looked down at her with satisfaction. "You look like a lovely, healthy girl," he said.

They took a short ride around the farm that day. Chris showed Nellie the different orchards of peaches, pears, and plums. "We grow mostly table fruit here," he said, "the best. It's an expensive crop and it takes a lot of care, so the orchards are relatively small."

In the following days, as Nellie became more confident in the saddle, they rode out further, one day taking a picnic with them to the Tuolumne River. Chris laughed as Nellie tore off her stockings and shoes and waded into the water, holding her gingham skirt not too carefully above her ankles. "How is the water?" He asked.

She flashed a grin as she turned toward him. "It's fine," she said. "It's all I can do to keep from diving in." That she didn't do, but when she climbed back up the riverbank, Chris took her handkerchief and dipped it in the water so she could cool her red cheeks with it. Famished for lunch, they attacked the fried chicken, boiled eggs, bread and fruit preserves that Caroline and Nellie had packed for them. "Soon, there will be fresh fruit," said Chris. "I'd like for you to taste it, Nellie. I'd like you to see the best that I can do."

Nellie smiled at him. "I'd like that too, Chris," she said.

As the days passed, Nellie fell into the rhythm of farm life. She didn't exactly rise with the sun as her mother and Chris did, but she got up early enough to help her mother get breakfast on the table, and then she usually spent some time with her in the kitchen garden. Caroline was happy to teach her daughter what she knew about growing things. Nellie had always liked going to the produce market in Oakland and taking the fresh vegetables home, but now she found that she loved pulling carrots out of the ground or cutting their own cabbage or lettuce. She could see that it was different, somehow, when you grew them yourself.

In the afternoons, Nellie rode with Chris, or, when he was busy with the orchards, by herself. She liked riding alongside Chris, talking about all sorts of things as she did with Mel on their walks, but she had to admit there was a special joy in going out for a ride by herself, just letting Sallie go, with no one to reign her in or tell her she was doing this or that wrong. It was exciting, a feeling of freedom she had never had before. She loved riding.

Nellie always returned to the house in time to help her mother with supper, and then they all sat together in the little parlor at night, the women with their knitting or sewing, while they talked. Each evening, they sang, or Chris read to them for an hour or so before they went to bed. Nellie had never seen her mother so relaxed and jovial. Living on the farm had stirred her memory, and she told stories about growing up in Indiana in the middle of the century as well as some hair-raising tales that Nellie had never heard before about coming west in the wagon train. Without the endless daily worries of running a household of twelve and a business on her own, Caroline seemed youthful and energetic. Nellie had never thought of her mother as good company before, but she was. And she came to appreciate Chris, not only for the authoritative figure he cut on the farm and his obviously superior knowledge as an orchardist, but as a good companion who seemed to be really interested in her ideas and feelings and anxious to make her happy.

On Sunday, Chris drove them in the wagon to church in Modesto. He obviously took great pleasure in introducing his guests to the other church members, a mix of farmers and townspeople. Nellie could tell that he was a respected figure in the town. Many people seemed anxious to make their acquaintance. Nellie met several of the farmers' wives, who seemed very warm and welcoming, and a couple of girls her age. They all sang the praises of Modesto as if they were a Chamber of Commerce delegation. No one stood on ceremony there.

On the night before they were to leave for home, Chris asked Nellie to walk with him. The moon was almost full, and they could easily see the road in front of them as they walked past the rows of fruit trees. They spoke of this and that as they walked, both chatting nervously, until Chris said, "Nellie, there's something I want to say to you before you go. I saw that you were a remarkable girl and wanted to make you my wife before these two weeks, but now that I know you better, I know that there is nothing that would make me happier in this world. I had promised myself that I would not press you for an answer while you were here, but I feel that I must speak of my love for you. I would like to lay everything that I have at your feet and devote all my efforts in the future to making a life and family together."

Nellie had thought Chris would press his proposal, but she had not expected anything like this. "I don't know what to say, Chris," she said. "I don't know if I could live up to that."

"I know you could, Nellie. You're going to be a very fine woman. I would be proud to have you by my side."

"Well, I would be proud to be by your side, Chris," she said before she knew it. And then she knew that it was true. This was a fine man, a respected man. He was offering her a good life, but most important, he really seemed to love her. "And I like it out here much more than I ever thought I would. I just don't know if I have it in me to be a farmer's wife."

"Believe me, Nellie. If you marry me, I will do what I can to make you happy. We can keep Maria on part time and save you most of the drudgery of keeping house. And of course, Sallie will be yours. You can go riding whenever you like and visit the neighbors. I wouldn't want you to feel that you were confined in the house or that you were alone out here. I know you will miss your family, but they can visit, and I know you will make nice friends here."

Nellie looked up at his earnest face. It touched her that he cared so much about her happiness. No one had ever given this much thought to her before. "I appreciate it, Chris," she said. "It means a great deal to me that you care so much. I can't give you my answer now, but I will say that what you offer is very generous. Let me go home and give it some thought. I promise to write to you in a week or so."

"That is all I ask," he said. "Give it some thought. Let's go back to your mother now."

Caroline left Modesto a little reluctantly. She was eager to see her children and to make sure that Tenie and Alice hadn't let the boarding house slide in her absence, but she had thoroughly enjoyed her holiday. "Nellie," she said, "you would be a lucky woman to live like that. I hope you know what he is offering you."

"I know, Mama," she said, and told her what he had said about hiring Maria and giving her the horse. "It's hard, though. It's far away. I would miss all of you and all my friends in Oakland. The choir in that church isn't much to speak of either." She looked at her mother, and they both burst out laughing. The choir had been terrible, with no apparent director and just a parlor melodeon to accompany it.

"Well, it's a little town. Maybe you could help them do something with the choir. And we can visit back and forth sometimes. It isn't that long a trip."

Alice and Tenie were amazed to hear that Nellie was thinking seriously about accepting Chris Tharsing. She told them every detail she could think of about the trip and Chris and the farm and what her life would be like. Finally, Alice said, "You know, you really seem to care for him, Nell."

"I think I do," she said, a note of surprise in her voice. "Chris Tharsing. Who would have thought it."

"I'm going to say something, and I hope you don't take it amiss," said Alice, "but what about Mel Chapman?"

Nellie had thought a good deal about this. "Mel doesn't really love me," she said. "We have fun together. We're good friends, but I don't matter to him the way I matter to Chris."

"Well," said Alice. "It's your heart and your life to live. You're the one who has to decide."

In the end, Nellie decided to marry Chris Tharsing. The wedding was set for October, just after her eighteenth birthday. In the two months leading up to it, Nellie and her sisters spent their leisure time on her trousseau. They descended on the dry goods stores in Oakland, and even made forays into the department stores in San Francisco. She needed fewer things for the house than was usual because there was a good deal there already. Mostly, they got to concentrate on her clothes. Nellie tried to be sensible and get clothes for the country, not the city. They made two nice dresses, one for summer and one for winter, which would mainly be for church, so they were modest, with high necks. For the most part, they bought and made dresses, waists and skirts that were light and cool, gingham or light cotton because it was so hot in the valley most of the time, with two linen skirts and one wool dress for winter. Nellie's married sister, Mary Shay, gave her a lovely warm shawl for winter and a pretty night gown. Her mother embroidered a set of pillow cases and a night gown, and she made her two practical sets of underwear as well. They all enjoyed "the sewing circle," as Alice called it, as they sat together in the evenings, working and singing and talking.

The day of the wedding was beautiful, with a crisp touch of fall in the air. Nellie looked lovely in her soft blue merino dress, with a lovely lace collar that was made for her by Mary Shay's Irish mother-in-law. Chris looked like anything but a farmer in his new black broadcloth frock coat, striped trousers, and silk hat.

They had a wedding photo taken, and Nellie smiled to see him strutting a bit as he greeted everyone. The wedding took place in the church that Nellie had attended all her life. She had sung in the choir since she was a young girl and was considered its lead singer now. They really put themselves out for her wedding, learning a new, complicated piece that they knew she would appreciate. Nellie was touched, but it was strange to hear the choir singing without her. After they had exchanged their vows with the blessing of the minister who had baptized her, they had a fine meal that Caroline, Tena, and Alice had been working on for days—everything from roast goose and ham served with several kinds of potatoes and sauces and all kinds of vegetables to a wonderful wedding cake made with brandy and chock full of dried fruit. When it was over, and they had changed into their travelling clothes, Chris shouldered her trunk, and the others helped to bring her bags and boxes out to the waiting cab. Soon they were on the train headed for Modesto.

Chapter 4

The first months of her married life were the happiest Nellie had known. Chris was a surprisingly skillful husband in bed, and Nellie found that looking forward to the night was a big part of her day. She took pride in her husband's stature in the community. The other farmers listened carefully to his views on agricultural matters, and he was treated with respect by the town folk as well. There was no question of respect or obedience to his orders on the farm. The men worked hard to perform up to his high standards.

In the house, Chris was more forbearing. Nellie gradually decorated their home a little more to her taste, hanging their wedding photograph and photos of her family as well as some watercolors by her sister Alice and drawings by her brother Willie. She livened up the parlor with a bright throw over the horsehair sofa and scattered touches of her family about in the form of embroidered pillows and antimacassars given by her mother and sisters for the chairs. She had bought a new bedspread for their bedroom and enough material so that she gradually made new curtains for all the rooms. Nellie had always liked cleaning and tidying. She kept the house spotless and inviting.

Cooking was not such a joy for Nellie. She was very happy to have Maria come in during the morning so she didn't have to prepare three meals a day. The girl came early and made up the fire in the kitchen stove, cooked breakfast, and did the dishes. She did the laundry, tended the chickens, and would take care of the garden in summer, and she helped Nellie with the heavier household chores. She helped with preparations for the noontime dinner before she left at eleven to cook for her father and brothers. She was also a girl to talk to, for Nellie, surrounded by men on the ranch, missed the companionship she had always had with her sisters.

In the afternoon, Nellie did the dishes and often went for a ride, sometimes visiting one of the other farmer's wives along Paradise Road, and sometimes just riding. She got home in plenty of time to fix supper for Chris, and they usually spent the evening in the parlor, Nellie with her sewing or knitting, Chris reading. He occasionally read stories or poetry to her in the evening, but more often he just read bits of the newspaper and expressed his opinion about them. Chris was a very conscientious citizen. He registered to vote every year and followed the political news—national, state, and local—very closely. Nellie looked out for information he would be interested in when she made her visits and always tried to remember the condition of the various farms she passed so she could tell him about them. By mutual consent, they usually went to bed early and enjoyed themselves after they got there.

Nellie took her mother's advice and joined the choir, which really just meant sitting with the choir during the service and singing one or two hymns. They were very happy to have her and delighted when they heard her sing. Nellie found that Ned Collier, the earnest young man who was the titular choir director, was capable of choosing the music and conducting the choir but had become discouraged because there was no time for them to rehearse. The farm families couldn't come to town in the dark on a weeknight just for rehearsal. As they were leaving the church one Sunday, Nellie suggested that the choir might rehearse in the hour before the service, while the children were in Sunday school. Ned said he'd thought of that, but the only accompaniment they had was the melodeon in the church, where the children would be. At this, Matilda McHenry spoke up. "We have a piano in the parlor, and I think it's large enough to accommodate the whole choir."

A few looks were exchanged at this. The new McHenry mansion was the biggest house in Modesto and certainly the most luxurious. Most of the choir members had never been inside.

"Why, thank you, Mrs. McHenry," said Ned. "If everyone is agreed, we can plan to meet at your house next Sunday at 9:00." When everyone quickly nodded assent, the tradition of morning choir practice had begun. After this, the choir began to improve remarkably. First, they worked on what was in the hymnal, but Ned began to take a real interest in finding other church music that the choir could sing, featuring Nellie's voice and that of Ed McCormick, a strong tenor. Before long, the choir had a reputation throughout the town. People began coming to the church for the music.

At first, Chris hung around with the other farmers, passing the time and talking crops and politics after driving Nellie into town. He took pleasure in her growing reputation as an accomplished singer. After a few months, he decided to join the choir himself, which pleased Nellie, not only because he was there, but because she no longer had to feel vaguely guilty that she was putting him out with the early trip into town on Sunday.

The winter passed pleasantly, and in March, Nellie watched with excitement as the orchard came alive. When she went riding, the rows of trees seemed endless, the colors a changing kaleidoscope of white, all shades of pink, and a little purple and yellow. As she rode between the orchards, the scent of peach, pear, plum, and apricot blossoms was overwhelming. But then in the middle of March, a cold snap came. As the temperature dropped down through the thirties during the day, Chris became more and more agitated, sending the men to check the thermometers in all the orchards and comparing temperatures on high and low ground. He hardly noticed his supper, and when Nellie asked him how bad the danger was, he didn't try to disguise it. "If it drops below the killing temperature, it can wipe out a whole crop. That's twenty-seven degrees for the peaches, plums, and apricots, and twenty-nine degrees for the pears. We're at thirty-three degrees now."

Chris went out right after supper with a lantern, checking the temperatures in key locations. At ten o'clock he told Nellie to go up to bed. He spent the night downstairs. She could hear him pacing in the kitchen and going out every hour to check the temperatures. When Nellie came downstairs after some fitful sleep in the early morning hours, Maria was there making the fire in the stove, and Chris was sitting at the table in an attitude she had never seen him in before, bent over, his head in his hands.

"Is it bad?" she asked.

He looked up. "Yes, it is bad," he said. "It went down to twenty-seven degrees in some places. The pears will probably be pretty much wiped out. I'm hoping that parts of the other orchards will come through all right. We won't know until we check the pistils."

Nellie put her hand on his shoulder. She didn't know what else to do. This was not her confident, blustering Chris.

Over the next few weeks, the extent of the damage became clear as what remained of the crop matured. The pears were almost a total loss, although a pretty good section of apricots and plums, and some of the peaches, had survived. Chris remained taciturn and subdued, hardly responding to Nellie's attempts to draw him out of himself. On an evening in April, they were sitting in the parlor when he said, "Nellie, I'm afraid our finances don't look good for this year. We're going to have to make some changes. We can't afford to keep Maria on in the house."

Nellie looked up from the sock she was darning. "But, Chris, Maria doesn't cost that much. Can't we cut back in other ways?"

"We will have to cut back in every way. You will have to grow everything you can for the kitchen and increase the chicken flock so we have meat and eggs. You will have to be careful with tea and coffee and sugar and everything that's store bought. It's going to be a hard pull to make it through the winter."

"I didn't realize it was as bad as that. What about the fruit that was saved from the frost?"

"That is less than half the crop, and it has to pay the lease on the land. We don't have anything to speak of in reserve." He set his jaw grimly. "This was supposed to be the year I started putting money away for the option to buy the land. Sometimes nature does not cooperate."

Nellie was dismayed to hear the state their finances were in. She hadn't known that a substantial farmer like Chris could be in such a precarious position. But she lifted her chin and looked at her husband. "We'll just have to see it through," she said.

The next months were the hardest Nellie had ever lived through. Gone were her afternoons of leisure, her horseback rides and visits, her pleasant mornings working in the house alongside Maria. She rose before Chris did now, in order to get the fire going in the kitchen to make breakfast before the men headed out to the fields. Chris had let most of the hands go, as well as their cook. Now Nellie cooked for four men in addition to Chris. In the morning, she cleaned up after breakfast and did the housework before she started the dinner. She expanded the garden and tried to save on groceries as much as she could. Luckily, she had had good training in her mother's boarding house. She made endless biscuits, bread, pies, and stews. She expanded the flock of chickens, and Chris made a second coop for them. She didn't like the chickens and hated the smell and the dirty job of cleaning out the coops. Chris insisted that they save the manure for fertilizer, so she had to scrape the roosting boards into buckets and empty them on the manure pile.

As the summer progressed, with its killing heat during the day, Nellie had a harder time keeping up with the work, and she watched helplessly as the spotless condition of her house and her clothes began to slide. "I have so much more to do now," she said to Chris one hot night in July. "Couldn't one of the men clean the chicken coops?"

"No," said Chris, sternly. "Keeping chickens is woman's work. The men have too much work to do on the farm." He softened a little as he looked at her dejected face. "I know it's hard, Nellie. This isn't what I had planned for you. But you will get used to it, and it won't seem so hard."

Nellie looked down at the shirt she was mending. She had thought of these last few months as a temporary hardship. She had not planned to get used to it. "How do you think our finances will come out this year?" she asked.

"If we're careful, we will have enough to pay the rent," he said.

"And next year we'll be back to normal?"

Chris was annoyed. "It all depends on the crop," he said. "If we get a good crop, we will have money to spare. If we have another year like this, we could be wiped out. It's the life of a farmer."

Nellie had a hard time facing up to the new reality that she now understood was to be their life. Why hadn't her mother explained to her how precarious a farmer's finances were? With the work and the heat, she became depressed and almost as taciturn as Chris. One morning in mid-July, Chris came out of the barn and saw two of his men just standing and looking toward the kitchen garden. A flash of anger hit him as he realized they were watching his wife.

"Why aren't you men at work?" he said gruffly.

Jed, the older one, turned to him and said, "Sorry boss. Just going now." As they got out of there in a hurry, Chris looked toward the garden to see what they'd been staring at. He was aghast when he saw Nellie bending over picking beans. She was wearing men's overalls and what looked like an old shirt of his with the sleeves rolled up. He strode angrily toward the garden.

"Nellie, where did you get these clothes?" he demanded.

She looked up at him under the broad brim of her straw hat, nervous, but determined. "I asked my sister Alice to send me some overalls," she said. "I told her it was for a joke."

"But why? How can you come outside dressed like that for the men and anyone who comes to see? It is not modest. It is an insult to your husband to go around like this."

Nellie took a deep breath. "I don't mean to be disrespectful to you, Chris, but working in the garden and cleaning the chicken coops was ruining my skirts. I know we can't afford to buy any new clothes this year, so I have to be careful with what I have. The overalls and this loose shirt are perfect for this work. I don't get nearly as hot, and it's much easier to keep clean."

Chris was livid. "Other farm wives manage to keep clean while wearing decent clothes," he said. "I will not have my wife parading about like this."

"Well, I can't afford to ruin the few dresses I have doing this work."

"Then we will buy some calico, and you will make a dress that is suitable for your work."

On their next trip to Modesto, Nellie made a show of buying some cheap, strong calico, but she continued to wear the overalls when she worked outside. At first, Chris asked her every day when the dress would be ready, but she made little progress, telling him she was too busy during the day to work on it and too tired at night. After a few days, the men took no interest, accepting the overalls as the new norm on the farm, and Chris stopped asking about the dress. Nellie felt that she had one small victory.

The summer went on with its stifling heat and endless work. Nellie tried to write at least a weekly letter to her family, but it was hard to keep up the pretense that everything was well with her marriage and she was enjoying her life on the farm. The visits back and forth that had been talked about didn't materialize that summer. Chris said they had no way to replace her if she went away for a week, and she didn't want her mother or sisters to come and see the reality of her life.

The one pleasure in Nellie's life was the choir, which continued to improve and be recognized in the little area around Modesto, largely through Nellie and Ned's collaboration. They grew excited when the sheet music for each carefully chosen piece of music arrived. In preparation for Sunday choir practice, Nellie practiced her solo parts all week as she went about her work on the farm. Chris continued singing in the choir. Ned, who obviously adored Nellie, praised her solos and offered her as an example of hard work to the rest of the choir. On the last Sunday in August, the choir sang its most difficult piece, one they had been working on for weeks. Nellie's solo was a showpiece, and she sang it flawlessly. She looked very pretty standing in her white muslin Sunday dress, her cheeks flushed and her eyes shining. Ned looked at her as she sat down, and they smiled at each other, a little private recognition of their shared triumph. As Chris Tharsing watched, a knot of fear formed in his stomach.

On the way home from church, Nellie asked Chris how he thought her solo sounded. "You sang well, Nellie," he said, "but I think the piece is somewhat vulgar."

She colored. "Vulgar! Why? It's a beautiful piece."

"But so showy for the soprano, don't you think? I'm not sure Ned has very good taste when it comes to music. To tell you the truth, Nellie, I have been thinking lately that Ned has placed you in a position that is unseemly. I don't like having my wife put out there on show for everyone to look at. I think we should tell him that you won't be performing any solos for a while."

"But Chris, it's not a show. It's the church choir. We're just making beautiful music."

"That's just it, Nellie. It seems like a show. People come to the church just for the music without caring about the service. I think Ned and Reverend Cooper are exploiting you just to fill the church. I don't want you to do any more solos. In fact, I think we both should quit the choir."

"Quit the choir! But it's my one pleasure in this awful life." Nellie had spoken without thinking, and she regretted it immediately. She glanced sideways at her husband.

Chris had stiffened, sitting up straight on the wagon seat. "I'm sorry you think your life is awful, Nellie, and you have no pleasure in our marriage."

"I didn't mean that, Chris. But life is hard right now, and the choir gives us a little joy and beauty and relief from work. What's wrong with that?"

"You make yourself a spectacle. That's what's wrong. Everyone in town makes jokes about you and that choir director."

Nellie was amazed. "Ned and me! Why that's ridiculous. We never see each other except at choir practice. You can't take anything like that seriously."

Chris's face set grimly. "All the same, it is insulting to me. You are disrespecting your husband by your behavior."

"What behavior?" Nellie cried. "All I do is sing in the choir."

"Well, clearly that will have to stop, then. I will not have this man driving a wedge in our marriage. We will not be singing in the choir. In fact, I think we should change to the Methodist church. They don't have a choir. Everyone signs together. That will give you every chance to enjoy the beauty of the music without making a show of yourself before the town."

Nellie was dumbfounded. She had seen instances of Chris's jealousy before, but nothing like this. She couldn't see anything to do, unless she defied him openly and went to church on her own, and she really feared for his response, he seemed so crazy on this point. She sat silent, her eyes straight ahead.

"Well, Nellie," he said after a while.

"Whatever you think is best, Chris," she said, without turning her head.

After this, Nellie's days followed one another in dreary monotony. With a lot of effort and considerable deprivation, they got through the winter, and 1886 was a better year for them financially. But Chris showed no signs of relieving the burden on Nellie. In fact, it increased because he hired two more full-time hands that she had to feed. She more than once reflected that she had fallen into the relentless life of keeping a boarding house, a life she had married Chris partly to escape. He was now obsessed with saving money. He did not want to buy this farm, he said, because the soil was not to his liking and the crop was too uncertain, but they needed money to make a move.

In April of 1887, Nellie found that she was pregnant. It was not the first time. She knew that she had had at least two miscarriages, one after two months, and one after three. Each time, she was sad but a little relieved that she hadn't had a baby to deal with in addition to everything else. Chris, she was sure, knew nothing about them. This time, Nellie was stronger, more used to the long days and the hard work in the heat. She had no morning sickness and felt better, somehow, about this pregnancy. In June, one unusually cool evening when they were sitting in the parlor resting, she told Chris. He was overjoyed.

"At last, my first child!" he said. "I was afraid you were going to be barren like my first wife, Nellie. This truly is a blessing for us." The thought of the coming child brightened things in the household. Chris began to plan seriously for a move to a better farm. He even began to help Nellie with some of the heavier chores. Nellie wrote to her family, and her mother offered to come and help when her time came. Her sisters were making things for the layette.

The harvest was good, ensuring enough money to live comfortably through the winter, but Chris had become fixed on finding a new farm where they would start their family. In September, he had narrowed the possibilities to three properties further up the valley, and he took the train to look at them. Nellie was worried about the prospect of leaving Modesto, which she had come to like, and the friends she had there. The neighboring women had already given her much needed advice and help in dealing with her pregnancy. She hoped that Chris would decide on a farm nearby.

When he came back from his trip, Chris announced that he had chosen a property in Yuba City, up in Sutter County, thirty miles north of Sacramento. Nellie could see that he was in high spirits. He talked with a confidence she hadn't heard in his voice since the early days of their marriage. "It is a beautiful piece of property on the Feather River," he said. "Plenty of irrigation, good soil. Everyone up there grows peaches for canning, and they are also drying grapes for raisins and plums for prunes. I will have to do that for a good cash crop. There is a fair-sized vineyard on the property. That's something I want to try, and I'm sure I could grow varieties of table fruit up there."

"How big a town is Yuba City?" Nellie asked. She had learned that it was best not to seem to question him or to pose objections, but she could learn what she needed to know with general questions that signified interest and enthusiasm.

"It's a small town, about five hundred people," he said. "But growing fast. It was started by John Sutter, the man who first discovered gold in forty-nine. He built it in the sixties as the trading center for that part of the state and it is the county seat, but it's quickly becoming an agricultural center because of the good growing conditions and transportation. It's a great place to start a new operation."

Nellie could see that Chris was thinking big, and she was glad to see him enthusiastic again, but she worried about moving even further from Oakland and her family, especially when the baby would be coming in a couple of months. "When are you thinking of moving?" she asked.

"To tell you the truth, I've already closed the deal," he said. "It is a three-year lease with an option to buy. There is a small house on the property that we can occupy right away, though of course we'll want to build something bigger soon. It will be nice to build our own house for our family, won't it, Nellie," he said.

"Of course," she said. "Our own house for our family." There didn't seem to be any choice at this point, so she tried to summon her enthusiasm. At least a smaller place meant less work for her.

Within a month, the Tharsings had packed up their belongings and sold the household goods and farm equipment they couldn't take with them, as well as the livestock. This included the little mare, Sallie. Nellie had hardly ridden her in the last year, and not at all since her pregnancy because she feared another miscarriage, but she was very sad to see the gentle little horse go. She had spent many a happy afternoon riding Sallie. Somehow her loss felt like severing the last connection with her girlhood. When they got to Yuba City, Chris replenished the livestock as part of setting up the farm, but there was no talk of a saddle horse for Nellie.

Yuba City turned out to be not much of a county seat. It made Modesto, with its four churches and handful of general and dry goods stores, look like a metropolis. It had a hotel, a couple of stores and little churches and several lawyers. There were maybe a hundred houses altogether. As they drove up to the little house on their farm, Nellie's heart sank. It was certainly small. It was one story, four rooms with a small attic. There was a bedroom, a sitting room, a small kitchen, and another small room that they could use as a dining room. The outside was whitewashed and weather beaten. The inside rooms had been roughly plastered and covered with paint that was chipping and peeling. "Well, I feel like a pioneer," said Nellie.

"The house will do for now," said Chris, sternly. "This is a start for us. You can have some money to buy paint and fix it up. It will look a lot better when you've hung the curtains and such."

Nellie worked hard on the house. She scoured it from top to bottom, including washing and scraping the walls. Chris helped her with the painting, and after she had placed the furniture and hung the pictures and curtains from the Modesto house, it began to look like home. It took her a while to get used to the small kitchen, with just the table to work at, but she had to admit that, at eight months pregnant, she was glad to have less house to take care of. Chris started in right away with his plans for the farm. It was mostly peaches and grapes when they arrived, but he planted plums and the pears that had always been his pride, often exhibited at the agricultural fair in Modesto.

During this busy and hopeful fall, some of the early spirit of their marriage was rekindled as they worked together on the new farm and looked forward to the birth of their child. True to her word, Caroline came in the middle of December to help. Nellie could see that her mother was taken aback by the house, even though she had tried to prepare her by telling her they were in a temporary little place until they could build their permanent home. But Caroline had seen, and lived in, worse. She praised her daughter's efforts at cleaning and sprucing it up. The baby, a daughter, arrived on the twenty-eighth of December. Nellie knew Chris had wanted a son, although he tried to hide his disappointment. She was glad her mother was there to be glad and excited.

Luckily, Hazel, as they called her, was a beautiful baby, with large eyes that became deep brown, almost black, like her father's, and her mother's abundant, dark curly hair. Chris quickly forgot his disappointment. Within a few months, his little daughter had become his pride and joy. In the evenings, he would sit holding her and singing little Danish songs as she gazed up at him with her serious brown eyes. As she grew, he bounced her on his knee and made up little games to play with her.

It was good for Nellie that Hazel was born in the winter, or what passed for it in Yuba City. There wasn't so much work to do, and she was able to spend a good deal of her time caring for the baby. But as spring came on, it was time to plant the garden, and Chris saw to it that she enlarged the chicken flock. From sun to sun, he was hard at work on the farm, taking care of the trees and cultivating the grapevines. In the evenings, after Nellie had put Hazel to sleep in her cradle and gone to bed exhausted herself, Chris would sit by the lamp reading agricultural journals and pamphlets about his new crops. As usual, he quickly became a favorite among the neighboring farmers with his hearty, friendly manner, and whenever they went to town, he got all the information he could about the local growing conditions and the techniques for growing the new crops.

As the heat rose in the valley, things became harder. The little house was not well ventilated, and as the temperature rose into the nineties each day, it became a little oven, impossible to stand, especially for the baby. Nellie spent as little time in the kitchen as possible, often cooking outside over a fire pit the previous owners had left behind. She put Hazel under the one shade tree they had next to the house as she worked over the fire or in the garden.

Chris was still spending every available hour in his orchards and vineyard, and things looked promising for a good harvest. But then something began to go wrong with the grapes. A pattern of dark spots broke out on the stems of two rows of the plants. Then the leaves and stems shriveled up and the unripe grapes fell to the ground. Chris was at a loss. He consulted his pamphlets, but nothing seemed to explain just this sort of disease. On the next Saturday, he went into town and talked to the group of farmers gathered in Hobbes's general store. "I'm new to grapes," he said, "and I've never seen anything like this. There are no pests that I see, and I can't find anything just like it in the agriculture pamphlets."

"You can't expect much out of those government pamphlets," said Elisha Boggs. "Them things are written for Eastern conditions, not for what we're dealing with out here." A couple of the other men nodded sagely, but it turned out they didn't agree on what was wrong. "Sounds like a fungus," said Elisha, "or black measles. That'll come from extra rain like we had this spring."

"Or it could be from over-fertilizing," said Tom Owens. "Happened to me one year till I cut back by half on what I was using."

After half an hour, Chris was more confused than he had been before he started. What he did know was that his grapes could be suffering from any one of several diseases or funguses, or from a mistake he had made in cultivation. He went home a dejected man, and, examining his vines, saw more cause for dejection. Many more plants were in one stage or another of the same condition. He was at a loss over what to do for them, and eventually, he lost nearly half the crop. The rest of the crops did fairly well, but the work he had put into planting pear trees would not bear fruit for at least another couple of years. 1889 was another lean year for the Tharsing family. Chris told Nellie there would be no new house for them that year.

Nellie was disappointed about the house, but she tried not to let it show to Chris, who would only resent her lack of faith in him. After the harvest, he remained dejected about the grapes, making every effort he could to find out about them. He finally decided it must have been black measles, which attacks mostly mature vines, and in January, he went ahead and spent the money and effort to plant new vines to replace the ones that had died. Still, he was dispirited and out of sorts. As the spring and summer went on, he complained constantly about Nellie's cooking, the state of the garden and the chicken coops, even her care of Hazel, who was kept as scrupulously neat and clean as any city baby.

Chris had a way of droning on and on in a monotone of complaint when he was alone with Nellie, quite different from his hearty manner with other people. Nellie did her best to ignore him and get on with things, but one day when he was haranguing her about the state of the kitchen, which she knew was in perfect order, she suddenly shot back, "maybe I could keep house better if I had a better house to keep, which we might have if you did *your* job better!" It was out before she knew it, and in the next moment, his hand had shot out and slapped her hard, on each cheek. She was too stunned at first to feel it. She looked up at him and saw a look of rage in his eyes that scared her to the bone.

She dropped her eyes. "I'm sorry, Chris," she said. "I didn't mean that."

He stared at her, his face grim. "Take it back," he said.

"I take it back," she said.

"All right. You'd better get this kitchen cleaned up then." He stalked out of the room.

Nellie was stunned. She could feel her face bruising and her right eye swelling where the knuckles had hit it. She wet a dish towel with cold water from the bucket and put it over her eye. Then she looked at the kitchen. "It's perfectly fine," she said.

Later that day, Chris apologized for slapping Nellie, and he did seem genuinely sorry about the bruises, which kept her from going to church that Sunday. "You just set something off in me," he said. "You should never say anything like that to me." Nellie promised not to, but something seemed to have been released in him, or some restraint taken off. Now when he was angry, he shouted at her and banged things around, often scaring Hazel, who cried, giving him something more to blame Nellie for. She resolved to keep her head down and give him as few occasions to explode as possible, but she knew that often he was just wound up tight and looking for an excuse. She told herself that it had nothing to do with her.

Over the three years of the lease, the farm did fairly well, about as well as the Modesto property had. Chris never became confident about grape cultivation. There were just too many unknowns there for him. The peaches and plums generally did well, but he was disappointed that his pears didn't seem to flourish in this soil. They never did make enough to build a house, although they made enough to pay the rent and make ends meet. For the most part, their life went along smoothly, punctuated by outbursts of Chris's anger that sometimes exploded into violence against Nellie. Through all of it, she kept a submissive posture and kept silent. She felt that there was nothing else for her to do. Hazel grew into a pretty but timid little girl. Chris never hit her and seldom shouted at her directly, but she clung to her mother. He was annoyed that she wasn't more eager to sit on his lap and talk to him or have him read to her. He blamed Nellie for tying her to her apron strings.

Chapter 5

Hazel was three-and-a-half the summer she got malaria. In 1892, it wasn't unusual to get malaria in Yuba City. People put it down to the miasma that arose from the reedy wetlands around the Feather River. Many of the adults in town had sporadic bouts of the disease, high fever alternating with shaking chills, body aches, and terrible upset in their stomachs and bowels. It was not taken lightly, but it almost always passed. With children it was different. They seemed to be taken harder with the disease, with a very high fever. More than one had lapsed into a stupor and died.

Nellie was terrified for her little girl and nursed her constantly, using cold cloths to bring down her fever or wrapping her in blankets to fight the chills, cleaning her up when she vomited, trying to get her to take as much water as she could, and doing what she could to ease the terrible aching in the little body. Chris was terrified too, but his fear took the form of tirades berating Nellie for not keeping their daughter safe from the disease and giving orders about her care. During his harangues, Nellie would put her head down and sit looking at her daughter, who was often crying in pain or out of her head with fever, and think, "Get better, Hazel, and we will get out of this place. I promise that I will get you out of this place."

Nellie formed her simple escape plan as she sat by Hazel's bedside. She was consulting the *Home Physician,* a book that Chris held in great reverence because of its scientific language. He had insisted Nellie follow its instructions to the letter in Hazel's care. As the little girl at last fell into a long, natural sleep, Nellie thought she should look at the section on the convalescent period. "In convalescence," it said, "the patient should be exposed to salubrious air if at all possible. Removal from a river valley or swampy area that is productive of miasma to the fresh air of the seaside or a higher elevation can be highly beneficial in recovery." As she read, she felt she had been given the gift that would save both Hazel and her. When Chris came in that evening, Nellie gave him the good news of Hazel's long sleep, which the *Home Physician* said was clear evidence of recovery. "She will need to sleep for a few more days and take nourishment regularly, but we can hope for the best now," she said, with a quick glance at Chris's face.

In this brief moment, Nellie could see Chris's great relief contesting with his need to assume control of the situation. "That is good news," he said. "Mind you follow the instructions carefully now."

"That's something I wanted to consult you about," said Nellie, keeping her posture submissive and her eyes resting carefully on Hazel. She picked up the book and read the passage about salubrious air to Chris. "I'm wondering if we shouldn't move her out of this atmosphere for a while once she's able to travel and take her on a visit to Oakland where she could get plenty of fresh sea air."

Chris reacted with his usual resistance to any suggestion of Nellie's. "I'm afraid that's impossible, Nellie. A holiday now is out of the question," he said sternly. "I couldn't leave the farm."

"Well, if you couldn't come, maybe I could take her on the train by myself and stay with my mother for a week or ten days."

"And who would do your work?"

"Maybe Hannah, Mrs. McMahon's oldest daughter, could come and help. She's a big girl now, and she does everything her mother does around the house and the farm. I'm sure she could cope for a week or two. It would mean so much if we could do that for Hazel. The book says that the better air is an important part of the convalescence."

Between his respect for the book and his genuine concern for his daughter, Chris's resistance was breaking down. "Well, we will see how Hazel's recovery goes," he said. I will send Jake to the McMahons' to see if they can spare Hannah.

Happy to help their neighbors, the MacMahons agreed to send Hannah over in a week's time. Nellie wrote immediately to her mother to expect them. Over the next week, as Hazel improved, Nellie gathered and packed as much of their belongings as she could without arousing Chris's suspicion. She packed their warmer clothes at the bottom of bags and bundles and made sure that her few keepsakes and Hazel's prized doll with the porcelain head and real hair, sent by Tena and Alice the previous Christmas, were carefully stowed away.

As he loaded the wagon for the trip to the railroad stop, Chris chided Nellie for not being more efficient in packing. "You don't need all of this for a ten-day stay," he said. "Why didn't you use your head? What do you have in these bundles?"

Nellie had to be careful here. If this set him off and he got angry enough, he was capable of pulling the bundles to pieces and demanding that she repack. She didn't know if she could explain some of the things in the bundles. "I thought I should bring some of our warmer things because you never know about the weather in Oakland at this time of year. It's so important for Hazel to be kept warm now."

"Well, you could have fit enough into the two bags if you'd had any sense."

"Yes, I suppose so," she said. "I've just been so anxious about Hazel that I haven't been thinking very clearly."

Nellie heard him mutter something about "the stupid cow" as he pitched the bundles into the wagon, but everything went with her. On the train to Sacramento, and then Oakland, she felt wave after wave of relief. She was free. Free of the relentless daily cycle of the farm, free of the heat and the mosquitoes, free of Chris's constant chiding and complaining—and his periodic outbursts of rage and violence. Hazel was safe, sleeping on the seat beside her. She was not going back.

In Oakland, Nellie and Hazel stayed with her sister Mary Shay's family because the Gotchetts' boarding house was full to bursting. Since she wasn't as close to Mary as she was to Alice and Tena, Nellie was disappointed at first, but the quiet order of Mary's house on Poplar Street turned out to be just what Hazel needed. The little girl was painfully shy and timid, the result, Nellie thought, of her father's strict standards for her behavior, very hard for a little child to live up to, his constant tirades, and his unpredictable violence toward her mother.

Hazel said nothing in the Shays' house, except when she and her mother were alone in their room, but she took quickly to the little bull terrier, Bruno. She also sat rapt in the evenings when her Uncle John read from Sir Walter Scott in his soft Irish voice. She would sit next to him, falling asleep against him as he read, something she never would have done with her father. She shied away from her cousins, eleven-year-old Frank and nine-year-old Roy, who were generally kind to her, but rough in the manner of growing boys. Mary, who had always wanted a daughter, was charmed by her pretty, delicate little niece, and determined to draw her out. She brought her to the kitchen when she baked, giving her a lump of dough to work and putting the end result into the oven to be shown off at the next meal. Hazel took this activity with great seriousness, doing her best to shape her little loaf of bread or, with her aunt's help, to roll out her pie dough and fill it carefully with peaches or apples. She listened to everyone's extravagant compliments with a solemn face and shining eyes.

Nellie did not tell her family right away that she was determined not to go back to Yuba City. Instead, she went to see Mel Chapman. She was aware from things her sisters had written to her that Mel had done well for himself. He had passed the bar and started a law practice, very quickly gaining a reputation as a trial lawyer, especially for his skill at oratory. He had won several high-profile cases, securing damages for a young woman against a street railroad company and getting an acquittal in a high-profile murder case. Another case was decided by the Supreme Court and affected cites all over the state. He had been elected to the state legislature. Now he was running for Mayor of Oakland and was expected to win. Back in 1887, he had married Lillian Childs, who was assumed to have brought him a tidy sum of money. The Chapmans lived comfortably on Eighteenth Street, near Mel's mother and brothers.

Nellie went to see Mel in his office on Broadway. As the office boy opened the door for her, she was delighted to see Mel's face light up with the eager expression of the old days. "Nellie!" he said, as he jumped up from his desk to greet her, "I didn't know you were in town." As he drew closer and looked into her face, his broad smile drew in a bit. "How are you, Nellie? You look—a little tired."

Nellie laughed. "Well, I can see the lawyer in you, Mel. I look terrible, but it's all right. I've just lost some weight and spent a lot of sleepless nights nursing my little girl."

"What's wrong with her?"

"Oh, she's much better now. She had quite a bout of malaria. It's pretty common up in Sutter County. I brought her down here to stay with my folks for a while and recuperate. You look well, yourself, Mel. It looks like marriage agrees with you. You certainly haven't lost any weight."

"No," said Mel, patting his well-filled vest. "On the contrary. Lillian sees to it that we do very well in the culinary department. But it looks like your daughter isn't the only one who needs to recuperate. Sit down, and we can visit a while. I don't have an appointment for another half hour."

Nellie sat in the chair opposite the desk and looked frankly at him. "I should tell you, Mel. This isn't purely a social call."

"Oh," he looked a little disappointed. "You need a lawyer's advice."

"Not a lawyer's advice. Advice from someone I trust very much, who is also a lawyer."

He leaned forward a little. "What is it, Nellie?"

"I want you to tell me what I would have to do to get a divorce and what my rights are."

His eyes widened. "Well, you would have to tell me the situation before I could advise you. Are you sure you want to do that?"

"Yes. I made the biggest mistake of my life marrying Chris Tharsing instead of waiting for you. I don't mind telling you that. You deserve to hear it. And I trust you with the secrets of my marriage more than I would trust any other man."

He looked down at the papers on his desk for a while, and then he looked at her. "Well, it's a strange situation, Nellie. But I do want to help you. Tell me why you want a divorce."

In the next half hour, Nellie emptied her soul to Mel, pouring forth the secrets she had been keeping for nearly seven years. She told of her husband's sporadic violence and constant verbal abuse, of the relentless burden of work he placed on her, of his tight grip on the purse strings and his refusal to give her money for the most basic things for herself and their daughter, and of the general misery of her life. "He even made me quit the choir," she said. "Remember how much I used to love music, Mel?"

"I remember," he said softly.

"There's no music in my life now."

Mel had listened with growing anger to Nellie's account of her life. This was someone he had cared for, a lovely, vibrant girl, who now looked ten years older than her twenty-five years, worn out by this cruel oaf who had no right to her. "I'll help you, Nellie," he said.

"I don't have any money now. But I have plans for making my living. I'm sure I can pay your fee soon."

"We won't worry about that now. The important thing is to get this done and get this man out of your life."

So Nellie had one of the best lawyers in Oakland to handle her divorce as well as a good friend who was not about to allow Chris Tharsing to push her around anymore. Between them, Mel and the Shays saw that Tharsing had no access to Nellie or Hazel during the divorce proceedings. At one point, when Tharsing threatened desperately to claim that Hazel wasn't his child, John Shay, who had grown very fond of the little girl, told him that he personally would beat him up if he made such a charge publicly. In the end, Chris Tharsing let it go. He had given up on the Yuba City farm and wanted to make a fresh start in Shasta County anyway. He too felt miserable in the marriage and blamed Nellie for that. There was no property to speak of, only Hazel. He knew he was in no position to try to take care of a three-year-old, but he hated to let her go. In the end, he got Nellie's promise to let him visit her when he was in Oakland. Nellie knew that, once Chris had plunged into his new farm in Shasta County, that would not be often.

Nellie and Hazel settled into life at the Shays', who told Nellie they could stay as long as they needed to. But she had already made a plan to support herself and Hazel. In San Francisco in the 1890s, the main legitimate business that was open to a woman on her own was keeping a boarding house, a business that, thanks to her upbringing, Nellie knew well. But unlike her mother, Nellie did not relish cooking, especially for a crowd of critical boarders every day. She did like taking care of houses, though. She liked making things clean and attractive, and she did housework with great efficiency. The chances she had had to transform her houses through cleaning and decorating had given her a great deal of satisfaction. She thought that maintaining a rooming house, with no meals, would be the right job for her. Between the boarding house and the farms, she had a lot of experience in dealing with single men. The prospect of a men-only rooming house did not scare her.

One morning early, Nellie took the ferry over to San Francisco and began scouring the city for rooming houses that were for sale or rent. After a few days of studying the advertisements and walking various neighborhoods, she found what she was looking for on O'Farrell Street. It was two blocks from Union Square, on the edge of the sleazy Tenderloin district with its noisy nightlife, but at the bottom of exclusive Nob Hill. The building had been built in the seventies as a rather exclusive small rooming house for bachelors. The façade was a little pretentious, but not vulgarly so, a light-colored brick, now covered with soot, and a double door flanked by two Doric columns, painted white, but now soot-grey. On a tarnished brass plate next to the entrance, she could barely make out the words "The Portals." It had three floors, with six rooms on each floor and two small rooms in an attic gable in the center of the building. Ten of the rooms were currently occupied, and the building was available for sale or lease.

When Nellie got the agent to take her through, she could see that the building had been allowed to deteriorate so that it had a seedy, down-at-heels look. There was paint peeling on the walls in the dirty stairways and halls. The two large public parlors for the residents were dark and dreary. On the street side, there were some nice large windows, but they were dimmed by years of dirt and hung with dusty, faded velveteen curtains. There were worn patterned carpets on the floor. A few mismatched sofas and stuffed chairs were scattered about, and there were some felt-covered card tables which obviously saw a lot of use. The two bedrooms without tenants had yellowing wallpaper, peeling in spots, that must be twenty years old at least, and cheap, worn carpets on the floor. Each room had a small bath, unusual in a building this old, a brass bedstead, a cheap and battered "matching set" of armoire and dresser, a small table with two wooden chairs by the single window, and one stuffed chair. Dingy Nottingham lace curtains hung in the windows. The overall effect was depressing. Someone would have to be either unable to afford anything better or immune to the look of his surroundings to rent such a room.

The attic rooms, clearly intended for maids, were the cleanest things Nellie saw in the building. They were a decent size and painted white. Each had an iron bedstead with a mattress, a small dresser, a diminutive wooden table and chair, and a secure lock on the door. The two rooms shared a bath and a little kitchen alcove. Nellie examined the attic walls and ceiling carefully to check for evidence of leaks and didn't see any. As Nellie and the agent were coming down the stairs, they ran into the maid, a girl of about sixteen who said her name was Kitty. She had a pleasant, freckled face with an upturned nose, and looked healthy and strong, though her unkempt hair and dirty apron made a slovenly appearance. Nellie asked her if there was an owner or manager on the premises.

Kitty laughed. "No," she said. "It's mostly just me and Mac, down in the cellar. He looks after the furnace and boiler and fixes things when they break. Mr. Butts comes around to collect the rents and pay us on Monday evenings."

"How do you like the roomers?" asked Nellie.

"We get along fine," Kitty said. "I try to do the rooms when I know they'll be out. I make the beds and tidy every day, and I clean three rooms a day so it's once a week for them. If they're in the room, some of them will talk your ear off. They're kind of lonely, especially the older ones."

The agent said the price for the rooms was four or five dollars a month depending on the location. The price of the building was $1,800. From having scoured the papers, Nellie knew this was a bargain if the building was in good shape, and it seemed to have good bones beneath the dirt and neglect. At four percent, a twenty-year mortgage on the property would cost about twelve dollars a month. It was possible. She knew there was no way a bank would lend her the money—a divorced woman with no down payment or business history. She went to see Mel, who was now the Mayor of Oakland, and put it to him purely as a business deal. She explained that her idea was not just to run the rooming house, but to gradually fix it up so that it could command higher rents and then sell it at a profit, using the money to invest in another run-down building, and do the same thing with it. She thought this would be a profitable, if labor-intensive business. She asked him to lend her the money at the going bank rate of four percent. Mel was happy to see Nellie so enthusiastic and excited about the future, more like her old self. If anyone could succeed with this scheme, Nellie could. On the following Saturday, he went to San Francisco and met Nellie and the agent on O'Farrell Street. After inspecting the building from top to bottom, including the roof and cellar, and closely questioning Mac about the condition of things, Mel decided to lend Nellie the money. She was in business.

Nellie asked the Shays to take care of Hazel while she fixed up The Portals. The little girl still needed fresh air and rest, and everyone agreed that she would be much better off in the Shay family's comfortable and orderly house in Oakland than in the rooming house while Nellie was spending all her time cleaning and fixing. The first thing she did was have a straight talk with Kitty, telling her that the standards for cleaning in the house were going to go up and she would be expected to work as hard as Nellie if she stayed on. Kitty was intrigued at the thought of a young woman owner who expected to work alongside her. She said she guessed she would stay awhile and see how it worked out. Not wanting to reduce revenue by taking up one of the prime rental rooms, Nellie moved into the other small room in the attic next to Kitty's. She proved equal to the task, despite the high standard for work that Nellie set, and the two formed the habit of cooking their meals together in the little attic kitchen. They gradually became friends, forming a little feminine fellowship at the top of the house full of bachelor men.

The first order of business was to clean the building. The two women started with the halls and stairs because they were the worst. Over several days, after the basic housekeeping of the rooms was done, they washed the walls and scrubbed the floors, taking off layers of dirt. With the money from the first month's rents, Nellie had the walls in the halls and stairways painted light blue with white trim. The floors and stairs she had painted a glossy grey. Then she hung mirrors in strategic spots to reflect the light, making the halls seem lighter and larger.

Nellie and Kitty tackled the two empty bedrooms, cleaning them until they shone and replacing the wallpaper. Nellie hired paper hangers for the first room, and she and Kitty watched the men carefully. They hung the paper in the second room themselves. Nellie thought the most important thing for elevating the general quality of the rooms was to replace the cheap, battered furniture. She began going to estate sales and scouring the city's second-hand shops for good furniture with little sign of wear. She had a good eye and found she could drive a hard bargain when she needed to. Before long, she was able to replace the furniture and rugs in the two rooms with some really elegant pieces salvaged from a few Nob Hill mansions. She advertised the rooms for six dollars, two more than they had been bringing in, and was able to rent them to two young men who worked in office buildings nearby. As additional rooms became vacant, Nellie went through the same process. She and Kitty became quite adept at stripping and hanging wallpaper, and she found she really enjoyed scouting out the furniture.

The big job was the two public rooms on the first floor. Nellie made a study of the nicer rooming houses in nearby neighborhoods, and she could see that her parlors were old fashioned. What the young bachelors wanted was more of a club atmosphere. In the nineties, poker, a part of San Francisco life since the gold rush days, was undergoing a surge in popularity among the young men who worked in the city. The downtown men's clubs had constant poker games, some of them for high stakes. She thought she could create a club-like atmosphere at The Portals by devoting one of the rooms to cards and designating the other a "club room" where the residents could relax and entertain friends. She was able to use the card tables she already had, just replacing the felt tops, and she gradually replaced the chairs at the card tables as she found good ones. For the club room, she found some richly upholstered stuffed chairs and gradually replaced the old horsehair sofas with some dark brown tufted leather ones that would wear well and, with the paneled walls, seemed to say men's club. She acquired some patterned carpets that looked like the oriental rugs she saw in the pictures of the fancier clubs. When she and Kitty had taken out the old carpets, waxed the paneling and hardwood floors, which were in good shape, and put the rugs down, the room had what she thought was a very clubby look. She continued to add touches like new brass lamps and potted plants, but overall, she was satisfied with the transformation.

Most of the residents were very happy with the changes. The Portals was becoming known as a desirable building for young professional men to live in. But some of the older residents were not happy. They missed the peace and quiet and felt estranged from the new class of roomers. As several of them moved out, Nellie redecorated their rooms and easily found new tenants who took the rooms at higher rates. Once she was finished with the general redecoration, she offered to redo the rooms of the remaining original tenants if they would agree to a one dollar increase in their monthly rents. All but two agreed to this, and she and Kitty went ahead with the redecorating.

At the end of the year, Nellie had almost realized her plan. The building had been transformed from top to bottom into a fashionable men's rooming house. She was now taking in twenty percent more in room rents than the previous owner had. The only remaining project was the outside of the building, which was still a sooty grey color. She was able to save enough money by the spring to have the façade of the building sandblasted to bring back the light color of the bricks and to have the columns painted a glossy white. She saw to it that Mac kept the brass name plaque shining.

Chapter 6

While her mother was building her business in San Francisco, Hazel was living in Oakland with the Shays. The separation had been very hard at first. In her short life, she had spent nearly every hour of the day with her mother. After living with the unpredictable brutality of her father, she was afraid of new situations and strangers. When her mother left for San Francisco, Aunt Mary did her best to comfort and distract Hazel, and the little girl sought the shelter of Uncle John, as if from a storm. In a sense, that was the way she regarded her cousins Frank and Roy, who invaded the house after school, laughing and shouting and tousling like two puppies. Hazel, who had seen other children only at a distance before, was scared of the loud noise and the rowdy play. Mostly the boys ignored her, but when they thought of it, they treated her as a kind of little pet who had come into their lives. "How ya doin,' Brown Eyes?" Roy would say, patting her curly head, and then run off to take care of some boy business.

Hazel's closest relationship in the Shay house was with the bull terrier, Bruno, a comical little brown dog with big ears and little legs. She treated him as a sort of live doll, and he was very patient about it. She would invite Bruno to a tea party, which meant dressing the dog in doll clothes and sitting him on a chair. She would get some food on a tin plate from Aunt Mary and set it on the floor, sitting herself down across from it with her own cup of milk. Then she would give the signal for Bruno to jump down and eat. Everyone in the family marveled at the control the little girl had over the dog, who was not particularly obedient to anyone else. It might have been a touch of jealousy that motivated Frank to run into the room and yell "Cats!" one day when he came home from school and saw the tea party going on. Bruno jumped up and ran wildly around the house in his doll clothes, looking for the cats, which made the boys double over with laughter. After that, it became a standing joke for Frank to yell "Cats!" whenever he saw a tea party, and Hazel resented him bitterly for it. She mostly kept her distance from both boys, relying on the protection of Aunt Mary and Uncle John and the companionship of Bruno.

Nellie visited on most Sundays, taking an early ferry to Oakland so she could sing in the church choir. Hazel looked forward throughout the week to these visits, asking Aunt Mary every day how many days it was until Sunday. When Nellie was there, Hazel clung to her or sat on her lap the whole day. She would hide in her mother's skirts while she was talking to a stranger at church and refuse to look up if she was told to say, "How do you do."

Nellie and Mary discussed Hazel's shyness and what to do about it. Mary tried to find other little girls for her to play with, but there were only older children in the houses around them. She thought things might improve when Hazel started school, but when she did, she stayed aloof from the other children and didn't seem to make any friends. Noticing this, Miss Boardman, her first-grade teacher, suggested that Hazel might profit from the elocution lessons she gave on Saturdays. The children were grouped by age. Hazel would be with other little ones who were just learning little poems and reciting them. "We often find that it brings the little shy ones out of their shells," she said. Mary spoke to Nellie about it the following Sunday and offered to bring her to the lessons if Nellie could pay the fifty cents a week. So Hazel started going to Miss Boardman's Elocution School the next week.

At first, Hazel enjoyed the lessons. There were always things to see on her walk with Aunt Mary, including several dogs who lived along the route and barked at other people, but always allowed Hazel to pat them on the head. She was proud of being one of the quickest to learn the voice exercises and the little pieces. But when Miss Boardman started calling on her little pupils to recite individually, Hazel began to dread the moment when she had to come to the front of the room and face the eyes of her classmates. She would look down at the floor and recite in a soft voice that was nothing like the confident tone she had when she recited with the group or at home. This response was nothing new to Miss Boardman, who was used to shy little girls and did her best to encourage her, but for more than a year, the recitals were torturous for Hazel.

Then Miss Boardman had an inspiration. She gave Hazel a special piece to learn, a little speech about Christmas by Carol Bird, a character from the popular book *The Birds' Christmas Carol* by Kate Douglas Wiggins. She told her that when she recited it, she must try to forget about being Hazel and concentrate on saying the speech as Carol Bird would say it. She must try to *become* Carol Bird. Hazel concentrated hard on this, and, by assuming a role, a sort of mask that stood between her and her audience, she learned a technique to combat her shyness that she was to use all her life. Hazel got Uncle John to read *The Birds' Christmas Carol* aloud in the evenings and listened, rapt, to every one of Carol's speeches. The boys said the book was sappy and refused to listen, but Aunt Mary said it was enjoyable.

Hazel found that playing the role of Carol was useful to her with strangers and teachers, and even her schoolmates. She became known as a very sweet girl. She recited so well in the class that Miss Boardman put her piece into the public recital, where the little children usually performed only as a group. The audience applauded enthusiastically for the curly haired, dark-eyed little girl with the pretty, earnest face reciting her piece about the meaning of Christmas. After that, Hazel's feeling about elocution school changed dramatically. She worked hard to get the chance to be in the recital every six months.

Hazel's shyness did not disappear when she started attending the elocution school, but it helped her to cope. She learned to look up and speak out when spoken to by adults, and she grew comfortable and confident around the other girls. Her role as something of a star in the elocution class carried over to Cole Elementary School as well. Miss Boardman was in charge of the school programs and plays, and she usually salted them with pieces already mastered by her elocution students. Hazel always played a central role in school performances.

While she was in elementary school, Hazel saw her mother on most Sundays, but saw little of her father. Chris Tharsing was doing well in Shasta County. A few times a year, he would come to Oakland and stay with his sister Sophie Dahl. Then he would bring Hazel to the Dahls to spend a day or two. These were always special occasions. Chris would take Hazel for a walk and out to a restaurant. As she grew older, he would take her to San Francisco for a day in Golden Gate Park or to a vaudeville show. He was always jovial and kind to her and paid her a good deal of attention, questioning her about her schooling and her interests. Hazel came to adore her father.

Chris Tharsing was proud of his pretty daughter, but he did not like the idea that Nellie, and through her the Shays, were in charge of her upbringing. When Hazel was nine years old, Chris convinced his sister Sophie that she and her husband Fred would be better guardians for his daughter than the Shays. The childless Sophie had grown fond of the little girl. The Dahls agreed to take on the responsibility as long as it was what Hazel wanted and Chris could get Nellie to agree. During his next visit, Chris lavished all his attention on Hazel, finally surprising her with two angora goats who pulled a cart that was trimmed in red Moroccan leather and shaped just like the carriage of a princess in her book of fairy tales. Chris told Hazel that the Shays' house on Poplar Street was no place to keep goats. The Dahl's place on San Leandro Road in rural Brooklyn Township was much better suited to it, so that was where the goats and the lovely little carriage would be, whenever she wanted to use them.

The Shays, who had come to view Hazel as their own daughter, were furious when they heard of this ploy, but they realized that, since they were not legally Hazel's guardians, there was nothing they could do. Nellie knew that she had become something of a visiting relative in Hazel's eyes and was afraid of alienating her daughter by criticizing her father. So Hazel was completely unprepared when Chris brought the subject up as they unhar-nessed the goats and staked them in the Dahls' big yard.

"Hazel," he said, "do you like spending time here with your aunt and uncle and me?"

"Of course, Papa," she said. "I wish you were here more often."

He took her hand, his black eyes looking earnestly into hers, "If you lived here, I could see you more. Would you liked to live with Aunt Sophie and Uncle Fred?"

She looked up in surprise. "You mean live here instead of with Aunt Mary and Uncle John?"

"Yes," he said. "I know they would like to have you."

"But Papa, I love Aunt Mary and Uncle John. They've taken care of me for as long as I can remember. I like Aunt Sophie and Uncle Fred, but I don't even know them really." She grew more and more agitated. "I would never want to move out here in the country and go to a strange school," she said, turning a pleading look on him. "I can see you just as often living in Oakland as I would if I lived here."

Seeing the intensity of Hazel's resistance, Chris gave up the idea for the time being and resolved to try it again when she was older. Meanwhile, Sophie didn't mind having some goats to supply her with milk for cheese.

When Hazel told Mary and John Shay what her father had said, and they relayed it to Nellie, they were all worried. If Chris Tharsing had gotten it into his head to get Hazel away from them, they knew this wasn't the end of it. He was like a dog with a bone. Nellie resolved to play more of a role in her daughter's life after this. To Hazel's delight, she began to come to the school programs she was in and would have her recite whatever piece she was working on each week, commenting seriously on her performance.

Hazel worked hard to present her latest piece to her mother each Sunday. When she was in the fourth grade, Nellie suggested that Hazel could be working on more advanced pieces than Miss Boardman was giving her. This was all the encouragement John Shay needed. He and Hazel began looking for pieces to suggest to Miss Boardman, who was only too happy to be relieved of that part of her job. Uncle John had always read a lot of poetry and Shakespeare in the evenings. With his help, Hazel began to recite poems by Tennyson, Elizabeth Barrett Browning, Joaquin Miller, even some speeches from Shakespeare. She took Miss Boardman's training seriously. The audiences at exercises and recitations were duly impressed with the powerful and beautifully modulated voice that came out of the delicate little girl.

By this time, John Shay's contracting business had become profitable enough that the Shays were able to enjoy some luxuries. For John, the first on the list was going to the theater, especially to see great Shakespearean actors. He loved taking the whole family to San Francisco for matinees. He would prepare them all beforehand by reading the play aloud, and they saw some memorable performances—Will Read as Richard III, Ada Rehan in *A Midsummer Night's Dream*, Helena Modjeska in *Antony and Cleopatra*, experiences they never forgot. Hazel watched and listened, rapt, and later tried to imitate their tricks of voice, their grand gestures. She would hold serious discussions with Miss Boardman about the effect of a specific gesture or how to deliver a particular line as a great actress had.

Chapter 7

By 1901, when Hazel was twelve years old, Nellie had done well for herself. Having sold The Portals for fifty percent more than she paid for it, she was able to pay off the mortgage from Mel and, with her successful business history, to secure a mortgage for a bigger rooming house. She had done this twice in eight years and was now living in a five-room flat on Geary Street, while Kitty served as the onsite manager of the latest rooming house two blocks away. She had done her best to leave her life with Chris Tharsing behind her and was now listing herself as a widow in the City Directory.

In each successive rooming house, Nellie had made sure that there was plenty of space for entertainment, so that comfortable poker and club rooms became the hallmark of her buildings. They attracted men from the theatre, newspaper men, young workers in the office buildings nearby, and others from the "sporting set." Each successive building had improved in quality, so for the present one, The Pillars, the only effort she needed to put in was redecorating. To help maintain a standard of decorum in her buildings, she made her presence known in the public rooms, walking through them each evening before she left for home, greeting the residents, meeting their guests, and occasionally kibitzing on a poker game. As her residents were now among the well-connected young men in the city, she became acquainted with many of the influential men in San Francisco in this way, and she had a couple of discreet romances.

On a rainy Friday night in January, there were two poker games going on. There were only four players seated at the table of young newspaper men. As Nellie came over to say good evening, Tom Wilts, who was a bit of a wag, said, "What do you say, Mrs. Tharsing. Help us out. Joe Sheets has stood us up, and we need another hand."

She laughed. "I'm sure you can do better than me."

"No, really, Mrs. T. You know the game. It's just for fun. Dime ante. Why not play with us?" With broad, welcoming smiles, the other players joined in a chorus of persuasion. "Come on, Mrs. T." "It'll be fun." "You know you'll clean us out."

Nellie was flattered to be thought enough of a sport by the young men to join their game, and she was not eager to go out into the rain to walk to her flat. She smiled. "Well, all right, gentlemen. But just for a few hands."

Having been trained long ago in the penny ante games with her sisters and Mel Chapman, Nellie held her own. Years of dealing with young men in her business made it relatively easy to read the players, and she had a pretty good poker face, developed during the years of trying not to betray her feelings to Chris Tharsing. The young men seemed to have no idea what she was up to. She had played for an hour before she noticed that the rain had stopped and told them she had to be getting home. She had won two dollars and was very pleased with herself.

The older men at the other table had kept a surreptitious eye on the game, and word quickly got around The Pillars that Mrs. Tharsing had played poker with the newspaper fellows and cleaned them out. After that, she was often asked to join a game by other groups who wanted to test her mettle. Mostly, she laughed off the invitations and said she needed to get home, but once in a while she joined a group that she considered convivial, and she enjoyed herself. Sometimes she won, and sometimes she lost, but she made a few rules for herself from the start to avoid big losses. She kept a kitty of her winnings and always quit when it was half gone. She never played for higher stakes than a quarter ante. If she won, she got out of the game as soon as she could without looking like she was taking the money and running. At first, the men enjoyed having her play as a novelty, but they soon got used to having her there. It was a while before they realized that she was a very good poker player.

Nellie gradually became a regular at a Tuesday table that included a couple of young lawyers, Josh Nesbitt and Jack Lawlor. One Friday morning, Josh stopped by her office on the first floor and asked if she would be interested in joining a game that evening. "It's with some of the big lawyers in my firm. One of the men can't play this week, and they put me in charge of recruiting a substitute. You're the best poker player I know, Mrs. T."

Nellie laughed. "Flattery will get you nowhere, Mr. Nesbitt, at least this time. I can't come to a gentlemen's club to play poker."

"But it's not in a club. We play right there at the firm. We go out to Smith's for supper after work, and then we go back and play in the conference room. It's not a high stakes game, or I wouldn't be able to play. Two-bit ante." He smiled mischievously. "To tell you the truth, they aren't that good. I think you could clean up. And seriously, Mrs. T, you would be doing me a big favor. You're kind of famous as a poker player, you know. Those big boys will love getting a look at your game."

This flattery Nellie could not resist. She agreed to play if Josh would escort her. "Sure," he said. "I'll skip the dinner and get a quick bite. I'll be here to pick you up at seven-thirty."

When Nellie entered the conference room at the G. W. Howe law firm on Market Street, she was amazed to see Mel Chapman sitting at the table. She had been well composed before that, prepared to treat these lawyers with the same cordiality she showed to the guests at The Pillars. But she was so surprised that she blurted out, "Mel, what are you doing here?"

"I see you two know each other," said George Howe. "Why don't we let Mel do the honors."

Mel was not the least ruffled. He introduced her to the others, explaining that they were old friends from Oakland. "Nellie and I used to play poker many years ago," he said. "I'm warning you, she's pretty good."

"So I've heard," said Howe. "Let's see how we measure up." The other men laughed, and they got down to the game. Nellie did all right. She won, but not a great deal. She could see that, except for Mel, the men had been condescending to her a bit at first, yielding a few pots they shouldn't have. But they soon saw that she knew what she was doing, and played as well as they could, which was pretty well. Nellie enjoyed matching wits with them.

As Nellie was preparing to leave with Josh Nesbitt, George Howe said that he hoped she would come to their little game again. Responding that she would be delighted, she said goodbye to each of the men. Coming to Mel last, she asked, "Do you always play in this game, Mel? It's a long way to go to play poker."

Mel smiled. "Well, you know Oakland. People get nervous about playing with the ex-mayor, thinking they're taking city money or something. Here nobody cares." The others laughed, and he explained that the two firms shared several clients with interests in both cities. "I have to come over here anyway," he said. "Might as well get some fun out of it."

"If it's fun losing money," said Howe.

After Josh had left her at her door, Nellie spent the rest of the night thinking about the past, about her time with Mel and all the things that had happened since. Except that she had his name and his daughter, Chris Tharsing was just a dim episode in her life now. She called herself a widow, and when anyone asked her about her husband, she said he had died years before of malaria from the bad air in Yuba City. It gave her pleasure to say this. None of the romances she had indulged in since her marriage were serious. Her current lover, George Clark, was a well-to-do undertaker from Sacramento who took her to Delmonico's. She had no interest in marrying again or being courted, but she felt nostalgic about Mel. She reflected with some surprise that he was the only man she had ever truly loved.

Nellie was invited to Howe's poker game occasionally when one of the men wasn't able to play. One evening, it was Josh who was absent, and Mel offered to see Nellie home. It was the first chance they had had since their business dealings to talk to each other alone, and Nellie took full advantage of the time to find out about Mel's life. He didn't talk much about Lillian, but he now, at fifty, had a four-year-old son, Mel Jr., whom he doted on. After his stint as Mayor, his law firm had done well, but Nellie assumed that it was with Lillian's money that they had bought their big house on Twenty-Third Street, not too far from the Chapman house on Eighteenth where his mother still lived. Mel asked her about her life as well, being careful not to pry. He was delighted to hear how her business had prospered. Nellie was well-off now. She had a sizable bank account and was thinking about the best way to educate Hazel once she finished elementary school next year. She wanted to send her to a boarding school where she would meet girls from society and learn how to behave with them. "No boarding house or rooming house for Hazel," she said. "I want her to be one of those pretty girls on the society page with a rich fiancé and not a care in the world."

Mel looked down into her eyes and smiled. "Who would have thought fifteen years ago that you and I would be among the substantial citizens of Oakland and San Francisco."

"I know, Mel. We've done it after all." She looked up at him. "Are you satisfied? Is this the life you wanted to lead?"

He returned her look. "It isn't something I think about much anymore. I love my son and I want to do the best I can for him and for Lillian. She's been my support every step of the way. And I love the law. Going to law school was the best decision I've made in my life. But it isn't everything. I guess you only have that feeling of all-consuming love once, Nellie, and I have to admit, I passed it up. You go down one road, and you never know where the other would have led."

"Amen," said Nellie.

During the fall, Nellie put a lot of time into planning for Hazel's education. She was due to graduate from Cole in December. Nellie planned to send her to boarding school, partly because she wanted her to make acquaintances in a better social circle than the public high school and partly because she wanted to move her out of the Shays' house. Mary and John had done very well by her daughter. In fact, they had all but made her their own, and deep down, that was what bothered Nellie. She was very proud of Hazel's looks and talent. She wanted her to be more than an Oakland housewife. Truth be told, she wanted her to be much more than Nellie was herself. Hazel, she knew, was going to be beautiful. She wanted to give her the best chance to marry into society, in San Francisco, or even beyond.

Nellie knew perfectly well that, however well she might know movers and shakers like George Howe, and even Mel Chapman, she would not be welcomed into the drawing rooms of their wives. She wanted her daughter to be able to walk proudly into any social gathering and to choose her husband from the highest echelons of society. What's more, she believed Hazel had the talent and the beauty to succeed on the stage, which had been only a girlish dream for Nellie. Hazel would have to be careful to avoid any breath of scandal if she pursued a singing career, but managed well, it could be the key to a brilliant future. Hazel needed a school that would provide her with good social connections as well as more training in singing and elocution. Singing was the Gotchett heritage, after all, and music was a more respectable career than acting. Nellie also wanted her daughter to go far enough away that the other students wouldn't be familiar with her family.

She finally settled on St. Gertrude's Academy in Rio Vista, on the Sacramento River about sixty miles northeast of San Francisco. It could be reached by boat from Oakland. Nellie chose St. Gertrude's partly because Alice's daughter La Veda had been happy there. Also, being a convent school, it was less expensive than most boarding schools. But it did not have the strictness of the typical convent. There were no uniforms or high walls, but beautiful grounds where the girls were free to roam, and the discipline was relaxed. It did not bother the Sisters if the students were not Catholic. Alice had told her there was no attempt to convert the girls, and a number of prominent San Francisco families sent their daughters there.

In shopping for her school clothes, Nellie paid more attention to Hazel than she had in all her twelve years. She had her come and stay in the Geary Street flat for three weekends while they planned and shopped and sewed. At the Cole school, it was usual for a girl to have two or three dresses, a light coat for winter, and a sweater knitted by a mother or grandmother. For St. Gertrude's, Nellie bought Hazel a full wardrobe of clothing the like of which she had seen only in magazines. She tried to impress on her daughter that it was important for her to be able to hold her head up with the girls from the best families, clothes being the central part of that. In a year when the Gibson Girl hour-glass figure and outsized hats with garlands of flowers and ostrich feathers were in fashion, Nellie avoided anything ostentatious for her daughter, anything that could be seen as vulgar or flashy. She bought her a small hat that set off her large brown eyes and avoided elaborate puffed sleeves or ostentatious lace or ruffles. Instead she explained the importance of buying the very best material—Japanese silk or lawn waists, heavy silk or linen skirts—with a pretty white dress for summer and a fine merino wool dress for winter. She bought a light cashmere coat and some beautiful gloves, both calfskin and cotton. Even the underwear was of the softest cotton and linen, tastefully finished with a little lace or embroidery. But she also bought middy blouses and skirts for play. She explained to Hazel that she shouldn't make much of her clothes, just act as if it was natural to choose the appropriate clothing for each activity.

Hazel was grateful to her mother for what she considered her extravagant wardrobe, but she also felt intimidated by it. What could St. Gertrude's be like that you had to wear all these fancy clothes there? She wished that she was going on to Oakland High with a simpler wardrobe and classmates who were familiar. On the last Saturday Hazel spent with her mother in San Francisco, Nellie took her out to Delmonico's. Partly she wanted to treat her daughter before her departure, and partly she wanted to see if her table manners needed any attention. She was happy to see that Mary and John had done their job. Although Hazel was unfamiliar with some of the refinements of fine dining such as finger bowls and fish forks, her deportment was perfectly acceptable for a boarding school. Nellie took the opportunity to give her daughter some advice.

"This is a new life for you, Hazel," she said. "A chance to make yourself into anyone you want to be. If you just act like the girl you want to be, people will assume that's who you are."

Hazel nodded, "Like playing a part."

Nellie was pleased that she caught on so quickly. "Yes. The thing to do is to be quiet and reserved, keep to yourself at first, and watch the girls everyone looks up to, the girls from the good families. Get to know them and try to behave like they do. I know you can do that because you're such a good actress. Your talent for dramatics is something that will make you stand out, but don't talk about it. Don't tell the girls how much you've performed. Just audition for dramatics like everyone else and be modest. They'll see pretty soon how good you are. And do the same thing with the Sisters. If you watch, you'll soon be able to tell which are the ones everyone looks up to. Those are the ones you should try to get to know. If the others see that you're in with the ones everyone respects, they'll respect you too." Hazel listened carefully to her mother's advice and remembered it. She was still somewhat in awe of Nellie's confident manner and her knowledge of the world. Her mother never seemed to suffer from shyness, or to be in doubt about how to behave.

Nellie had waited until the very last minute to tell Chris Tharsing where his daughter would be going to school, in case he would try to sabotage the plan, but he seemed to be happy enough to have her at St. Gertrude's if Nellie was willing to pay for it. He sent Hazel a white fur piece, which was the most ostentatious thing she owned. Hazel was tearful when she said goodbye to Uncle John, who gave her a little leather-bound volume of Shakespeare, and Aunt Mary, who had knitted her a lovely cashmere scarf—expensive yarn, she knew. Frank and Roy really seemed to be sorry she was going. "It won't be the same without you, kiddo," said Roy.

Bruno was an old dog now. He wasn't well and spent most of his time lying on a little mat in front of the fireplace. When she petted him before she left the house to meet her mother in San Francisco, she did cry a little despite her determination not to. She felt it would be the last time she saw him.

Chapter 8

Before leaving the Shays' house, Hazel had packed a few personal things in a small bag. She had the Shakespeare book and the *Golden Treasury of Verse* that she and Uncle John had chosen her recital pieces from. She had her two necklaces, one of coral and one gold chain that held a locket. She also brought three framed photos—a picture of her and her mother when she was three years old, a recent picture of her holding Bruno, and a picture of the whole Shay family, including Hazel, that had been taken two years earlier on the occasion of Frank's graduation from Oakland High. When Hazel met her mother at the dock, she found that Nellie had had all her new clothes and her supplies for school packed into a new trunk and brought to the boat that would take them up the Sacramento River to Rio Vista.

On the boat, Nellie reminded Hazel that she was beginning a new chapter of her life, and it was hers to write. She thought a good deal about her mother's advice as they traveled up the river. When they got to Rio Vista, she saw a little of what Nellie meant. As they approached the school building, Nellie became another person from the down-to-earth, jovial mother she was used to. She stood straighter, held her head erect. It was almost as if she'd grown taller. Nellie always dressed well when she went out in public, but Hazel noticed that she had given particular attention to her appearance that morning. True to her principles, she wore clothes of the finest material, from her navy blue merino traveling suit to her light blue crepe de chine waist and neat navy hat with one strategically placed feather. She wore no jewelry except her gold watch and chain.

"How do you do, Mother," she said with gracious intonations when Mother Camillus greeted them. "It's so nice to meet you at last after your kind correspondence." After Mother Camillus had spoken to Hazel and the two women had exchanged pleasantries, she handed them off to Sister Bernardine, who brought them to

Hazel's room. It was a large room with two big windows, for four girls. Sister Bernardine explained that they liked to put the new girls in with students who had been at the school for a term. Hazel was in a class of fifteen high school freshmen, twelve of whom were boarders. Sister Bernardine introduced Nellie and Hazel to the girls and said she would leave them to get Hazel settled. After chatting pleasantly with the girls for a few minutes, Nellie told Hazel she would have to be saying goodbye in order to catch the boat home. As they walked down the hall together, she said, "I don't think you need to bother much with Adelaide and Mary, but Clarisse Huntington looks like someone you should get to know. She's a San Francisco girl. She may be related to *the* Huntingtons."

Hazel had given a lot of thought to the role she would be playing at St. Gertrude's. She knew without her mother saying it that it would not be a good idea to expose her family circumstances to the other girls. Her plan was to be quiet and reserved, creating a little mystery around her background. She told the other girls that her mother was a widow and her father had died years before. She put only the photo of her with Bruno on her dresser, keeping the others in a drawer. And as her mother had instructed, she watched the other girls.

It soon became clear to Hazel that Clarisse Huntington was looked up to, not only by their roommates, but by the other girls in the school. She made a point of confiding to Clarisse that she was shy and would appreciate her advice. Clarisse was a kind girl and well brought up. She took her pretty new roommate under her wing. As Nellie had suggested, being attached to Clarisse led to spending a lot of time with the other girls from prominent families. But Hazel was careful not to get too close to any of the girls. She watched and learned and kept her private thoughts to herself.

St. Gertrude's was what passed in the West in 1902 as a finishing school. More than the basic academic curriculum, it stressed "accomplishments," and offered a wide range of optional instruction in painting, drawing, singing, piano, and elocution. Mrs. Graham, the elocution teacher who came from San Francisco once a week to give lessons, was in charge of the annual play, which was put on by St. Gertrude's and St. Joseph's, its brother school for boys. Nellie had enrolled Hazel in singing and elocution, of course, and Mrs. Graham was impressed with the vocal training she had already had. She was not as impressed with the pieces she had chosen to perform.

Mrs. Graham was a professional who sometimes worked with San Francisco's actor-managers to bring their newly hired actors up to snuff. She chafed at the suggestions of the Sisters, who would have preferred it if the girls recited only works like Cicero's Catiline Orations and the more serious Shakespearean monologues. On the other hand, the things the girls wanted to do were usually pure fluff. She tried to steer a middle course between the two, giving the girls monologues or poems that had some depth and range but were within the convent's moral compass and still intriguing to girls in their teens. Hazel wasn't always happy with the pieces she was assigned, but she had to admit that Mrs. Graham was a good coach. And when she performed Antigone's monologue beginning "Tomb, bridal chamber, eternal prison in the caverned rock" before the whole school at the midterm exercises, the admiration of the Sisters and the other girls made her a complete convert.

The spring play that year was *Coriolanus*. After reading the play, Hazel was hoping for the role of Volumnia, the hero's mother who had some of the most important speeches in the play, but instead she was cast in the lesser role as his wife, Virgilia. Making the most of it, she found that as a freshman with a leading role, she received the kind of attention from her classmates that she had come to crave in elementary school.

Up to this time, Hazel had been known as a shy, pretty girl who moved in the shadow of Clarisse Huntington and some of the other popular girls. After her surprising confidence on the stage was revealed, she cultivated an aura of mystery. When she was asked about her acting, she would say that she had been on the stage since she was a little child and occasionally dropped the names of actresses as if they were acquaintances.

Seeing that the mystery was having its effect, she extended it to a general air of greater sophistication than the other girls. They recognized that she dressed well, but differently from the typical high school girl. When someone praised her neat and becoming little hat, she might say that it was chosen for her "by someone who knows fashion very well," who they assumed to be a famous actress. This led the other girls to want to exchange their expensive, big hats with ostrich feathers and flower garlands for a "sophisticated little hat like Hazel's." When she got a box of treats from her mother or the Shays, she would just smile and look mysterious if someone asked her who had sent it. She began signing her name in people's memory books as "Jane C." which she said was going to be her professional name when she went on the stage. When asked what the "C" stood for, she would say, "You'll just have to wait to find out."

The "C" was Hazel's real secret. One Saturday evening while she was staying at her mother's flat, Melvin Chapman had come to call. Hazel knew very well who he was. He had been the Mayor of Oakland, and Hazel had heard her Aunt Tena say more than once to Aunt Mary what a pity it was that Nellie had married Chris Tharsing when she could have had Mel Chapman. Nellie had welcomed him formally, as if she was a little surprised he had come, and introduced Hazel to him. He was a tall man with a big mustache and kind blue eyes. He looked down at her and smiled warmly. "So this is Hazel," he said. "I hear you're off to school soon."

"Yes," she said. "I'm going to St. Gertrude's."

"Well, I hear it's a very good school for young ladies. I think you'll like it there."

Then Nellie said, "You had better go into the dining room and finish writing your letters while I talk with Mr. Chapman about business," and closed the pocket doors that divided the two rooms behind her.

Since then, Hazel had devised a whole story for herself about her mother's romance with Mayor Chapman. She was sure that they had never lost the fire of passion that had burned between them even while they both were married to another. She imagined having been Chapman's daughter instead of Chris Tharsing's, with her father a kind and dignified lawyer and the ex-mayor of Oakland instead of a fruit farmer way up in the country whom she hardly ever saw. Someday, she thought, it would all be as it was meant to be.

During the three years Hazel was at St. Gertrude's, her image of her mother changed radically. Having followed Nellie's advice, she had indeed gotten to know the girls from the "better" families, although she had not become intimate friends with any of them. She watched the mothers carefully when they came to visit, taking note of their speech and manners, and their attitudes toward their daughters, as if she were preparing to play the part of Mother from a Prominent San Francisco Family. She could see that Nellie was different from these women, even when she was putting on her best social manner. She was brusque, businesslike, straight-forward, not charming and feminine and affectionate like these ladies.

Hazel knew that Geary Street was not a good part of San Francisco for a lady to live in, and she kept her address from her friends, along with any reference to the Shays in Oakland. To fend off questions, she generally said that she spent most of her time with her Aunt Sophie Dahl in the country. She also realized fairly quickly that a woman who kept a rooming house was not socially acceptable to the better families. Like the address on Geary Street, this was connected to not having good morals. Hazel did not tell anyone where she was living during the first summer vacation, when she was mostly in the flat on Geary Street helping her mother with some of the simpler business tasks and making visits to the Shays and her grandmother. She told everyone she would be visiting various relatives all over the country and there was no use in trying to track her down with a letter.

After Hazel had dropped many hints about the desirability of a good address, Nellie moved to a much better one during the following year, the Audubon Apartments on Ellis Street, which was a few blocks further from the rooming house, in a nice residential area. From there, Hazel could write back and forth to the girls from school, and even have them visit. But as she grew older and took on more of the secretarial tasks for Nellie's business during the summers, she became more aware of the things that were associated with rooming houses. She knew about the poker games and that it wasn't socially acceptable for a single woman to spend the evening in a men's clubroom, even if she owned it. Her mother might be very comfortably off, but that didn't mean she was acceptable in San Francisco society.

Hazel understood that Nellie wanted her to go further than she had been able to do, to walk with pride into the drawing rooms from which Nellie was barred, perhaps marry into one eventually. But she didn't think her mother understood that, in order to do that, Hazel would have to be cut off from her. Visiting a friend in Sacramento or Oakland was one thing, but she would never be accepted into San Francisco society as her mother's daughter.

And then there was the question of Nellie's romantic life. As she grew older, Hazel understood that there had been more men in her mother's life than Chris Tharsing and Mayor Chapman. Chapman continued to call on them occasionally, and he always took an interest in what Hazel was doing. He asked what she was reading and what play she thought they might do at St. Gertrude's the next year. But eventually, he and Nellie would end up alone in the parlor together. Then there was George Clark, a wealthy undertaker who was around quite a bit, playing poker with Nellie and taking her out for late night suppers. Clark had a coarse sense of humor, which Nellie seemed to enjoy. She kept very late hours with Clark. But Hazel never cared for him, and she was aware of how shocked the world of St. Gertrude's would be by her mother's behavior.

All of this went into Hazel's careful crafting of her mysterious, sophisticated, and aloof persona during her school years. The other girls knew Hazel had her secrets, but she made them believe that it was because she wanted to, not because she had to. Speculate as they might about her among themselves, the other girls observed the boundaries she set up and respected her for them. Partly because of this air of mystery, she became someone the other girls wanted to confide in. This surprised her at first, but then she figured out that they trusted their secrets to her because she kept her own so well. It was thought a privilege to be invited to confide in Hazel, and she did keep secrets faithfully.

In the end, Hazel liked her position at St. Gertrude's. She had no really close friends, but never having had them, she didn't miss them. She valued the other girls according to their usefulness. She learned how to cultivate the useful girls with compliments and flattery and thoughtful little gifts. She associated with the most prominent girls in the school, and the Sisters recognized her as a school leader. She was always the first girl in line when they walked anywhere, conversing easily with the Sisters who accompanied them. And she made progress with her elocution and acting. After the first year, she always had the female lead in the play. In her senior year, Mrs. Graham gave her the role of Calpurnia in *Julius Caesar*, the most ambitious production that had yet been mounted by St. Gertrude's. The role fit Hazel, with her abundant dark hair and classical profile. All her training went into the powerful, well-modulated delivery of her lines and her distinguished air on stage. High compliments on her performance came from students, faculty, and guests alike. Nellie, who had made the trip from San Francisco just to see the play, fairly glowed with pride.

When Hazel met with Mrs. Graham for her private elocution lesson on the Tuesday following the play, the teacher sat in her accustomed straight-backed chair, her salt-and-pepper hair smoothed back into a neat bun, her posture perfect. Hazel took a deep breath and went through with her plan to ask for advice. "I'd like you to tell me frankly, Mrs. Graham, no need to worry that my feelings will be hurt. I know that you work with some of the best managers in the city to train their actors. Do you think I have the talent to succeed on the stage professionally?"

Mrs. Graham looked at Hazel kindly, motioned for her to sit down and spoke softly, with perfect diction. "Hazel," she said, "every year I have someone who asks me that question, and I try my best to discourage her gently. But you deserve to hear my best and frankest judgment. Could you succeed on the stage? Yes, I think you could. You have the physical assets of a beautiful face and a distinguished profile, lovely hair, extraordinary eyes. Your hands are small, and your arms could be more graceful, but you could train yourself to disguise these defects. You have a very good voice. It is a powerful instrument, and I think we've trained it well. You have very good vocal range and modulation. Your singing voice is not as strong as your speaking voice, but with more training, it would be adequate, I think. You are quick to see the possibilities in a role, although you have a lot to learn about the nuances, both of human character and of performance. I think you've improved in movement and gesture onstage, but you are still very amateurish in that department. On the whole, you need more instruction in the craft of acting and in dramatic literature, perhaps just a greater level of maturity before you can understand and act certain motives and emotions, but with a lot more hard work I do think you could be a successful actress."

Hazel's ivory cheeks flushed a deep rose, her dark eyes shining. She considered this high praise from Mrs. Graham, and a kind of permission to think about her dream as a genuine possibility. "How would I get the training I need?" she asked. "Should I try auditioning for some of the managers?"

Mrs. Graham looked her in the eye. "Let me tell you Hazel. I said you have the talent, but that doesn't mean I think you should go on the stage in San Francisco. You read about the stars in the papers and you think it's a glamorous life, but for a young girl starting out, there is nothing glamorous about it. You would start with walk-ons, learning stage business with maybe a line or two. You would be paid next to nothing and spend your time in crowded, dirty dressing rooms with half a dozen other girls who are competing with you for the most meager attention from the manager. And, unless you are very careful, it is not a life for a nice young girl. There are too many temptations and too many reasons to give in to them. Do you understand what I mean, Hazel?"

Hazel reddened to the roots of her hair, but she nodded. "Yes, I do," she said. "I'm not as naïve as most of the girls here. My family background has exposed me to more of life."

"Well then, you understand that it is not what I would want for you, Hazel. And if you really want to be a serious actress and not just a singer and dancer, San Francisco is no place to start. You notice that the actresses who come here to perform in Shakespeare and other serious plays come from New York and London and Europe. You don't see San Francisco actresses going the other way."

"There are some. What about Lotta Crabtree?"

Mrs. Graham smiled. "If I could tell you the number of times I've heard that. But there is only one Lotta Crabtree, and frankly, Hazel, you are nowhere near her level. Maybe someday, but not yet."

"But what can I do if I want to become a serious actress?"

"There are two choices as I see it. You could study at a local school, perhaps the Paul Gerson School of Acting, and try to join a company here, work very hard, and perhaps you would succeed in your ambition against all odds. My guess is that your beauty would take you a good way, although since you are dark, you would probably be cast in the femme fatale or vamp roles in melodrama, villainess rather than heroine. I haven't seen that you have any particular talent for comedy, but then we haven't given you much chance for that at St. Gertrude's." She smiled. "That is a line you might develop. In any case, it would mean years of taking direction from managers, watching more experienced actors, and learning what you can from them. If you're lucky, someone might take you under their wing. I could do what I can to help, of course, and we could continue our lessons with more of a practical eye to the stage. But it would be a long, hard road."

"What is the other option?"

"The other option is to get out of San Francisco. If you went to New York, you would be at the center of things. There is so much more activity, more than a hundred new plays a year, but of course there is more competition as well, and away from home you would be even more at the mercy of the theatrical life." She looked at her frankly. "If you are determined to try this and you want my best advice," she said, "it is to go to London. There are schools there that teach you the things you have to pick up catch-as-catch-can in the theater here. Herbert Beerbohm Tree has opened a school for the dramatic arts that teaches the best of the English techniques. You could not only continue your singing and vocal training there, but study dramatic literature, languages, movement and gesture, even fencing. Tree is one of the most respected actor-managers in London, and success at the school would almost certainly lead to employment on the stage there. In any case, coming back to this country as an English-trained actress would put you in a much better position than coming from San Francisco. Of course, that would be expensive. I don't know what your family's financial situation is, but they would have to be willing to invest in your career."

"Yes, of course," said Hazel. "Thank you very much, Mrs. Graham. I appreciate your frankness. You've given me a great deal to think about."

Mrs. Graham looked at her curiously. "I've given it to you straight, Hazel, because I want you to understand that this would not be an easy path for you. Are you still determined to try it?"

Hazel's lovely brown eyes widened in surprise. "Oh, yes," she said. "Of course I am."

Chapter 9

The more she thought about it, the more Hazel realized that she had never wanted anything as much as she wanted to go to London and study at Herbert Beerbohm Tree's Academy of Dramatic Art. She reflected that she had had no say in any of the decisive events in her life—her parents' divorce, living with the Shays, coming to St. Gertrude's—even her first elocution lessons had been her Aunt Mary's idea. She was determined to find a way to study in London, which meant getting Nellie both to allow her to go and to pay for it. She planned her campaign carefully.

Hazel of course played a conspicuous part in the June 1905 graduation exercises at St. Gertrude's, reciting her prize-winning oration to great applause. She could see that Nellie was proud of her lovely, poised daughter, who took everyone's congratulations graciously and said goodbye to her friends without the girlish giddiness that was on display around them. She knew her mother was congratulating herself on having made the right choice in sending her to St. Gertrude's.

After graduation, Hazel went back with her mother to the Audubon Apartments and made a point of behaving as a mature young lady. She did the secretarial work for the business and took on many responsibilities of running the household. She made sure to read the newspaper every day, engaging her mother in conversations about the events in the city and the world. On their first Sunday evening, after they had returned from visiting the Oakland relatives, Hazel made a light supper of creamed oysters on toast, one of Nellie's favorites. After the meal, she washed the dishes as Nellie rested in the parlor. Then she brought in some tea.

"You're spoiling me, Hazel," said Nellie.

"I'm happy to, Mama," said Hazel, "I need to have something to do." She kept an eye on her mother as she sipped her tea. Nellie looked relaxed and comfortable drinking her tea and looking at the Sunday paper. "Mama," Hazel said, "what did you have in mind for me now that I've finished at St. Gertrude's?"

Nellie looked up in surprise. "Why I thought you would stay here in San Francisco with me. It's been very pleasant having you here, Hazel."

"But what sort of life do you see for me?"

"Well, I'd expect that you can be a help to me in the business and still have a busy social life. Some of your friends from school are from the best families in the city. With all of their connections you should have lots of invitations."

Hazel turned a troubled face toward her mother. "I'm not sure you exactly understand my position, Mama. Those girls were happy enough to be my friends at school, but that doesn't necessarily carry over now that we've graduated."

"Why ever not?" asked Nellie.

"Mama, they're all debutantes. Now that they've graduated, they will be coming out, which means tea parties and balls and other events, all with their own set. Six months from now, I won't be hearing from any of them."

Nellie looked uncomfortable. "It can't be as bad as that," she said.

Hazel looked her mother in the eye, the delicate lines of her face just perceptibly hardening. "To be perfectly frank, Mama, you know that we are not in that class. We read about those people in the Sunday Supplement. We don't socialize with them. Those people are snobs. They don't live on Nob Hill for nothing. With my—background—they can't let me into their drawing rooms without compromising their own standing. You know how that works."

Nellie knew very well how it worked, but she had hoped that sending Hazel to St. Gertrude's would change things for her.

"But friendship counts for something. I can't believe they would just throw you over."

Hazel's eyes didn't waver. "Mother," she said, "you are friendly with a lot of men from that class through your rooming houses. The young men ask you for advice and invite you to play poker with them. Do you ever get invited into their families' drawing rooms?"

Nellie colored and looked away. "No. But it's not the same thing. I don't know the women, and they control the social events."

"Exactly," said Hazel. "And we aren't part of that world. If my mother isn't welcome in their homes, neither am I. I have to think of a different future for myself."

Nellie looked at her. "Did you have something in mind?"

"Yes, Mother," Hazel said. "I am thinking seriously of a career as an actress." At Nellie's impatient movement, she said, "Before you say anything. Just let me finish. I asked Mrs. Graham to tell me frankly whether she thought I could make it. You know she works with some of the best actor-managers in town to help train their actors. She says that I have a way to go in learning about stage movement and gesture, but that I have a very good voice and," Hazel went on with determination "she says I have the looks to make it on the stage."

Nellie nodded. "I agree with her," she said. "But I don't want my daughter to be an actress. That's a step back for us, Hazel. You know how actresses are thought of."

"But not the serious actresses who do legitimate plays. Look at the paper. Every week there are stories of actresses who retire and marry stock brokers, or even English aristocrats."

"Of course, but those are the exceptions. That's why they're in the paper. They're usually English. They're not girls from a humble background in Oakland, California."

"That's just it, Mama. If I go abroad to study, I can come back to this country as an English actress. My background won't matter. I can make up any background I want and make people believe it."

"But where would you go? We don't know anyone in England."

"Mrs. Graham told me about a school in London that's run by Herbert Beerbohm Tree. He's one of the most prominent actor-managers in England," she said. "Mrs. Graham thinks he would take me as a pupil. I could learn the things I still need to learn from the best. With his connections, I could go on the stage in England, or I could come back to the U. S., maybe to New York, and launch myself as an English-trained actress. That's so much better than being an unknown girl from San Francisco."

Nellie nodded. "I can see that," she said. "But it sounds like an expensive proposition. There's not only the tuition, but the travel fares. And your wardrobe would have to be replenished." Nellie was not parsimonious. In fact, she could be generous to a fault. But she was a businesswoman. Before she put out a hundred dollars, she wanted to know exactly how it would be spent and what the results would be.

"I know it's asking a lot," said Hazel, "but it's the one thing I care about doing. I don't want to marry a carpenter or a clerk and be a housewife all my life, like Aunt Mary. I love Aunt Mary, but her life is so humdrum, so small. I'm your daughter, Mama. I was made for action. I want to do something in this world. To be someone, not someone's wife."

Nellie was flattered by the comparison, but she was not yet convinced about her daughter's going so far away. "I sympathize with you, Hazel," she said. "And I'm proud of you wanting to work hard to make your mark on the world. Let's look into the school and see how the cost comes out."

A warm smile softened Hazel's classic features. "Thank you, Mama," she said. "I've already written off for a school catalogue. I'll look into the fares and write to Aunt Alice. She was in London when she and Roy took that trip to Europe a couple of years ago. I'll ask Clarisse Huntington to meet me downtown for tea one day this week. She spends a lot of time in London. I'll ask her if she knows any good places where a single girl can stay."

Now that action was being taken, Hazel's studying for the theater moved from hypothetical to reality. It quickly became The Plan. After thinking through what her daughter had told her, Nellie began to fall in with her enthusiasm and excitement. Deep down, she had always worried that St. Gertrude's would not be enough to get Hazel into those Nob Hill drawing rooms. She was no more eager than Hazel was to see her married off to a carpenter or grocer, the way her own sisters were, or worse, to a farmer, living a hard and unspeakably boring life. It had been a blow to have the brutal light of day shone on her buried worries, but she was relieved to find that Hazel had already learned the hard truth and thought of a way around it. And as long as it didn't undermine her reputation, she was pleased to think about her pretty and talented daughter on the stage. But she was concerned about the money. She knew there would be the tuition fee and the fares, and housing in London, which could not be cheap, and she would need to buy her daughter a generous wardrobe as well. Nellie's business provided her with a comfortable living, but she was not sure she was up to all this.

After their first conversation, Hazel acted quickly, partly out of eagerness and partly to make sure her mother didn't have time to change her mind. She met with Clarisse, who didn't know of any places to live right off but was excited about the prospect of Hazel's going on the stage. She happily took on the assignment of finding one. Within a week, she had asked around her circle and found two places where a nice young woman might live on her own in London. One was a residential hotel. The other was a residence for women students in Bloomsbury not far from the Academy, which was run like a college dormitory. It had small private rooms for the residents, large attractive parlors for dining and entertaining guests, and, importantly, chaperones who were on guard when young men came to call. Hazel immediately wrote off to the hotel and the residence.

By the end of October, Hazel's plans were made. She had secured an audition for the school's Lenten term, which began at the end of January. To prepare, she was taking classes at the Paul Gerson School of Acting in San Francisco, where she was concentrating on comedy, and she was working with Mrs. Graham on audition pieces. Nellie decided that the Bloomsbury residence would do more to assure Hazel's social respectability in London than a hotel. Clarisse had told her that the social forms were much stricter in London than in San Francisco, and both Hazel and Nellie thought it was wiser to err on the side of too much propriety than on not enough until she knew the lay of the land. There was still the passage to book and the journey to New York to arrange. It would cost a lot of money.

Nellie kept tabs on Chris Tharsing through his sister Sophie. She knew that he had finally made a success of fruit farming up in Shasta County. His 300-acre farm outside Anderson was providing a good living for him and Ada, his latest child bride, and he had recently been named a county Horticultural Commissioner. She thought that, for once, he could shoulder some of the responsibility of educating his daughter. But it would have to be Hazel who asked him for the money. Nellie decided to put the situation squarely before her as they ate supper one evening. "Hazel," she said. "We need to talk business. I'm happy to help with your school tuition and your wardrobe, as well as giving you an allowance to cover things when you're in London, but I can't do that and cover your travel too. You will have to ask your father for the money for that."

Hazel heard from her father once a year, at the end of December, when he sent a combined Christmas and birthday remembrance to her and enclosed a small check. He always wrote a short letter, telling her his triumphs on the farm that year, and she sent back a thank you note describing her progress in school and her singing and acting activities.   Before his remarriage, he had always said that he hoped she could visit the farm in the summer, but that had never happened, and he hadn't mentioned it since 1902.   To ask him for a large sum of money seemed to her like writing to the man in the moon, but so determined was she to go to London that she wrote a letter explaining her plans, stressing that it was on Mrs. Graham's advice that she had chosen this course, and emphasizing the eminence of Herbert Beerbohm Tree, the superiority of the singing instruction in London, and the respectability of the arrangements in Bloomsbury.   To her surprise, Chris sent a check for a hundred dollars with warm wishes for her success.   He had always known she had talent, he said, and he was proud to help nurture it.   Her hard work over the years had proven to him that this was not a passing fancy, but perhaps a true vocation.   This response was not without bitter irony for Nellie, but she was happy for Hazel to have the check.

Chapter 10

As 1905 came to an end, Kitty Smith thought with satisfaction that she had come a long way since Nellie Tharsing had agreed to keep her on at The Portals fifteen years earlier. At Nellie's side, she had learned the rooming-house business from the bottom up. By the time she was twenty-five, she had been ready to go on her own and had bought her first building with Nellie co-signing the loan. Kitty had gone a different way than Nellie in developing her business, though. She didn't care about the ever-increasing social status that Nellie craved. Kitty bought her first rooming house on Geary Street, on the edge of the red-light district, because it was run down and dirt cheap. After fixing it up to the point where it was one of the most comfortable houses on the street, she was happy to raise the rents moderately and take on another building in the same neighborhood. Now, at thirty-one, she derived a comfortable income from three low-rent rooming houses in the Geary Street area.

But Kitty was getting tired of the business and tired of her life in San Francisco. Outside of a few other single businesswomen who had worked as hard as she had to build a comfortable life, she had no friends in the city. Her parents had died when she was in her early teens, and, no one being much on writing letters, she had lost touch with the two brothers who made up the rest of her family. She was thinking of seeing the world beyond San Francisco. She thought about her parents picking up stakes and leaving New York State to come West when they were in their twenties. What a spirit of adventure that had taken back in the 1860s, when they had to come by wagon train from Missouri. She thought about reversing the trip to see what the country was like. The idea of taking on New York City had shaped itself as a worthy adventure for 1906.

When Kitty told Nellie that she was thinking seriously of selling out and going to New York, her first response was dismay.

Out of habit, she started counseling her protégé, questioning whether she had thought this out, whether it was a good time to sell, what she was going to do in New York. As usual, Kitty listened to everything Nellie said, and then went her own way. Coming up against this resistance to her plan only made her realize that she had already decided to do it. Once Nellie had seen this, she also saw that there was a big boon for her in Kitty's plan. She asked if Kitty would be willing to take Hazel with her to New York. The cross-country train journey had been weighing on Nellie's mind. She could not imagine sending her convent-bred eighteen-year-old daughter on the week-long trip alone, but she had no desire either to make the trip there and back herself or to spend the extra money on Pullman car fares. Both Kitty and Hazel were enthusiastic about the idea, Kitty for the company and Hazel because she knew that Kitty would be the most cheerful and permissive chaperone she could ask for.

As the fall went on, the plan fell into place. Kitty sold her rooming houses at a good price, banking a healthy amount for what she called her New York stake and keeping out enough for a comfortable vacation trip, the first of her life. Hazel and Nellie put together Hazel's wardrobe with careful eyes on all the photos of New York and London fashion they could find in newspapers and magazines. As always, Hazel kept her clothing simple, with good materials and clean lines, although this was no easy task with the hourglass silhouette and all the pleats and flounces that were in style. They stayed away from the enormous, elaborately trimmed hats that defined the season, deciding to buy just two simple traveling hats and letting Hazel wait until she got to London to see what the other students were wearing before they made this investment.

Nellie gave Hazel a hundred and fifty dollars, which was to cover her twelve-guinea tuition and her first three months' expenses. In return she asked two things, that Hazel write home weekly and that she continue her singing and piano lessons.

Hazel had never been enthusiastic about singing. In fact, she refused to sing in public, a marked difference from her attitude toward acting and reciting. But music was important to Nellie. She considered it Hazel's Gotchett heritage and was certain that her daughter would be good at it if she applied herself. She believed that there was only a slim chance of Hazel's dreams for her acting career coming true, but she thought she could always support herself teaching music, a respectable profession for a young lady, even if she didn't have a stage or concert career. And Nellie thought that a career in music would be much better for Hazel's marriage prospects than an acting career.

In early December, Kitty and Hazel set out on the first leg of their journey, having decided on parlor car tickets and making stops in Ogden, Omaha, Chicago, and Niagara rather than the forbidding expense of Pullman cars. Sleeping cars would have made the train journey cost three times Hazel's thirty-five-dollar second-class fare on the ship to England, and besides, both Kitty and Hazel were eager to stop and see a little more of the country as they traveled. Crossing the San Joaquin Valley, Hazel looked out the window at its seemingly endless expanses of dead brown stubble broken by rows of stunted, bare fruit trees. Stopping in Sacramento, she thought of her father. She had not seen Chris Tharsing in years, but passing through this country where she had spent her earliest childhood unsettled her with vague memories of being cold and afraid, her mother clutching her too tightly against her father's loud voice and angry red face. She was grateful that Chris had responded generously to her pleas for money, but the days when he had paid her special attention, almost courted her, during his visits to Oakland were long gone. With a show of girlish enthusiasm, she turned to Kitty and said, "Let's jump out and see if we can get something good to eat here." Kitty was happy to oblige.

During the trip, Hazel behaved as the same demure, quiet girl she had learned to be at St. Gertrude's, but she watched with interest as Kitty made friends with many of their fellow passengers as well as the conductors and porters and waiters. It was different than traveling with her mother, who tended to imitate the manner of a society lady when she was in a strange situation and remained aloof from her fellow passengers on a train or ferry. Watching Kitty interact easily with all sorts of people just by remaining her hearty, open self, Hazel began to see the advantage of her Western ways. Business travelers especially enjoyed being in the company of the cheerful Western woman and her pretty young companion. They did what they could to entertain and treat them. Kitty had no trouble getting helpful directions and advice on hotels from their fellow passengers, and she made immediate friends of desk clerks and waiters.

When they got to Grand Central in New York, even Kitty was a little overcome by the sheer size of the station and the crowds. They were glad to have made a reservation at the Hotel Gerard, just a few blocks away from the station, on the advice of Mel Chapman, who had stayed there when he had business in the city. The hotel was large by their standards, thirteen stories, and handsomely decorated with bay windows and gables. It was an apartment hotel where Kitty planned to stay until she got settled in the city, so while the parlor room was crammed with their trunks and luggage, they still had room to move in the bedroom, as well as a private bath. They found that the cramped quarters didn't matter during the first week, for they seemed to be in the hotel only to bathe and sleep.

Kitty was determined to explore every neighborhood where she might find a rooming house to buy, from the Bronx to Chinatown. Staying clear of the Tenderloin and Hell's Kitchen, they made their way methodically, first walking south to Gramercy Park and Chelsea, a little too rich for Kitty's blood, and then to Madison Square and Greenwich Village, which was a possibility, down through the Italian and Chinese sections to the Lower East Side, a maze of tenements that was daunting even to

Kitty. They took the subway north to Columbus Circle, both delighted by Central Park after several days among the noise and the crowds and the traffic. They wandered in the quiet neighborhoods on both the east and west sides of the park, which Kitty determined were nice but pricey, more Nellie's kind of place than hers. They took the subway up to Harlem and the Bronx, both of which had a nice neighborhood feel to them, but Kitty thought she would like to be closer to the center of things.

In the evenings, they went to the theater. Mel Chapman had told them the hotel was in the theater district, but they hadn't realized what that meant until they saw it. Kitty left the choice to Hazel, who was dazzled by the offerings on the newspaper's Amusements page. They saw Minnie Maddern Fiske, the famous cousin of Hazel's friend from the Paul Gerson acting school, Merle Maddern, in *The New York Idea*, a daring play about divorce. They saw William Gillette, the legendary Sherlock Holmes, in *Clarice*, Eleanor Robson in Clyde Fitch's *The Girl Who Has Everything*, and the great John Drew in *His House in Order*. To make sure Kitty stayed interested, Hazel took advantage of several hit plays about the West, David Belasco's *The Girl of the Golden West* with Blanche Bates, William Vaughn Moody's *The Great Divide*, and Rachel Crothers's *The Three of Us*. They saw *Madame Butterfly*, and of course they went to see Maude Adams as Peter Pan. No matter the play, Hazel sat on the edge of her seat, studying every gesture, every vocal trick of the actresses she had read about for years. Kitty had never seen her so animated or so emotional. She alternated between an exalted inspiration to put her wonderful new knowledge to use and despair that she could ever approach this level of her art.

Kitty was truly sorry on New Year's Eve when she took Hazel to the pier to board the *Baltic*. As she had promised Nellie, she saw Hazel and her luggage safely aboard and went with her to the small stateroom she was to share with another young woman, Jane Merrow, who was already installed. For her part, Hazel was sadder to say goodbye to Kitty than she ever had been to see her mother go at school. Kitty was fun, and she always made things easier. Before she left, she struck up a conversation with Jane, who was English and a few years older than Hazel, going home after a visit to some relatives in America. She had never met anyone from California before and seemed to think that San Francisco was the Wild West. When the time came, Hazel walked with Kitty to the gangplank, and waved energetically to her before she turned, disappearing in the crowd on the pier. Then she took a walk around the second-class area of the ship, looking at the dining room with its long banquet-style tables, the drawing room where the ladies could sit, the bathrooms, and the promenade deck. To a boarding-school veteran it all looked comfortable enough.

As she walked slowly back to her stateroom, Hazel decided to emulate Kitty on this voyage. Since she was out of her element anyway, she thought it would be better to act the role of a straightforward and friendly California girl than a demure, convent-bred young lady. And she saw that she could have some fun testing how far Jane's credulity would go when it came to stories about California. By the time they embarked from the ship, Jane had found herself enchanted with this seemingly ingenuous and forthright Californian. She made sure to get her address, so she could invite her to meet some of her friends in London. And Hazel had a strategy for presenting herself to the British. It was not to try to be like them, but to be someone they would be intrigued to know. It made her smile to think that all the things Nellie had tried so hard to rub off her daughter were just the things that might help her achieve the social success that Nellie was so eager for her to have.

Hazel dressed carefully in her traveling suit for her arrival, having noted from Jane's wardrobe and observing the other young ladies on the ship that her instinct for simple lines with good fabric and tailoring would serve her well in London. When the hansom cab pulled up at 69 Torrington Square in Bloomsbury, Hazel's first impression was that it was not what she thought of as a square, but just a place where three roads converged in front of the Church of Christ the King. Her future residence was a four-story brick building, or rather a block of five buildings with individual doors. When she knocked at number 69, she was admitted by a young maid dressed in modest black with a cap and a spotless white apron, who announced her to Mrs. Merritt, the manager and chaperone of the residence.

Mrs. Merritt was a middle-aged lady with carefully arranged silver hair. She was dressed simply in black, her only ornament a gold watch on a chain. She rose from her desk with dignity and came forward to meet Hazel. "How do you do, Miss Tharsing," she said. "We have been expecting you."

Hazel controlled her impulse to drop her eyes and murmur her thanks. Instead, she looked Mrs. Merritt in the eye, took a step forward, and put out her hand with a broad smile. "It's very nice to finally be here, Mrs. Merritt," she said. "It's been a long trip from California."

Mrs. Merritt returned her hearty handshake with a little smile. "We have a number of residents from America here," she said, "although no one from the Far West. We are very glad that you found us."

After a little interview in which she acquainted Hazel with the rules and customs of the house, she led the way to her rooms on the second floor. Hazel was pleased to find that she had a little sitting room as well as a small bedroom. Bathroom facilities were shared, but there was a washstand in her bedroom. Everything was comfortably arranged, with a white chenille bedspread on the little bed and cheerful chintz covers on the chairs in the sitting room.

"After you have unpacked your trunk, we will have it moved to the cellar for storage," said Mrs. Merritt. "Then you will see that the rooms are quite comfortable."

Hazel smiled. "Oh, I'm very happy with the rooms," she said. "They're much nicer than the ones I had in the convent school where I was raised."

"Are you Catholic, Miss Tharsing?"

"Oh, no. My family is Protestant. My father was Danish, and my mother's family is Swiss and Dutch. But there are not many boarding schools in the West, so most people go to a convent school."

"That is most interesting," said Mrs. Merritt. "I understand that your mother is a widow?"

Hazel was so used to this lie that she responded smoothly without thinking, "Yes, my father died several years ago. He was a horticulturalist who had come from Denmark to do experimental work with fruit in California. Fortunately, he left us well off, so I can pursue my education."

At this point, some of the other residents looked in the door to be introduced, and Hazel was spared any further interrogation for the moment. She greeted the other young women with the same open and cheerful manner she had shown to Mrs. Merritt, and before long, the chaperone left them chatting away, asking about California and Hazel's plans for her time in London. When she said she was scheduled to audition for the Academy of Dramatic Art the following week, the others were impressed. With some carefully hidden dismay, she gathered from them that the school was very selective. She had never seriously considered the possibility that she might be turned down. They told her that some of the girls in the residence had auditioned unsuccessfully in the fall and were studying elocution or music with private teachers in the hope of being admitted in January for the Lenten Term. Hazel started immediately to build a hedge against failure.

"Of course, I'm really here because my mother wants me to continue with my singing," she said. "It's in the family. My mother is quite a well-known soprano locally, and my uncle is a professional basso profundo." She didn't say that her uncle Fred

Gotchett was with a minstrel show. There were limits to the simple California act. "If I don't do the course at the Academy, I have some music teachers in mind."

Despite her offhand manner with her fellow residents, Hazel went through the entrance examination process with intense focus and determination. She had no idea what the standards were, but it turned out that she had been well coached by Mrs. Graham. Her highest grades were in elocution, where she was placed ahead of many English students, despite the work she still needed to do to eradicate the vestiges of her American accent. And again, playing the California role helped. The directors found her frank, ingenuous air refreshing, and they valued diverse backgrounds among the students, particularly when they could serve as models for dialect. As she had expected, she did not do as well at singing. Despite her mother's hopes, she knew her singing ability was limited. Although she had a rich contralto voice, she had only a mediocre range, and her projection was weak for the stage. Her lowest marks were for her dance and stage movement, which the directors considered wooden and amateurish.

Hazel left the examination feeling anxious. It was all she could do to keep up her relaxed, cheerful manner with her fellow residents on Torrington Square. After a tense week, she was tremendously relieved to be accepted into the Academy of Dramatic Art for the Lenten Term beginning January 16, 1906.

Hazel blossomed at the Academy in a way that she never had at St. Gertrude's. In a world where everything was performance at some level, Hazel flourished. Instead of putting her acting talent into creating a role of mystery and concealment, she was putting it to use to shape a California character who was likeable and attractive to the other students and the Torrington Square residents. With her sharply observant eye, she quickly learned the prevailing manners and modulated her behavior to fit within the norms while still appearing refreshingly frank and easygoing. In

London, Hazel always walked into a room with a broad smile and a greeting. Her wit, which had only been seen before by a few close friends and family members, was now put on display, and with her general demeanor, no one ever suspected that her teasing or comments were anything but good-natured. For the first time in her life, Hazel was popular. At Torrington Square, she acquired the nickname of "The Girl of the Golden West," after David Belasco's play. Little did they know how much of her behavior was actually modeled on Blanche Bates's performance.

The Academy also gave Hazel a new perspective on her looks. She had always known that she was pretty. But her upbringing had brought confusing messages about how to regard that. Her mother was proud of her looks, and of course her father had doted on them, but Aunt Mary, in her strict Methodist way, had downplayed Hazel's appearance and cautioned her against vanity when she thought the little girl was taking too much pleasure in her appearance. At St. Gertrude's, the other girls professed their admiration for Hazel's classic profile and envied her beautiful dark eyes and long lashes, luxuriant gold-highlighted chestnut hair, luminous ivory skin, long, graceful neck, and perfect teeth. But Hazel also absorbed the prevailing attitude of the Sisters that one should be modest about one's looks, dismissive of compliments. Dressing simply and wearing her hair parted and drawn back rather severely into a bun or looped around her head in braids had become her habit at a time when clothing and hair were big, elaborate, and set off by huge hats.

In one way, Hazel's classic beauty was emphasized by the lack of distraction, but that didn't mean it couldn't be enhanced with some artful help. At the Academy, one's looks were regarded as a tool in the actor's chest. Getting maximum benefit from them was a matter of professionalism. Hazel soon adapted to this way of thinking, finding ways to emphasize her eyes and loosening her hair in more becoming styles. Learning to do her stage make-up professionally made a dramatic difference in her appearance on stage. She began to consider her beauty a major professional asset and had several photographs taken for later use, always sending prints to Nellie so she could see what her money was buying.

Chapter 11

In her first year, Hazel followed the basic curriculum of the Academy. She worked especially hard at dance and stage movement, which was taught in both the classical way for period drama and less formally for contemporary plays. She also studied dramatic history, Shakespeare, in which the students prepared recitations, and French drama, in which the students staged scenes in French. Keeping her promise to Nellie, she took extra singing lessons and made progress, although her teacher told her she would never be a really strong singer.

At the end of the term, Hazel was among the Academy students invited to audition at the prestigious Daly's Theatre for the chorus of *The Geisha*, a musical comedy that had been wildly popular in the 1890s and inspired a fad for all things faux Japanese, including Geisha hats, frocks, cigars and cigarettes, waistcoats, bows, and ties. The new show was to star May de Sousa, an American actress who had taken London by storm in the current season. Hazel already had the looks to match the musical comedy version of a Japanese woman. It only took a few tricks with make-up and hair to assure her being cast for the chorus despite not having the strongest voice. When the show opened in June, she wrote proudly to Nellie that she had her first professional engagement after just six months in London.

In the fall, Hazel continued with the regular curriculum as well as with her singing lessons. She did well, even in classical stage movement, where she was able to learn the series of gestures that were traditionally matched with particular emotions. The stiffness she had on stage was actually helpful in period drama. Everyone said that no one could act an eighteenth-century duchess like the Girl of the Golden West. But the graceful movements of dance and the modern parts of society ladies eluded her. A little exasperated, Mr. Willett, her dance instructor, said she should find more ways to practice movement.

"What can I do?" she asked, "I'm taking all the courses and acting in as many pieces as I can."

"Why don't you try fencing? It demands great agility and teaches one to be aware of one's body."

She smiled at him. "I would love to learn to fence," she said, "but will they let me in?"

"Why not? If we find another girl who's willing to be your partner, you can be in the class. I suggest Lili Forbes. She could use the practice too, and she seems like a game young woman."

Lili was a game young woman. She was ten years older than Hazel, the sturdy daughter of a country squire who had finally agreed to let her try the acting school after her mother had failed to marry her off. Lili had a gift for comedy and made friends with everyone in the school, regardless of background or talent. She always said she would try anything once. When Hazel told Lili what Mr. Willett had said, she smiled and said she would be delighted to take fencing with Hazel. She had fenced a little with her brothers at home, so she thought she could even take on a Californian. So Hazel and Lili became "those two girls in the fencing class" to the young men at the Academy, who looked on them with amusement or disapproval depending on their background and disposition.

One of their fellow fencing students was a rather tall, well-built man who looked to be closer to thirty than twenty, with close-cropped sandy hair, blue eyes, and regular, if somewhat heavy features. All during the class one day, he seemed to be staring at Hazel every time she turned her head, but he turned away when she looked at him. "Who is that?" she asked Lili at the end of the class, nodding toward the other side of the studio.

Lili glanced that way and said, "Oh, that's Jack Moffat. He's here for elocution. He's in politics. I think he just does the fencing for the exercise. I was at school with his sister Edith, and we've visited back and forth."

"Does he always stare at people that way?"

"He always was a little eccentric. He's a Scot, but very much the gentleman. There is a lot of money and some titles in his family, but he's a younger son, so they're making a politician out of him, although he doesn't seem to have a natural talent for it. He put his foot in it and made something of a scandal when he stood for Parliament last year with the Liberal Unionists."

"What happened?"

"It would take too long to explain that now," said Lili, as she packed up her fencing gear. "But I followed it all because I know the family, and I'm rather interested in politics. I'll tell you later." The class had been a strenuous one. Both of them were tired and hungry.

"Let's stop for tea," said Hazel.

"I'm keen for that," said Lili.

When they were settled into Munson's tea room and Lili had helped herself to a generous slice of bread and butter, Hazel said, "Entertain me, Lili. Tell me about the scandal of Jack Moffat."

Lili laughed. "Oh, it's nothing shocking. It was all political. It seems that Jack was out on the hustings attacking Balfour and the Conservative government, which didn't go down well with the higher-ups in the party."

"But why not, if he was running against the Conservatives?"

"It's not quite that simple. The Conservatives and the Liberal Unionists have a long-standing alliance that kept the Conservatives in power for years. The Liberal Unionists sit with the Liberals, but they vote with the Conservatives."

Hazel shook her head. "I will never understand British politics," she said.

Lili laughed. "You're not alone. The short version is that the Unionists broke off from the Liberal party because they join the Conservatives in opposing Home Rule for Ireland."

"Does Jack Moffat support Home Rule?"

"Oh, no. He's quite conservative as far as all that goes," she said. "He just didn't think Balfour's government was any good.

You have to go back a bit," she admitted. "Before the current Prime Minister was elected in the Liberal landslide earlier this year, the last two PMs, Balfour and Lord Salisbury, were Conservatives. Jack was the designated Liberal Unionist candidate from Paisley, in Scotland, where his mother's family is very prominent. Anyway, last year, while Mr. Balfour was in office, Jack gave a speech in Paisley attacking him and saying that he should be replaced as PM by Joseph Chamberlain, who is the leader of the Liberal Unionists. This made the local Conservatives furious, and they refused to support him in the coming election, which of course was seen as a breakdown of the long-standing alliance between the two parties."

"But that was just a local election, right? It couldn't have been too much of a scandal."

"That's where you're wrong," said Lili with a grin. "This is a small country, and news of that kind travels fast. In the end, Chamberlain himself had to write a letter to the *Times*, saying that Jack's attack on Balfour and the Conservatives was uncalled for and unjust, and reassuring the public of his support for the alliance and Balfour."

"I would think that would be the end of Jack."

"Jack is not one to back down, I must say. He wrote an answer to Chamberlain in the *Times*, essentially saying that he still thought he should replace Balfour. He said he thought the rest of the party really shared his view and that he had no intention of resigning his position as Unionist candidate of his district."

"So he is still the candidate?"

"Oh, no," said Lili. "The local Unionist party in Paisley held a meeting and voted unanimously to turn him out. But even then, he stuck to his guns about Chamberlain and Balfour. It wasn't until last summer that he resigned his position as candidate. He said that in the future, he intended to be active in politics as a Liberal."

"And is he?"

Lili laughed. "You would have to ask him that. He was not a candidate in the election this year. Paisley already had their Liberal candidate, who won quite handily. I think his move to London is part of a plan to get in with the party leaders a bit, perhaps get an appointment in one of the ministries. His people are all Conservatives and Unionists, so he has no natural connections except Eton and Cambridge friends and so on. And I don't know how eager the Liberals are to embrace him, since he is known now as something of a loose cannon. It would be good if he could get a government position and show that he's capable of hewing to the line and quietly working away so they might learn to trust him."

Before the next fencing class, Lili came up to Hazel with a mischievous gleam in her eye and Moffat in her wake. "Miss Hazel Tharsing," she said, "may I present Mr. John Moffat."

Hazel put out her hand, and in her warmest Western manner, said, "Pleased to meet you, Mr. Moffat. What is your view of women who fence?"

Moffat's face reddened a little, but he smiled and said, "If they are as lovely as the two ladies in this class, I'm all in favor."

Hazel laughed, and the three of them chatted for a few minutes about the class. As the instructor arrived, Moffat turned to Hazel. "Miss Tharsing," he said, "Miss Forbes has agreed to join me for tea tomorrow after the two o'clock recitation class if you would consent to join us."

Hazel smiled. "Of course, I would love to have tea with our gallant defender. I have my French class next door at the same time."

As Moffat made his way across the room, Lili sent Hazel a merry glance. "This is going to be interesting," she said.

The tea proved to be more of an event than Hazel had expected. Rather than one of the little tea rooms the students frequented on Gower Street, Moffat took them to a hotel on Russell Square. After being shown to a table in the beautifully appointed dining room, they had a luxurious tea, with exotic little sandwiches and French pastries as well as the lightest scones and freshest butter Hazel had eaten in London. She was enchanted. She sat back and looked around at the beautiful room filled with stylish ladies and immaculately groomed gentlemen and thought with satisfaction that she was in the midst of British society at last.

"Your smile looks very mysterious, Miss Tharsing," said Moffat.

Hazel turned her smile on him. "I was just thinking what a lovely room this is. It's not the sort of place where we students usually take tea."

Moffat glanced around at the light-filled room with its pale green walls and white decorative trim, the white plaster medallion on the ceiling, the little domed alcove at the end of the room. "Yes, it is a nice room. I like this revival of the Adam style. I suppose it reminds me of my home in Scotland. No one has messed about with the original Adam interior from the 1790s, so we're quite stylish now."

Hazel had no idea what the Adam revival was, but she listened attentively as he and Lili went on talking about its architectural and decorative principles and the various country houses they knew. She felt as if she had stepped into a novel by Henry James, and John Moffat would make a good Lord Warburton.

As the fall term went on, Hazel and Lili and John Moffat made a regular threesome, sometimes at tea, sometimes at a concert or lecture. Moffat also took them to the theater, where, disdaining the balcony seats that were supplied to the Academy students, he bought tickets in the dress circle. Once, he invited them to sit in his cousin's box at the opera. Unlike the other male students, who lived in rooming houses if they didn't live with their families, Moffat lived at his club. It made Hazel feel very sophisticated to have a friend who spoke of his club with such nonchalance.

Hazel had only encountered the likes of John Moffat in novels, or in stories in the society pages. Although he was Scottish, having gone to Cheam and Eton and Cambridge, he was at home in the highest London social circles and had many friends with country estates where he went hunting and shooting—two different things, Hazel came to understand—and trout fishing. He was also what was known as "very sporting." He owned several race horses and raced yachts and automobiles as well as playing tennis and golf. One day he surprised her by mentioning his novel.

"I didn't know you'd written a novel, Mr. Moffat," she said.

"It was a bit of a lark. I wrote it with Ernest Druce, a friend from Cambridge. It was illustrated by Hugh Thomson, who has done Shakespeare and Dickens and Jane Austen. It is really quite a nice little volume. I will bring one for you."

"What is it about?"

"That's a little hard to say. It's called *Ray Farley: A Comedy of Country Life,* and we were rather under the spell of your Mark Twain five years ago when we wrote it. You will have to judge for yourself."

Hazel was a little dismayed when she read *Ray Farley.* The book was clearly written by very young men. It was about a lazy young gentleman who runs up his debts at the university and, after failing to get his father and his uncle to pay them off, gets a lucky inheritance from America that saves him from prison in the end. Some of the scenes that were meant to be humorous disturbed her, for it was a cruel physical humor. She thought it showed the worst traits of Mark Twain, without his sentiment or his innate morality, although the hero was insistent about the code of the gentleman. The book didn't seem to her to express the spirit of the Jack Moffat she had come to know. She thought that his co-author must have been the one who was responsible for the "humor." But Jack was pleased when she told him that it was very much like an English version of Mark Twain.

"It was fun to do," he said. "But I'm not really that sort of writer. Journalism is more my kind of thing. Although I'm so busy with politics at the moment that I haven't a chance to do much of that."

As the two girls were walking from the Academy toward Torrington Square that afternoon, Lili asked Hazel whether there was an actress in Moffat's novel.

"Not exactly an actress, but there is a pretty dancer."

Lili laughed. "Does she get the hero?"

"No, she doesn't. The hero actually gives up the chance to inherit his uncle's fortune, which he would have gotten on the condition that he married the dancer, who happens to be his uncle's wife's niece. "

"Whom does the hero marry?"

"He marries the virtuous girl who is the ward of the local Baronet."

"And what happens to the dancer?"

"She turns out to have been already married in Paris to another Baronet who had traveled with her on the continent and then abandoned her. After the hero inherits his millions from his American relative, he makes sure that the Baronet does right by her and acknowledges the marriage."

"Hmm," said Lili. "Food for thought. For someone who considers himself a Liberal, our Mr. Moffat seems to be full of aristocratic sentiments and Tory sympathies—but not too particular about where the money comes from."

"It seems that way," said Hazel.

During the fall, Hazel got to know Jack Moffat better. He was unfailingly courteous and gentlemanly. Always careful of pro-priety, he made sure they were chaperoned, usually by the willing Lili, and never placed her in a position that could bring on any kind of social censure. She also learned that he was something of a hypochondriac, viewing any sniffle or pain with alarm that often led to a doctor's visit. As the season wore on, he was constantly worried about the cold, both for Hazel and for himself. He wore an overcoat on the mildest fall day, and he dressed in more and more layers as the winter approached—a wool suit and knitted waistcoat beneath the overcoat, and a thick muffler around his neck. Hazel, who didn't find London all that cold even after her California upbringing, expressed her surprise to Lili that someone who grew up in Scotland should mind the cold so.

Lili smiled. "I think it's his mother's influence. Mrs. Hay is very solicitous of her children's health. I suppose that living in big, drafty old country houses made her especially aware of the cold and damp. I remember that when I visited at Somerby House, I had the largest bedroom fire I have ever had, and I was smothered in eiderdowns and hot water bottles. She would ask me every morning if I had been warm enough. Jack seems to have taken her concerns to heart more than the other children. Edie and her husband alternate between two old castles in Scotland now, but I don't notice that she is overly concerned with heating them."

To Hazel, who had imagined living in castles and manor houses as a luxurious existence, the aristocracy's concern about keeping warm was eye-opening. She began to revise her assumptions as she listened to details that Moffat or Lili would drop. During the Christmas holidays, she had a chance to see some of this life for herself. Jack Moffat went home to Somerby House in Leicester-shire where his mother and stepfather lived, and then on to Dalraddy to shoot grouse on the Scottish moors. Lili invited Hazel to her home in Dorset. "Don't expect anything as grand as the Hays and Moffats," she said, "we're just simple country gentry living in a country house."

The Forbeses' beautiful Georgian manor, with what Hazel now recognized as an Adam interior, was grander than any house Hazel had been inside. Her capacious guest chamber was richly furnished, and there were a bewildering number of servants about who seemed to be waiting for her to ask for something. She had been schooled enough in etiquette while acting in period pieces that she was not worried about how to address people or which fork to use, but she had to look to Lili for cues about what to expect from the servants and how to speak to them.

Lili took pleasure in introducing her California friend to the family circle, especially when she could tell they were bemused by her actions or her outspokenness. Even when she was reigning herself in, Hazel was far more assertive and talkative in company than a well-bred English girl of her age would be. Lili enjoyed having someone further from the norm than herself for once, and her family took Hazel on as a kind of colonial project. They were very kind to her.

Chapter 12

Early in May of 1907, just as the term was finishing up at the Academy, Hazel received a cablegram from her mother. It rather cryptically informed her that she had been entered in a beauty contest run by the *San Francisco Call* and had won first prize. Hazel was first dumbfounded, then angry that her mother had done this without asking her, and then curious about the details. She soon received another cablegram, this time from the newspaper, informing her that she had been judged the most beautiful woman in California and asking her to send more photographs, so she could be submitted as the California candidate in the national contest, which would be held in Chicago the following June, sponsored by the *Tribune*.

Hazel thought about it. Now that it was done, she didn't see that being judged one of the most beautiful women in the country could hurt her stage career in America. She decided to take it in stride, making clear that it was her mother's doing and not hers. Her answer to the Cablegram was published in the *Call* on May fourth. "Many thanks for the honor conferred on me," she wrote. "I think you could easily have found more beautiful girls right at home. Of course I feel tremendously flattered. Thank the judges for me. I was surprised when I got mother's cablegram about my winning. Mother thinks I am better looking than I am. I will send the photographs you ask for. Be sure to let the sisters at Rio Vista convent know about this. They will be pleased." She thought this set the right tone. To her mother, she wrote a letter that she knew would probably be published in the newspaper. She tried to main-tain her breezy attitude, reflect her new London sophistication, and send Nellie a clear message to write and tell her what going on. "Do write and tell me all about it, for really such a thing is incredible to me," she wrote, "I think yet it must be a mistake. Isn't it silly? If they ever saw the original the judges would change their minds, I am very much afraid."

The next day, a young man named Herbert Williams appeared at 69 Torrington Square and asked to see Hazel. The maid went up to inform her and then came back to lead him to her apartment. In accordance with the rules of the house, she left the door of the apartment open after depositing Herbert in Hazel's sitting room. He looked carefully around the pleasant little room, with its bright chintz curtains and chair coverings, and waited expectantly for the door to the other room to open. As Hazel walked into the room, she held out her hand in her best Western manner and, as Herbert described it in the *Call*, "gripped me in an honest shake. Her manner was distinctly affable and approachable, but peculiarly dignified in so young a woman. There was no doubt in my mind that she was really the fairest of California women, or the fairest woman anywhere. I had never seen anyone so radiantly beautiful." So overcome was Herbert that he forgot for a minute what he was there for and became tongue-tied. In her best newly acquired English society manner and a rich, mellow voice that reminded Herbert of the great actress Julia Marlowe, Hazel said, "To what do I owe the honor of this visit?"

The question focused Herbert on his task once more. He explained that he had come to interview Hazel for the *Call* about her being judged the most beautiful woman in California. Hazel regarded him with a smile and said, "All the pretty girls I used to know in California must have gone a long way off if they have to choose me as a beauty." When Herbert saw that she was not going to take the matter seriously, they soon relaxed into what felt like a social call between two young Californians. Hazel offered Herbert tea, saying, "I only drink it because I know that all London is doing the same thing at this time of the afternoon, and I don't like to feel out of things." She said she didn't take cream because she had learned to drink tea in Chinatown at home, and she always took it straight.

As the hour went on, the casual sociability of the residence revealed itself. Several of the other young ladies stopped by and were introduced. Mrs. Merritt came in to say hello, fulfilling her role as chaperone. Hazel talked the whole time, mostly about the recent Cambridge-Oxford field meet where several Americans, friends of all the girls, had done well. Hazel confessed to having been "wildly excited" at the meet. And she said she'd come home simply covered in American flags. She told Herbert that she was studying music to please her mother. As Hazel spoke of her mother, Herbert later wrote for the paper, "I saw the full depths of her wonderful eyes. She was between me and the evening light that came in through the window. The gold in her dark hair lighted, her face was strong lines and deep shadows. I felt as if I were in the seclusion of a convent and were an intruder." When he rose to go, Hazel appeared to be lost in thought, leaning against the door, "Imagine the judges choosing me!" she said. "I wonder what mother said! I wish I were at home—at home in dear old California." Herbert left in something of a daze, with the vague hope that she had invited him to call again. Hazel's feeling that she had given a very effective performance was confirmed when she read the article in the *Call* that Herbert sent her.

Herbert's interview appeared alongside other stories about the contest, which included an account of Hazel that had been drawn from interviews with her mother, and written statements from the three judges of the beauty contest, two painters and a sculptor, who explained the principles of beauty they had used to choose among the hundreds of photographs that had been sent into the *Call* from all over the state. The newspaper story described Hazel as a "tall, strong girl with perfect health. Her complexion is fair with an olive tinge. Her hair is chestnut brown with a slightly golden sheen. Her eyes are large and expressive.

The breadth of her forehead, the strength of the curve of her eyebrow, the power and magnetism of her beauty as shown in her chin and mouth can best be seen in photographs of her." The sisters at the convent, it said, had taught her to be humble, so that she regards her beauty as a "gift in which she must not take too much pride." In keeping with this humility, it read, "her manner is as simple as her heart. She is always at home wherever she goes." Nellie had told the reporter that Hazel seemed unconscious of the people who stared at her. Nellie also told the reporter that Hazel always had perfect marks at school, often getting up at 4:00 a.m. to study.

In order for Hazel to be entered in the national final for the contest, she had to be present at the event in Chicago where the ten finalists would meet the judges. So invested in the story was the *Call* that it paid Hazel's fare to return to New York on the White Star liner *Oceanic*, first class, to meet Nellie and then travel by train to Chicago. The reporter who met the ship wrote that his expectation of seeing a typical beauty, "imposing and statuesque," was completely upended when he saw Hazel, who was "not of the conspicuous type." Instead, he saw "just a slender girl, radiantly healthy, buoyant, glowing; a girl of trim, lithe figure, stylish, typical of young American womanhood." In contrast to the elaborate hairstyles that were in fashion, Hazel's "small, well-shaped head" was "crowned with a glory of dark hair, parted on the forehead and caught up at the back in a knot after the simple, old fashioned style that makes a plain woman look plain indeed, but adds new charm to beauty. Her face is oval. Her wondrous eyes, black as coals and surmounted by delicately penciled brows, are fringed with large dark lashes. Her lips, half parted in a smile, reveal perfect teeth." In her eyes, he wrote, "invariably shines a merry, roguish light that makes no small part of her charm. Miss Tharsing's beauty is essentially girlish, the beauty and the promise of the budding rose . . . it grows upon you and convinces you more and more as you observe it."

Hazel kept up her breezy, self-deprecating attitude about the contest as she spoke to reporters, saying that the whole thing still seemed like a joke, "the idea of my being entered in the beauty contest! But I'm grateful to the *Call* for bringing me home." She spoke humbly about the beauty of the other candidates and said she hoped she would be able to live up to her photographs. After a quick overnight in New York, Nellie and Hazel and the *Call* reporter boarded the Twentieth Century Limited for the eighteen-hour trip to Chicago. In her excitement, Hazel spent a fairly sleepless night in a Pullman car, arriving at noon. She barely had time to bathe and put on the new evening dress her mother had brought before she joined the other nine contestants for a social event with the judges. Hazel's training and London experience served her well, as she presented an open but dignified appearance. She was friendly to everyone in a subdued version of her Western persona, but she exercised all her knowledge of English manners. Hazel charmed the judges, as she usually charmed older men, but there were some more experienced charmers there. In the end, it was a Southern Belle from Nashville who won the judges' votes. Hazel was a little disappointed, mostly for the *Call* and for Nellie, who had so much invested in the contest, but she was happy enough for herself not to have to live up to the title of America's Most Beautiful Woman.

After two days of social events and sight-seeing, Nellie and Hazel took a slower train back to New York and stayed for a week with Kitty at her home in the Bronx before Hazel boarded the ship for London. She had no professional engagement that summer, but she was due to start rehearsals for several Academy productions, including one that was to be presented by Herbert Beerbohm Tree at Her Majesty's Theatre. Each year since he had started the Academy, Tree had taken one or two of the best graduates into his company, and these showcase performances were highly prized chances to come to his attention. Hazel was not going to miss her opportunity.

Alone on the ship, Hazel had ample time to think about the events of the last few weeks, which she had taken in only as a whirlwind fantasy. Traveling first class was a delightful novelty for her, not to mention being photographed and interviewed, with serious people hanging on her every word. She came to the realization that her beauty was a much greater asset than she had given it credit for. Talent was something that would take you far in the theater, and you could develop it if you worked very hard. But if she thought about it honestly, she knew that her talent for both singing and acting was a modest one. Beauty she clearly had, much greater beauty than she had imagined, and if used intelligently and shrewdly, beauty could take her farther, both in the theater and out of it.

Hazel knew better than to talk about the beauty contest in London, except in a joking, self-deprecating way, as a fancy of her mother's that she had indulged. But it did not pass notice that she had been judged one of the ten most beautiful women in America. Now viewing her beauty as her major asset, she worked hard at enhancing and emphasizing it, changing her hairstyle and wearing flattering colors and trimmings. The changes were subtle, but when Jack Moffat returned to London from his summer of fishing, tennis, golf, and auto racing, he noticed them, or at least he noticed that Hazel seemed to grow prettier each day. Since he was a socially well-connected man who was almost always at hand, she tended to focus her efforts on pleasing him. When he said she looked lovely in a rose-colored silk shirtwaist, she began to place rose-colored accents on her white shirtwaists. She experimented with her hair, and when he complimented it, she remembered the style and sought to enhance it.

Hazel also practiced what she thought of as the "womanly arts." She gradually transformed her California manner into a quieter, more reserved presence, using fewer, more restrained gestures, and talking in a softer voice. Always a good mimic, she imitated the talk of upper-class people like Lili, reining in her American accent and distinguishing between a British formality on formal occasions and up-to-date slang among her friends. She was learning to play an English society girl.

Chapter 13

When he returned to London in the fall 0f 1907, Jack Moffat found that he was in love with Hazel Tharsing. She seemed to have profited a good deal from her time in London and at the Academy, and, he flattered himself, from the time she had spent with him. Not only did she seem more beautiful with each passing day, but her manner, especially toward him, was changing from that of a rather hoydenish American girl to that of a charming and modest English lady. She was still an uncivilized little thing, but her animal spirits showed a cheerful, optimistic nature. He felt that she was at heart a warm and responsive woman, capable of great love if given the proper chance. The problem was that he had no idea what to do about his feelings. He held Hazel in such regard that he could not imagine her in one of those casual romances that one would typically take up with an actress, but it was equally unimaginable to present Hazel to his family as his bride to be. For the time being, he resolved to live in the moment and enjoy the time he spent with her.

As the days passed, Jack tried to think of more ways to expand Hazel's social sphere without demanding too much of her. He confided in Lili, who fell in eagerly with his plan, suggesting that a large tea or evening reception would give him a chance to introduce Hazel to society without the need for a great deal of personal conversation. Lili was confident that Hazel's theatrical training and her experience with the Forbes family in Dorset had given her enough knowledge of manners and etiquette that she would be comfortable in such a setting. When an invitation arrived for a Friday evening crush at Apsley House, the London residence of his cousin, the Marchioness Douro, Jack thought it was just the thing. There would be a great many people from all ranks of society, from the aristocracy to the middle class. He could bring Hazel and Lili and introduce them where he pleased, moving on if the conversation became difficult.

When Lili agreed with the plan, Jack made the invitation to Hazel, who was excited by the prospect of attending an evening party at a great London house.

Hazel had only one suitable evening dress, the one she had worn for the reception in Chicago. It was honey-colored silk, with a tastefully embroidered skirt and a stylish square-necked bodice trimmed with black lace. As usual, Nellie had chosen well for her daughter. The gown flattered her coloring, and the dressmaker at home knew Hazel's figure. It fit her perfectly. Lili observed that the dress would be quite the thing, and that Hazel looked well in it, as she did in everything. Lili wore a simple light-blue dress with lace trim. When Jack came to the door of 69 Torrington Square, he was impeccably groomed, his tall, athletic figure set off by his perfectly tailored evening dress. Watching them descend the steps at Torrington Square, Lili thought they looked like an illustration in one of the more fashionable magazines.

At Apsley House, Jack took his guests immediately to meet his cousin, who bestowed her hand and a polite smile on the two girls. "Miss Tharsing and Miss Forbes are classmates of mine," said Jack. "I'm studying public speaking at the Academy of Dramatic Art."

"Good for you, Jack," said the Marchioness. "I hope you will stand again for Parliament. I know you will do the family proud this time."

Jack blushed a little. "Well, we'll see," he said, and took his leave as new arrivals came up behind him.

Lili spotted a school friend across the room and told Jack she would meet them later.

"Near the big clock at the back of the great hall," he said. "There shouldn't be such a crush of people there. We'll meet at 11:00 if we don't see you before."

As Lili went off happily to talk to her friend, Jack steered Hazel toward the dining room and refreshments. "It's best to get something early, I find. There's such a mob of people that the table is quickly decimated, and you can't get anything to eat or drink after ten o'clock."

Soon they were sitting next to a little corner table in the enormous drawing room, drinking Champagne and eating bon bons and candied orange slices while the room filled with people. Jack was in his element, pointing out various people whose names Hazel knew from the newspaper—government officials, artists, writers, famous beauties. When they had finished their wine, Jack offered Hazel his arm and took her on a slow tour around the rooms, introducing her to friends and acquaintances and showing her the most important paintings and *objets d'art.*

Hazel was dazzled and did her best to perform well. She noticed that Jack introduced her as "Miss Hazel Tharsing, my American friend," and did not elaborate. She could see that some of the people were curious about her but were too well-bred to pry. Other than to inquire how long she had been in the country or whether she was enjoying London, they did not ask her anything personal. For the most part, she just stood quietly gazing around at the scene while Jack exchanged remarks about politics with the other guests. Everything there was of interest to her, from the decoration of the rooms to the ladies' gowns, jewelry, and hair, to the manners on display and the relationships she could discern. When 11:00 came, she was surprised to find that they had been there for two hours. She would happily have spent another two, but Jack said they should collect Lili and go, or they would be caught in the crush at the door.

The ride back in the cab was a slightly giddy one. Lili had spent the whole evening gossiping with old friends and was in high spirits. Jack was delighted at the obvious admiration Hazel had inspired in friends and acquaintances. And Hazel felt that a world she had read and dreamed about for a long time had been opened to her. Looking at Jack Moffat, she saw him no longer as a handsome but rather awkward, sometimes boring man who bought her lovely teas and squired her around town, but as a comfortable habitué of the world where she dearly wanted to live. They all talked and laughed and made plans to have tea on Monday afternoon.

As he walked back to his club, Jack thought hopefully that a future with Hazel might just be possible. In the following weeks, he escorted her and Lili to several other large parties and was amazed at what a quick study Hazel was when it came to fashion and conversation. Each evening showed her more attractively turned out. Besides acquiring a stylish new gown, Jack could tell she had made subtle but telling alterations to her dress and hair. She could converse about the weather like any English society lady or nod quiet encouragement during a political discussion. Her lovely face glowed with a special vitality at these parties. He had never seen her more beautiful.

After the Apsley House party, Hazel could tell that Jack's feeling for her had left the realm of friendship and become romantic. She wondered whether her own feelings would eventually match his. There was no doubt that she felt attracted to him, but she didn't know how much of that was being dazzled by all the trappings of wealth and British society. She smiled to think how ignorantly she had spoken to her mother of acting as a route to marriage with an English gentleman. Now she knew how far-fetched that was, but here she was, all but being courted by a wealthy gentleman who might soon be an MP and spoke nonchalantly of the castles his mother and sister lived in. And this was before her career had really started. She enjoyed the Academy and took pride in her accomplishments there, but when she weighed marriage to a man like Jack against an acting career, there was no doubt which she would choose. He could offer her a life the American girls on the society pages would envy. Weighed against the hard work, the uncertainties, and the difficult conditions starting out in the theater, it was ridiculous to think there was a choice to be made.

The autumn weeks passed quickly for Jack and Hazel. To spend more time together without the need of a chaperone, they started walking in the afternoons, strolling through Gordon Square and the other Bloomsbury parks. During these walks, Jack told Hazel about his life, which seemed to her a round of weekend parties in castles and country manors, fox hunting and grouse shooting, tennis and golf and horses and fast cars. "Don't you need to work?" she asked him one day. "I know you're involved in politics, but don't you practice law?"

Jack laughed. "I know I must seem a lazy lout," he said. "I did read law at Cambridge, and I spent some time in my cousin's office, but I never took to the solicitor's work. Now that I've become so interested in public speaking, I'm thinking that I might train to be a barrister if I don't get into Parliament this time. I think I would quite enjoy that. I've been living on an inheritance from my father while I try my hand at this and that, but as I'm nearing thirty, I do think it's time to settle into something."

Hazel thought this was a very casual way to approach one's career, but she supposed that if you had all the money you needed, it must not seem all that urgent to get started on making more. It was an entirely different frame of mind than she was used to in San Francisco.

As Hazel became more familiar with Jack, she grew more fond of him. He really was like a big boy, enthusiastic and eager to please. He would jump through hoops to satisfy any little whim she expressed. If she was unhappy or depressed over some setback at the Academy, he did his best to cheer her up with flowers and little gifts. He was most generous with the entertainments he devised for her and Lili, with dinners and after-theater suppers and even a lavish Champagne picnic on one fine September Sunday when they went on an outing to the country. It got so that Hazel could not imagine her life in London without him.

On an unusually bright and warm October afternoon, Jack and Hazel decided to walk in Gordon Square after their classes at the Academy. Strolling slowly along the path, Jack nodded absently as Hazel chatted on about the day's events. He had been revolving a speech in his mind for weeks, and he suddenly decided to come out with it. "Miss Tharsing," he said. "May I speak to you about something important?"

"Why, of course, Mr. Moffat," she said. "Let's sit on that bench over there."

After they were seated, he turned to her and took her hand. A little startled by this unaccustomed intimacy, Hazel looked up at him. Looking into her deep, innocent eyes, Jack felt a wave of love such as he had never felt before. It was intense and urgent, but also protective. "Hazel," he said, "if you will permit me, I would like to tell you how I feel about you."

Hazel's hand moved a little in his, but her eyes did not flinch. "Of course you may, Jack," she said.

He went on, each sentence having been carefully considered. "I think you know that I have been drawn to you since the first time I saw you. You were beautiful then, but you have grown ever more so over the last year." He smiled at her. "Remember that you were *my* beauty queen before you were America's."

Hazel smiled, but cast her eyes down, shaking her head a little.

Jack went on. "But you must know that it is not only your physical beauty that I appreciate, Hazel. You have all the fine qualities that a lady can have. You are soft and sweet and sympathetic, but you are also intelligent and strong. I think you have a beautiful soul. You would do me the greatest honor if you would consent to be my wife."

Hazel blushed and looked up at Jack. The proposal was not unexpected, but now that it was in front of her, she was not sure how to respond. "Oh, Jack," she said, "it's you who honor me. I'm just a nineteen-year-old American girl, and you are an English gentleman, with so many accomplishments. I don't know what to say."

"I hope you can say that you are fond of me."

"Yes, of course. I think you are a wonderful man. I've never met anyone as kind and generous and thoughtful as you."

"I'm afraid I haven't a great deal to offer you in a material way just yet. I have just a thousand a year from my father and thirty thousand from my grandmother that becomes mine to invest next year. But I do have prospects, as you know, and I would work very hard with you to inspire me." He looked down at her face, which, with its perfect lines and slightly heightened color, had never seemed lovelier.

Hazel turned to him. "I know you have ambitions for your career, and I don't care about the money, as long as we would have enough to live on comfortably," she said. "I would never want us to descend to quarreling about money. But I am concerned about your family. Would they accept me? I'm young to marry, and I think I know just enough about your world to know that I would need to know a lot more before I could live in it."

Jack looked relieved at this shrewd judgment. "I've thought about this, Hazel, and I think there is an answer. Many American girls who come to London, and English girls, too, go to a finishing school in Paris to improve their French and German and perhaps study music or painting, and by the way to learn what they need to know to flourish in London society or country life. If your mother would be willing to send you to Paris, I'm sure you would have no qualms about fitting in after a year or two."

This was something Hazel hadn't thought of before. She wasn't at all sure that Nellie would be willing to finance another school abroad, although the prospect of Hazel's marriage to an English gentleman would certainly be an incentive. "That's something we've never even considered," said Hazel. "Of course, Mother wants me to get my musical education. I don't know how she would react to news of my engagement to begin with. She doesn't believe in early marriages."

"That may be something in our favor. We wouldn't need to announce our engagement formally yet. If it was put to her simply as a chance to continue your musical education in Paris, your mother might agree. It's very important to know French and German if one is to pursue music seriously."

"That's true," said Hazel, "and Mother would much rather have me pursue music than acting. I could certainly propose it to her."

"Then suppose we have an understanding, Hazel. I will not ask for your promise now, but next year, I will ask you again, and we will see where we are. Meanwhile," he said, kissing the hand that he held, "I reserve the right to visit you in Paris."

Hazel wrote to Nellie, laying out the whole plan. She doubted that her mother would be willing to finance another year in Europe without some tangible expectation, so the proposal was an important element in the calculation. Nellie wrote back cautiously, telling Hazel to find out all the necessary information about the school that Jack suggested. She said she had been planning to surprise Hazel by coming to London in December, and they could discuss it then. So Nellie arrived in mid-December in time to see Hazel's final performance at the Academy and spend Christmas and Hazel's birthday in London. More importantly, she met Jack Moffat, who did everything he could to entertain Mrs. Tharsing and demonstrate his high regard for Hazel.

To Hazel's surprise, Jack and Nellie hit it off from the start. Jack had spent some time in San Francisco during his world tour after leaving Cambridge. He knew more of Nellie's type than either she or Hazel suspected, and he liked it. Nellie put on a little show of being the grand dame, as she did with strangers who intimidated her, but it didn't take long to break it down when she felt at ease. Jack could see that she was a smart, shrewd woman and a straight shooter, who enjoyed a good time. He thought she was quite a character. For her part, Nellie had been dealing with the San Francisco version of Jack Moffat for many years. She could see that he was a young man who liked his pleasure, whether it be sport or wine, but he took life seriously in the end, and she expected that he would soon settle down to work at something, given all the opportunities and advantages he had. Besides, he clearly adored her daughter.

Chapter 14

Jack Moffat was able to secure an introduction for Hazel from one of the English patrons of the *Pensionnat de Mme. Yeatman* in Neuilly-sur-Seine in Paris, and she began her studies there in the beginning of 1908. Madame and her husband Thomas, an American professor, had begun the school in the 1880s, calling it the French Protestant Institution. At the beginning, it was a religious school whose patrons were the Bishop of Carlisle and the Bishop of Down as well as other prominent English and French Protestants. Its purpose was to educate the children of the large English expatriate community of Paris in the English Protestant tradition. After Thomas's death in 1890, Mme. Yeatman had changed the character of the school, turning it into a secular boarding school for young ladies who wished to finish their education while "improving their French" in Paris and benefitting from the cultural riches of the continent. By 1908, when Hazel enrolled, it had become a popular training ground for well-off American girls who hoped to enter European society. In the school, they were able to mingle easily with the upper-class British girls and form useful social connections.

Although it was rather permissive for a French boarding school, Hazel found it difficult to adjust to the restrictions of the *Pensionnat* after the last two years at the Academy of Dramatic Art, where male and female students took classes together and associated freely, and where she had her own rooms apart from the school with only the rules of the house to follow. At the Academy, not only had the classes been interesting to her, but there had always been the excitement of an upcoming production, with all the behind-the-scenes drama attached to rehearsals. The *Pensionnat* was more like a sophisticated version St. Gertrude's, with a regimented daily schedule and all the little boarding school rituals and relationships that Hazel had already gotten thoroughly tired of in high school. She resolved to make the greatest use she could of her opportunities there and leave as soon as possible.

Hazel knew that her American school-girl French was wholly inadequate, not only in France, but in English society, where people seemed to slip in and out of French as if they were born speaking it. She was determined to concentrate on her French in addition to the music that was her ostensible subject. She also took German, European history, and dancing, something she always needed to work on, and a course in etiquette, general training for American and English middle-class girls in the niceties of upper-class social behavior. After they had been instructed in table etiquette and conversation, the students, or "young ladies," had regular luncheons and dinners with many fussy courses, where they sat five to a table along with either Mme. Yeatman or one of her designated assistants—upper-class girls who had learned all their manners from governesses and mothers. During the meal, the young ladies practiced the art of conversation and were gently reproved if they picked up the wrong utensil or made some other gauche move. Most of the American girls dreaded these meals and were terribly embarrassed if they made a mistake. Hazel just took them as an elaborate acting course, getting everything she could out of them. By the end of the term, Mme. Yeatman said she was ready to become an assistant herself, the highest mark of approval she could win.

None of the courses Hazel took at the *Pensionnat* were either exciting or challenging intellectually, and she found most of the other students immature and quite limited in experience. She behaved toward the other girls much as she had at St. Gertrude's, but with a clearer plan. Her California manner was gone, replaced by the smart, sophisticated air of the Londoner. She talked of her life in Bloomsbury, and while she made it clear that she had no intention of becoming a professional actress, the other girls were impressed that she had studied at the Academy and had appeared in *The Geisha* with May de Sousa. After carefully scouting the other students, Hazel formed a little clique with two of them, Mabel Glenn, a pretty and good-humored steel heiress from Pittsburgh who was game for anything and thought she might as well take on Europe, and Jane Baird, a blue-eyed, golden-haired beauty from Glasgow whose family wanted her to debut in London. The three of them were not only a little older and more sophisticated than most of the girls, they were recognized as the most beautiful girls in the school. The others looked to them for cues about style and dress and generally deferred to them in most matters. After a few weeks, Hazel enjoyed her position at the *Pensionnat*.

As part of their education, Madame Yeatman thought it was important for her young ladies to take part in the cultural life of Paris. She often brought them to lectures, museums, and galleries, or to an occasional matinee if a classic was being performed at the *Comédie Français*. Hazel made the best of these outings, and she took every opportunity to spend time in the city. The young ladies were not allowed to leave the *Pensionnat* grounds on their own, but Hazel spent almost every one of her free Saturday afternoons with Mabel and Jane, shopping or just strolling along the Champs Élysées and sitting in a café for an hour. The three beautiful, stylishly dressed girls were aware that they drew a lot of attention from people around them, or passers-by if they sat at a sidewalk table, but they were clever enough to enjoy it without showing it.

While she was in Paris, Hazel and Jack Moffat wrote faithfully to each other every week. His letters, which began "My Dear Hazel," or occasionally "Dear One," were signed "Affectionately, Jack." They were not particularly interesting letters, mostly accounts of his various activities, which had a great deal to do with visiting and racing and gossip about politics or people they knew from the Academy. He was making headway in the Liberal social scene and had hopes of standing for Parliament in the next election. Hazel wrote a good deal about what she had seen and done in Paris and not much about the school and its doings.

Hazel planned carefully for the second week in March, when Jack was coming to spend a week in Paris. With the help of Mabel, who had an unerring eye for what was becoming, she spent most of the money her mother had given her for her birthday at the Galeries Lafayette on her first Paris evening gown. It was a filmy dress in the new slim silhouette, with no bustle effect, a deep rose color with just a hint of ivory lace trim. Hazel felt like a sylph in it. When Jack wrote to ask what she would like to do on the Saturday evening they would have together, she answered that she would love to go to *Le Théâtre Sarah Bernhardt* to see the great actress perform with her new young partner, Lou Tellegen. Jack responded by inviting Hazel and Mme. Yeatman to join him at the theater.

The week of Jack's visit was everything Hazel could have hoped for. On Sunday afternoon, he came to the school, making a tall, handsome figure in his dark suit. The young ladies were impressed with Hazel's visitor, whom she had given them to understand was her fiancé. As always, Jack's manners were perfect, and he paid due attention to Mme. Yeatman during afternoon tea. On Wednesday afternoon, when there were no classes, Hazel obtained permission for Jack to escort her and Mabel and Jane into Paris, ostensibly to attend an exhibition. They made quick work of the pictures and spent most of the time at the *Café Royal*, where they all hit it off marvelously. As Jack had more or less grown up in Scotland, he and Jane turned out to know many of the same people and places. Jack was delighted to find that Mabel was an avid golfer and tennis player. On Saturday afternoon, he took them all to a tea at the British embassy. In the evening, he arrived in impeccable evening dress to escort Hazel and Mme. Yeatman to the play.

Hazel took in the atmosphere of the evening theater audience with rapt attention, and even Mme. Yeatman seemed to be impressed. She said it had been quite some time since she had been on a Saturday evening theater party. When the play began, Hazel couldn't take her eyes from the stage, but she barely noticed any of the performances except Sarah Bernhardt's. She was astounded by the power of the little actress, who was not particularly beautiful, to hold the audience in thrall. Every gesture, every vocal trick, realized its calculated effect to perfection. The audience not only smiled with her and wept with her but breathed with her. Jack, on the other hand, watched Hazel. He was delighted and touched by her excitement and the play of emotions on her lovely face. After he had bid good night to Mme. Yeatman, Jack lingered in the parlor with Hazel, quite sure that there would be no disapproval expressed after such a lovely evening. "I think your French has already improved a good deal, Hazel," he said. "You seemed to be following the play without any trouble."

"I followed every word," she said. "Sarah Bernhardt is the cleverest actress I have ever seen. Every single thing she does hits its mark. I can't imagine thinking of myself as an actress after seeing her."

This was something of a relief to Jack, who always worried that Hazel might be drawn back to the stage. "What did you think of the production?"

"I hardly noticed anyone else. Lou Tellegen is a handsome prop for Bernhardt, and the rest of them said their lines all right. It's quite a bit different from English theater. I don't think anyone would chastise Bernhardt for standing at center stage or hogging the limelight."

"They say there is a romance between her and Tellegen even though she's thirty-seven years older."

"I can believe that, can't you? She could convince anyone she was any age."

He looked dubious. "I don't know. I think I would have to see her close up."

Hazel looked up at him and burst out laughing. "Well, at least I don't have to worry about you going off with La Bernhardt."

"No," he said. "You certainly don't."

After the visit, Hazel felt surer about her attachment to Jack. The other girls treated her with the respect they afforded someone who was engaged. Mme. Yeatman also thought of Jack as her fiancé, which made things much easier during subsequent visits. They were allowed to go about the city and to the theater unchaperoned, and Jack introduced Hazel to café society. For a treat during each visit, they had a long, exquisite meal in a fashionable restaurant like Fouquet's or Maxim's, with the accompanying wines chosen carefully by Jack, who was developing into quite a connoisseur. On these occasions, Hazel dressed to the nines, often in clothes borrowed from Mabel, and often received the distinction of being placed at a table near the front windows, tacitly reserved for beautiful women. Mostly, though, they ate at brasseries or had a little supper at a cabaret. Hazel loved these visits—the luxury, the attention, the entertainment, the comfortable, chatty conversations with Jack, who was an enthusiastic gossip and, true to his agreement to wait, never pressed her with ardent words or actions.

On the whole, the two years at Mme. Yeatman's passed much faster and more pleasantly than Hazel had expected. At the end of her four terms, she had confidence in her ability to hold her own, not only in French and German, but in British society. She had studied British history. She read the *London Times* regularly. And, with Jack's help, she felt she understood the political scene fairly well. She also read many novels by writers like Mrs. Humphry Ward and Henry James, which made her comfortable with the idea of country house life. With her training in etiquette and the art of conversation, she was no longer daunted by the thought of being placed next to a lord or an MP at dinner or being left with the ladies in the drawing room.

What Hazel worried about was getting the money that she knew was needed in order to flourish in this new world before she married. In the years since the San Francisco earthquake in 1906, Nellie Tharsing had done very well as a businesswoman. Her big stroke of luck was that her apartment building was on the western corner of Van Ness Avenue and Ellis Street. The line of the horrific fire that had destroyed the core of the city after the earthquake ended on the eastern side of Van Ness. While the building required a lot of attention to recover from the smoke and ash, it was still standing and was rentable when the demand for housing was at its peak, and she was able to make some profitable investments as the city was rebuilt. With her business flourishing, Nellie was able to finance Hazel's education without strain. But it would be another matter for Hazel to live in London as a young lady of Jack Moffat's social class. Hazel knew that this would be essential if he was to get his family's approval for the marriage. Men of Jack's class married American women, but they were women with money. His family would never approve of his marriage to Hazel if they knew her background and her financial state, and if they were going to live in comfort as a couple, they would need the support his family could provide.

During his final visit to Mme. Yeatman's in the fall of 1909, Jack asked Hazel again if she was willing to marry him. This time, she did not hesitate. "Yes, I will," she said, her face coloring slightly and her dark eyes lifting to his. "But on one condition. Our marriage has to be acceptable to your family. I know how much family means to you, and I could never be the cause of alienating you from them. If we have your mother's blessing, I will be honored to be your wife."

For the first time, Jack put his arms around Hazel and kissed her fervently on the lips. "I will win my mother's blessing or die trying," he said.

Later, as they talked over the future, Jack suggested to Hazel that often young ladies whose families did not own a London house or have an accommodating relative would live in a small flat or an apartment in Mayfair for a social season. It was convenient and perfectly proper as long as someone lived with them. "Perhaps your mother could come for a visit," he said. "It would be well for people to know she was on the ground."

Hazel was surprised when Nellie was enthusiastic about the plan. She was anxious for Hazel to be married to Jack after all the money and effort that had been invested in her preparation. Nellie had told Mel Chapman how much she liked Jack and how impressive his family was. "You should go, Nell," Mel said. "You deserve a nice trip. You can get Hazel set up in a flat and enjoy London for a while, get to know Jack better and maybe meet some of his relatives. I'm sure that's important to them over there. Put on your best clothes and your best behavior and let them see that Hazel has a formidable mother."

Nellie laughed. "I don't know about formidable, but I suppose I could do my best so she wasn't ashamed of me."

So it was decided that Nellie would meet Hazel in London, and they would stay at the Hotel Welbeck in Mayfair until they were able to find a suitable apartment. Hazel was of two minds about this. She was relieved that she would be able to afford the kind of fashionable address that would be acceptable to Jack's family, but she was worried about what to do with Nellie in London. Although her mother always dressed well and looked dignified when she wanted to, Hazel knew that she would be even less presentable in London society than she herself had been in 1906. She relied on Jack to negotiate the social moves, and as he had been with Hazel, he proved equal to the task.

After helping them to find a small but well-appointed apartment on Welbeck Street, Jack attended to their social life, making sure that Nellie was introduced to his relatives at large teas and receptions. Hazel attended to her Mother's appearance, and Nellie was happy to go on a little shopping spree at Harrods, buying two appropriate afternoon dresses and an evening dress. Always attractive with her healthy complexion and abundant chestnut hair, Nellie in her early forties made a handsome figure next to her beautiful daughter, and Jack, with his athletic good looks, completed the trio. At large parties and receptions, Hazel was especially animated in conversation, trying to keep Nellie's participation to a minimum, and Jack kept them moving so that a conversation didn't go on beyond the introductions and the usual pleasantries. People remembered them as those good-looking Americans of Jack's. They thought the daughter unusually well-mannered for an American, but rather chatty for a young girl.

As the weeks went by, Nellie and Hazel found it necessary to watch their expenditures. They economized on food, cooking simple meals in the apartment's little kitchen when Jack wasn't squiring them around. Nellie complained that they would soon be living on tea and bread and butter like most Londoners. Always shrewd about the rental market, she scouted around and decided that they were paying far more than was necessary for the Mayfair apartment. "We really should move before I leave for home, Hazel. You can't afford this place, and you can find the same accommodations for much less a little further out in Paddington or Bayswater."

Hazel was shocked. "But that's impossible, Mother," she said. "One can't have an address in Bayswater."

"Well, how about Bloomsbury, where you lived before? It's pricey, but not as bad as Mayfair."

"Bloomsbury is too bohemian. It's where the unconventional artists and writers live. I can't afford to be associated with anything like that."

Nellie cocked her head and looked at her daughter. "Well, we certainly have become quite the snobs in London."

"I know it seems that way to you, Mother, but as an American, my living arrangements have to be perfectly *comme il faut.* It's important for Jack's family to believe that, even if I am American, I move in the same social circles they do."

"But you don't. What will you do when they find out?"

"They won't find out if I play my part well. Or not until after we're married. And once that's done, it's for life. The British take marriage very seriously. They have to make the most of it."

Nellie shook her head. "I know there's no point in arguing once you've set your mind on something," she said, "but I hope you know what you're doing."

Hazel stayed in Mayfair, and she simultaneously solved the problem of having a female companion once Nellie left and paying the rent by asking her friend Lili to share the apartment. Lili had done well at the Academy but had not been successful in landing an acting job with a provincial company as she had hoped to do. Hazel could tell from her letters that, after nearly a year of country life in Devon, Lili was champing at the bit to get back to London, and her family would be glad to have her go for a while. When Hazel wrote to her, Lili jumped at the chance. Her parents were relieved to find she would be staying with someone they considered more practical and level-headed than their Lili. So Hazel had her friend's company and maintained her address at twenty-seven Welbeck Street, just on the edge of Mayfair.

Chapter 15

In January of 1910, Nellie returned to San Francisco, reasonably happy that Hazel was in a nice place in London where she would have a friend with her and only be paying half the exorbitant rent. The Parliamentary election was in full sway when she left. With the Paisley seat in the capable hands of the local Liberal Party chairman, Jack had been sent to help with the campaign in Leicestershire, near Somerby, his mother's family home, where he was well known. His classes in public speaking had been worthwhile. He gave several rousing speeches to warm up the crowd for the candidate, and as word got around, he was invited to speak in several other districts as well. He was busy from mid-January until the election ended on the tenth of February, with the Liberal Party pulling off a surprise victory. Jack returned to London with great hopes of joining the government in some capacity, but when the list of nominees came out, his name was not on it. Apparently, he had not yet convinced the Liberals that he was one of them. Although he kept up his Party connections, his hopes of joining the government were fading.

On the other hand, Hazel and Jack felt that they had laid the necessary groundwork for their marital campaign by showing Hazel's presentable mother to various relatives and giving them to understand that Hazel came from plenty of money. The next step was for Hazel to be invited to stay at one of the great country houses. For Jack, the choice was obvious. He had confided in his sister Edith two years before, writing that he had fallen in love with an American girl, and she knew about Hazel's enrollment at Mme Yeatman's. Edith was as eager to invite Hazel as Jack was to bring her. They settled on the week after Easter, when a small party of friends was joining the family at their castle in Scotland, the hereditary home of Edith's husband Henry. Edith invited both Hazel and her old school friend Lili, which helped to put Hazel at ease and delighted Lili. "Now you'll see the Scottish aristocracy in all their splendor," she said. "Prepare for bagpipes."

As Hazel and Lili were packing for the trip, Lili told her to be sure to bring some sheet music. "These country house parties can be work, you know. You'll be expected to sing for your supper."

Hazel hadn't thought of this. Despite her years of musical training and her love for performing on the stage, she still did not like to sing in public. She did not trust her singing voice in the way she trusted her acting ability. She looked a little anxiously at Lili. "What sort of thing, do you think?"

"Oh, nothing too ambitious. You'll just be entertaining the country gentry, not London connoisseurs of music."

"I've done some Scottish songs, 'Auld Robin Gray' and 'Ye Banks and Braes.' Would they do?"

"They would love that. And there will surely be someone who can accompany you. Bring the sheet music. I can do it if need be. They're sure to ask you more than once when they find that you can really sing. What else do you have?"

"I don't know what I have that's appropriate. Mendelssohn hymns?"

"They're not *that* bad. Any light opera?"

"The *Mikado*. I know Katisha's songs."

"Perfect. I can play those."

"I know some of Sullivan's parlour songs too. I'll bring them along. I can accompany myself if necessary."

Lili nodded. "Now for my job, which is dramatic entertainment. I thought we could do that dialogue between Célimène and Arsinoé from *Le Misanthrope* that we did for French class at the Academy."

"Oh, I could never remember that!"

"No need to worry. I have the book right here. It will come back after a couple of readings. And your French is much better now. I'm sure it will put mine to shame."

Once they were on the train with Jack, heading for Scotland, Lili showed the extent of her preparations. "I have a dramatic reading for the last night," she said. "We'll make everyone participate, but I have the best parts for us. It's Shaw's *Major Barbara*. Hazel will be Barbara, I'll be Lady Britomart, and you, Jack, will be Adolphus Cusins."

Jack thought Adolphus Cusins a bit of a milquetoast for him to be playing.

"But he's the hero," said Lili. "He outsmarts all the others. It will be good for your image. And he gets the girl"

Jack laughed. "There's no denying you," he said.

As she had planned, Lili's concentration on Hazel's strengths put her in a cheerful and confident frame of mind as she approached the weekend. But her confidence nearly evaporated when, as they were being driven through the estate, the enormous castle appeared, complete with twin towers and crenellated walls. "How old is this place?" she asked Jack.

"Don't worry," he smiled. "It's not a medieval castle. It was built in the 1760s with all the modern appurtenances of the Enlightenment. Luckily, my sister and brother-in-law value modern living, so it has plenty of bathrooms and all that."

"No central heating, though," said Lili. "I suppose it would be like heating a train station. But they will make you comfortable."

Once Edith had greeted them and they had entered the house, Hazel began to relax. Edith was very much like Jack, forthright and a little brusque in manner, but thoughtful and kind. She was especially welcoming to Hazel, inquiring solicitously whether she was comfortable in her chamber when they came down to tea. "Quite comfortable," said Hazel, for whom the room, with its beautifully carved, canopied bedstead, its ornate mirror, its marble fireplace and Turkish carpets and lovely paintings, represented the height of luxury. She was next door to Lili, with whom she was to share a maid to help with dressing. Hazel had laughed with Lili over this as they walked down the elaborately curved staircase together, since they were used to serving as each other's ladies' maids.

The rest of the house was up to the same standard as the bedrooms. The drawing room where they had tea was lit by full-length windows and warmed by enormous carved marble fireplaces. There were full-length portraits in gold frames decorating the walls and *Louis Quinze* furniture arranged in conversational groupings. In the architectural details, Hazel recognized the Adam style, and when she commented that the room was a beautiful example, Henry was pleased to tell her that the Adam brothers themselves had designed the house in the 1760s and the family had done their best to keep up the style.

Assuming she had an interest in architecture, Henry conducted her on a tour of the house, during which she learned a good deal, and felt she had made a friend. The library was the homiest room, with its comfortable chintz-covered furniture, convenient tables spread with the latest issues of magazines, and reading lamps everywhere. It clearly was a room where books were read, not just displayed. The fanciest was the dining room, so large it dwarfed the table of twelve guests, with its decorated ceiling and wall panels, enormous chandelier, and elaborately carved marble fireplace. Hazel kept reminding herself that she was in a private home, her fiancé's sister's home.

Having been awed into unaccustomed silence by her surroundings in the dining room helped Hazel to make a good impression on the family. When she noticed that Lili, who was almost as talkative as she, was quiet at the table, leaving the conversation to the men and the older women, she was careful to follow her lead, only responding to questions that were put to her and making the occasional polite remark. In the drawing room with the ladies, she opened up a bit as Edith tried to draw her out, but she was circumspect in answers to questions about her family and California. She told her usual story about her father, that he had been a Danish horticulturalist who had come to California to experiment with fruit and had died when he was young, although she felt a twinge of guilt as she thought of the hearty Shasta County farmer who was very much alive. She was vague about her mother, saying only that she had planned to spend a year with Hazel in London but had been called back to San Francisco to tend to some family financial business.

"Is your mother very active in managing financial matters?" asked Edith. "I've heard that women have much more control of such things in America than we have here."

"Oh yes," said Hazel. "She's very clever about things like that, and she enjoys it. I must confess I don't follow it at all. My eyes glaze over after five minutes' discussion." After spending several summers working for her mother, Hazel actually had a fair sense of the business, but she was not about to reveal that to Edith.

Lili was helpful in steering the conversation to London and gossip about the social season and the theaters, which Edith loved as much as she did. "What do you have planned for our entertainment this week, Lili?" she asked, with a little smile.

Lili laughed. "You'll see," she said. "I think you're going to enjoy it. Just let me arrange things."

From all points of view, the house party was a great success. The men were satisfied with their deer stalking and had a number of stories to tell. Lili managed the evening entertainments skillfully, with an eye to showing Hazel at her best. And Hazel shone. Following Lili's prompting, on the first night she sang the *Mikado* songs, which everyone found delightful. With her dark hair and eyes and olive-tinted ivory skin, Hazel found it easy to simulate the British person's prevailing idea of a Japanese girl, and she used all the tricks she had learned in *The Geisha* to embellish it. Lili and Hazel did their Molière scene the next night, amid recitations by other guests. They were the only ones to perform in French, and those who understood, which was most of the group, laughed delightedly at the scene. The others just enjoyed the two animated girls. Lili had a true gift for visual comedy, and Hazel just looked lovely and vivacious. On the next evening, wearing her simple rose-colored gown with a single white rose in the bosom, Hazel sang her Scottish songs, the stillness of her demeanor drawing attention to her lovely face and her vibrant contralto bringing tears to the eyes of her Scottish listeners.

The *Major Barbara* reading was on the last night of their stay. Lili had enjoyed herself, not only casting Hazel in the showy part of Barbara and Jack as her successful suitor, but Henry as Andrew Undershaft, the munitions maker. She filled out the other roles by doubling Jack with the cockney Snobby Price and herself with Rummy Mitchens, having Edith play Sarah Undershaft and Jenny Hill and enlisting other guests for the rest. Having been well supplied with wine at dinner, the players had a hilarious evening, and the reading was pronounced Lili's best effort yet. Jack felt that Hazel had made a most favorable impression on his sister and brother-in-law. Hazel was delighted to have sung well and to have been showered with attention and accolades. If this was country house life, she felt that she was more than ready for it.

When Jack wrote his thank you letter to Edith, he asked her to tell him candidly what she thought of Hazel. Since it was obvious to her that Jack adored Hazel, Edith simply wrote that she was a charming and accomplished girl, and very beautiful. Privately she reflected that Hazel was an American with most of the rough edges buffed off. She was indeed accomplished, and far cleverer than Edith's poor brother. She had the kind of looks that would only get better with time, and she knew how to use them to best advantage. Edith felt that Jack was overmatched. She hoped this girl was sincere about her feeling for him. She also hoped she had plenty of American money, because Jack would never have much more than his thousand pounds a year to live on, and he enjoyed spending it.

Jack's next and most important step was to bring Hazel to stay at Somerby House, where his mother and stepfather would pass judgment. When his mother invited him to come up to Leicestershire for a week in May, he asked if he could bring Edith's school friend Lili Forbes and his young American friend Hazel Tharsing along. As Edith had warned Mrs. Hay to expect some-thing like this, she was full of curiosity about Jack's "American friend." She was quite sure it was not Lili who was the object of his interest. He had treated her like a cousin since childhood. In fact, rarely had her son evinced a particular interest in any young lady. Although Mrs. Hay was not acquainted with many Americans, her impression of them was not good. She thought of loud, aggressive men and overdressed women who chattered like magpies. She hoped that Miss Tharsing was not of this type.

When Hazel arrived at Somerby House, she was less intimidated than she had been at the castle. After her experience there, the large proportions of the house and the grand scale of living did not seem so overwhelming. But she was now facing Jack's mother, not his sister. In her first encounter with Mrs. Hay, she did her best to play the demure English young lady, smiling and giving soft replies to direct questions, but otherwise remaining still and quiet as she followed the conversation. Mrs. Hay was not as intimidating as she had expected. She had the same forthright manner as Jack and Edith, a family characteristic, obviously, and Hazel was used to that. Mrs. Hay had more of Edith's genial, somewhat wry attitude than Jack's stolidity. Hazel felt welcome in her home and enjoyed listening to her conversation with Jack and Lili, who was an obvious favorite.

The visit was a more relaxed occasion than the house party at the castle had been. The guests were mostly family members, and except for one dinner when some of the neighbors were invited, the meals were not formal. Hazel was asked to sing and play on several evenings, and Lili was asked to perform some comic monologues that were favorites of the family, but there was no organized performance. The women went on several excursions in the countryside while the men were fishing the Eye Kettleby lakes. Mrs. Hay also enjoyed conversation. Hazel learned a good deal about the family by listening to her and Lili casually gossiping about this person and that. On the fifth day of their stay, Jack got up from breakfast when Hazel did and steered her into the garden. As they strolled along a path between flowering hedges, he told her that he intended to explain their future hopes to his mother that afternoon. Hazel gave him encouragement and a quick kiss on the cheek. "I have confidence in you, Jack," she said.

Watching Mrs. Hay at dinner, Hazel found it impossible to tell how she had responded to Jack's news. She was an English lady, well-practiced in the art of emotional concealment and able to carry on socially under almost any conditions. After dinner, the ladies retired to the drawing room as usual, and Mrs. Hay asked Hazel to play some music. When the men came in after their port and cigars, she organized tables for cards. The evening passed pleasantly for her guests, however Mrs. Hay may have been feeling. Just after Hazel had retired to her room, one of the maids delivered a note which said,

Dear Miss Tharsing,

Might I ask you to join me in my boudoir for a chat after luncheon tomorrow? I think we have much to talk about.

Yours faithfully,

Jessie Hay

The note was perfectly non-committal. Hazel would have to find out from Jack what to expect.

But she did not see Jack at breakfast. His stepfather had asked him to breakfast early and come with him to check on one of the farms. Whether this was a calculated move, Hazel could only imagine. She spent the morning in her room, supposedly writing letters. The small group at luncheon was convivial, with no sign of trouble on Mrs. Hay's part, at least that Hazel could see. She waited fifteen minutes after everyone had left the table, most for a country walk, before she knocked on the door of Mrs. Hay's room.

"Come in, Miss Tharsing, and sit in this chair next to me," said Mrs. Hay. "It is good of you to make time for a little *tête-à-tête*."

Hazel moved toward her. "Of course, Mrs. Hay. I'm delighted to have the chance to talk with you."

After she was seated, Mrs. Hay looked her directly in the eye. "Now, as I'm sure you have noticed, our family is not much given to beating about the bush." Hazel nodded. "Jack has told me of his desire to marry you and has said that you are willing if his family approves. His stepfather leaves that question to me." Hazel reddened, but kept her hands folded in her lap and her eyes on Mrs. Hay's. "I will be blunt with you, Miss Tharsing. Although, as you see, we live quite comfortably here, Jack's means are limited. He has a thousand pounds a year from his father and a legacy of thirty thousand from his grandmother that has just come under his management. This is perfectly adequate for a bachelor who lives in his club and his family home, but not much with which to set up a domestic establishment. I'm afraid Mr. Hay is not in a position to do anything for him. I have a little of my own from which we will make him a small wedding gift when he marries, but I'm afraid this is the limit of his expectations."

"I understand," said Hazel. "Jack has made his financial situation clear to me. We're prepared to live simply until he gets established."

Mrs. Hay looked at her keenly. "What do you mean by established?"

"He still hopes to get a government appointment and rise in the Party."

"I hope you know that will pay next to nothing. In general, politics costs more money than it pays. Jack was sponsored by people in the family as long as he was with the Unionist Party, but he won't be finding that kind of support now. In fact," she smiled a little, "some of his cousins still haven't recovered from the election of 1905."

"To tell you the truth," said Hazel, "I don't think his chances of getting into the Liberal government are very great. I think it's a much better idea for him to train to be a barrister. But it means so much to him that I've agreed that he should try."

Mrs. Hay looked skeptical. "Jack has had many plans in the past that have not come to fruition. He is thirty years old. I don't think we should count on his plans to be any more tangible this time. Forgive my bluntness, Miss Tharsing, but I'm sure you know that I am concerned about my son. Would you be bringing any financial assets to the marriage?"

Despite herself, Hazel blushed. "My father didn't leave me anything directly," she said. "We are not wealthy by your standards, but my mother has a number of business assets in San Francisco, which is what we live on. I'm afraid I know nothing about the details. I'm sure she would be willing to make us a gift when we marry."

"Your mother approves of the match?"

"Yes, Jack insisted on asking her permission before he proposed to me. And I insisted that we would not marry unless you approved."

"I appreciate that, Miss Tharsing. May I ask you something very personal?"

"Yes."

"Why do you want to marry Jack?"

This was something Hazel hadn't expected, even from the blunt Mrs. Hay. Before she had a chance to think, she said, "I *like* Jack."

Mrs. Hay nodded. "But you are not in love with him."

"I do love Jack, Mrs. Hay. And I admire him. He is the kindest, most generous man I've ever known, and he has spirit. He's not afraid of anything he has a mind to try. I enjoy his company more than anyone else's. But to be perfectly honest, I don't know if I'm in love with him."

Mrs. Hay nodded. "That is a good basis for marriage. Personally, I think passion is overvalued. In most cases, it cools quickly, and then one is left to make the best of the person one's chosen with little regard to his character or disposition. I will tell you something about the British upper classes. Many of us marry without passion, and the marriages are perfectly serviceable and often very happy, like my own, I'm pleased to say. Passion may crop up along the way, in another quarter. It is sometimes indulged, and one looks the other way as long as there is no public scandal. I don't think that is a failure of the marriage so much as a means of preserving it. We take marriage, the contract, very seriously in Britain, you know. There is almost no divorce here. It's not like your country."

For a second, Hazel wondered if Mrs. Hay had somehow heard about her mother, but there was nothing personal in her remark. "Yes, I know," she said. "I'm quite sure about the commitment I am prepared to make to Jack."

Mrs. Hay had a great deal to think about after this conversation. It was time that Jack was married, and he was so set on this girl that she knew it would be foolish to oppose the marriage. He would either go through with it anyway, and she would lose him, or he would not, and he would resent her for the rest of her life. There is no love like a thwarted love. This little American was perfectly presentable, actually quite a beauty, and provided with all the requisite accomplishments. By putting the financial question out in the open, Mrs. Hay had satisfied herself that the girl was not gold-digging. She did wonder what sort of "business assets" one had in San Francisco—gold mines? Ships? But she had been exaggerating the limitations of Jack's prospects. It would be perfectly possible for the young couple to live comfortably on his income if his capital was invested well. And she hoped he would soon see that he needed to buckle down to practicing law, whether he trained to be a barrister or not. At any rate, this girl did seem to have the backbone that would be needed to keep her dilettantish son working at something. And Lili liked her. That was comforting. She sighed. If only Jack had proposed to Lili, things would be so much simpler.

Chapter 16

On the day following her conversation with Hazel, Mrs. Hay told Jack that she would give their marriage her blessing if he and Hazel were willing to wait until Christmas to announce their engagement. "I would like to get to know Hazel better, to have her here for a long visit in the fall, and I want to see you settled at some kind of work before you marry, Jack. You know that you will need to add to your income to support a household, and it doesn't look as though a political appointment is in the cards for you just now. Why not take up Dickie Coats's long-standing offer to train as a barrister with him? You two have always gotten on, and his practice is quite well established now."

Jack was not excited about the idea of deviling for his cousin, but he had to admit the good sense of his mother's suggestion. "I suppose you're right, Mother," he said. "I didn't take to the solicitor's sort of work, but I think I might like presenting cases in court. I quite enjoy public speaking now."

So Jack went to work in Richard Coats's firm, learning to be a barrister. It was difficult and exhausting work for someone who was not used to it. It had been years since Jack had worked as a solicitor, and he had to bone up on the law at the same time he was learning to be a barrister by deviling under his cousin. Dickie did not spare him because he was a relative and older than the other pupils. "I'm sorry to be working you so hard, Jack. I don't want you to think it's hazing," he said one day. "But this is the way the profession is. You had better get used to it."

"I can manage the work," said Jack, "if I can just get the law through my head."

Jack's new occupation meant that he had very little time to see Hazel. She kept up her singing lessons, and, with a donation from Nellie and Lili's help, she went to work assembling her trousseau. After spending several weeks at Somerby House in the fall, she came to like Mrs. Hay a good deal. She found that, inside the lady of the manor, there was a practical, straightforward woman who wanted the best for her children. She was not so different from Hazel's Aunt Mary, but more worldly-wise. On her side, Mrs. Hay found Hazel more sophisticated, opinionated, and shrewd about the world than an English girl of her age would be. Once she became used to the family, Hazel's emotions showed themselves as powerful and rather close to the surface. Beneath the delicate beauty of her face and eyes, Mrs. Hay saw glimpses of a strong will, which she hoped Hazel would be using to support her son rather than to fight him. But she was pleased to see that Hazel was clever and had a sense of humor. She was good company.

The fall went by quickly for Hazel, but for Jack, these months were simultaneously a blur of frenetic activity and a long succession of tedious days and evenings. What he most enjoyed was occupying the second chair when Dickie presented a case in court. Having done the grunt work, Jack was in awe of his cousin's ability to shape all the information into an elegant courtroom plea seemingly instantaneously. He was very quick on his feet, tailoring his rhetoric to the response he detected in the judge or jury.

At the end of his first two months, Jack sat down with Dickie to review his progress. "Are you sure you want to do this, Jack?" his cousin asked briskly. "It seems to me that the pace is a little faster than you are comfortable with."

"It is fast," said Jack, "but I think I will be much more comfortable when I'm more on top of the law. I have to do a lot of legal research on each case now."

"Mmm. But it's not only that. As a barrister, you have to put the case together on the fly, and you have to keep several cases in mind at once. It helps to be able to jump from one thing to another very quickly."

Jack reflected. Had Dickie just told him his mind was too slow for this work? "You might as well be blunt," he said. "It's what our family is known for. Do you think I have the ability to be a barrister?"

Dickie smiled. "Well, to be frank, I think there are less talented barristers around than you, certainly. It will be a way to make a living if that is what's wanted. But I don't think it's your natural bent. You must love constant frenzy to do this well. I think you would be happier as a solicitor, not in general practice, but attached to a firm or something. Somewhere you can master the general legal landscape and concentrate on one or two cases at a time. It's a much less frenetic life."

Jack nodded. "Thank you for clarifying in your inimitable way the inchoate feelings I have had about this work. As it happens, Tom Miller has been asking me if I would be interested in taking on the position of legal counsel for a new investment firm."

Dickie looked up. "Tom Miller? Do you know that area of the law?"

Jack smiled. "As well as I know any. I can work at it. Tom invests in mining stocks and mineral interests, something I know a bit about."

Dickie shook his head. "Make sure you look carefully before you leap there," he said. "I don't mean to suggest you are not welcome here, you know. I'm just not sure it's the way you would want to spend your life."

"I understand, Dickie. Thank you for this advice and for all you've done for me. I will have a great deal to think about."

In the end, Jack decided to give up the idea of becoming a barrister and take Tom Miller's offer. When he considered his talents as impartially as he could, he realized that he did not have the quickness of mind that he would need to advocate in court as effectively as Dickie did, no matter how eloquently he could speak. Being a barrister was more than making speeches. As he told Hazel, the job with Tom Miller would give him much more regular hours and more leisure time to spend with her, and he was interested in what the firm did. Hazel was disappointed that her husband was not going to be a barrister. But having missed Jack's company over the last two months and seen how uncharacteristically anxious and tired he was, she agreed that he was making the best decision. So Jack went to work for Tom Miller and immersed himself in mines and minerals.

The 1910 holidays were upon them before they knew it. Because Christmas was on Sunday, Jack was able to come up to Somerby House on Christmas Eve and stay through Boxing Day before he had to be back at the office. Hazel came a few days earlier and was to stay through the hunt in January, when Jack would come up to ride to hounds for two or three days. Having been riding regularly when she was at Somerby, Hazel hoped to be able to surprise Jack by joining the hunt. If her instructor didn't think she was ready, she planned at least to be among the onlookers.

For Hazel and Jack, the central event was that they would at last be able to announce their engagement. At the Christmas Eve party, the family held for all the people on the estate, Mr. Hay made the announcement, and Jack was delighted to receive hearty congratulations from many of the local people he had known since boyhood. On Christmas Day, Jack, and especially Hazel, were the center of attention among the family and guests. The happy couple had never looked so handsome. Hazel's beauty and charm and accomplishments were quietly noted among the guests, as she and Jack fairly glowed with happiness. On boxing day, when Jack presented Hazel with his engagement gift, a diamond and sapphire broach that had been in his mother's family for a hundred years, Hazel's eyes filled with tears. "Your mother gave this to you for me?" she said.

"Of course," said Jack. "You are her daughter now."

The engagement was followed by many congratulatory letters from family members whose complex web of relationships Jack was sometimes hard put to explain to Hazel. "They're cousins," he would finally say, "a few times removed." In January, they made a weekend visit to Edith and Henry in their castle in Scotland. As they drove up, Hazel was not intimidated, as she had been during their first visit. She was now comfortable with Edith and Henry and enjoyed their well-behaved little son, Henry. Except for one dinner when Edith invited friends of Jack's to celebrate the engagement, this was a much more relaxed visit than the house party had been, with mostly just the family, including Mr. and Mrs. Hay and Jack's half-brother Charles, at home. Unless she was performing, Hazel was always more comfortable when she could deal with one or two people at a time. Large group conversations made her nervous. Going on walks or sitting with Edith and Mrs. Hay and discussing her trousseau were activities Hazel enjoyed.

During this visit, Hazel really began to feel part of the family, but she also began to realize how complicated it was becoming to plan her wedding. She and Jack had always talked of a simple wedding in London, with just his immediate family and a few close friends present and breakfast in a restaurant afterwards. When she described their plans to Edith and Mrs. Hay, she could tell from the looks on their faces that the idea was even more unorthodox than Jack had given her to understand. "But no wedding gown, no bridesmaids, no guests? The family would be so disappointed," said Mrs. Hay, "and people might think there was something wrong."

"It does sound a little *declassé*," said Edith. "It looks as if we weren't willing to make an effort. You could certainly be married from here, or from Somerby House."

Hazel could feel the control over the wedding slipping from her fingers. The situation was beyond her. She wished Lili were there to give her a cue about how to handle it. She said it was really up to Jack and left it to him to deal with his family. But Jack was not much help when it came to his mother. When she told him that of course he must be married from Somerby House, as everyone would expect, he could think of no good reason why not. He told Hazel that might be the simplest thing after all, as his mother and stepfather would take care of the whole thing, and they would only need to show up a couple of days before and then leave on their wedding trip. Hazel began to think that she might be able to manage it if she could find someone to make her a gown that was dramatically simple, without a lot of expensive lace and beading and embroidery. She thought she could get away with it if she did the right thing with her hair and veil, and Mrs. Hay had already told her that she wanted her to wear her own wedding jewels. Hazel suspected she was covering for the fact that Jack could not afford to give her the customary bridal gifts. She began to feel that she might enjoy the chance to be a dramatic bride. She knew she could give a good performance. She felt excited as she wrote to Nellie about their plans and asked if she would make a gift of the wedding dress.

When Hazel received her mother's reply, it was as if someone had flicked a finger at her house of cards. Nellie wanted to come to the wedding. In fact, she wrote that she was determined to come and see her only daughter married. This struck Hazel as a disaster in the making. It was one thing for Nellie to have met some of Jack's relatives for five minutes at a reception, but to have her at Somerby House, getting through formal dinners and sitting in the drawing room afterwards, not to mention the wedding itself, was something Hazel could not imagine happening without Jack's family, especially the keen-eyed Mrs. Hay, seeing her for what she was. Jack might find Nellie an entertaining character, but Hazel was quite sure that Mrs. Hay would not, and everything Hazel had implied about her family's social status would be exposed as false. Hazel's position in her husband's family would be unalterably lowered. They might take her for a gold-digger. She could not let that happen.

Hazel's solution was to tell Jack that Nellie was insisting the wedding be held in America, the bride's home, and that she be there with her only daughter. Giving one of her best performances, she turned her anxious face to him, her large eyes brimming with tears. "I don't know what to do, Jack," she said. "How can we possibly please everyone?"

"I don't know," said Jack. "It does seem a difficult problem."

"I wish we could go back to our original idea, and just have a simple wedding. It's the promise we make to each other that matters, after all, not all the trappings."

He nodded. "I so agree, Hazel."

A lovely smile crossed her face. "I just thought of a way," she said. "You are supposed to make that trip to New York next month to finalize the negotiations about the copper mines in Arizona."

He looked quizzical. "Yes."

"Why don't we both go to New York, and get married there? I can tell Mother to meet us, and we can have a simple wedding at an Episcopal church. That would be the same as an Anglican church, wouldn't it? We will tell your family that we felt we had to get married in the States as it meant so much to Mother. We don't have to tell them the circumstances exactly, just that we're being married quietly in New York. We can do it in an hour, and then be off on a honeymoon somewhere."

Jack brightened. "I certainly do like the idea of avoiding all the fuss."

"And I would like to take a little trip home to America. You should be able to get Tom to give you some extra time in the States if you're getting married."

Jack laughed. "Of course. I'm sure he'll come up with some sort of bridal suite for us on the ship coming home."

Hazel took his hands and looked up at him, her face lit with happiness. "Let's do it, Jack," she said. "It's a way of doing things our way without putting anyone else out, and I know Mother will appreciate it."

"I'm game," said Jack, with a conspiratorial smile. "I think it will be a first-rate caper. We'll honeymoon in Niagara Falls."

"Niagara Falls! But it's such a cliché."

"Exactly. American wedding, American honeymoon. It will be great fun."

Hazel smiled. "It will be our wedding."

Chapter 17

Mrs. Hay made a show of regret that Jack and Hazel would be married so far away, but she was relieved to be free of the social dilemma. After they had made their decision, the preparations for the wedding proceeded quickly. Jack's meetings in New York were scheduled for the last week in March, and they only had about a month. Hazel cabled Nellie, telling her they had decided to marry in New York and inviting her to meet them there. They reserved their tickets for a ship that was to arrive on March 20, which would give Hazel and her mother a few days with Kitty to organize Hazel's clothes for the wedding and honeymoon, and they could tend to the details of organizing a little celebration of some kind.

Jack thought it would look best at home if they were married in a well-known church, so he used a family connection to arrange for a simple wedding at Grace Church. He was given a time of two o'clock on Friday, March 31. This date proved to be crucial, because the day before he and Hazel were to board the ship, there was a major complication in the negotiations over the mine, and Tom Miller told Jack he would have to stay in London for a few more days to help sort it out. Jack quickly found a ship that was arriving in New York on the thirty-first and booked a ticket. He told Hazel she should sail as planned and spend the time with her mother. He was determined that their marriage would not be put off again. So Jack saw Hazel off and returned to a week of frantic negotiating.

At nine o'clock on the morning of March 31, 1911, Hazel and Nellie laughed and waved from the dock as Jack fairly bounded down the gangplank toward them. He scooped Hazel into his arms and kissed Nellie on the cheek. After they had jumped into a taxicab and told the driver to make for the Registrar's Office as fast as he could, Jack said, "I have another complication for us. The negotiations have been moved to Chicago, and they begin the day after tomorrow. But I'm determined not to wait another day to marry my beautiful Hazel. What do you say, my darling? Are you willing to take a night train to Chicago after the wedding?"

Hazel laughed. "Why not?" she said. "It will be the perfect ending for our madcap wedding."

Nellie looked from one to the other and laughed. "Luckily Hazel's honeymoon clothes are ready and pretty much already packed. We'll go back to Kitty's, so she can change into her dress and pack her overnight bag for the train."

Jack smiled joyfully back at her. "I knew you and Hazel would have everything in order. When we have the license, I'll go and buy the Pullman tickets for the Twentieth Century Limited." As he helped Hazel out of the taxicab, he leaned down and whispered, "I hope you won't mind spending your wedding night in a Pullman car."

Hazel looked up at him with a beaming smile. "I think it will be fun," she said, "and it's just the first of thousands of nights."

The license obtained, they scattered to perform their tasks and collect the surprised Kitty, who was to be the second witness. After a quick but merry lunch at the Hotel Brevoort, they presented themselves respectfully before the rector at Grace Church, and Jack and Hazel were married at last. Outside the church, they thanked the Rector, kissed Nellie and Kitty, and jumped into a taxicab for Grand Central, where their luggage had already been sent. When they boarded the train, Hazel was surprised to find she had her own Pullman parlor. Her overnight bag sat on the seat. But, she reflected, that was just like Jack. The perfect gentleman. He didn't want to have an awkward wedding night where they were at close quarters for dressing and sleeping and so on. So Hazel spent the first night of her married life in a Pullman birth, and after an hour of the day's events whirling in her mind, she fell asleep and didn't wake up until she heard the porter calling.

The business in Chicago went well, better than Jack had expected after the frenzied activity in London during the previous week. At the end of five days, he had concluded the final contract negotiations, and he and Hazel still had nine days left in the U. S. before their ship sailed. They decided to go to Niagara after all. It was the final piece to the story. Once installed in the town's nicest hotel, they spent two days strolling around, trying the different vantage points on the falls, American and Canadian, and watching the tourists. Hazel hoped they were not as obviously newly married as the other couples she saw. She and Jack took to counting them and wound up laughing hilariously together as they argued over this or that couple. The hotel was comfortable enough, but the food, they agreed, was ghastly. There didn't seem to be a decent restaurant in the whole place, and Jack had no use at all for New York state wine. They decided to go down to Saratoga for a couple of days, where they found a quieter and more refined crowd, and better accommodations. It was out of season, so the hotel was half empty. They were glad to at last spend some time together quietly.

It was in Saratoga that Hazel began to realize she was actually Mrs. John Moffat. After all the years of planning and preparing and waiting, they were truly married. The only problem was sex. After the first night on the train, they had slept in the same bed, but Jack never went beyond a good night kiss or two. They would talk for a while lying next to each other, then he would fall asleep. Hazel didn't know what to make of this. When she had asked her mother what to expect, Nellie had just said to relax and let Jack take the lead. She knew he was a gentleman and would be considerate. But this was beyond considerate. She thought maybe he was not comfortable being ardent in their strange surroundings. She tried to forget about it for now and just enjoy their trip together. As she had told him, there would be thousands of nights.

Hazel and Jack came back to New York three days before they were to embark for London. Jack invited Nellie and Kitty for a fine meal at Delmonico's, telling them it was the delayed wedding celebration, and they all had a wonderful time, especially Jack, who had a new appreciation for Delmonico's wine cellar. Seeing them off on the ship, Nellie was duly impressed with their enormous state room. "The company is paying," said Jack, "and after what I've been through for them lately, they owe us this."

Hazel came back down to earth as they approached London on the train from Southampton. She could hardly see through the murky fog. In the U. S. Hazel had forgotten the fog, and the air felt close and fetid after the clean atmosphere of western New York state. Even New York City was bright and clean compared to this. They went to their temporary home at the Palace Welbeck Hotel in Mayfair, where they stayed until they found a reasonably-priced flat in Portland Place near The Regent's Park. It was not far from the City, where Jack had to go each morning, but thanks to the park, it had a quiet, suburban feel. They grew into a habit of strolling there in the evening when Jack came home, as they exchanged accounts of their days and relaxed sufficiently to enjoy their dinner. It was a little bit of country life in the city. They became fond of several restaurants in the neighborhood, especially a small place rather grandly called the Café de Paris. When Jack had asked for a wine list on their first visit there, the waiter had said, "There is the red wine and the white wine," which Jack found endlessly amusing. In the end, he thought both wines rather good, considering the price.

Hazel was happy in Portland Place, with her flat to decorate and her adoring husband to look after. But the sex problem had still not resolved itself. Jack would kiss and caress her, but that was all. Finally, after they had been married for six weeks, she decided she had to say something. One Friday evening as they were walking in the park, she asked him quietly, "Jack, do you find me attractive, physically?"

"Why of course I do, darling. I should think you would see that every day."

She continued as gently as she could, "Is there some reason why you are refraining from—marital relations?"

Even in the dusk, she could see him blushing. "Not at all," he said. "To tell you the truth I have been thinking I should see a doctor to make sure everything is all right. I had expected that things would have started by now."

Hazel nodded. "Perhaps you should see a doctor. There's no shame in that. And if there's something wrong, we should know about it."

When Jack returned from the doctor's office the following week, he was looking much relieved. "There's nothing wrong," he said. "Apparently it's not always—spontaneous. There are things one can do to—prepare. He gave me this book. I'll read it, and we can give it a try, shall we?"

Hazel was surprised to find that Jack seemed to know as little about sex as she did. "Of course, darling," she said. "I would like nothing better."

On Friday night, Jack was more ardent than usual, kissing Hazel for a long time before they got into bed. Once there, he undid her nightgown and caressed her breasts, something he had never done before. Hazel felt an unfamiliar excitement. Then he disappeared to the bathroom, saying "I'll be back in a trice." When he came back a few minutes later, he got into bed and whispered to her to open her legs a little. Then he moved between them and she felt something stiff pushing against her. "Open a little farther, dear," he said, and she did. He gave a thrust and she felt what she took to be his penis driving up between her legs. There was a sharp pain that caused her to cry out a little. He stopped and looked down at her. "Are you all right, Hazel?"

"Yes," she said. "It was only for a second." She felt him moving some more, and then he gave a moan and pulled away.

After lying for a moment next to her, he raised up on his elbow and kissed her tenderly. "Thank you, my darling. The next time will be better for you."

She kissed him. "It was lovely, dear," she said. "I felt so close to you." Then she got up and went into the bathroom. There was a little blood, and the other stuff. She cleaned herself and came back to bed. Jack cradled her in his arms and fell asleep. Hazel lay awake wondering. Was this what she had waited for all this time? The thought suddenly struck her that she could become pregnant now. She did not feel ready for children.

As the weeks went by, they both became more skillful, and Hazel came to enjoy and look forward to sex, especially the kissing and caressing beforehand. After they had become more comfort-able with each other, she asked Jack what he was doing in the bathroom before he came to bed. When he explained what the book had said, she asked if that was something the wife should be doing. He said the book did suggest that. So he showed her, and they experimented, and soon Jack had no problem performing. But Hazel did worry about getting pregnant. She suggested to Jack that they should perhaps try to wait for a while to have children because she didn't feel quite ready. "Can you get some of those covers they use?"

"All right," he said. "If you don't feel ready yet." It was good news to him. He was enjoying their life and having Hazel all to himself. There was plenty of time before they needed to turn things upside down with a child.

As the summer and fall passed, Hazel fell into a comfortable routine. She took care of the housekeeping in their pleasant flat with the help of a cook and a maid who came in for half the day. She usually went shopping in the morning to buy flowers or a special treat for their dinner or to look at clothes. In the afternoon, she often had some social engagement or other. Jack's wide network of family and social connections had meant many invitations both for the couple and for the new bride alone.

Hazel was doing her best to keep up her end. In the evenings, they often went to the theater, as they had in the old days. Hazel missed the company of Lili, who had finally managed to get an acting engagement with a provincial company, but she enjoyed the theater as much as ever. The young couple were also invited to a number of weekend parties in the country. Although Hazel sometimes found it a strain to get through the formal meals and evening rituals, she enjoyed performing as much as ever. She also looked forward to the chance to get out of the city, especially during the summer months, and she enjoyed the outdoor activities. Her riding had improved enough now that she could keep up with the others on a country ride. The young couple spent Christmas with Edith, and, in January, Hazel was proud of being able to ride to the big Somerby hunt for the first time.

Chapter 18

In February 1912, a serious blow struck the seemingly charmed existence of Mr. and Mrs. John Moffat. Jack came home early one afternoon and asked Hazel to walk with him in the park. "I don't know, darling," she said, "it was a little raw when I was out earlier. Can't we just sit here?"

"Please, Hazel," he said, "I need to get out and walk and I would like your company very much."

Hazel looked at him. His face was uncharacteristically troubled. She could not very well refuse such a request. "All right, dear," she said. "Just let me get my warm coat."

Once they were walking along in the dusk, Jack told her that he had given up his position with Tom Miller.

Hazel could tell from his voice that he was very upset, although he would never admit it. She did her best to speak calmly despite the knot of fear in her stomach. "What happened?" She asked, trying to keep her voice flat and neutral.

"The short of it is that Tom asked me to do something that would not be honorable and might very well be illegal. I told him so, and he told me that I could choose not to do it, but if so, he expected that I would not be comfortable working at the firm any longer. I told him I could not imagine working at the firm for one minute longer and left."

"I'm amazed at Tom," said Hazel. "He should have known better than to ask such a thing of you."

"It surprised me too. I've seen him play a little fast and loose with contracts and regulations, but never something as overt as this. I see clearly now that he is not an honorable man, Hazel. I simply could not work for him any longer."

"Of course not," she said.

"I'm sorry that it will make for something of a financial hardship for us."

"I'm not too worried. We can live on your income until you find something else. We'll just have to cut out the little extravagances like expensive restaurants and new clothes for a while."

With a little surreptitious gesture, Jack took her hand and drew it into his coat pocket as they walked along. "Thank you for understanding, my darling."

She squeezed his hand. "Of course, Jack. I know you are too principled a man to get involved in something that isn't right."

Jack decided not to look for another position for a few months. He and Hazel agreed that he had been working too hard, and they decided to take this as an opportunity to travel and make the visits that were expected of a newly married couple in his family. After Jack wrote of his new freedom to several relatives, and in the spring, they spent many weeks in castles and manor houses. As she grew used to the rhythms of these weeks, Hazel became accustomed to what Jack's family referred to as "country life." Word of her performances had made its way around the family network, and she was always asked to sing. She and Jack also prepared several scenes they could do together, which were a big hit. Jack gradually lost the tension that had built up over the time he was working for Tom Miller and became what Hazel thought of as his old affable self.

In the spring, Edith invited them to come on a trip to the Jersey and Guernsey Islands and to the *Côte Basque* in France. Henry was busy with the House of Lords, and she felt they all could use a sunny holiday. Away from the castles and the display and the family rituals, they settled into a new rhythm together. They played tennis and sat at outside cafés and sailed and had long, wonderful dinners that lasted until midnight. Hazel found that she really enjoyed Edie's company in her vacation state, and she and Jack agreed this was the best time they had had together, far more like a honeymoon than their honeymoon had been.

In June, Jack told Hazel that he had decided not to take another position as a solicitor, but to put his energy into investing in mining and mineral stocks. "I know the business now, and I may as well put my capital to good use," he said. This made sense to Hazel, for whom talk of such investments had been part of life in her mother's house. But it turned out that Jack didn't understand the business quite as well as he'd thought. It seemed that one had to be on the ground in New York if one wanted to really know what was going on in the market. By the end of July, he was convinced that he needed to relocate to New York for a while. When he put it to Hazel, he was pleased to find that she was enthusiastic. She had been missing the States and admitted that she always felt a little alien in British society, no matter how kind people were.

"It would be a relief to spend some time at home," she said. "When shall we go?"

"As soon as possible," he said.

Jack booked the tickets for the *Cedric*, and they sublet their apartment, gave notice to the servants, and embarked for New York in late August. They enjoyed the first few days in the city. Hazel did some shopping with Kitty and had lunch with her old San Francisco acting partner Merle Maddern, who had just finished the run of a hit play, *Kismet*. In the evening, they dined well and went to the theater. With Kitty's help, they were able to find a reasonably priced four-room apartment in a residential hotel near Central Park, with services included, so Hazel had no worries about domestic help. The comfortable and confident feeling she had in New York made her realize that she was always a little on edge in England. Here there were no society people to impress, no worries about doing and saying the correct thing. It was her own territory.

But it was in New York that things began to go wrong between Hazel and Jack. He didn't discuss the financial situation with her, but she could tell from his demeanor that it was not going well. He took to going to Wall Street nearly every day, and when he came home at night, he was aloof and taciturn. He spent more and more time away from the apartment. Left alone most of the time and unable to get Jack to talk to her about what was bothering him, or about anything, really, Hazel began to worry that his love for her had faded. She became alternately over-animated, trying to spark Jack's interest with all the feminine wiles she could summon, or withdrawn, revealing her resentment through a distant and sulky manner. Both irritable, they began to bicker over little things. Almost without their realizing it, these little spats grew into arguments. Hazel could hear her voice getting shrill and cutting, but she seemed unable to stop it. After a while, she no longer tried, since she seemed to feel better after an outburst.

At first, Jack met her outbursts with silence, sometimes stalking out of the apartment. But one day he shouted at her to mind her tongue or face the consequences, which only infuriated Hazel more. They shouted at each other until Hazel went into the bedroom, slamming the door, and Jack walked out, not to return until after midnight. They spent three days not speaking to each other in the close quarters of their apartment until Jack finally apologized for his behavior and Hazel forgave him. This proved to be the first of many such altercations. Although both of them wanted to stop the fighting, they were unable to control what they said to each other once they had begun. Without many friends in town to relieve the pressure of their constant friction, it was a long and difficult winter.

In the spring of 1913, the business situation exploded. Jack appeared in the apartment earlier than usual one afternoon and asked Hazel to walk with him in the park. They had done this often during the first weeks of their New York stay, but it had been many days since he had made the invitation. Hazel started to make an excuse, but when she caught sight of his face, pale and tense, she said, "All right, Jack." As they walked toward the park, an un-spoken tension between them, Hazel was reminded of the walk in Regents Park a year earlier, when he had told her that he had quit his job. This was clearly the same kind of crisis, but how differently they felt about each other now. Hazel prepared to protect herself from whatever bombshell he had for her this time.

As they were walking along the lake, Jack, his eyes on the ground, started to explain to Hazel that their financial situation had gone from bad to worse. Since Jack rarely explained his business dealings and she only half paid attention when he did, she really had no idea what their situation was. She only knew that occasionally he had spoken of a good day in the market when he had sold something at a good profit, and once or twice insisted on taking her out for an expensive dinner to celebrate. Now as he droned on about margin calls and debit balances, she only got the sense that his mining stocks had taken a tumble, and somehow that was costing more money.

"I don't understand, Jack. What's happened to the money?"

He looked at her impatiently. "If you would listen, Hazel, you would understand. As I just explained, it turns out that some of the mines are worthless. They've been covering it up for months with shady accounting. The stock price has dropped to almost nothing, and because some of it was bought on margin, with a loan, I have to produce the amount of the loan as well as the interest."

"But where will the money come from?"

"I don't have any cash on hand to speak of. The brokerage will liquidate my other holdings to pay for it."

"Is it a lot of money?"

"Yes, a lot. My capital is nearly wiped out."

Hazel stopped and looked up at him. "Your capital? Gone?"

"Yes, I'm afraid so." He tried and failed to keep the emotion from his voice. He looked down at her. In his face was bewilderment, shame, a plea for solace.

Hazel felt her stomach contract as if a fist had hit it. Panic, a physical force, rose in her. Before she could think, she heard her voice, strident, accusatory, "You stupid fool!" she shrieked, "You stupid bloody fool! You've ruined us."

His head jerked back as if slapped. He looked at the ground. "I deserve what you say," he said finally. "But we aren't completely ruined. I still have my income, which is fixed, although I may have to make periodic payments from it if there is not enough money realized from liquidating the other assets."

Fear and anger mounted in Hazel. "I can't believe this!" she cried. "What will we do? We can't stay in New York, and we can't go back to London, not without money. I want to go back to San Francisco, to my mother," she said. She looked at him defiantly. "Will you give me the money for that?"

"Hazel," Jack said. "You are not going anywhere by yourself. We are not destitute, and I will take care of you. We should not try to make plans until we can do so calmly."

Hazel's red face contorted in anger. "In one minute, you pull the earth from beneath my feet, and now you talk about being calm? How can I be calm? I will not be calm, you cold-blooded Scotsman!"

"I can't blame you," he said. In his eyes was a plea for compassion. "It will be better, though. You'll see."

Hazel turned to walk back to the apartment. "Don't follow me," she said. "I'll make my own way home." But he did follow her, at a distance, until she was safely out of the park and on the brightly lit street. Then he walked in the park by himself. He walked in the park for hours, and at the end he had a plan. They would go to San Francisco. They would visit Hazel's family. It would be good for her to be with her mother until she was over the shock. And he had liked San Francisco ten years earlier—a bustling city, alive with opportunity. A real American city. It was a place where he could look around and start again.

Once she was over her initial shock at their changed circumstances, Jack presented Hazel with his plan for making a new beginning in San Francisco. Hazel took stock of her situation and came to the conclusion that a trip to California was not a bad idea. Having the option of her mother's house would allow her to take a hard look at her marriage and decide whether Jack really was someone she wanted to spend the rest of her life with. She was grateful that she had put off children and that she had been married in the United States, where a divorce was so much easier to get than in England. The more she considered it, the more she thought that a career on the stage might be a better future than marriage to an improvident Englishman who couldn't seem to hold a job or manage money. So Hazel wrote to Nellie and told her that they planned to come for a long visit. Hazel packed their trunks, and Jack bought the tickets.

Chapter 19

Nellie Tharsing received Hazel's letter with mixed emotions. She had not seen her daughter since that crazy wedding, and she often wondered how the marriage was faring. She liked Jack Moffat, but she wasn't sure how sensible he was. What's more, the letter hinted at financial problems. Nellie wondered what sort of financial problems a wealthy Englishman who divided his time among clubs and castles and manor houses might have. She knew that, as a younger son, Jack would not inherit the family fortune, but the money situation he had laid out for her when she was in London was certainly adequate to maintain the young couple in style.

She also worried about Jack's reaction to her living arrangements. Things had changed since Hazel's last visit to San Francisco. Mel Chapman's wife had died in 1909, and his twelve-year-old son, broken-hearted, had insisted on his promise that he would not re-marry. But Nellie didn't really care whether she and Mel were married. She would have liked to join the ranks of respectable Oakland society as Mrs. Melvin Chapman, but she was also as wary of marriage as ever, and she valued her independence.

Nellie had sold her rooming houses and, with Mel's help, bought a substantial office building on a prestigious corner in Oakland. Mel moved from the Montecito Avenue house he had shared with Lillian, building a new one in a new neighborhood out on Santa Clara Avenue. Nellie moved from San Francisco to Oakland and bought a house on Stanley Place, two blocks from Mel's house. No one in the neighborhood thought anything about the two old friends and business partners, Nellie a substantial widow in her late forties and Mel a pillar of the community in his early sixties, spending time together. There were some whispered comments about Nellie's really being a grass widow with something of a past, but most people just thought it was nice that Mr. Chapman had an old friend to give him solace after the death of his wife. This situation would not be a surprise to Hazel, but Nellie hoped that Jack would not be scandalized once he figured it out.

It turned out that Nellie need not have worried. Jack took to Mel immediately, regarding the successful lawyer and politician with admiration and disarmed by his open and unassuming manner, which Jack thought the essence of California. He would sit with Mel in Nellie's parlor by the hour, getting him to talk about politics and the landmark legal cases he had been involved in. Enjoying the attention of the young English lawyer who made such an appreciative audience, Mel held forth in a way that Nellie, who didn't observe him at his club, had never seen.

Mel defended Jack from Mel Jr. and others who thought he was a strange duck. He had to admit that Jack certainly stood out in Oakland, with his Scots accent and deeply ingrained British ways, which sometimes embarrassed Hazel. He wore tweed suits in the summer, and when the Chapmans went for a long walk in the Presidio with the Moffats, he insisted on wearing woolen knickers, with argyle socks. Mel Jr. was particularly sensitive to the sight of a grown man in knickers. He was embarrassed by the stares that Jack attracted. Jack's accent led to the nickname of "Scottie" among family and friends, which he enjoyed, never having had a nickname before, but Mel noticed that Hazel never used it.

After a few weeks, Jack confided in Mel about his financial situation and his worry that Hazel had not taken it well. "I would like your advice about how to proceed," he said. "I'd like to get back in the game again."

"Do you mean you'd like to practice law in the U. S.?"

Jack shook his head. "No, I've learned that I have no particular talent for the law. I listen to your own experiences, and I realize that I would be even less successful here than in Britain."

From what Mel had learned of Scottie, he had to agree. He was not the sharpest tack he had ever seen, and he couldn't see him arguing in a California court with his Scots accent and his British manners. "What do you have in mind?" he asked.

"I enjoy business," he said. "I got myself in a muddle with these mining stocks, and I am now acutely aware of the dangers of trading on margin, but I like the stock market. Never a dull moment."

Mel regarded him carefully. "Well, I've never taken to that kind of thing myself. I prefer to invest in solid real estate, bonds, safer investments. I don't make huge returns, but I prefer not to worry about the alternative."

"Perfectly understandable," said Jack. "But there is some active trading here, isn't there?"

"In San Francisco, yes. There's a stock exchange. Mining stocks are a big factor, of course. Are you thinking of becoming a broker?"

"I think I have the requisite experience for it, yes."

"Of course, investing and brokering are two different things."

"Of course, but I made quite a study of it in New York. I think I would like to give it a try."

"Well, I have a couple of friends in the business I can introduce you to. Can't promise anything, though."

When Jack was interviewed by Mel's friend Harry Mitchell, he found that he knew less than he had thought about the brokerage business. Mitchell suggested that he could start in with the firm at a lower position and then work his way up to actual trading, and perhaps become a broker someday, but Jack felt that at thirty-four he was too old for that. He thanked him for his advice, and Mitchell told him he could call on him anytime.

At the club that evening, Mitchell took the easy chair next to Mel's. "Saw your Scotsman today," he said. "Nice fellow. But he doesn't have a clue about the business. Maybe it's different in London."

"Maybe," said Mel.

Shortly after this, Jack received a remittance from London that was considerably less than he was expecting. When he wrote to his solicitor about it, he was reminded that the settlement on the New York fiasco required him to repay his remaining debt from his monthly income. He would be receiving only about half of his regular income for several years. Jack had known that he would owe more money, but he had no idea that it was this much. He dreaded telling Hazel, but he knew that he must. He told himself that it was the right thing to do, and she would have to find out about their reduced income eventually. Hazel's response to this news was not as explosive as her outburst when he had first told her about his losses. She simply said, "We'll have to make the best of it, then. It looks as though we will not be leaving Oakland soon."

With no other real option, Hazel and Jack stayed on in Nellie's house. Jack seemed to lose interest in pursuing any other occupation, although Mel tried to bring him together with men who could help him find employment. Nellie found the living situation difficult as Hazel and Jack grew more at home in her house and reverted to the bickering and arguing of the last few months. Nellie was used to Hazel's volatility. Her daughter had always been high strung, even as a child, when she would burst into tears if she was spoken to sharply or erupt in a tantrum after hours of brooding over some perceived injury. Nellie attributed it to spending her early years with Chris Tharsing. But she had thought Jack a remarkably even-tempered and patient man. That was one of his chief attractions as a husband for Hazel as far as Nellie was concerned. Now Jack responded to Hazel's off-hand taunts and quick, disparaging remarks in a heavy-handed way that Nellie thought was out of proportion, and the argument over some little thing would escalate until they said things to each other that couldn't be taken back. More often than not, the fight would end with one of them stalking out the door. Nellie tried to talk to Hazel about it, but she just said that Jack got on her last nerve these days, and she couldn't help herself.

Finally, Hazel told Nellie that she wanted to divorce Jack. "We don't get along, Mama, and frankly I'm afraid of him when he loses his temper. And I don't think he will ever support me properly. I try to get him to look for some kind of employment, but he thinks everything is beneath him. He can't practice law in this country, and we couldn't possibly live in England on his income. What if a baby should come? I'm just so hopeless and unhappy." Hazel burst into tears, seeking her mother's comfort in a way she had not done since she was a little girl. "Can you help me, Mama?"

When Nellie described the situation to Mel, he was surprised to hear that Scottie was capable of such behavior. He suggested some mitigating circumstances. "He's under a lot of strain, with the financial problems and all. His pride has been tremendously damaged. It can't be easy for him to live off his mother-in-law."

"It's not easy for Hazel, either. Or for me. I'm afraid of what might happen."

Mel looked at her sharply. "Has he been violent in any way?"

"No, not yet," she said, "but I certainly know the signs."

"Let me talk to Hazel," he said.

When Hazel had her conversation with Mel, she told him about her unhappiness, her despair of her husband's ever getting a job to support them, her fear of becoming pregnant in an impossible situation. Mel thought she was in a very fragile emotional state. "Would you be willing to try a separation?" he asked. "Sometimes people find that the situation looks different when they aren't right in the middle of things."

With very little persuasion, he got Hazel to agree to a trial separation. But then he had to convince Jack, who was extremely reluctant to separate from his wife, even temporarily. "To tell you the honest truth," said Mel, "I think this is the best you can do just now. Hazel and Nellie are both talking divorce, and you know it's not hard to do in California."

After Mel had explained the legal situation and outlined what he had in mind, Jack agreed to the separation, but he had a very difficult time following through with it. He violated the agreement several times by trying to contact Hazel directly. Once, Hazel had tried to escape the pressure by going camping with her childhood friend Celia, who was now engaged to her cousin Frank Shay, out on the country property that her Uncle John and Aunt Mary now owned. Jack somehow got wind of it and showed up. John had to order him off the property, much as he had Chris Tharsing in the old days.

As Jack became more desperate to get Hazel to return to him, Hazel became more determined to pursue the divorce. Pondering her situation, she came to think that she had lost herself trying to conform to someone else's rules for living during the entire time she was involved with Jack. Whether it was Mme. Yeatman's code of comportment for young ladies or the complicated social rituals of the British gentry or Jack's own expectations for their home life, she had been constantly trying to meet standards that were alien to her, to live a life that was not her own. No wonder, she thought, that her nerves had been constantly overwrought. Since Jack had left her mother's house, she had returned to herself. She felt a freedom and a confidence about her future that she had not experienced since the Academy days. She came to believe that nothing would make her happier than being on her own again, pursuing her original ambition of a theatrical career, which had been cut short by this whole disastrous detour into British society.

It fell to Mel to convince Jack to agree to the divorce. When he finally accepted the fact that Hazel was not going to return to him, Mel appealed to him as a gentleman. "Hazel is not asking for alimony or any kind of settlement. She just wants to part friends if possible and be free. Don't you owe her that much?

It's time to acknowledge that this marriage was a mistake and go on with your lives."

In the end, Jack gave in and did not contest the divorce. At Mel's request, he boarded a train in San Francisco that would take him to New York, en route to London. Mel assigned the divorce to William Wells, a junior member of the firm of Chapman and Trefethen. It was a simple matter to publish the summons in the *Oakland Tribune* several times and for the judgment to go to Hazel as plaintiff when Jack did not appear to answer the summons.

For the first few months after her marriage had ended, Hazel was happy just to be free. Free of what had become the constant irritation of Jack's company, free of the pressure of expectation, free of anxiety about the future and Jack's ability to support them. She did not feel a particular stigma as a divorced woman in Oakland. Even though the summons had been published in the newspaper, she listed herself as a widow in the City Directory, as her mother did, and people continued to call her "Mrs. Moffat." She had no interest in entering San Francisco society or taking up with the women she had known as girls at St. Gertrude's. She was happy to spend time with her family and Frank Shay's fiancée, Celia, who had become a loyal friend and close confidant. Mostly, however, she and Nellie spent their time with the Chapmans. Mel Jr. was now a tall, nice-looking boy of seventeen, and he adored Hazel. Nellie and Mel were amused to see him so in thrall to a young woman who was eight years older than he. But his infatuation with Hazel had gone a long way toward easing the resentment he had always harbored against Nellie, so they were grateful for it. The four of them went casually back and forth between the two houses as if both were home.

Hazel treated Mel Jr. as a younger brother, taking shameless advantage of him to run errands and do little services for her. Mel Jr. was happy to do these things. He knew about the *Call* beauty contest, and he agreed with the judges that Hazel was the most beautiful woman he had ever seen. With her clean, sophisticated sense of style and her New York and London clothes, he thought her of another order than the girls his age, who were all flounces and curls when they were dressed up and all boyish simplicity on the tennis court or the golf links. Hazel was sophisticated and sleek all the time, but she never looked as though she had taken trouble to dress up. And she had a sophisticated way of talking, and of joking, too. As if she were a character in a fashionable play. When he was with Hazel, he felt himself to be a man of the world and soon-to-be-lawyer rather than a recent high school graduate who was just beginning to study law.

When Hazel needed an escort, Mel Jr. was always delighted to go along. As their parents had thirty years ago, they often took long walks in the Presidio or along the coast on Saturdays, and they played golf and tennis at the country club. For Hazel, the summer and fall of 1914 was almost like a rest cure. But toward the end of the year, she began to feel a familiar restlessness. As she contemplated her future, she could not see a path in San Francisco to what she had decided was her goal, a successful stage career. She knew that what she wanted was Broadway. For that she would have to get to New York, and she would need money. Money to get there, money to buy a theater wardrobe, and money to live perhaps for several months before she landed a part. She knew that Nellie was not enthusiastic about the acting idea. If it were a case of money for more vocal training or to get a start in opera, it would be different, but Hazel now knew the limits of her voice. She could sing in a chorus, or do musical comedy if the role was right, but she would never have the power or range for opera. What's more, she didn't want to go on with singing. What she wanted was to act, to command the stage as a leading lady. She knew she was no Sarah Bernhardt, but she thought she could play on the same stage as Minnie Maddern Fiske or Eleanor Robson.

After considering various approaches, Hazel decided to ask her mother for a business loan, to be repaid weekly when she won her first salaried part. This was familiar ground for Nellie, who was quite generous when it came to helping young women get their start in business, as long as she could see a return in the long run. When she made the proposal, Nellie laughed.

"It's not what I would call a sure thing, Hazel," she said. "I've made better business investments."

Hazel had expected this. "I know that, Mama," she said. "But look at all you've already invested in this, all the training at the Academy as well as all the singing lessons. Think of this as one way to make good on your investment."

Nellie laughed again. "Well said, dearie. We'll make a business-woman of you yet." In the long run she knew she was incapable of refusing her daughter, who had become increasingly restless and unhappy in Oakland during the dreary winter months, but she took advantage of the situation to exert some control over her. She got Hazel to promise that she would stay with Kitty Smith when she got to New York, and she would not invest in a theatrical wardrobe until she had secured a role, although of course she would be buying some new clothes when she got to the city.

Part 2

Carlotta Monterey

Chapter 20

On the first of March 1915, Hazel found herself in the waiting room of the offices of Chamberlain and Lyman Brown, the most prestigious theatrical agency in New York. She wore a new suit in a fashionable shade of green that was meant to set off her eyes, hair, and skin tones. It was cut in the newest, slimmest silhouette, not short enough to show her ankles, but short enough so that her feet in their new pointed shoes peeked out below her skirt. The jacket's neckline plunged to the waist, revealing her thin silk blouse. Cocked to the right side and displaying her glossy dark hair to advantage, she wore a small green hat with a wispy white feather attached to the turned-up side brim. From head to toe, the look had been carefully planned to present Hazel's new identity as a sophisticated, slightly exotic actress. To match it, she had chosen a stage name, Carlotta, a vaguely Mediterranean name with a nod to her girlhood idol Lotta Crabtree, and Monterey, which suggested Tenerife and was also a tribute to her northern California roots.

Hazel had an appointment, but she understood that it was not uncommon to spend several hours waiting, appointment or no. As she sat in the crowded waiting room, she studied the other aspiring actresses and decided that she had been right in her choice of dress for Carlotta Monterey. She knew her sleek, sophisticated look stood out among the big hats with ostrich feathers and the fussily trimmed suits in the room. Among the raft of pretty, blonde American girls, she looked European and chic. She was pleased to have seen the much-harassed receptionist bring her portfolio of pictures to an inner office to which, occasionally, someone was admitted. Like the other heads in the waiting room, Hazel's turned automatically when the outer door to the room was opened, admitting a thirtyish man in a fashionably slim suit and a high collar. He hustled past the receptionist with a slight nod and went straight into the inner office.

The young man was Jimmy Potter, from the producing firm of Lee and J. J. Shubert, one of the largest and most powerful in New York. As he burst into Chamberlain Brown's office, he muttered, "sorry to barge in."

Brown looked up without surprise. "What can I do for you, Jimmy?"

"We need a girl quick. The one who was playing the vamp in the new Lou Tellegen thing just quit on us and we're starting rehearsals day after tomorrow."

"What's she like?"

"French. Coquettish. Daring. Maybe a touch exotic. Good figure is a must. There's a scene with Lou where she's in a negligee, obviously post-hanky-panky. It's a bedroom farce with a twist—he's a bank robber."

"So you want a brunette. Someone who just came in this morning might fill the bill." He rummaged through the stack of portfolios on his desk and pulled one out. "Here she is. Carlotta Monterey. Sounds right, doesn't it? And she looks the part." He handed a stack of photographs to Jimmy. Looking at the resumé, he said, "Impressive credentials. She studied at the Royal Academy of Dramatic Art, if you please, and she was a national beauty contest finalist."

"I can see that. Let's have a look at the real thing."

Brown pressed a buzzer on his desk to summon the receptionist and told her to send in Miss Monterey. Hazel was startled to hear the name called. Just like that, she had become Carlotta Monterey. She rose and walked coolly into the office, aware of the eyes that were trained on her from the waiting room. She extended her hand gracefully, looked up at Chamberlain Brown through her long eyelashes, and said, "Good morning, Mr. Brown."

A little taken aback, Brown took her hand and said, "This is Mr. Potter from the Shubert organization. He might have a part for you."

"I'm very pleased to meet you, Mr. Potter," she said, extending her hand. "What sort of part is it?"

"It's a good speaking role in the new play with Lou Tellegen," said Brown. "You would be playing a French actress. Do you think that's something you could manage?"

She smiled. "Oh, yes, that's quite in my line," she said. "I was educated in a finishing school in Paris. I'm well acquainted with the French theater. I saw Lou Tellegen perform with Sarah Bernhardt."

A broad grin lit up Jimmy's face. "Okay, then, Miss Monterey," he said. "Would you like to read for me right here and now?"

Carlotta smiled at him. "Why not?" she said. "May I study the script for a few moments?"

"Of course," said Jimmy. He handed her some pages, and Brown showed her into a little room with a table and a few chairs. "We'll be back in fifteen minutes," he said. "Jimmy will read with you."

The pages were the beginning of Act Three in a play called *Taking Chances*. As the curtain opened, Lucy Gallon, the character Carlotta would be playing, was clad in a negligee and slippers, perched on the corner of a desk where the Count de Lastra, presumably Lou Tellegen, sat trying to write a letter. They clearly had just spent the night together. She kept trying to interrupt him and get his attention as he wrote, pouting and flirting and finally kicking off her slipper to wag her bare foot at him. Then he tried to get rid of her because he was expecting a visitor. As he finally pushed her out of the room, she held her foot up through the open door and he put the slipper on it. Quite *risqué* stuff, she thought, but she knew she could make something of it.

When the men came back, Carlotta said, "I think I can do something with this. Did you want a French accent?"

"Oh no," said Jimmy. "Lou Tellegen is trying his best to sound American, so everyone else should too."

Carlotta read the scene with a pouty little attitude that made the men smile. "I think we can go somewhere with this, Miss Monterey," Jimmy said. "Mr. Brown and I have agreed upon terms, so if you want it, the part is yours. Any questions?"

"I have just one concern," said Carlotta. "This is rather racy material. May I ask how far the part goes along those lines?"

Jimmy grinned. "This is as racy as it gets," he said. "She also appears in Act 1, but she's just running away from her boyfriend and flirting with all the men at a party. "

"So she's a somewhat *louche* woman?"

"Loose woman? She's not a prostitute, just an actress who likes a lot of men."

"Well," Carlotta smiled. "It's a wonderful chance, but I don't know whether I should be quite so daring when I'm just starting out."

Brown shot Jimmy a look. "Will you excuse us for a minute, Mr. Potter? I should speak with my client before she decides."

When Jimmy had left the room, Brown said, "Look, Miss Monterey, normally I would spend a little time explaining the way things are in the New York theater, but we don't have that luxury. If you're worried about tarnishing your reputation with a little *risqué* material, then Broadway is not for you. This is a golden opportunity. Your first role would include a scene alone with the leading man, and not just any leading man, Sarah Bernhardt's leading man. Lou Tellegen is a big film star. Everybody is looking at this play to see how he'll do in English. The Shubert organization controls a big, important hunk of New York theater, and they own theaters in every decent-sized city in the country, so they control most of the road bookings. They're offering you a honey of a part. Believe me, you will not have a better chance than this. And they're offering a decent salary because they're up against it. Rehearsals start tomorrow."

Carlotta squared her shoulders and looked at him directly, her voice an unconscious imitation of her mother's. "What is the salary?"

"Thirty dollars a week. That's very good for a supporting role."

Carlotta reflected that it was a start. And he was right that a chance like this would not come around often. She could tell that from studying the girls in the waiting room.

"All right," she said, and she was a Broadway actress.

Carlotta soon found that nothing had prepared her for the Broadway theater. Everything went much faster than it had in Academy productions. There were two weeks for rehearsals, start to finish, and most of the actors were involved in other shows, so the process was as efficient as the stage manager could make it. She was glad she had spent the day and evening before rehearsals learning lines. She had all she could do to follow the blocking, especially in the party scene, when she was entering and exiting and moving all over the stage. And she got little help from her fellow cast members, who all seemed to know each other and were not particularly welcoming to a newcomer with a good role. The women looked at the attractive outsider warily. The men either ignored or tried to flirt with her. This was dismaying to Carlotta, who missed the camaraderie of the Academy productions. Her sense of isolation intensified her natural shyness, which the other actors seemed to take as arrogance or superiority, and resented. She could sense their pleasure when she was chastised by the stage manager for missing her mark or messing up a piece of stage business. Lou Tellegen was polite and patient in rehearsals, but, preoccupied with his own transition to the American stage, he was no help to Carlotta.

At first, she found it difficult to act with Lou Tellegen, especially in the Act Three scene. When she had seen him on stage at the *Théâtre Sarah Bernhardt*, Carlotta had thought him a handsome prop for Bernhardt, but a mediocre actor. Dealing with him on the stage was another matter. With his athletic body, his flawless, classically modelled face, and above all, his intensely beautiful eyes, she found his physical presence overwhelming. When she was perched on his writing desk in her thin negligee, their bodies nearly touching, she felt a sexual tension that made it difficult for her to play the light comedy of the scene. She found the physical tussling as he hustled her out of the room exciting in a way that was not intended for the scene and, she reflected, not very professional of her. She realized with some chagrin that, like probably hundreds of women before her, she had fallen for Lou Tellegen.

Through a determined generosity on stage and good humor off, Carlotta slowly made her way to acceptance by the rest of the cast. Lou Tellegen welcomed her little suggestions for improving their scene and was delighted when one of them resulted in a big laugh. He insisted that the change remain in the show. In return, he talked to her about acting, relaying many of the tricks that Bernhardt had taught him. Off stage, Carlotta paid more attention to her appearance than she ever had in her life and took every chance she could to talk to Lou. She felt like a fan, waiting at the stage door for him to come to the theater every day. Her interest was not lost on Lou Tellegen. One night after the show, he came up beside her as she left her dressing room. "Carlotta," he said, "I have an idea for improving our scene."

"What is it, Lou?" she responded eagerly.

He looked down at her with a smile. "Don't you think we could play it more effectively if we had actually slept together?"

Carlotta was taken aback, but she did her best not to show it. "I think it might be helpful," she said, looking up at him through her long lashes. In a few weeks, they had drifted into an affair, which was a new experience for Carlotta, but as natural as breathing for Lou. She found that his store of sexual knowledge was far vaster than Jack Moffat could ever dream of, and for the first time in her life she knew what it was to be sexually satisfied. She was amazed at the physical response that Lou evoked in her, at the passionate abandon she was capable of. She agreed when he told her that her love-making was making her a better actress. She had a new awareness of her body, a new sense of freedom in its movements and power in its attractiveness. When she was married, she had hidden in the dressing room or bathroom to change her clothes, emerging each night in a nightgown and dressing gown. Now she displayed her body proudly for Lou, her glossy hair down about her waist, her ivory skin glowing, excited by his excitement.

"You have changed, my lovely Carlotta," he said one night. "When I first saw you, I thought, 'that's a cold woman.' But now I know you were just waiting to be awakened. Your husband must have been a brute."

"Not a brute," she said, "just not sensual. He had no idea what he was missing."

"That is right," Lou laughed. "But there is more for you to experience too. Depth of feeling. Womanliness. I don't think any woman can be a truly great actress unless she experiences motherhood."

Carlotta bristled. "I don't know. I think Maude Adams is a pretty good actress."

Lou smiled. "Yes, pretty good, but not great. A woman must unlock all of her emotions to be great."

"And what about a man?"

"A man must try his best."

Chapter 21

When *Taking Chances* closed in mid-May of 1915 after a three-month run, Carlotta and Lou went their separate ways. He went to Hollywood to make a movie about the French Foreign Legion called *The Unknown*. Eight months later, he was married to the opera diva Geraldine Farrar. Carlotta stayed in New York, auditioning for acting roles that proved difficult to get. Although it was a small part, her performance as Lucy Gallon had been well-received, with one critic singling her out as a "picturesque, petulant and pouting adventuress." But there were hundreds of pretty and talented young actresses in New York. As she saw the same ones over and over at auditions, she began to appreciate how truly lucky she had been to land her first role. And May, at the end of the theatrical season, was a bad time to try to find a new role. Most of the Broadway actors who were working were in shows with long runs that weren't over yet. By the middle of June, there really was no point in looking for work, but Carlotta went to Chamberlain Brown's office every week or so to remind them she was there.

Carlotta was glad she had saved enough from her *Taking Chances* salary to stay in New York for the summer, but in July she was sweltering along with the rest of the city. Although it was not a fashionable activity, she was happy to go with Kitty Smith on weekend ferry boat excursions to get a little relief from the heat. With her old friend Merle Maddern, who was free until rehearsals for *Mrs. Boltay's Daughters* started in the fall, she went to the Jersey Shore for the last week of July. When they returned, the theater scene was starting to come alive. Many new shows were being cast for the next season, which would begin at the end of the August. On the twenty-eighth of July, Carlotta received a note from Chamberlain Brown's office telling her to come in right away to discuss a major opportunity. Arriving promptly at nine the next day, she was admitted to the inner office immediately.

"I have big news for you, Miss Monterey," said Brown. "Oliver Morosco is in town from Los Angeles, casting the new road company for *The Bird of Paradise*, and you were recommended to him for the lead by Lou Tellegen, out there in movieland. I assume you know the play?"

Like everyone else in the theater, Carlotta was familiar with the phenomenon of *The Bird of Paradise*. It had originated in Los Angeles and very improbably made its way to Broadway from there. Since the New York show had closed in April of 1912, companies had been touring with it across the country, sometimes two at once. Carlotta had seen it in San Francisco and thought it a bad copy of *Madame Butterfly*, set in 1890s Hawaii. In its far-fetched plot, a research scientist came to Hawaii intending to work on a cure for leprosy and fell in love with Luana, a Hawaiian princess. He married her and lost all his ambition amid the tropical lassitude and pleasure-loving life of the island. When someone else discovered the cure, he attempted to leave the lazy island life behind him, taking Luana to live in the colonial enclave. But in this foreign environment the charm was broken, and Luana found that he no longer loved her. Heeding the call of her people, she returned to find that they needed her as a sacrifice to the god of the Kilauea volcano. The play ended with her throwing herself into its fiery mouth, spectacularly represented on stage. The badly written play had been saved by the lavish production and the illusion of Hawaii that a group of Hawaiian dancers and musicians were able to create onstage.

"Yes, I've seen it," she said to Brown. "It isn't a very good play."

He smiled wryly. "No, it's not a very good play," he said, "but it's a honey of a role for the actress who plays Luana. The New York production made Laurette Taylor into the toast of Broadway. Bessie Barriscale has had two Broadway leads since she came from Los Angeles with that show, and it launched Lenore Ulrich on a big movie career. This role could be the thing that makes you into a Broadway leading lady."

Carlotta became businesslike. She looked him in the eye and asked, "What does the offer entail?"

"It's a road company. You would start touring in the Midwest in September and you would be out in California by November. That's where you're from, isn't it? It looks like you would be spending the holidays in Sacramento, San Francisco and Los Angeles. They love the play out there. Then you'd continue the national tour. It's pretty much booked through the summer."

"I would be touring for a year with this play? Isn't that a long time to be away from New York if I'm trying to build a career?"

"Normally, I would say yes, but this show is a juggernaut. There will be all kinds of advance publicity every time you come to town, and if you're creative about it, there will be stories and interviews that are picked up across the nation. You could be coming back to New York with a name."

Carlotta was skeptical. "I came to New York from the West Coast because everyone said it was impossible to establish a career from there."

"You're right. You don't get stars coming to New York from the sticks very often. But you would be coming from New York *to* the sticks. Entirely different thing. Just make sure you present yourself as a New York actress. Look, Miss Monterey, you are not going to get another offer like this very soon. A leading role in a play that's guaranteed to be a hit. Most girls would kill for this. If nothing else, it's a year of work at a leading lady's salary. That's really something at this stage of your career. And you'd get the star treatment on the road—Pullman cars, your own dressing room, the whole bit. Not bad at all for touring."

Carlotta reflected that she needed the money, and if Brown was so sure that it wouldn't injure her career, truth be told, she was glad to try her first leading role on the road rather than under the glaring lights of Broadway, where any flaw could mean the end for her. She was quite sure she could handle the role of the simple and sexy Luana. And travelling as a diva might be fun. "What exactly is the salary?" she asked.

"I would have to negotiate that with Morosco, but you can be sure it would be at least three times what you were making in *Taking Chances*, and a lot of your living expenses on the road would be paid."

"Do you have the script? I would like to read it before I give a definite answer."

He handed it to her. "Take this overnight," he said, "and give me your answer in the morning. We have a meeting set up with Morosco in the afternoon. Have something prepared to read for him if you want the part. And really, you'd be crazy not to."

Reading the script, Carlotta found that the play was not quite as bad as she remembered. Its author, Richard Walton Tully, was a literary man, and there were some good speeches, although hers were mostly in broken English. She would have to come up with a Hawaiian accent. She had a love song to sing, which would not be too taxing and would show off her vocal training, but she would have to dance, not her strong suit. She found a scene with Wilson in Act Three that she could read for the audition. She just hoped they wouldn't ask her to dance.

When she met the producer, Oliver Morosco, they understood each other immediately. He was impressed with her mix of California roots and London and Paris training. "We can use all of that with the newspapers," he said. He was pleased with her reading and told her not to worry about the accent or the dancing. "We have people to help with that," he said. "It took Laurette a while to find the accent that worked for her. It's not like there are a lot of Hawaiian people around who will be checking to see if it's authentic."

In the middle of September 1915, Carlotta appeared as Luana in Cleveland. Chamberlain Brown had been right that the fame of the show would precede her, which made for abundant press coverage. Carlotta had a good time with the press agent. She went along with the most farfetched stories he created to suit the audiences in the various parts of the country. To use in the Midwest, he had come up with a campaign based on her being a wholesome "farmer's daughter," and the *Cleveland Plain Dealer* featured a photo essay in the Sunday paper about a farm called "Happiness" she supposedly owned in Oakland. The photo shoot included poses of her wearing overalls or a middy blouse and skirt and holding a hoe, riding home on the hay rack, or petting a calf. Carlotta had spent enough time in the country to know how ridiculous the whole thing was, but it seemed to make audiences in the region disposed to welcome her.

Meanwhile, Carlotta was working earnestly on her part, trying to get her performance to its highest level before she reached the West Coast. She had learned the lines easily enough, and her richly modulated voice and projection had always been her strong suit, but consistency in the pseudo-Hawaiian accent took concentration, even after intensive coaching. And then there was the singing and the dancing. Luckily her contralto voice was suited to the love song she had to sing. It went all right, although she never received any particular praise for it. The dancing was something else again. The Hawaiian dancers in the cast gave her models to emulate, and they were kind and generous with their help, but she could not manage anything like their lithe fluidity, even in the simplified form of the dances she was required to do. Practicing every day, she felt she got better, but she knew she needed to reach a higher level for the West Coast audiences for whom the play was already a cherished institution.

Carlotta felt she did well in Colorado Springs and better in Salt Lake City, so that she was fairly confident in the role when the play opened in Sacramento. She was nervous, though, because she half hoped, half feared that Chris Tharsing would be in the audience. In a moment of bravado, she had written to tell her father about the engagement, inviting him to come and see whether his investment in her career had paid off. On opening night, Chris indeed appeared, and made sure that the reporter from the *Sacramento Union* knew that Carlotta was his daughter. The story in the paper duly identified her as "the daughter of a Shasta farmer," under the headline "New Star Rises in Tully Play," noting that "C. N. Tharsing of Anderson, Shasta County, father of Miss Monterey, saw his daughter appear for the first time in her part as leading lady." Characteristically, Chris, who was not too clear on the details of his daughter's life, went on to embroider in his interview with the reporter, who wrote that Carlotta had been "awarded a prize as the most beautiful girl in the United States" and that she was married to "a titled Frenchman" who was fighting in the trenches in France.

When Chris came back to Carlotta's dressing room after the show, he was impressed with the crowd of people, including the most important men of Sacramento, who were anxious to convey their congratulations to his daughter, and to him. He stood by her side, beaming, while businessmen and legislators and successful farmers slapped him on the back and told him he must have done something right, although the looks must be from her mother's side. Carlotta, playing the unspoiled hometown girl, received their compliments with a grateful smile and basked in her father's pride.

The San Francisco opening repeated the Sacramento one on a larger scale. Not only was the theater bigger, but the crowd included many of the glitterati of the city, come out to see one of the Bay Area's daughters starring in a California play that had become a national phenomenon. Seated prominently in the front rows, of course, were Nellie Tharsing and Melvin Chapman, along with Mel Jr. and a large contingent of the Gotchett clan, including the Shays, who were as delighted for their Hazel and as proud of her as Nellie was. This opening night was celebrated much more lavishly than Sacramento's. Mel and Nellie had arranged a supper where the family and a number of friends from Oakland and San Francisco greeted Carlotta with their congratulations. San Francisco socialites who might not have invited her into their drawing rooms ten years earlier were delighted to be seen with her now. Mel Jr., now a young law student, was positively dazzled by her theatrical success. He came back to see the play every night of its two-week run and eagerly took her to supper on any night when she didn't have another engagement. He made no secret of his devotion, lavishing praise on her performance and her appearance at every opportunity. Apart from his adoration of Carlotta, he showed a surprisingly shrewd and knowledgeable sense of the theater, which he seemed to attend almost nightly. He offered suggestions that might improve the show here and there, and Carlotta thought many of them were not bad ideas.

Carlotta was able to spend Thanksgiving of 1915 in Oakland with her mother and the Chapmans, surprising herself with her pleasure at being in the family circle. Her mother, feeling both proud and vindicated for the many years of monetary support she had provided for her daughter's career, was in her best mood—warm, affectionate, joking and laughing with all of them. Mel Sr., who had been supportive of launching her theatrical career, was much relieved as well as pleased for Nellie and Carlotta. Mel Jr. was more than ever Carlotta's devoted admirer. Carlotta basked in the admiration and approval that permeated the atmosphere at 76 Stanley Place.

After the heady experience of Sacramento and San Francisco, Carlotta approached Los Angeles with less trepidation than she had expected to a month earlier. This city, where the *Bird of Paradise* phenomenon had begun, was clearly the test for any new actress playing Luana. It was where Bessie Barriscale had originated the part, and where Lenore Ulrich had scored such a big hit, touching off her film career. This was Carlotta's chance to make her mark. She approached it now with excitement as well as nerves. To prepare the way, the press agent had gone all out with stories meant to present Carlotta as an intriguing figure to her potential audience and to suggest the art and craft behind the "primitive" character of Luana. In an interview with Grace Kingsley, theater and film columnist for the *Los Angeles Times*, Carlotta stressed her education and theatrical training. The resulting story called her "one of the most brilliant and accomplished women of the stage," with a "tremendously fascinating personality." Kingsley wrote that Carlotta had mastered four languages, was "a musician of attainments," and dabbled in sculpture and painting. Carlotta, she wrote, was a graduate of the London Academy of Dramatic Art and had been trained for grand opera but had given up that career when she strained her voice "with overwork in Paris." A few days later, another story in the *Times* described Carlotta's exercise regimen, which consisted of "several hours every day" of fencing with the men in the company. The article called her "one of the few expert women fencers in the country." Photos of Carlotta posing with a fencing foil were prominent.

This was all background to the December 20 opening itself. Carlotta, who was prone to stage fright, became more nervous as the hour approached, resulting in a performance that was stiffer than usual, particularly when it came to dancing. The reviews generally praised Morosco's spectacular new production of the play, with its tropical rainstorm and volcanic eruption, and were tolerant, but not complimentary, about the acting. The *Herald* said that Carlotta's performance was inferior to Lenore Ulrich's, but that on the whole she did very well. In the *Times*, however, Henry Christeen Warnack wrote a review that was devastating to Carlotta because he hit on all the things she most worried about in her performance. "It is to be regretted," he wrote, "that the casting of this splendid work should be of a nature distinctly disappointing to those familiar with previous productions of this successful piece. While a little lady of charm and talent, Miss

Carlotta Monterey is not in any particular satisfying as Luana. She has not the accent or the motion and, in this particular role, she lacks the quality of the right emotion. She declaims too much and this causes her voice to become deadly monotonous in its over-intonation, and she has not caught the subtle fluidic motion which makes the grace and lure of the role. The latter defect is emphasized by some of the other girls who attend Luana's party in the first act and who seem to be much more at home in its atmosphere."

Carlotta had received some harsh critiques in drama school, but nothing had prepared her for this matter-of-fact laying bare of all the weaknesses in her performance. To some extent, she had expected the criticism of her dancing, but she prided herself on her voice, her second-best asset, as she saw it. After anger and tears, she appeared at the theater for the second night with a brave face that could not hide her obvious fear and anxiety about going on. Oliver Morosco and Richard Tully, on hand for the Los Angeles premiere, both tried to console her. The fundamentals of her performance were strong, they said. These were just the kinks that still had to be worked out. Her voice and movement would become more natural as she got used to the part and felt more confident. It had taken Laurette Taylor a few weeks to get her accent and vocalization down in New York, Morosco told her, and of course this was much more difficult on the road with the constant travel and adapting to new theaters.

Carlotta appreciated the support from the producer and the author. At least she didn't feel her job was in jeopardy, but her stage fright was worse than it had ever been. Keenly aware of the situation and seeing the state she was in, her fellow actors, who had not been particularly friendly up to this point, did their best to put her at ease and make her appear to advantage on stage. There was a general air among the company, led by the older, road-hardened veterans, that "the show must go on." Hooper Atchley, who played her husband Paul Wilson, had come in for some harsh criticism as well. They tacitly agreed to brave it out together, which gave a new depth to their scenes. They worked hard, and Morosco and his assistants worked on endearing the company to the public. On the twenty-third, the *Herald* said that the theater had been crowded at every performance and that "indications point to the two largest weeks that this pretty play has ever enjoyed in this city." It went on to say that "Miss Carlotta Monterey, the new Luana, has made many friends on this, her first appearance, as an actress in this city."

For Christmas Eve, Morosco had already planned a free matinee for a thousand "needy children of the city." He had arranged for a fleet of automobiles donated by the likes of Charlie Chaplin and De Wolf Hopper as well the Elks, Masons, and Los Angeles Athletic club to ferry the children to the theater. All of the cast and crew were to donate their services for the event, and Carlotta was to help distribute candy to the children. She told Morosco she was willing to do whatever he thought would help to make this event stand out. They put their heads together and came up with a plan that demanded an enormous effort from the actress. On the morning of December 24, Carlotta visited the Los Angeles Children's Hospital and an orphanage, The McKinley Home, where she talked to the children and handed out candy. Then she went back to the theater, and, as the children arrived for the matinee in the donated cars, she stood at the entrance, personally handing each of more than a thousand children a bag of candy and a small toy.

The performance was a raucous affair, but the cast went on gamely, and Carlotta could not help but smile when, in her most intense scene with Hooper, a little boy said loudly, "when is the bird going to show up?" The children were finally awed into silence by the volcano's eruption. They emitted a loud simultaneous gasp when Carlotta mounted its fiery rim, about to cast herself into it. The applause was wild, and someone handed her a large bouquet of pink carnations during the curtain calls, which she kissed and held out to the audience as she bowed, earning another outburst. Carlotta was exhausted at the end of the performance, but as she had promised, she went to the Jewish Children's Home afterwards, distributing more candy to the children.

The ample press coverage of these events did a good deal to endear the cast, especially Carlotta, to the people of Los Angeles. As Christmas week went on, the theater remained full, and the audiences were enthusiastic in their applause for Carlotta. She received bouquets and curtain calls after every performance. As the shock of the review passed and Carlotta felt the warmth of the audience's applause, she began to relax, and her vocalization, her chemistry with Hooper, and her physical movement were the better for it. She actually began to enjoy the performances. In the end, the *Times* reversed its judgment a bit, conceding that "Carlotta Monterey, as Luana, the lovely Hawaiian girl, appears to have established herself in the hearts of all who have seen her." On December 30, it reported that *The Bird of Paradise* would be held over for two performances beyond the scheduled two-week run because "Carlotta Monterey is scoring a big success as Luana." It was a triumph not only for Morosco and Tully's play, but for Carlotta, who had stood up to what she felt as a devastating personal attack and done what she needed to do. After Los Angeles, the cast was not only better in performance, but a happier and more unified company on the road.

A less eventful but successful run in San Jose followed Los Angeles, and then a return to Sacramento, where the *Sacramento Union* said that there was "a noticeable improvement" in Carlotta's work. After that, the company left California for new environs. As they approached Portland, with its generally more intellectual, artistic and bohemian audience, Carlotta took a new approach in interviews. One interviewer reported that she was a disciple of Buddha and a feminist. In the interview, she came out against the double standard of sexual morals for men and women, a hot feminist issue in 1915, as well as the "excessive masculinism" in ethics and religion, although she stopped short of calling herself a suffragette. The image-making, the intense work she had put into her performance in Los Angeles, and the new confident energy she had for acting seemed to pay off in Portland. The *Morning Oregonian* called her "an intensely dramatic actress, full of repressed fire and passionate utterances, a flame-like Luana, a veritable gypsy of the tropics and buoyantly, gloriously young and lovely."

When the press agent suggested that it was time to lighten up a little, they released a story calculated to endear Carlotta to much of her audience. Like many a diva, she traveled with a little dog, Pom-Pom. Carlotta told a reporter that he was a Hawaiian dog, and that she was so fond of him that she kept him with her always. One day, the story went, a train conductor had insisted on putting the dog in the baggage car, and both Pom-Pom and Carlotta had endured such a miserable trip that she was determined never to be separated from him on a train again. So she had a giant muff made with a pocket that held Pom-Pom and a flap that could button over it, keeping him hidden from conductors and porters until she was safely in her berth. Not only did this story endear her to theater audiences in Portland, it originated a fad, as it was picked up in a string of other papers, and many women tried to recreate the muff. A number wrote to Carlotta to ask for the pattern, so they could copy it. As it turned out, the image of dog lover, which was the most authentic of the many versions of Carlotta the press agent put out, was also the most popular. During the early months of 1916, Carlotta had to show her "dog muff" off at every city and town on the tour, and there were many.

Chapter 22

When Carlotta left San Francisco for Los Angeles in the middle of December, Mel Chapman Jr. began writing to her. He had occasionally written in the past—short, breezy letters about his activities and the events in Oakland. But the new letters showed a change in his feeling toward her. Alongside the infatuated fan of the last few weeks was a thoughtful young man Carlotta had seen only in occasional glimpses before. When he was not abashed by her physical presence, he seemed to be freer to reveal this side of himself. He followed the Los Angeles papers while she was there and wrote consolingly about the poor reviews, reminding her of her triumph in San Francisco, and praising the strongest points of her performance. When things turned around for her, he rejoiced that LA had finally woken up and seen what any informed theatergoer should see. Although Carlotta wrote one letter to four or five of his, and then only short notes, she began to look forward to Mel's letters as an unfailing support when she grew depressed by her day-to-day life on the tour, which was often seedier and more boring than glamorous.

After the Portland run, the tour made its slow progress across the upper West and Midwest in the dead of winter. It was then that Carlotta began to realize the jaunty slogan "the show must go on" masked a sometimes grim and dreary reality. It took a determined effort to cope with the conditions in Oregon and Washington—the dirty trains and stuffy hotel rooms, the bad food and the nighttime journeys, the constant adjustments to different cold, drafty theaters where the actors stood in the wings in their overcoats while they waited to go on in their skimpy costumes.

When Carlotta stepped down from the train on a bitterly cold February day in Anaconda, Montana, the realities of the road seemed to smack her in the face. Anaconda was essentially an enormous copper mine with a town of ten thousand souls attached. Its claim to fame was that it had the biggest smoke stack in the world. A biting wind assaulted the actors as they walked down the ugly main street toward the single hotel. Carlotta's hands were warm in Pom-Pom's muff, which she held against her chest, providing some protection from the wind, but she had nothing but a thin veil over her ears and face, which ached with the cold before she had walked a single block. Her feet in their fashionable pumps immediately froze so that she envied the fur-lined galoshes that Anne Henry and Fanny Yantis, veterans of the road, had thought to bring. By the time they reached the hotel, even Pom-Pom had begun to shiver inside his muff.

Carlotta was standing over the radiator in her dingy room, trying to get back the feeling in her hands and feet when a bell boy knocked on the door. He handed her a telegram from Mel Jr. and a box. The telegram read, "Been following the weather. Stay warm and radiant." The box contained a lovely, warm cashmere scarf. Carlotta nearly broke down in tears. Never had she received a gift that showed more thoughtfulness. That night she wrote Mel a real letter. Dispensing with the pose of breezy sophistication, she wrote to him honestly and directly of the hard time she was having on the road, not only the physical trials, but her loneliness and depression, her doubts about her ability to become a serious actress, her boredom with the play. It made her feel better that she was communicating the truth to someone who she knew would be understanding and sympathetic.

Mel rose to the occasion. At almost every new town afterwards, there was a letter from him answering her last one. He was supportive and encouraging about her career, but took her complaints about the road very seriously, urging her to take care of herself and try not to let the physical trials affect her stamina or her emotional health. She had the sense that he was really worried about her and tried to reassure him that she was coping even while she complained about the rigors of Duluth,

Minnesota, where it was six degrees below zero when they arrived on February 27.

Although she soon supplied herself well with winter clothes, including long silk underwear, Carlotta was plagued by a stubborn cold at the end of March. It reached a crisis during the first week in April, when her voice was completely gone, and she could not go on in Peoria, Illinois. From Peoria, the company had to go to New York for one day's performance so the judge who was adjudicating a plagiarism suit against Richard Tully could see the play. Morosco decided that Carlotta should remain in Peoria to recuperate and join the show when it returned from New York. Feeling cold and lonely and deserted in the second-rate hotel, Carlotta telegraphed her mother to ask if she could come and spend a week with her while she recuperated. Nellie telegraphed back to ask how sick her daughter was. She was much relieved to hear it was only a cold and laryngitis. She told Carlotta she was very sorry, but she had to be in San Francisco to close a real estate deal later in the week.

As the sky began to darken the next afternoon and her hotel room was at its dreariest, there was a knock on Carlotta's door. Expecting the bell boy, she called, "Come in!" To her surprise, in walked Mel Chapman Jr., the anxious look on his long face melting into a sunny smile when he saw Carlotta standing there in her dressing gown with her waist-length hair loosely braided and looking as beautiful as ever.

"Mel!" she cried hoarsely, the surprised delight showing on her face before she had a chance to mask it with any conscious effect. "What are you doing here?"

Mel spoke off-handedly, although his dark brown eyes were lit with joy at this reception. "Well," he said, "your mother said you were sick, and she couldn't come to look after you, so I decided to chuck my law school classes for a week and come myself."

Carlotta tried to capture a bit of her older-sister role toward him. "But Mel, this must have cost a lot of money, and you shouldn't be missing your law classes."

"Not that much money," he said. "I can make up the work, and now that I see you're among the living, I think we can make a decent holiday of it, even in these luxurious digs in Peoria. I have an equally splendid room just down the hall."

She smiled in spite of herself and dropped the older sister pose. "That's a claim I challenge you to meet," she said, and looked up at him with a genuine smile.

"I accept the challenge with pleasure, Madame," he said, "but my first mission is to help you recuperate, so no moving around."

She sat in the armchair and found a good deal of amusement in his clumsy attempts to settle pillows behind her back and tuck a blanket around her. "Now," he said, "I will read to you until you get sleepy, which shouldn't take long, and then I will scout out some first-rate fare for our dinner."

"Good luck," she said. "I've pretty much experienced third-rate fare from the hotel so far."

"Never fear," he said. "My food-hunting instincts are impeccable."

So Mel picked up the novel Carlotta had been languidly making her way through and read with such gusto that she told him she would never get sleepy at that rate. After an hour, though, drowsiness overcame her, so Carlotta went to bed as Mel ventured into the streets of Peoria in search of its best restaurants. The desk clerk told him that the two best things to eat in the city were fresh fish from the Illinois river and, of course, steak from the stockyards. He pointed him toward the best steak houses in town, and Mel was off in search of beef. After looking around a bit, he decided on a place just a block from the hotel that the desk clerk swore by and that would deliver a hot meal to the room. He ordered a meal that would easily serve four normal appetites and spent an hour walking around the city to see what else it had to offer in the way of food and entertainment. Then he went back to his room to spruce up for his dinner with Carlotta. When he knocked on her door at six o'clock, Carlotta was awake and waiting for him. He told her dinner would be arriving soon, and they waited companionably.

The meal was a surprise to both of them. They thought the steak every bit as good as Delmonico's in San Francisco, and Mel had chosen well with the sides of creamed spinach and potatoes au gratin. Carlotta said there was too much of everything, but Mel's youthful appetite proved adequate to the task. "You should let me pay, Mel. It must have cost a fortune," said Carlotta.

Mel laughed. "Not nearly as much as Delmonico's," he said. "And it's my pleasure. We have to build up your strength. Besides, you ate about one-tenth what I did."

The first few days of Mel's visit went on in a similar way. He would come to Carlotta's room in the morning and have breakfast with her, always supplying some hard-to-find food that would aid her recovery, like fresh oranges or grapefruit. Then he would read to her, keeping conversation to a minimum to save her voice, until she was ready for a nap. The same routine would follow with lunch in the afternoon. During Carlotta's afternoon nap, Mel would scour the streets of Peoria looking for interesting food for dinner, and books and magazines that she would find amusing. He kept her well-supplied with hot lemonade, honey and tea, and her voice gradually came back, so that by the fourth day, they could sit and converse comfortably. Their conversations on these long, slow winter days ranged far and wide. Carlotta was impressed with the breadth of Mel's interests and the depth of his knowledge in some subjects that he understood much better than she did. On Saturday, the day before he was to leave, Mel was surprised to find Carlotta fully dressed with her freshly washed hair done up. "I'm officially recovered," she said. "It's a beautiful day today, and I want to go out."

Mel was delighted, but a little concerned. "I think that's a wonderful idea," he said, "but as your nurse, I have to insist that you don't overtax yourself. How about a short stroll in the park, followed by lunch and a matinee?"

"Yes, please," said Carlotta, "anything except *The Bird of Paradise*." They immediately went to the newspaper to see what was on offer. It was a charmed day. Coming out of the hotel into the bright, unseasonably warm weather, Carlotta felt her spirits lift. Mel's were already as high as a kite, and during their stroll in the park, the smiles on people's faces, the children running on the grass, the general sense of life being renewed as they walked arm in arm gave Carlotta a feeling that was both comfortable and completely new. Mel had scouted a bright and cheerful restaurant, where they agreed their light lunch was exactly right, and they went to see *Daddy Long Legs*, a sentimental comedy that completely suited their mood. After the show, Mel insisted that Carlotta rest while he went in search of dinner, and finding that she was more tired than she had expected, she slept until his return.

Mel returned with flowers, which Carlotta used to decorate the table. It looked very pretty when their dinner of fresh bass, followed by steak with béarnaise sauce and vegetables, arrived. Today, Carlotta had an appetite. She tucked into the bass with relish while Mel polished off most of the steak. When the meal was over, and they were sitting in the room's two comfortable chairs on either side of the fireplace, Carlotta turned to Mel and said, simply and sincerely, "I'm going to miss you, Mel. This has been the nicest week I've had in a long time, even though I was sick."

Mel looked at her without the characteristic glimmer of humor in his eyes. "I don't need to tell you that I will miss you. I would chuck it all, law school be damned, if I could be with you like this all the time."

Carlotta looked at him, her brown eyes gleaming. "Do you really mean that, Mel?"

"Yes, I do," he said. "And there is something I've been wanting to tell you. I've planned and rehearsed it every day when I've been out walking, and I ask you to please just listen and not interrupt until I've finished. "

"All right."

He looked down at the floor for a moment, and then looked into her eyes and began. "What I have to say is this. You know that I have adored you since I was a boy, but in this last year, that feeling has deepened into a love that is the strongest, most compelling thing I have ever felt in my life. You are the only woman in the world to me, Carlotta. I don't believe that I could ever be happy away from you. I am asking you to consider marrying me. I know it will seem ridiculous to you to begin with, but I can tell you that you could never have a more devoted husband. If you want to stay on the stage, that's all right with me. I will do everything in my power to help with your career. If you don't, I promise to provide a comfortable home for you always. I have money through my mother from the Dargie estate that will support us until I join the law firm. I'm sure my father would want us to live with him, but if you would prefer an apartment in the city or a small house of our own, either of those is possible. We can have a fine life together, Carlotta. Imagine a future when every day is like today."

In spite of herself, Carlotta had to smile at that. How little this earnest, lovesick boy knew of marriage. "Oh, Mel," she said, "I'm so grateful to you for all you've done and all you offer, but you really don't know what that is. I'm not a girl, as you well know. I've been married, and I know how hard it is after the first glow wears off. I must say that you know me better than almost any man I could name, but you don't know all my moods. When I feel trapped, I can be a termagant, just ask Jack Moffat."

"But you won't ever be trapped by me. That's just what I'm trying to say. I want to offer you a future where you are free, whether you choose to be an artist first or a wife and mother. I know you better than you think, Carlotta. I know you wouldn't last long in Oakland if the stage still beckoned. Well, that's all right with me. I will support you wherever the road takes you."

She shook her head. "You may say that now, Mel, when you don't have a career yet, and you're bored with law school. But how will you feel when you're a successful lawyer like your father? Will you still be willing to have an actress for a wife when you have all the disapproving matrons of Oakland looking at you and judging, keeping their husbands from sending business your way?"

His face set with a determination she had not seen before. "Yes," he said. "I've been thinking about this for a long time, and I don't see that there's so much to value in Oakland society that I wouldn't give it up to be your husband."

"What about our families?" she said. "What would your father say?"

"My father would not like me marrying so young. I can't deny that. But you know he's very fond of you, and when he sees that I'm determined to marry you no matter what, I think he will give us his blessing."

"Maybe, but I don't know what my mother would think of this." She looked at him sincerely. "I really don't know what to say," she said.

"Don't say anything right now if you aren't ready. I know this will take a while to sink in. And I want you to think about the future, both as we could make it and as it would be otherwise. I know the stage hasn't been as satisfying as you had thought it would be. Of course, part of that is the grind of touring and the effect on your health. Only you can say what the theater means to you. But I don't want you to have to face it alone anymore. I want to be with you to face whatever the future brings."

There were tears in Carlotta's eyes. "Thank you, Mel," she said. "I frankly don't know what will come of this, but I will be forever grateful for what you have said to me today. For now, I think you should go back to your room."

With that, Mel stood up and said, "Good night, Carlotta. I'll knock on your door tomorrow before I go."

Chapter 23

The next day, they both got on trains, Mel for Oakland, and Carlotta to meet up with the company in Wilkes-Barre, Pennsylvania, where they were opening on the twenty-fifth of April. As she sat alone on the train, Carlotta felt the loss of Mel much more than she had expected to. It was not easy to do without his sunny presence and constant attention once she had had it. Encountering a chilling rain as she stepped off the train in the dreary coal-mining city did not lift Carlotta's spirits. She barely looked around her as she rode in a taxi to the hotel, where she unpacked what she needed and ordered dinner in her room.

As she sat alone trying to eat the greasy beef stew that was finally delivered, she thought of the comfortable evenings she had spent with Mel during the last week and of the long weeks stretching before her of trains, hotel rooms, solitary meals or quick bites in restaurants with people from the company she didn't much like and didn't like her, and performance after performance in a play she had come to loathe. The excitement of being treated as a leading lady had long since died away. "Why am I doing this?" she thought. The answer was not nearly as clear as it once had been. After almost a year's experience on the road, she no longer dreamed of being a great actress. She knew that she was no Sarah Bernhardt, no Eleanora Duse, not even a Lotta Crabtree. She knew that if she kept working at it, she could become a competent actress within a limited range. She was a still a beauty, and audiences responded to that, but she was twenty-seven years old now, and her looks would not last forever.

What the immediate future would bring, Carlotta had no idea. The tour was nearly over, and none of the offers that had made careers for previous Luanas had come her way. She had left Los Angeles with a good deal of popularity, even acclaim, among audiences, but no motion-picture offers. She had heard nothing from Chamberlain Brown's office about theater roles for next year. The prospect of continuing to tour in *The Bird of Paradise* next year, if the offer were to come from Morosco, was utterly disheartening.

Carlotta began to think seriously of Mel's offer. Yes, there appeared to be a ridiculous difference in ages. He was twenty, and she was twenty-seven. But, of course, nobody would think anything of that if the ages were reversed. Mel had convinced her in his letters and in their time together during the last week that he was no longer a boy, but a young man who could function effectively in the world. She believed he was fully capable of doing what he said he would do. She had no doubt that he loved her as she had never been loved. She knew that ardor like this could never last, but she thought it was enough to get them through the rough patches of the first year, and then it was pretty much a matter of will anyway. As for her feeling about him, she was fond of him, a feeling that she had to admit still had something of the maternal in it. But she had a growing respect for his mind and his practical capabilities, and she enjoyed his company. They had the same background, the same way of looking at things, something that, as she well knew after Jack Moffat and his family, counted for a good deal in a marriage. And marriage would mean security, comfort, enough money, and, if she were to leave the theater, even a rise in social status for her and her mother. She had no desire to act in San Francisco. If she went to live in Oakland, it would be as Mrs. Melvin Chapman, Jr., not as Carlotta Monterey.

As she and Mel wrote back and forth during the rest of the tour, Carlotta came to feel that he was the only stable thing in her life. When the tour was winding to its end, Oliver Morosco told Carlotta that he had decided to look for a new Luana to make the show "fresh" for the new season. Carlotta doubted that she would have taken the part in any case, but she would like to have been offered it. When she contacted Chamberlain Brown's office, she was told that they had nothing in mind for her, but if she came to New York, she would be positioned to take what came up. Carlotta had saved enough money so that she could spend another summer in New York if she needed to, but the thought of the stifling city, the loneliness of a hotel room or tiny apartment, broken by weekly visits to the agent's office alongside the other actresses in search of work—humiliating to her now that she had been a leading lady—and the general anxiety of being unengaged, was daunting. But to go back to Oakland, to live with the Chapmans and her mother, in the shadow of the stultifying atmosphere of the Bay Area's version of "good society," that was not a pleasant prospect either. She could not see herself living a life where her greatest ambition was to be the belle of the ball in Oakland.

When the tour reached its final stop in Rhode Island and the company was preparing to disband, Carlotta still had not decided what to do. Listening to the other members of the company talking about their plans for the summer and fall, she found she envied the ones who were already engaged for the next season, their futures decided at least that far. When Fanny Yantis and Anne Henry asked if she wanted to join them on the afternoon train for New York the next day, she found herself saying, "No, I'm going to go home to California this summer. I need to get away from the theater for a while." It was not something she had planned to say or had even thought of, but it came out as naturally as if it had all been worked out in advance. The next afternoon, before the last performance of *The Bird of Paradise*, she went to Western Union and sent a telegram to Melvin Chapman, Jr. It said, "Tour is over. I am yours if you want me. Love, Carlotta." When she got back to the room after the show and a little farewell supper for the company, an enormous bouquet of red roses and a telegram awaited her. The telegram read, "You are my heart's desire. Come on the next train. I adore you. Mel."

After receiving Carlotta's telegram, Mel had rushed immediately to the Western Union office and sent his answer. It was almost as if he had to claim her before she took her offer back. He didn't remember a thing about the walk when he got home. All he could think of was that Carlotta would be his. His night was spent lying awake and planning the many ways he would prepare for her arrival. Although sleepless and a little punchy the next morning, he was determined to tell his father the news, and he sat a while over several cups of coffee while he thought about his approach.

He knew it would come as no surprise to Mel Sr. that his son had proposed to Carlotta. He had made no secret of his devotion in the last year, and his father saw the letters going back and forth and knew of his trip to Peoria. What he did not know was that his father, having seen this coming long ago, had thought a good deal about what his reaction should be, and had discussed the situation with Nellie. When, with a show of manly gravity, Mel Jr. came to his office and sat across from his desk as he told him that, not only had he proposed but Carlotta had accepted, his father was a little taken aback in spite of himself. He hadn't expected to be dealing with a fait accompli. He leaned back in his chair and said, "I'm happy for you, son. I was expecting something of the kind. It's no secret how you feel about Hazel—Carlotta."

Mel Jr.'s face relaxed into a smile. "Yes, I know it's obvious, Dad, but I couldn't care less about that. Today I'd like the whole world to know how I feel."

His father smiled in return. "That's how it should be, son. If you don't feel that way before you marry, you have some hard times coming afterwards. I've thought about this a good deal, and I can make all the objections you're expecting. You are very young to make this decision. You haven't even finished law school. You aren't in control of your money for another year, so it's up to me to see that it is spent wisely. And of course, Carlotta is seven years older and has a great deal more experience of the world than you. And, of course, she's Nellie's daughter. Your expression is telling me you know all that. And I'm telling you I know you know it. What I want to tell you is that I made a mistake myself when I was not nearly so young as you, but almost in the same position. You know that I loved your mother and that we made a good life together. You're the best part of that life. But I was not completely fair in marrying her. As I'm sure you know, I had never gotten over my first love, Nellie, whom I gave up because I didn't think I was ready to marry. That decision affected not only Nellie and me, but your mother and you and Chris Tharsing and Hazel. I'm not the man to stand in the way of your marriage. The only thing I worry about is whether Hazel cares for you as you do for her."

Mel Jr. laughed a little. "Nobody could care for anyone the way I care for her," he said. "I'm gone on her, I know, but I'm not a raving lunatic, Dad. I know that she's not in love with me the way I am with her. But I can tell she's sincere when she says she cares for me and I believe she wants to be with me. I know it's a strange pairing from the outside, but we are good together. We see things the same way, laugh at the same things, think a lot of the same things. And we complement each other. She gives me something to work for, a purpose to my life that I've never had before. I know I will be a better student, a better lawyer, a better man, because of her. And I give her the unquestioned love and support she has always needed and never quite found."

His father nodded. "I know you've always had something special between you, and it's taken on a new depth in the last year. And I can see that you've matured a good deal in that time, but you're still only twenty years old. Let me ask you, are you intent on establishing your own household, or would you be content to live here and keep me company in this enormous house after you're married?"

Mel smiled. "I knew you'd want that, Dad, and I've talked with Carlotta about it. She's happy to live on Santa Clara Avenue for now."

"And she's willing to give up her career?"

Mel looked at him. "I think she's ready to give up her career, but I told her that if she finds she can only be happy on the stage, that's all right with me. I won't keep her here in domesticated misery. This isn't the nineteenth century."

"Well," said his father. "That's a complication I hope you don't have to face. I think you're right not to hold her back. Nothing good comes of that kind of situation. But it might make difficulties for you, both personal and professional."

"I know that, Dad. And I hope I won't be the cause of any problems for the firm. But it's only the real old fogeys who look down on actresses in that way now."

His father smiled. "Well, I'm afraid we have a few old fogeys on the books who bring in quite a bit of money. But we'll have to face that situation if and when it arises. Let's hope that Carlotta has had enough of the acting bug and is ready for some peace and quiet in Oakland." He spoke with more confidence than he felt, but there was no point in belaboring this hypothetical situation. "You have my blessing, son, for what it's worth. I hope you will be very happy together." He put out his hand, and Mel gripped it.

"It's worth a great deal to me, Dad."

When Carlotta's train pulled into the station in Oakland, Mel had already been waiting on the platform for half an hour. He had engaged a porter and guessed at the car she would be in. He was on hand to swoop her from the steps and lift her to the platform. In five minutes, he had organized the transfer of her luggage to Stanley Place, and they were on the way to his Maxwell touring car, parked next to the station. He managed to contain himself until they reached the house, but once they were inside and the maid had gone in search of Nellie, he gathered Carlotta in a fierce embrace and kissed her with a passion that fairly took her breath away. "Welcome home," he said. Carlotta's face flushed to her hairline, but she smiled up at him with shining eyes.

Walking into the hall, Nellie smiled wryly. Mel Sr. had prepared her for the situation. "I see you two haven't wasted any time," she said.

"I feel that we've wasted a lot of time," said Mel. "But I'm very happy with the result." Nellie laughed, Hazel beamed, and they all went into the front parlor for a celebratory glass of Champagne, which Nellie had been keeping on ice.

As they sat down, Nellie in her accustomed arm chair, Mel and Carlotta, appropriately, on the love seat, Nellie asked about their plans for the wedding.

They looked at each other and burst out laughing together. "We have no idea," said Carlotta.

"The sooner the better," said Mel.

Nellie smiled and shook her head. "I suppose it should be small and simple, since it's Hazel's second. Does that suit you?"

"It suits me fine," said Mel. "What about you, Carlotta?"

Carlotta smiled at him. "Fine," she said. "I'm very tired of being on display. A simple wedding with just the family will just suit me. You can sing, Mother."

"We'll have a Gotchett family choir," said Nellie. "Everyone will sing."

"A small weekday six o'clock wedding with supper afterwards, and then we'll be off," said Carlotta. "Where should we go, Mel?"

Mel laughed. "Now that's something I *have* thought of," he said. "But it's a secret."

"You see, Mother," said Carlotta, "we do think of the important things."

They chatted a while longer, the young people in a mood of hilarity and Nellie cheerful and tolerant. When the luggage arrived, she banished Mel and told him to bring his father back for dinner, so they could celebrate. Once they were alone, her talk with her daughter took on a different tone. "Hazel," she asked. "Why are you marrying Mel? It's not just because you're tired of touring, is it?"

Carlotta bridled. "Of course not, Mother. Mel is the kindest, most thoughtful person I know, and that's from knowing him since he was a boy. But he's grown up now. The week we spent together in Peoria showed me how much he loves me, and that I really do care for him. Spending time with him is the most natural, most restful thing in the world for me. We see things the same way. He understands and appreciates me far more than Jack Moffat ever did, even after three years of marriage. And he's much deeper and more intelligent than we've given him credit for, Mother. With me to help, I know he can have a successful career in the law."

"And are you willing to give up the theater for this?"

Carlotta looked her mother full in the eye. "I am, Mama. Just now, I can't imagine ever setting foot on a stage again. But if I ever should want to go back to the theater, Mel is willing to support my decision. He can't bear the thought that I should be unhappy. He says that if I want to act here or go back to New York, he will stand behind me."

"He says that now, but of course he may feel differently if it actually happens."

Carlotta smiled. "I'll make sure he promises in writing. But in all sincerity, Mama, I really don't expect it to happen. I know now why so many good actresses retire from the stage when they marry. It isn't just because the husbands insist on it. There is a great deal to loathe about the theater, even when you're a leading lady. It is so lonely when you're touring, or even when you're in a play in New York. On the road, I thought a lot about how wonderful it would be to be raising my own family in a comfortable home."

Nellie suppressed a smile at the thought of Hazel pining away for the domestic life. "But that can be confining too, as you know."

"Yes, but I'm older and wiser than I was the first time around. I'm more willing to make compromises."

"Well, dear, you know yourself best. I want you to be happy. And you know I have never been enthusiastic about your being on the stage after you gave up on your singing."

Nellie was far more skeptical about the future of this marriage than she gave away in her conversation with her daughter. But she could tell, both from her communications with her and from what Mel Jr. had said, that Hazel was deeply unhappy in the theater. She thought that was probably the real source of her illness in the spring, and that the appearance of Mel, so devoted to her and always ready to do anything he could to please and amuse her, was what had led to her recovery. That kind of devotion was what her daughter seemed to need. She knew that infatuation like young Mel's would not last forever, but she reflected that the two young people had always gotten along well together, and if he was willing to give her the loving attention she craved, maybe this would be the stable future she needed. And Nellie had another reason for approving the marriage. With her daughter living in the Santa Clara Avenue house, especially if a baby came along, there would be an obvious reason for Nellie to move in as well, without the social censure that could ruin the Chapman Trefethen law firm. There was a chance that, at long last, she and her Mel could live under the same roof.

The young couple settled on an early fall date for their marriage. Carlotta enjoyed this engagement a great deal more than she had her first. There was no worry about her trousseau. She needed very little, and she had saved enough money so that she could buy the lingerie and other new clothes she wanted, without a lot of sewing. The Chapman house was well supplied with all the household goods they would need. With Mel Sr.'s blessing and financial backing, she redecorated the bedroom and sitting room that would be hers and Mel's after their marriage. She had the flowered wallpaper stripped and replaced it with a soft eggshell paint on the walls, got rid of the dark, heavy Victorian furniture and replaced it with a bedstead, tables, and dressers in the fashionable Queen Anne style, put up light blue curtains, and bought comfortable upholstered chairs and a sofa for the sitting room. Both father and son agreed it was a big improvement. Carlotta felt it would be their little island within the big, old-fashioned house.

There was no lack of social activity during the summer. Mel was delighted to show off his beautiful fiancée at the various social events the Chapmans, as one of the first families of Oakland, had on their calendar. Carlotta had officially shaved off several years from her age when she went on the stage, and she made a point of dressing and styling her hair to look young so there seemed to be no comment on the difference in ages. As far as official social events went, Mel Jr.'s choice of a wife had not altered the Chapmans' social standing at all. Any fallout from Carlotta's career or divorce would come in more subtle ways. And she had learned so well under the tutelage of the Moffats that no one in Oakland society could suggest that she had anything but the most refined manners. To the few society matrons who tried to high-hat her, she behaved with such aristocratic hauteur that they never tried it again. Soon the couple was considered a catch at dinner parties among Oakland's young professional and business class, and Mel Sr. felt he could relax about the effect of the marriage on the firm.

Meanwhile, Carlotta had renewed her friendship with Celia Shay, the wife of her cousin Frank, now a lawyer. Celia had been her best friend and confidante during her last year with Moffat. It was she who had taken Carlotta camping out on the Shays' rural property to get away from Jack when she had felt threatened by him. She had stood by her staunchly in the spring of 1914 as she went through the humiliating process of having the divorce summons printed in the newspaper. With Celia as her confidante and guide to the social landscape, Carlotta did not feel as isolated in Oakland society as she might have, and the two couples had a lot of fun together outside the stuffy social scene.

Chapter 24

On Thursday, October 12, 1916, Hazel N. T. Moffat was married to Melvin C. Chapman, Jr. in a small service conducted by the Rev. F. J. Van Horn. As Nellie had promised, the Gotchetts did sing, making a much better choir than the church's regular one. Mel Sr. and Nellie provided a Champagne supper afterwards for an increasingly jovial group of family and close friends. The bride and groom were having such a good time that it was hard for them to make up their minds to leave, but finally they made their way to their first night together at the Fairmont hotel in San Francisco.

Mel's passion for Carlotta had only increased during their engagement, and she had put aside the conventional idea of waiting for sex until after they were married. She was not about to repeat the mistake she had made with Jack Moffat. This time she would be sure that her new husband was as interested in sex as she was and was capable of performing to her satisfaction. During the summer and fall, she and Mel had taken to spending their free afternoons driving or walking in the country. The isolation pro-vided plenty of opportunity for privacy, of which they took full advantage. Mel was delighted to find that Carlotta not only was a willing partner, but often took the lead in their lovemaking. He was an ardent but not an experienced lover, and Carlotta enjoyed sharing the techniques and tricks she had learned from that self-described expert Lou Tellegen. They tried every position they could think of in the Maxwell, and they took a blanket with them on their walks, which made for a greater luxury of space in the countryside. Sex proved to be the best part of their relationship. Mel simply could not believe his good fortune, and Carlotta looked forward to a richly satisfying marriage.

As they rested in each other's arms in the middle of their wedding night, Carlotta found herself laughing out loud.

"What's so funny?" asked Mel, smiling down at her.

"Nothing. Only this is a lot different than my first honeymoon."

"For the better, I hope."

"Oh yes, definitely for the better."

The next day, they took their time driving to Half Moon Bay, where they were to spend the weekend. Aside from the name, Mel had chosen the little coastal town because he wanted privacy on their honeymoon, and Carlotta had no wish to get on a train or to go anywhere she had toured in *The Bird of Paradise*. He had found a little inn in this beautiful setting on a motoring tour down the coast, and he knew Carlotta would appreciate the privacy. They spent three days in a romantic idyll such as only the California coast could provide. The combination of warm sunshine, a beautiful view of the ocean, and a simple, comfortable room were all they could have asked for as a background to their first days together. They took walks on the beach and short drives to look at the scenery, but they were always delighted to get back to their room, where they made jokes about the novelty of making love in a bed.

On Monday, they drove back to Oakland and began their married life. Mel went back to his law classes and Carlotta began the process of becoming Mrs. Melvin Chapman, Jr. To smooth the way socially, Carlotta informed Chamberlain Brown that she had married and retired from the stage. The agency duly gave out a press notice, which was printed in many of the California papers. Preparing the way for Carlotta to take her place as mistress of the house, Mel Sr. had let his housekeeper go. She asserted herself with the servants, trying to train a reluctant California cook, maid, and chauffer into the ideal of British service as she had seen it practiced. She got advice from Nellie about managing the household budget and proved to be good enough at it to cover up her periodic extravagances. And she and Mel attended a good many social events.

In early December, Carlotta was deep into plans for redecorating when she began to feel sick. At first, she dismissed the nausea and general lethargy as a touch of food poisoning or a light case of the grippe, which was going around. But when the symptoms went on for a week, she began to get a little worried. When Nellie came by to have tea and look at fabric swatches, Carlotta told her the symptoms and asked if she thought she should see a doctor. Nellie cocked her head and looked at her daughter.

"Are you running a fever?" she asked.

"No, I don't think so."

"Is your monthly regular?"

"Why, I don't know, Mama. It isn't due for a few days."

Nellie grinned. "Well, wait and see, but I don't think you're sick, my darling, I think you're pregnant."

Carlotta's eyes widened. "But I can't be pregnant. It's too soon. We take precautions."

Nellie's wry smile emerged. "Apparently not precautions enough. I could be wrong, of course, but if nothing happens in the next week, you should go to the doctor."

Nellie proved to be right, as usual. Just six weeks after she was married, Carlotta was pregnant. She and Mel had planned to wait at least until after he had finished law school and they had a regular income, but this thing had happened regardless. When she broke the news to Mel, Carlotta was surprised at his reaction. Since he had agreed enthusiastically about birth control and putting off the pregnancy, she had assumed he was as reluctant to bring a child into the marriage as she was. But he was delighted by the news, and so were Nellie and Mel Sr. For the next nine months, Carlotta found herself the uncomfortable center of attention in the house on Santa Clara Avenue. Her nausea intensified so that she felt sick and miserable throughout the first four months of her pregnancy. Because the nausea was so bad, she gained very little weight during that time, but afterwards, she developed a voracious appetite and watched helplessly as her body grew and grew till she found it unrecognizable. It was not only her belly but her hips that spread. She felt as though a whole new layer of fat had suddenly appeared on her body.

Carlotta did not believe Mel for a minute when he told her how beautiful she looked, nor did she appreciate her father-in-law's references to "our little Madonna." But it was Nellie who got on her nerves the most. The mother who had never had time for her own daughter as a child suddenly became obsessed with her coming grandchild. She offered endless maternal advice, and as the due date drew nearer, she badgered Carlotta about making preparations for the baby. Carlotta put off her mother as much as she could with complaints that she was tired and didn't feel well. After the first four or five months, she exaggerated this and privately wondered what was wrong that she could summon no interest in preparing for this baby.

When Nellie realized that her daughter was not going to do anything, she took the bull by the horns and did it herself. She designated the room next to Carlotta and Mel's as the nursery, ordered baby furniture for it, and decorated it with nursery rhyme illustrations and what Carlotta thought of as sappy pictures of babies. Then she set about putting together a layette. She bought the best when it came to clothing, bedding, receiving blankets, and all the other accoutrements. Carlotta was amazed one afternoon during her seventh month to come into the parlor and find her mother knitting.

"Mother, what are you doing?" she asked.

Nellie gave her a preoccupied look. "I'm knitting a cap and booties for baby," she said. "We'll need them at first, even though it will be August when the baby is born."

Carlotta looked at her as though she had said she was painting a fresco on the dining room wall.

"When did you learn to knit?" she asked.

Nellie glanced up in surprise. "Why I learned to knit as a girl," she said. "I used to knit all the time when you were little. Don't you remember? I sewed and knitted all your baby things and your little clothes. There was nowhere to buy them and no one out there in the middle of nowhere to help me."

"I thought you hated that kind of domestic work."

"Well, it's different when you're doing it for the little one." She looked at her daughter. "You know you used to do such lovely embroidery at St. Gertrude's. Don't you want to make a Christening dress for the baby? I never could do any fine work like that."

"I'm too nervous for that, Mother. Now that I don't feel deathly exhausted or nauseous all the time, it seems that I can't sit still." She turned away. "I'm going to take a little walk before we have tea. "

Nellie sent a concerned look after her. She had known that Hazel wouldn't take well to pregnancy. Her daughter had been looking forward to a carefree few years once she had made up her mind to give up the struggle of the theater. The pregnancy had come as a shock, and the changes in her body and forced seclusion from social activity were bound to tell on her. But Nellie was beginning to think her daughter's lack of interest in the baby was unnatural. Nellie had been nervous about her own pregnancy, but by the seventh month, she had been eagerly looking forward to seeing her baby. She had thought it was the same with every girl.

Nellie wondered if her own behavior toward her daughter was somehow to blame. She had done what she thought was best for Hazel in leaving her with Mary and John, and then at St. Gertrude's, while she did everything she could to earn a comfortable living for her, but she had never had time to pay much attention to her when she was little. She knew now that Hazel resented this, feeling that her mother had deserted her as a child, and she was afraid it had left her without a real sense of what it was to be a mother. She hoped that would come during those first few weeks that brought love to a mother's heart. Meanwhile, she would do what she could to prepare a home for the child. She felt that being a grandmother was a second chance of sorts, to do things right this time. The child would know that it had loving grandparents at least.

Carlotta's baby girl was born on the twentieth of August 1917, and named Cynthia Jane, after Mel's grandmother. Nellie and Mel Sr. were as delighted as if the child of their son and daughter were their own child. Mel Jr. was happy when the baby arrived, but mostly relieved that Carlotta was all right. Carlotta felt slightly disgusted when the nurse first showed her the baby. Its twitching body was a blotchy red color, its squinched little red face topped by a pointed head with a swatch of black hair. She turned to her mother with a look of dismay.

"Is something wrong with it?" she asked.

"No, no," said Nellie. "They all look like that at first. You'll see how sweet she looks once she's really cleaned up." Exhausted from the long delivery and still groggy from the gas they had given her, Carlotta fell asleep. When she woke, her mother was gone and the nurse, holding a tightly wrapped pink bundle, was squeezing her shoulder. "Your daughter is hungry, Mrs. Chapman," she said. "Would you like to feed her?"

"Oh, I won't be nursing her," Carlotta said sleepily. "There must be some mistake."

"Yes, I know that, but we like to give our mothers the chance to feed their babies themselves. It gets things off to a good start."

Carlotta looked at the pink bundle and shook her head. "I'm sorry nurse," she said. "I'm much too sleepy to manage that now. I might fall asleep and drop her."

The nurse was taken aback. "Would you like to hold her for a few minutes before I take her away?"

Carlotta lay back on the pillows. "Not now," she said.

"All right," said the nurse. "I'll bring her in for the next feeding."

Carlotta saw that she was not going to escape this forever, so the next time the nurse came with the baby, she agreed to feed her. The nurse put the baby carefully into the crook of her arm, telling her to be sure to support her head. She showed her how to test the temperature of the formula on her wrist and how to hold the bottle to keep the baby from swallowing air bubbles. "If she gets sleepy," she said, "just jiggle the nipple a little and she'll get back to work." Then she left her alone with the baby.

Carlotta looked closely into the pudgy red face as it sucked away at the nipple. This baby looked nothing like her, or Mel for that matter. Nellie had told her that the blue eyes would turn to brown in a few weeks, and then she would see the resemblance, but she doubted it. She watched for a while as the baby sucked away, but then her arm grew tired and she wondered if it was all right to shift her around a little. She tried to hold the bottle upright, so the bubbles would stay at the top, but her wrist would get tired and it would sag. The minutes were leaden. She just wished the nurse would come back. Suddenly the baby pulled back from the nipple and let out a yell. Carlotta was amazed to find that something this small could emit a sound that loud. Then she let out another and another, and Carlotta had no idea what to do. She tried to shush her by rocking her, but she just got louder. In a few minutes the nurse returned and said, "I see Baby is exercising her lungs."

With an expert movement, she picked her up and put her over her shoulder, thumping her on the back. Soon a loud burp came out, and the baby began to quiet down. "It was just gas bothering her," she said. You have to be careful that she doesn't take in the bubbles."

"I thought I had been," said Carlotta.

"Well, no need to worry. You'll get it right next time." And with that she left with the baby, to reappear in four hours.

In this advanced hospital, Cynthia was kept on a strict schedule of feeding every four hours, which Carlotta was told must be enforced until she was four months old. Sometimes the baby was asleep when she was brought in, and it was hard to wake her up to feed her. Sometimes she was yelling at the top of her lungs and latched onto the bottle as if she were starving. The nurse told Carlotta not to worry, that Baby would get used to the schedule eventually and wake regularly, ready to feed. For Carlotta, the feeding schedule was relentless. Every four hours— two, six, ten, two, six, ten—the baby and bottle were presented to her, and she must do her best to deal with them, whether it was in the middle of the night or at dawn when she was falling asleep herself. During afternoon visiting hours, Carlotta was relieved to have Nellie do the feeding, cooing over the little bundle and talking baby talk so that Carlotta hardly recognized her brusque, businesslike mother. But the rest of the time, it was just her and Cynthia. She felt as if she were in a long, dark tunnel with the time closing in on her in waves of four hours, four hours, four hours.

At the end of her week in the hospital, a great burden was lifted when Carlotta turned the baby over to Oto, the Japanese nurse they had hired to care for her. She told Oto to decide what the feeding schedule should be. An experienced and capable nanny, Oto was as happy to take charge of the baby and the nursery as Carlotta was to have her do it. Before long they established a routine that was based on what Carlotta had seen in the great English houses during her marriage to Moffat. In the morning, she would come into the nursery to check on the baby and discuss the schedule for the day with Oto, just as she discussed the day's menu with the cook. At about four in the afternoon, when Nellie had taken to coming for tea, Oto brought the baby down for her grandmother to hold and play with for an hour or so. When Mel came home, he and Carlotta would go up to the nursery to visit the baby and get Oto's report on the day, and often Mel Sr. would look in when he arrived later in the evening.

Carlotta had little to do with Cynthia directly, although she did accompany Mel as he proudly and somewhat self-consciously wheeled his daughter up and down the street in the baby carriage, accepting compliments on her from the neighbors. She also went with her mother to take the baby on visits to the Gotchett relatives. She was a little embarrassed on these excursions, for despite being done up in spotless ruffled and embroidered caps and dresses, Cynthia was not a very attractive baby. Her eyes had turned brown, as Nellie had predicted, but they were not the infinite black pools of her mother or even the warm brown of her father, but a muddy brown with green flecks in it. Her hair did not grow curly and luxuriant like Carlotta's, but thin and lanky and straight as a poker. Oto could never get a bow to stay in it for long. Despite people's compliments, Carlotta did not think Cynthia's face was attractive either. Her skin was sallow rather than her mother's glowing ivory, and her features were not in perfect balance. She was a plain baby who would grow up to be a plain woman. Carlotta had hoped to be able to take an interest in planning for her future, perhaps avoiding the missteps and detours of her own career to do something really extraordinary. But she thought the best this child could do would be to marry a man who was a "good provider" and live out her life in Oakland. It pained her to think that the life she was settling for was probably the best her daughter could achieve.

Chapter 25

As the fall of 1917 dwindled into a cold, rainy winter, Carlotta's disappointment in the baby, the tedious routine of the household and nursery, and her now less than exciting sex life with Mel set off an urgent need to change her circumstances. Rather than the refuge from the theater that she had thought it would be, this domestic life was turning into a new kind of trap. She was becoming that cliché of clichés, a middle-class wife and mother, and not a particularly successful one. She had an unattractive baby to bring up, a callow law student for a husband, and no real home of her own for years to come. She began to feel that, as trying as it could be, the theater was better than this. There, at least she had her own identity and the applause of the audience for her work. With an eye toward enforcing the agreement that she and Mel had about her returning to the stage, she thought she might test the waters by writing to Chamberlain Brown to see if there would be anything available for her.

During a particularly dreary spell in February, Carlotta wrote a letter saying breezily that she was becoming bored with her retirement into domestic bliss and asking whether there would be any interest in her returning to the stage. Within the week, Brown wrote that the agency would welcome her back, but she would have to work her way slowly at first after having retired. "We don't want to make a big splash about your return and give everybody the idea that you're divorced. You can't keep giving farewell performances and coming back. You're not Sarah Bernhardt." Carlotta knew that very well, but she wished people wouldn't remind her of it.

Now came the difficult part. She began by talking to Mel for several days about how depressed she felt and how restrictive the domestic life was, ending their conversations in tears. By the third day, he was really paying attention. Worried about a downward turn in her always volatile emotional state, he told her he would do all he could to help her break out of her depression. "I would love to just jump in the car and drive off somewhere," he said, "but this is a really tough time with my studies. At the end of the semester, I'll be through with school, and then we'll do something exciting. Can you hold on till June? In the meanwhile, we can liven things up by thinking of exotic places to travel to."

Carlotta looked at him with a brave smile. "Thanks, Mel," she said. "You always do your best for me. I'll have to try and bring myself out of this melancholy."

As the days went by, Carlotta did one of her best acting jobs, ultimately convincing her young husband that she was showing alarming signs of depression. Finally, on a darkening Sunday afternoon, she told him that she felt she needed a complete break from routine to shake off her melancholy. "If I went to New York and plunged into the theater for a season, I'm sure it would revive me."

Mel looked at her in dismay. "You want to leave us and go to New York? Are you thinking of taking Cynthia with you?"

It was Carlotta's turn to be dismayed. She hadn't considered this. With an effort, she gathered herself together and said quietly, "No, Mel. I've thought that through, and I think the best thing for Cynthia is to be here in her home with Oto to care for her, and you and Mother and your father to watch over her. I couldn't possibly do a good job of that with all the demands on me in the theater."

He looked incredulous. "You would leave your daughter behind?"

She tried to look self-sacrificing. "I think it would be better for her."

"But you're a wife and mother, Carlotta. You can't just go off and leave us like this."

Carlotta felt the anger rising, but she controlled herself by keeping the end in view. She straightened her back and said, "We have an agreement, Mel. You promised that you would let me go if that is what I need to do."

His bewildered look met her determined one. "But that was before Cynthia came. Everything is different now."

"Some things are different, but unfortunately, I seem to be the same. I can't stand this confining life any longer, Mel. And if I can't go back to the theater, I'm sure something more drastic will happen."

In the end, Carlotta was successful in convincing Mel to let her go. This meant selling some of his property, an apartment that his mother had left him, to pay for her expenses and supplement her theatrical wardrobe. He was not happy about this, but he had to admit that he'd agreed to her going back on the stage if she needed to—had, in fact, suggested it. At some level, he had always known that she would not be content to stay in Oakland for long, and if he had a hope of holding her in the marriage, he would have to concede her a certain amount of freedom. It was with difficulty that he explained this to his father, but in the end, Mel Sr., who knew Carlotta nearly as well as his son did, saw that letting her try the New York theater again was probably the best course to take. He agreed to give her an allowance out of his income from the law firm until she was earning enough to live on.

The changed circumstances in the Santa Clara Avenue household meant a change for Nellie and Mel Sr. as well. The need for someone to take charge of Cynthia while Carlotta was away created a perfectly acceptable rationale for Nellie to move into the house with her granddaughter. She and Mel could live under the same roof at last. It was also a good war time strategy. Before the spring of 1918, World War I had not had much material impact on the Chapman and Tharsing households. Like other patriotic Americans, they avoided canned goods and observed "Meatless Tuesdays" and "Wheatless Wednesdays" in order to conserve meat, fats, wheat and sugar so they could be sent overseas, but their lives continued pretty much as always. Mel Jr. was not yet twenty-one when the first draft registration was held on the fifth of June in 1917, so, for the moment, the family was not worried that he would have to leave law school to go and fight in the trenches. But they knew it was coming. And Mel Sr. could foresee shortages not only in food, but in coal, gasoline, and other necessities if the war continued for long. He and Nellie agreed that it made sense for them to consolidate their households and invest the money from Stanley Place house in commercial real estate.

After a good deal of discussion, it was decided that Carlotta would go to New York as soon as she was ready, get settled in an apartment, and make contact with Chamberlain Brown in order to take advantage of any summer parts that were available at the end of the season. When the academic year ended, Mel Jr. would join her in New York, and Nellie would take charge of Cynthia for the summer. This arrangement made all parties reasonably happy.

After spending a few weeks putting her basic wardrobe together and making a determined effort to shed what was left of her baby weight, Carlotta took the train to New York and enlisted Kitty Smith to help look for apartments. They found an attractive and comfortable place, fully furnished, for just thirty-five dollars a month in the Bronx, near Kitty's. Carlotta moved in with just her luggage. After her trunks were delivered, she closed the door to her little foyer and surveyed the sitting room, bedroom, kitchenette and bath with pleasure. For the next few months at least, this was her private little domain. She unpacked her clothing and placed it in closets, wardrobes, and dressers with her usual efficiency. The very next day, she paid a visit to Chamberlain Brown. Twenty minutes later, she was invited into the inner office and could not help preening a bit when she walked by the other actresses, some of whom had been sitting in the waiting room for hours.

"Welcome, Miss Monterey," said Brown, taking her gracefully extended hand. "We're glad to have you back."

"I'm glad to be back, Mr. Brown," she said with a dazzling smile. "It seems I simply could not stay away from the theater."

He offered her a chair and got right to business. "It looks like we have a part for you right away," he said. "It's not much, but it's a start to kind of get your feet wet again. You know Philip Bartholomae? He wrote *Very Good Eddie*."

"That's a musical."

"Yes, but this one isn't. It's a comedy called *All Night Long*, just a little farce about exchanging a wedding present and trying to get it back when the person who gave it shows up to visit. It's a summer play, light stuff. If it doesn't go in New York, the Shuberts are planning to put it on out of town."

Carlotta tried to mask her quick panic with a show of nonchalance. "It's not a tour, is it?" she said, leaning back elegantly and crossing her legs. "I'm really not interested in another long tour."

He smiled. "No, no, not a tour. They just plan to put it on nearby. In Philadelphia, and maybe some summer theaters in Jersey. It's a show for the summer. It opens in the middle of June. It will keep you busy until they start casting for the big shows in the fall."

"That sounds like a possibility," she said. "I should tell you, though, that I'm married to an attorney now, from a very prominent firm in San Francisco. He doesn't approve of the gypsy life of the theater and does not want me to enter into a business arrangement without a contract."

"I understand, Mrs. Chapman. We would be interested in a five-year contract as your agents if that would be satisfactory to you. The reports on *The Bird of Paradise* from the West Coast and some other cities were very positive. I know you made quite a hit in some places. I'm pretty confident that, down the road, we could arrange a long-term contract with the Shuberts. But you have to understand that New York producers are interested in success in New York. You did well here in *Taking Chances*, but you'll need to get some more credits before we can look for any kind of long-term contract for you."

"That seems reasonable to me. I'm not interested in touring anyway. I think I've more than paid my dues there, and my husband would be much more comfortable if I'm established here in New York and not traveling all over the country."

"Very well. I'll have the contract drawn up and you can have your husband review it if you like."

"That sounds agreeable."

"Meanwhile, you can take a look at *All Night Long*."

Carlotta found that "light stuff" didn't begin to describe the silly froth that was *All Night Long*. But it was a paycheck, and it would get her through the summer. She would be busy and earning money, justifying her absence from Oakland. But after the show played for just four performances in New York, Carlotta found herself on the road again, with much less comfort than in the *Bird of Paradise* days. Her bit part did not entitle her to any amenities, and she had the most basic accommodations, but this had its compensations. Fortunately, the show only went to Philadelphia and two towns on the Jersey Shore. She found that without the responsibility of the lead, she could relax and enjoy herself with the other cast members, who treated their time on the shore as a kind of paid vacation. With her new feeling of freedom, she behaved more like the free-spirited California girl of her youth and felt some of the old camaraderie of the Academy days revive. Adopting this new persona with the other show people, she began to think she could find her way to really enjoying a life in the theater.

Because the show was touring, Mel did not join Carlotta until the run was over, toward the end of July. His circumstances had changed when a second draft registration was held on June 5, 1918, signing up everyone who had turned twenty-one in the last year. Now he was subject to being drafted at any time. When he arrived in New York, he had to notify the local draft board. He and Carlotta planned for his stay in the city to be a temporary one. To make the best of things, they moved into a new, rather luxurious apartment, on Sixth-Third street, overlooking Central Park, and set out to enjoy a couple of weeks in the city before Carlotta was to start rehearsals for *Mr. Barnum*.

The play was a big spectacle about the circus, including several of P. T. Barnum's acts, like the Wild Man, the Living Skeleton, a snake charmer, and two lady bareback riders, one of whom was known as "The Queen of the Arena," and played by Carlotta Monterey. She did not actually have to ride bareback on stage. She was there to bring complications to the plot as a seductive and jealous vamp. Mel found this a waste of her talent. She agreed that it was not the part to make her career, but it was a big show that would attract attention, and it was work. Because Carlotta's part was so small, she felt no particular strain during rehearsals or the brief run of twenty-four performances. She and Mel were able to enjoy the city and even plan little overnight excursions for Sundays.

When *Mr. Barnum* closed at the end of September, Carlotta went right into rehearsals for a play that was much more important to her. The playwright Clare Kummer was a rising star in social comedy who had made a big hit the previous year with *Good Gracious Annabelle*. Critics used adjectives like "gossamer" when describing her plots but applauded her fresh take on up-to-date characters and her witty dialogue, which kept audiences laughing. In the new play, *Be Calm, Camilla*, Carlotta played Celia Brooke, a sophisticated and heartless high-society rival of the young heroine for the hero's affections, a "woman of the world" who torments the poor girl and is vanquished, to the delight of the audience.

The play was ultimately well-received by both critics and audiences, and it ran in New York from Halloween through the holiday season, providing Carlotta with a steady income. On the whole, she was happy with the employment, but unhappy to be cast once again as a heartless vamp, out to steal the leading man from the darling young heroine, what one critic called "a touch of evil in a Cinderella story." She thought that, in the final analysis, Celia was unnecessary and unimportant to the play. She longed to be cast as a leading lady again.

Be Calm, Camilla's popularity was partly based on its providing some escapist comedy during wartime. The dress rehearsals were held before audiences of soldiers who were appreciative both of the laughs and of the pretty women. The fact that the war was winding down did not complete assuage Carlotta's worries when Mel was called up and inducted into the army on the eighth of November. When the Armistice was signed three days later, ending the fighting, she joined in the jubilation that was felt everywhere in the city. She did not know how long Mel would be kept in the service, but she was very happy that her husband would not be going over to fight in the trenches and come back maimed or shell-shocked or with his lungs destroyed from poison gas. To her relief, it turned out that Mel was sent to Camp Johnston in Florida and discharged after spending only a month as a private in the U. S. Army.

Chapter 26

Mel's month in the army proved to be a watershed for him. Although he was only twenty-one himself, he found that he had little in common with most of the other draftees, who were young men without responsibilities. Their talk was all about food and sleep and beer and fast women and how they would spend their pay if they ever got leave. As a husband and father, with a wife in New York and a daughter in Oakland to bring up, Mel found that he had other things to think about. During his month in the army, he came to the conclusion that it was time he stopped dangling after Carlotta and hanging around the theater and assume the responsibilities of a man. He decided that he would have to join the firm and become the breadwinner if he was ever going to take care of his family. After spending the holidays with Carlotta, he returned to Oakland early in January to join Chapman and Trefethen as a clerk and prepare for the bar exam.

During Mel's visit to New York, Carlotta made it clear that she had no intention of leaving the city. She was directing all her effort toward securing a long-term contract with the Shubert Organization. As she saw it, *Be Calm, Camilla* was her ticket to security and ultimate success in New York. When the play had finished a respectable run on Broadway and the touring company was being put together, she had to face a decision. Most of the company was to remain intact for the upcoming engagement in Chicago. Arthur Hopkins, the play's producer, offered Carlotta the role of Celia Brooke. Instead of accepting right away, she asked Chamberlain Brown to see whether the Shuberts would be willing to offer her a long-term contract. He thought it was premature, but when he talked to Lee Shubert, he found him enthusiastic about Carlotta. Selling the idea to his brother J. J., Lee said, "She's original, a new take on the vamp. She's not only beautiful and sexy, she's sophisticated, classy. We can use that now with all these high-society bedroom comedies that have to titillate the matinee audiences but not be banned in Boston. And she's trained. She has some range. I think we could do something with her."

J. J. thought that Lee's enthusiasm might have something of the personal in it. "Tell you what, Lee," he said. "Let's give her some parts, some variety, over the next year or so. That should give us time to see what she can do. If she catches on, we can get something in writing. Let's see how it goes." So Carlotta was not in the Chicago cast of *Be Calm, Camilla*, which proved to be a big surprise hit there, running for weeks and kicking off a year-long tour for the company.

Inspired by the smash hit *Up in Mabel's Room*, the 1918–1919 New York season featured a craze for plays that set up the heroine in an apparently scandalous situation that would lead to social ruin if it was found out, but then showed her to be purely innocent. The twist in *A Sleepless Night* was that a blonde ingenue played the lady who was compromised by going to a man's bedroom and the dark-eyed brunette, Carlotta, was the wife. In a racy touch, both actresses appeared in the new fashion fad of boudoir pajamas during most of the play, Peggy Hopkins in pink, Carlotta in blue. During a lot of frenetic action, the two young women hid in various parts of the room, including under the covers and under the bed, to avoid discovery, affording a lot of chances for physical humor.

Although performing in lingerie was an old story for Carlotta, the physical comedy was a novelty, and she received a good deal of praise for it. The newspaper critics mentioned not only her "deep tones and clear diction" and her "altogether brunette loveliness," but her clever comic timing and the "lithe movements of her plump body" as she dove under the bedclothes or the bed.

Peggy Hopkins was a revelation to Carlotta. She had known many actresses who considered the theater a useful venue for accumulating presents from admiring men and eventually capturing a wealthy benefactor one could marry, or perhaps not, and achieve ease and security in retirement. Carlotta herself had plenty of experience with stage door Johnnies who made theater life more pleasant with flowers, luxurious suppers and little presents. But she had seen nothing like Peggy Hopkins. Although five years younger than Carlotta, she was many years older in worldly wisdom and experience. Having run away from home with a vaudeville performer when she was fifteen, she had immediately dumped him for a millionaire she met on the train. Thus began her career of marriages, engagements, and liaisons with ever richer men, who compensated her with lavish gifts of jewelry, and, when she demanded it, hard cash.

Peggy laughed at Carlotta's romantic notions about love and insisted that true love was a heavy diamond bracelet, preferably one with the price tag still attached. "You've got to make some hay, Carlotta," she would say. "I may have sex appeal, but you're a classic beauty. Men will give a lot for that. You have maybe ten years to really cash in." Carlotta didn't like to think in those terms, but she had to admit that Peggy had a point.

In June of 1919, Carlotta went on to Chicago with *A Sleepless Night*, happy enough to fill these summer weeks with a tour and avoid a return to Oakland. After a plan to take the play to London fell through, she thought she was to have her chance at last. The Shuberts commissioned Owen Davis to write a play with a Spanish locale, featuring Carlotta. To have the lead in a serious play that was written for her by a prominent playwright was Carlotta's dream. But the deal soon fell through, and the play was never written.

In the fall, Lee Shubert agreed to lend Carlotta to the newly announced producing firm of Dodge and Pogany, so she could star in *Esther*, a biblical epic. The producers said that the beauty of her speaking voice was what had made her such a desirable choice for the role, and she was hoping to make her mark with it.

But the theater being what it was, the plans for the producing firm foundered, *Esther* was never produced, and Carlotta was left high and dry for the fall, still contracted to Dodge and Pogany.

Although Carlotta did not have a high regard for movies, when the chance came to fill the empty time with a role in *The Cost*, a film adapted from a novel by the distinguished David Graham Phillips, she decided to take it. Since she considered the movies a form of pantomime that required only the crudest of acting techniques, she had a hard time taking the job seriously. What's more, the medium deprived her of her two chief natural assets as an actress, her carefully trained, richly modulated voice and her luminous beauty, which had never completely come across in photographs. But movies were the coming thing, and from the careers of Lou Tellegen and other people she knew from the theater, she was keenly aware of the fame and fortune that could be achieved in the movies with relatively little effort.

In October, Carlotta found herself at the Eastern Studios, newly opened by the Famous Player–Lasky company at Pierce Avenue and Sixth Street on Long Island. To her chagrin, she was cast once again in the familiar vamp role, as a sophisticated society woman who has an affair with the husband of the virtuous and dutiful wife, who also happens to be her best friend. Carlotta found that making movies was a fast-paced and sometimes chaotic activity, but she also learned that there was more to the silent acting technique than she had thought, and she picked up a great deal by watching more experienced performers. She was pleased to find that she was given a first-rate wardrobe, something that had worried her when she considered the costuming in the few movies she had seen. In the end, the weeks in the Long Island studio turned out to be more interesting than she had expected, but she had no intention of making a career of the movies, however much money there was to be made. Her ambition was to be a leading lady, an actress to be reckoned with.

Carlotta discovered that one nice thing about making a movie was that once it was filmed, it was over. There was no uncertainty about how long it would run, no tour hovering on the horizon. Plans could actually be made in advance. At the beginning of November, she decided to go to Oakland to rest for a few weeks. The Shuberts planned for her to go into a new play, *The Trickstress*, in January, so she would have to be back in New York before Christmas, but she would spend Thanksgiving with the family. Mel had worked very hard in the time that she had been in New York and Chicago. He had passed the bar exam and his father had been very proud to make him a full member of the firm of Chapman and Trefethen. Both he and Nellie had been writing regular reports to Carlotta about Cynthia's progress and what a dear and clever little girl she was becoming. Carlotta was interested to see the development in her young husband and her two-year-old daughter. And she felt that her return to Oakland as a successful Broadway actress would be a much happier occasion for her than the last one had been.

The visit to Oakland proved to be both gratifying and disappointing. Mel had made all sorts of plans to keep her happy and amused while she was there. She saw that he had a great deal more confidence in himself now that his professional role was secure. He carried himself with a quiet assurance, almost dignity. He was also a doting father. It was clear that he and Cynthia adored each other. But Cynthia was a disappointment. She was not much more attractive at two years old than she had been as a baby, and Carlotta did not see the great evidence of cleverness that Mel and Nellie often spoke of. Although it had clearly been explained to her that Carlotta was her mother, it was Nellie Cynthia looked to for security and affection, regarding Carlotta shyly as some sort of dazzling visitor who had been set down mysteriously in their midst. Carlotta had occasional moments when she remembered feeling this way during Nellie's had visits to the Shay household so many years earlier. She resigned herself to the fact that she had no particular feeling of affection for the child. She didn't know how Nellie had felt about her as a little girl, but she took comfort in the fact that her mother had come to care for her later on. Perhaps she would feel the same about her daughter eventually. On the whole, Carlotta enjoyed her time with the family and all the attention she received from other relatives and family friends, but the dominant feeling she had when she boarded the train for New York was relief. She was happy to be going back to New York and work and her own apartment and to be free of emotional entanglements and confusion.

Chapter 27

Carlotta was listed twice in the 1920 census. For 57 Santa Clara Avenue in Oakland, where Mel Chapman Sr. was listed as head of the household, Hazel Chapman, at her true age of thirty-two, was listed as daughter-in-law, her profession as actress. Also listed were her husband, daughter, and mother (as a "roomer"). For 28 West Sixty-Third Street in New York City, Carlotta Monterey, aged twenty-eight, was listed as head of a household of one, her profession as theatrical. This was the state of her identity at the beginning of 1920. With her return to New York, she was determined to leave Hazel behind her and make her mark as Carlotta Monterey. She reflected that her prospects were bright. Partly to make up for the disaster with *Esther*, Lee Shubert had commissioned a play by Clare Kummer's former husband, a fashionable popular novelist, that would feature Carlotta's first starring role in New York. It was a much more congenial part for her than the biblical heroine Esther, and she was looking forward to beginning rehearsals. But just when she returned to the city, she received a letter from Shubert saying that the show had been postponed because Paul Kummer was still working on the book for the new Victor Herbert operetta.

Initially, Carlotta was devastated. It had not occurred to her that this could happen again. She had thought this role would be the making of her career at last. Instead she was left once again with nothing. But this time she had no intention of sitting out the rest of the season waiting for something to happen. She spent most of the next morning preparing to visit the Shubert office. When she arrived, she was the image of sleek sophistication, her stylish cloche hat framing her famous profile, flawless ivory skin, and bee-stung lips, her tastefully fur-trimmed coat just revealing her ankles and hand-made English pumps. She looked more like a fashionable young society lady than an out-of-work actress. This was the effect she needed in order to carry out her strategy for Lee Shubert. She knew that he was attracted to her and that part of the attraction was her distinction from the run-of-the-mill actress.

"Mr. Shubert," she said, sweeping into his office and extending her hand, "please don't get up."

Shubert hadn't thought of getting up, but at this, he made a half-rising motion in his chair and took her hand. "Sorry about the Kummer play," he mumbled, hoping there wasn't going to be a scene. He had a busy day ahead of him.

Carlotta dropped gracefully onto a chair and gave him a rueful smile. "What can one do," she said. "That's show business."

He smiled back, grateful for this reprieve from the expected emotional outburst and the tedious explanations.

"The question," she said, "is how can we best make use of this time? I hate to be idle, and I am determined to fulfill my commitment to you by working. You must have something that could make use of my talent."

He leaned back in his chair and looked at her. "Under the sleek society schtick," he thought, "this is a very determined broad." Then he thought of a nagging issue that had just come up again that morning. The Grace George play was still foundering a little in Washington. He was sure it could use somebody like her. "Tell you what," he said, "there is something that's right up your alley if you want to work right away. There's a honey of a part in the new Grace George play that we're trying to recast."

She shot him a quick, shrewd glance. "Why is the part being recast?"

He looked away and shook his head. "This play is by Frances Nordstrom. You may know her. Good character actress. Well, she insisted on playing this part, and it's all wrong for her. It's a sophisticated society lady, very worldly-wise, who gives some straight advice to her friend, Grace George, about trapping her fiancé into a quick wedding. Frances doesn't look the part, and I think we could spice up the play by having someone with your looks and flair playing it. I think we've finally convinced her that she has to give it up if her play is going to go anywhere. The thing is it's already in tryouts. You would be joining the cast in Baltimore next week, and it would be opening in New York the week after that."

Carlotta leaned toward him, all intelligent concern. "This could be a touchy situation. It's never easy to join a cast that's already formed, and it is certainly not much notice. Are there a lot of lines?"

"Enough. It's the second female role. She has one big scene. You're a pretty quick study though, right?"

"Yes, a week would probably be sufficient."

A happy grin spread across his face. "You know the more I think of this, the better I like it. I think you'd be perfect for the part, and a great contrast to Grace George. If you take this on, we'll owe you one."

She cocked her head and regarded him with an answering smile. "I'll see that you don't forget it," she said. "After all, I have my own way to make in the theater and a little daughter in California to think of."

When Carlotta joined the cast of *The "Ruined" Lady* in Baltimore, she found the situation even more difficult than she had expected. Not only had the cast already formed one of those quick familial bonds that are so common in the theater, but Grace George, for whom Frances Nordstrom had written the play, was devoted to her friend and felt her ill-used by the Shuberts. Carlotta was not exactly embraced by the other actors. But this kind of thing was not new to her. She resolved to put the best face on it, do her work, and hope her relationship with the rest of the company would work itself out over time, as it usually did. She welcomed the role of Olive Gresham as at least not a vamp or an exotic princess, and she was mentioned favorably by several reviewers, who were agreed in their acclaim for Grace George and their indifference to the play, which was just one more bedroom farce with an innocent heroine placed in a compromising position, a premise that was getting very threadbare.

After a New York run of just thirty-three performances, *The "Ruined" Lady* opened in Chicago on the first of March, but Carlotta was not in the cast. Grace George had made it a condition of her taking on the tour that Frances Nordstrom be restored to her role. Since Carlotta's performances had not garnered appreciably better reviews than Nordstrom's, Shubert felt he had no grounds to refuse. Like *Be Calm, Camilla*, the play proved to be a hit in Chicago, where it ran for two months, launching a year-long national tour.

In New York, Carlotta went to see Lee Shubert for what she called a heart-to-heart talk. "I'm just so disappointed and frustrated," she told him. "I've spent so many years, so much hard work, training for the theater and paying my dues, but it doesn't seem to get me anywhere. It's the same old supporting roles over and over, nothing challenging, nothing to show off my talents. You gave me such hope when we had our talk a year ago that you would find roles for me that would make me a leading lady, but nothing seems to work out."

Shifting a bit uncomfortably in his chair, Shubert said, "It's not for lack of trying, you know. It's just the luck of the draw that a couple of shows fell through. You're a real trouper, and believe me, we appreciate your willingness to help us out the way you did with this last show. It's just been a run of bad luck."

Her face flushed, and her eyes betrayed the emotion she was barely keeping in check. "I believe that too," she said. "But I need to have a chance to make my mark with a good role. Time is passing quickly. I won't be twenty-eight forever. I've given up this time with my little girl to concentrate on my profession. I know you may think this is corny, but I really believe that acting is an art. I trained in London with the Royal Academy and in

Paris with vocal instructors from the Opera. My goal has always been to be considered a real artist one day. Not to be vain, but I believe I'm every bit as good as the young actresses who get all the critical praise, like Ethel Barrymore and Helen Hayes. And I *know* I'm as good as Grace George. What I need is a role that will show my range and showcase my talent."

During this speech, the air of cool sophistication Carlotta assumed when dealing with Lee Shubert had given place to a passionate insistence. Her ivory cheeks glowed, her deep brown eyes shone, and her face was alive with emotion. Shubert thought that she looked magnificent, but she seemed overwrought, on the verge of tears. He hated tears from actresses.

"Look, Carlotta," he said. "We know you're good. We think you have a lot of promise. And you've had some tough breaks with us. You've been a real trouper, stepping in when we needed you, and you've never had really bad reviews. I will personally promise to find you a role that shows off more of your talents than you've had so far. But there's nothing like that on the horizon just now. I suggest that you take advantage of the situation with this play to get a few weeks' vacation. Relax and forget about the theater for a while. Go and see your little girl. We'll have some new shows starting in the spring, and there is bound to be something promising for you."

Carlotta knew there was no use in further pleading. She could tell from his body language that he had reached the limit of his patience. But she knew she had made an impression. With an effort of will, she relaxed into a sophisticated attitude, the cool mask once again descending over her features. She bestowed a bewitching smile on him and offered her hand. "Thank you for listening to me," she said. "I hope I haven't bored you with this talk. I just get carried away occasionally when I talk about the theater. I suppose it means more to me than I like to admit."

"Nothing wrong with that," said Shubert, taking her hand. "Take some time off and be sure to give Maggie an address and phone number where we can get in touch with you."

A few days later, Carlotta was not entirely unhappy to be on the Twentieth-Century Limited en route to Chicago, and not to perform in *The "Ruined" Lady*. Soon she was in Oakland, greeted eagerly by her young husband, shyly by her little daughter, and a little reluctantly by her mother, who had a new appreciation for the disruption she must have caused in the Shay family with her visits to Hazel years ago. Carlotta found that Lee Shubert had been right. She had not realized the nervous state she was in before she left New York. Between the situation with *The "Ruined" Lady* and her worries about the future, she had been under a great deal of stress. With Mel's devoted attention and the soothing monotony of the day-to-day life in Oakland, she could feel herself becoming calmer. The obsessive worry about her career began to fade. Toward the end of February, though, she had a new source of anxiety. She suspected that, despite the precautions she and Mel were taking, she might be pregnant. This filled her with dread. She simply could not endure another pregnancy, another birth, another year in Oakland. Within a week, she was sure. She went to see a doctor in San Francisco, who agreed that she was probably pregnant, although it was too soon to know for certain.

Having spent time in San Francisco show business circles, Carlotta knew the names of doctors who would perform abortions, and she also knew the going rate for the best ones, one hundred dollars. She did not have that much money at hand, and she could not ask Mel or her mother for it. There would be too many questions. But she was owed that much by Dodge and Pogany from her contract for *Esther*. She had tried to get the money several times but was always put off with some delaying tactic by their lawyer. Mel could probably get the money, but then she would have to account for it. She decided to enlist Lee

Shubert's aid. She wrote him a letter explaining that she needed the money for an emergency appendectomy and asked his help in prying it loose from Dodge and Pogany. Several telegrams later, Lee Shubert had advanced her the money himself, on the condition that his lawyers would recover it for him. One morning in early March, Carlotta went to San Francisco, telling the family that she was going to stay with an old school friend for a couple of days. She went to a house on Highland Avenue, where the abortion was performed and she was able to recover overnight. When she got back to Oakland, she kept to her room for a few days, pleading a touch of flu. Mel joked about too much Champagne while living the high life in San Francisco but treated her with indulgence. Nellie said nothing. If she suspected the truth, she did not let on.

Carlotta felt an overwhelming sense of relief. Spending time alone in her room, she realized that being trapped in Oakland indefinitely was the greatest dread she had in life. It drove her actions and fueled her ambition in the theater. She faced the fact that her theatrical career had been a great disappointment to her, and not only because the Shuberts had failed to make her a star. She did not really like acting. She still suffered from stage fright and supposed she always would. She minded the physical discomforts of the theater and of touring more and more as she grew older, and, although she had developed a good-humored, earthy manner that helped her fit in around the theater, she had never been comfortable with the quick and casual intimacy of theater people. She never truly felt she was one of them. All of this was endurable in exchange for the freedom to direct her own life, the chance to someday earn the world's acclaim on her own terms, but time was getting short. Although she easily passed for twenty-eight at this point, she was already beyond the ingenue in terms of casting, and pretty much stereotyped as a sophisticated vamp. In a few years, they would start offering her middle-aged character roles, and then the chance for stardom would be over. She resolved to push more for roles than she ever had.

As a start for her new campaign, in mid-April of 1920, Carlotta wrote to Lee Shubert, thanking him profusely for his help in arranging for the money for her appendectomy, and assuring him that she was fully recovered and ready to take on any new challenge he could offer her. He responded with a telephone call and a completely unexpected offer to appear in a musical. He remembered, he said, that she had a lot of singing background, and said there was the perfect part for her in a new musical with a book by Owen Davis. It had already been tried in Atlantic City and Baltimore as a straight play called *A Weekend Marriage*, but it had a few problems, and they were rewriting the show as a musical and recasting it. It was going to open in Brooklyn and move to Philadelphia before a New York opening early in June.

"What would my part be?" she asked. "I'm a contralto, you know, not a soprano."

"Yes, we have that information," he said. "It's not the lead. It's the second female part. The lead is married and runs into trouble when her husband falls for her friend. The friend, a sophisticated interior decorator, that's you, sets out to save the marriage by luring the lead's husband to this cottage in the Adirondacks. This is all a ploy to show how hopeless she is at housekeeping compared to her friend. The husband realizes his folly and they all end up living happily ever after. It sounds kind of dumb, I know, but it's actually pretty fresh, and it has a lot of good songs."

"How much singing would I do?"

"Your character has, let me see here, three songs. There are two trios, one with two women characters and one with the two leads, and then one duet with the male lead. We've got Ernest Truex—you know, *Very Good Eddie*. I think he'll be great. And we have Marjorie Gateson for the lead. She was wonderful in the earlier version. The only member of the cast we've held onto. And she can really sing. You two should be great together."

Carlotta was unnerved by this prospect, but she tried not to show it. "You know it's been quite a while since I had a singing role," she said. "My last one was in *The Bird of Paradise*."

"That's one reason why I thought of you for this. You said you wanted to stretch yourself, and you have this singing background. I thought this would give you a chance. Do you think you're up to it?"

Carlotta had spent enough time around her poker-playing mother to know that her bluff was being called. It was put up or shut up. "Well, I will certainly give it a try," she said.

"Good. You can start working on the songs when you get to New York. I think they have them ready. Then we'll see how it goes. How soon can you get here?"

"I can be there in five days."

"You're a trouper. Just stop by the office and they'll have the sheet music for you and hopefully a more or less final version of the script. We're hoping to open in Brooklyn on May seventeenth."

After making her train reservations, Carlotta spent the rest of the day exercising her voice and packing. She had not attended to her voice in years, and it was quite creaky, but she planned to hire a voice coach as soon as she arrived in New York. Her mother, delighted to hear that she would be onstage in a musical at last, began making plans with Mel to come to New York for the opening. Mel saw her off on the train with a good deal more confidence in her future than she felt.

Chapter 28

When the musical *Page Mr. Cupid* opened in Brooklyn on May 17, 1920, Ernest Truex and Marjorie Gateson were applauded for their singing. If reviews mentioned Carlotta, it was as barely adequate. This did not surprise her. She had a pretty good sense of the caliber of her voice. It was fine for the chorus, but not strong enough to withstand the spotlight of a featured role. But she kept working away with her vocal coach during the week in Brooklyn. The show was scheduled to open at the Shubert Theater in New York the following Monday. Ads had been placed in the newspapers. Tickets were on sale. But Lee Shubert decided to postpone the opening and do another tryout week in Philadelphia.

Carlotta thought her singing improved during the week, and, as everyone got more familiar with their roles, the show got much better. Even so, after the second tryout week, Shubert decided to cancel the opening. He didn't think the show would go. Truex and Gateson were fine, he told J. J., really good, but the supporting cast wasn't strong enough. He was especially disappointed in Carlotta Monterey, who had, he thought, sold him a bill of goods about her voice. It wasn't going to get any better than this, and this wasn't good enough for Broadway. Privately, he suspected that she had sold him a bill of goods about a lot of things.

Lee Shubert was not available when Carlotta called on him to discuss her next role. When she suggested to his secretary that she could make an appointment, Maggie responded that there was no use in that because Mr. Shubert was so tied up with the new summer shows that he wasn't keeping his appointments anyway. Carlotta wrote him a note, reminding him that she was available for anything suitable in the new plays. It went unanswered. She had never gotten the cold shoulder from Lee

Shubert before and was really beginning to worry about the future. She went to see Chamberlain Brown.

"I wouldn't push Lee Shubert," said Brown after hearing Carlotta's account of the situation. "If something has put him down on you at the moment, the best thing to do is stay away from him for a while. You aren't under any written contract with them. Why don't we find you something from another producer if you want a summer part? If it's a success, that will make Shubert take notice, and if not, no real harm done."

"What do you have in mind?"

"Well, A. H. Woods is casting like a house afire. He's got a bunch of new shows for the summer and a lot more planned for the fall. I think he's out to give the Shuberts a run for their money. Why don't I see if they have anything that would suit you, and I'll let you know in a day or two."

As eager as she was to get some kind of explanation from Lee Shubert, Carlotta knew that Brown was right. The best thing to do was to walk away, take a part from someone else, and hope he would see her making a success of it. "All right," she said.

The next day, Carlotta received a call from the Woods office, inviting her to come in and discuss a part in a new play that would be opening in July. When she entered Peter Stone's little room, Carlotta was surprised to find that he was very young, even younger than her husband. But she was used to dealing with a younger man, and, having taken the usual amount of care with her appearance before going to a producer's office, she flattered herself that she could overwhelm him. "How do you do Mr. Stone," she said in her most mellifluous tones, "how very nice to meet you."

He was a small, pudgy man in a tight suit with sandy hair, not very well groomed. He looked up from the paper he was reading, his blue eyes looking a little glazed in his round pink face. When she extended her hand over the desk, he grasped it for a moment and pointed to a chair behind her. "Have a seat," he said.

This reception was not what she had envisioned, but she lowered herself gracefully onto the chair and said, "I was happy to receive your call about the new play. I loathe being idle in the summer."

"Yeah," he said distractedly, looking through the pile of papers on his desk. "Here it is. *The Sacred Bath*. It's a Polynesian princess role. Mr. Brown said you would be perfect for it because you had so much experience with that kind of thing in *The Bird of Paradise* a few years ago."

Carlotta's heart sank, but she maintained her mask of cool sophistication. "What is the play about?" she asked.

He grinned. "Well, I haven't read the whole thing, but it's about a New York show girl who gets shipwrecked on an island called Pukapuka, or something. All these island people have never seen a white person before and they make her their white goddess. She teaches them to talk slang like Americans and names them all after movie stars. There's a big storm effect at the end of the first act. Then an American aviator lands on the island, out of gas. Of course, he falls for the show girl and they're married in a big native wedding ceremony. Then some pirates show up with some gasoline and they fly off into the sunset together."

This was worse, far worse, than *The Bird of Paradise*. "Who wrote the play?" she asked.

"Crane Wilbur. You know, *The Perils of Pauline*? I think he's trying to get back to the stage a little after the movies."

"What would my part be?"

"Let's see." He looked down at his paper. "You're Lakatoola, the High Priestess, otherwise known as Theda Bara. She's kind of a vamp. In love with the captain of the temple guards. She wears a costume of feathers and looks very exotic."

A visceral anger rose in Carlotta's body. She saw the demise of her acting career being spread before her. Another vamp. A terrible play. A costume role. Feathers, no less. What could

Chamberlain Brown possibly have been thinking? With an effort, she controlled her voice and looked at the boy. "Mr. Stone," she said, "I don't think this role would be right for me at this stage in my career. When I starred in *The Bird of Paradise*, I was a young actress just beginning."

"Well," he said, "Mr. Woods thinks you can still pull it off. He said to tell you this role is all we have to offer you this summer. But there is a show he's planning for October that he thinks you might be right for."

She understood. It was almost like starting over. She was no longer a favored actress in the Shubert gallery, given special treatment by the producer himself. This humiliating role was a penance she would have to serve if she wanted a career. At least it would be short. The play could not possibly succeed. She made an effort to pull herself together. "What is the show in the fall?" she asked.

Stone shuffled through the stacks on his desk but couldn't find what he was looking for. "I think it's called *The Jury of Fate*," he said, "by C. M. S. McClellan. A serious play. A kind of— modern morality play. It was done a few years ago in London, but not here. Mr. Woods is very high on it."

Carlotta considered. At least it would be a serious role, and McClellan was a respected playwright. "Do you know anything about the role?"

He tipped back on his chair and looked at her. "Well, I only got a quick look at the summary, but from what I understand, it's pretty wild, sort of like a modern Faust. The hero is a successful playwright who has lived a life that was, let's say, not too virtuous. He's staggering home from the tavern one night when he meets the figure of Death on the road. There's a big scene with the Jury of Fate, full of special effects, that ends with him getting another chance to live his life. So we next meet our hero as a young bridegroom who has stolen his bride from an honest working man. On his wedding night, he meets the reincarnation of a woman he had seduced and abandoned in his earlier life. She gets even by luring him into an affair and ruining his marriage to his dewy-eyed bride. Then he becomes a labor leader who stirs up the workers and causes all kinds of trouble. They attack the foundry where his wife's first love is now the manager. Long story short, he shoots at the man and hits his wife instead. Then the Jury of Fate convenes again in a wild night scene in the forest, and Death deals the final blow to our hero."

Carlotta stared at him. "You say Mr. Harris is very high on this play?"

He lowered his chair and looked earnestly at her. "Oh, yes. There's a lot more to it than a summary like this can get across. It's very high-flown and literary really. Lots of juicy dialogue for everyone."

"And what part would I play?" She hoped it might be the wife, but she already knew better.

"Oh, you're the beautiful temptress. It's just made for you, Miss Monterey," he said, looking at her appreciatively. "You're such a famous beauty, people will believe he'd be tempted by you. You get to pull out all the stops with wardrobe and everything."

Carlotta sighed. "Well," she said. "It's something of a curse to be typecast by your looks."

He grinned disarmingly. "Not as bad as not having them, though."

She grinned back, disarmed. "I suppose you're right," she said. "But I would like to see the script."

"As soon as we have copies," he said. "This show isn't scheduled until September or October, so there's time. We'll get your sides for *The Sacred Bath* right out to you."

Carlotta had almost forgotten *The Sacred Bath*. She could see now what Chamberlain Brown was thinking. This would be a quick summer stint she could do in her sleep. Then she would be going into a featured role in a serious play, not quite the female lead, but a part she knew she could make something of. Lord knew she had enough experience playing dark, alluring temptresses, and it seemed there would be some chance to show off her vocal skill. Hopefully the play would be enough of a *succèss d'estime* for Lee Shubert to take notice.

"All right, Mr. Stone," she said, "but I want to make sure the engagement is for both plays."

"Great," he said, with his winning grin. "We'll work out the contract for both plays with Mr. Brown." He put out his hand. "It's been nice to meet you, Miss Monterey. I've been a fan of yours since I saw *Mr. Barnum* as a kid."

She smiled and took his hand, thinking ruefully that that was two years ago. "Goodbye, Mr. Stone," she said. "I hope I'll see you again soon."

In the end, Carlotta was relieved to find that she had been right about *The Sacred Bath*. It played a summer circuit in Atlantic City and Long Branch, New Jersey, then went to Buffalo and closed, mercifully, without coming to New York. In September of 1920, she was back in New York and waiting to begin rehearsals for *The Jury of Fate*. But the play kept being put off. It was announced for September, then delayed until the middle of October, when the Astor Theatre would be freed up from the movies. Then it was delayed again, until the spring. Carlotta was seeing the signs of another cancelled production, and she was determined not to waste this season. She asked Chamberlain Brown to see if the Shuberts had anything for her that she could do right away. They knew that she was a quick study and had stepped in to rescue them in the past.

Brown came back with an offer for Carlotta to replace Betty Murray in a new production that was already in tryouts in Washington. "It's a detective show called *The Dauntless Three*," he said, "just a slight revision of a play that ran for quite a while in Chicago a couple of years ago. It was called *Mr. Jubilee Drax* then. Lee Shubert said to tell you that you will be playing the good girl and you get the hero in the end."

Carlotta smiled. A lead at last. Perhaps the strategy of playing hard to get had overcome whatever prejudice Lee Shubert had conceived against her. "What is the play about?" she asked.

"The hero, George Drax, is a detective who's trying to find a big diamond that's been stolen from a mine in South Africa so his wealthy employer can buy it for his wife. He chases all over the world and uses a lot of disguises to get hold of it. It's a very high-energy play. There are scenes in England, Constantinople, Paris. Your character, Elaine Gordon, is a very modern woman, the detective who is hired by the mining company to get the diamond back. You are out to beat George to the diamond through most of the play, but then you fall in love with each other and end up happy ever after."

"It sounds like fun, but why is it called *The Dauntless Three* if there are just two of them?"

"Well, 'the dauntless three' actually refers to a gang of high-class jewel thieves who are in the race for the diamond against the detectives."

"So my character is the only female role?"

He looked down at the papers on his desk. "No, the leader of the thieves is a woman, Lady Angela, sort of a beautiful, sleek, sophisticated villain. This review from 1917 says 'she is of the sort who, beautiful and sinuous, says the most dreadful and ominous things, with gorgeous, melodramatic diction and a glittering smile.'"

"But my character is the lead, isn't it?"

He glanced up at her. "Well, Lady Angela has more lines and appears in a few more scenes, but it's not a normal play that way. You're definitely the heroine who fights for the good and ends up with the hero. You will be the lead in the audience's eyes."

"Who plays Lady Angela?"

"Estelle Winwood has been playing the role, and they're happy with her as I understand it." He added a little sheepishly,

"She's getting lead billing after Robert Warwick." He might as well get it all out on the table.

Carlotta could see what Lee Shubert had been up to now. Here at last was the leading role tailor-made to showcase her talent as well as her beauty, and instead he was offering her what amounted to a sappy ingenue role. Lady Angela clearly commanded the stage, while Elaine Gordon was a prop for the male lead. She could feel her muscles tighten and the color rise to her cheeks as she thought about it.

Chamberlain Brown could see the signs of dissatisfaction in Carlotta's face. "It's a good part, Carlotta," he said. "The Shuberts wouldn't ask you to do it if they didn't have confidence that you can step right in and make something really good of it. What's more, you would be doing them a favor. That should get you back on Lee's good side if you're not there now."

Her dark eyes shot him a piercing look. "I've done them favors before and look where it's gotten me. I don't think Lee Shubert believes in me. He doesn't think I'm a leading lady."

He shook his head. "I don't think that's true, Carlotta. He couldn't put you in the leading role in this one. He can't just fire a star who's doing well in the role. He's offering you a good part, and you can use the work if *The Jury of Fate* isn't going to appear until the spring."

Carlotta's face was still flushed, and her body had not relaxed its rigid pose, but she gave a sigh and said, "You always present things so sensibly, Chamberlain. I suppose I will have to do it if I ever hope to get into the Shuberts' panoply of stars."

He sat back and smiled as he drew the contract out from under his desk blotter. "I think you'll enjoy it," he said. "The show is a lot of fun, and for once you will have the audience on your side."

She gave a little answering grin. "That will be a nice novelty," she said.

Carlotta dove right into *The Dauntless Three*, joining the company in Washington in early November. She was judged more than adequate in the role but watching Estelle Winwood play Lady Angela every night heaped coals on the fire of her anger at Lee Shubert. She was sure she could have made a much better thing of Lady Angela than Estelle, and Estelle was far more suited to the part of Elaine. It was sheer perversity on Lee's part, as if he had just given her the part to taunt her. She still could not understand what he had against her, and it was eating away at her. Without consulting Chamberlain Brown, who she knew would talk her out of it, she decided to write to Lee Shubert directly and ask what had happened to undermine his faith in her.

In planning the letter, she meant to be terse and businesslike, but once she started writing, her pent-up emotions poured out and drove the pen relentlessly over page after page of her bonded writing paper. She said she was bewildered by his unwillingness to help her make good after he had been so interested in her career before. She knew she could act as well as the women he was favoring over her, and she looked better than most, so there must be some other reason for his neglect. She went so far as to plead with him to help her for the sake of the baby she had to support but said she would rather go hungry than play any more of the rotten parts she was being given. She reminded him of their earlier relationship in various ways and said she relied on what she had felt to be their friendship in taking such a personal tone. In a final touch, she said she hoped that he would come to believe in her once she did *The Jury of Fate* for Mr. Woods.

Carlotta felt much better when she was finished, but she hesitated over mailing the letter. Something told her that Lee Shubert was not the man to be moved by such an appeal. But he had responded to an emotional appeal the year before, when she had needed the money for the operation. If nothing else, he would be reminded that she was a woman with strong passions and emotions, and there were limits to what she could be expected to endure. She mailed it.

Carlotta heard nothing from Lee Shubert. When *The Dauntless Three* closed in early December without making it to New York, she was not surprised. She thought of writing him another letter suggesting that the play might have been a hit if he had put her in the leading role, but she held off from it. She decided that her special relationship with the Shuberts was over, but it wouldn't do to make an enemy of one of the most powerful men in the theater.

Chapter 29

With nothing happening in the theater until the spring of 1921, Carlotta had no excuse to avoid spending the holidays in Oakland. It proved to be a difficult time. Worried about her career, she was hard put to keep up the pretense that all was well in New York. She found Cynthia no prettier at three-an-a-half than she had been as a baby and given to prattling on and on in a lisping voice that Carlotta longed to correct. The child's father and grandparents seemed to be charmed by everything she said as well as the way she said it, but Carlotta found it tiresome after twenty minutes or so. And the holidays made the focus on Cynthia all the more intense. The house had been turned upside down to make a festive Christmas for her. The family living room was dominated by an enormous Christmas tree. Between them, Nellie and Mel seemed to have bought everything in the Oakland Emporium's toy department. Carlotta's role in this scenario was to play the doting mother. It was not a role that came easily to her.

Amidst all the holiday preparations, Carlotta was repeatedly surprised at the extent to which Nellie had become involved in family life. She seemed at last to have found her ideal, if unorthodox, family grouping of herself and Mel Sr. with Mel and Cynthia as their children. They lived with each other naturally and happily. This left Carlotta out, of course, except for ceremonial purposes. Not that she would have wanted to be more involved with Cynthia. She was a little dismayed to find that she could not help feeling twinges of jealousy when she saw Nellie with her daughter, but it was because Cynthia was getting the attention from her mother that she had missed as a child.

Nellie's new embrace of family included the whole Gottchet clan, and a family party on Christmas Eve was part of the Christmas festivities, so Carlotta had to face numerous aunts and uncles and cousins who were curious about her New York career.

It took all her energy and inventiveness to present the last year as one of successes. More than one of her relatives commented that it sure took a long time to get going in the theater and they all admired Hazel for sticking to it. The only one she enjoyed talking to was her uncle John Shay, who cherished every bit of theatrical gossip she could come up with and still had a firm belief that she would be recognized as a really fine actress in her next production. As was their custom, the Gottchets sang in various combinations during the party. The one nod to Carlotta's professional career was that, at Uncle John's request, she was asked to recite rather than to sing.

Carlotta's relationship with Mel was another source of anxiety during this visit. He was no longer the adoring boy she had married, anxious to do anything to please her and eager for any approval or attention. He no longer saw the holidays as a time to arrange a series of amusements for Carlotta. Like Nellie's, the center of his world had shifted to his daughter. He was delighted to have Carlotta there, but he took it for granted that she too would be taken up with Cynthia and not interested in amusements that would take her away from the daughter she saw so seldom. What's more, Mel followed Carlotta's career closely, and, although she tried to put things in the most favorable light when she wrote to him, he knew that the last year had been a series of failures. Over the several weeks she was there, he hinted several times that perhaps Carlotta had exhausted the possibilities the theater had to offer and might be happier with her family in Oakland. He told her several times how well he was doing in the practice and made sure she knew that he was only staying with the old people for Cynthia's sake. He said they could have their own house whenever they wanted it. Carlotta got the message that he and his father were getting tired of financing her failing career just to keep her in New York, so far away from him and Cynthia.

On an unusually cold January day a week before Carlotta was scheduled to leave for New York, Mel asked her to go for a long walk in the Presidio. She suggested they wait for a warmer day, but he was uncharacteristically insistent. They drove over to San Francisco and bought a picnic lunch to eat in the park. The day was bright and windy, with the sun glittering on the water from their vantage point high above it. As their parents had so many years ago, they felt inspired as they walked along taking in the grandeur of the landscape and feeling the brisk wind battle the warm sunshine. They spoke little until they were eating their lunch in the shelter of a big boulder that cut off the wind and radiated a comfortable warmth from the sun. As they ate the grapes they had bought for dessert, Mel said it was time they had a serious talk about their future. Seeing him gather himself as if he was about to deliver a speech, Carlotta was reminded of the day in Peoria when he had proposed. Things were different now.

Mel looked down at her with affection. "You know that I believe in you and your talent more than anyone," he said, "and I know you have worked like a dog and fought tooth and nail for decent parts and recognition. But the theater is doing you in, Carlotta. You were obviously worn out when you got here. You could hardly summon the energy to play with Cyndy. I could see it. Another year like this would be very hard on you, and I have a responsibility to take care of you as best I can. I have to ask if it's worth it. I mean working so hard and fighting for parts and all the while being separated from your family. I don't mean myself, though I miss you terribly when you're in New York. But your child is growing up without you. You of all people know what that means for a little girl. We're getting to the point where we have to ask if it's worth it to pursue your career."

Carlotta felt a wave of panic surge through her. She looked up at Mel with defiance in her eyes. "You promised!" she cried. "You said you would support me as long as I wanted to pursue my career in the theater."

Taken aback by her sudden vehemence, he said, "I'm not going back on that promise. I'm just saying we should think about the future a little. Maybe give it to the end of the season, and if nothing has happened for you, then give up on New York and look at other possibilities."

She shot him a scornful look. "What other possibilities? Oakland? San Francisco? I might as well give it up altogether. I won't do it, Mel," she said, her voice rising. "I've worked too hard. I'm so close to the top. How many times this last year has the role that would make my career been in my grasp and been snatched away for this or that stupid reason."

"But that's just it. You can't count on anything. You know I haven't lost my faith in your talent. It's the theater I'm losing faith in, the playwrights and producers and your agent. They give you such trash to play in. I don't want you throwing away the best years of our lives on this trifling stuff. I know you will feel terrible if you get to be forty and that's all you have to look back on."

She straightened up and looked at him, her eyes flashing. "I'm not forty yet. Far from it. And I have big prospects in front of me. *The Jury of Fate* is a great work of literature. I will get recognition for my work in it whether the production is a hit or not. And I plan to build from there." Suddenly the tears rose in her eyes and a soft, almost pleading tone replaced her defiance. "You do believe in me, don't you Mel? I sometimes think you're the only one. You've been so steadfast. My Rock of Gibraltar. You won't abandon me?"

He reached over, gathered her to him in a fervent embrace, and kissed her shining hair, touched with golden highlights by the sun. "Of course, I believe in you, my glorious Carlotta, and I will never abandon you. But we have to think about what's best for you in the future. Let's say this. You go back and keep working. We'll give it a year and then think the situation over again. If you started to make money again, it would help a lot. Dad's beginning to think your allowance is a big drain just now. Not that he begrudges it, you know. It's just not a good time to be taking money out of our earnings from the firm."

Carlotta had no patience for talk of the firm's affairs. "If your father can't afford it, you can, can't you?" she said.

Mel looked uncomfortable. "You know I'm not a partner yet, and we can't afford to take any more out of the Dargis legacy. That's Cyndy's money now. It should be used to make a home for her, and we have to think of her future."

When he saw Carlotta's expression darkening, he said quickly, "We don't need to bother about this now. Dad will pay your allowance for the next year. We'll just have to take stock again at the end of the year. And by then, you'll be a big star," he said, kissing her. "How can the world resist this beautiful face?"

Mel was tender and attentive for the rest of the afternoon, but Carlotta felt she had been put on notice, and as long as Mel controlled the money, he called the shots, however gently he might do it. He was no longer a schoolboy she could wrap around her little finger with a glance and a word. He was a grown man, a lawyer, and getting to be a good one if she could judge by the rather neat way he had managed putting her on a year's notice. But a year was a year, and she was determined to make the most of it.

1921, the decisive year, did not start well. At the end of January, a week after Carlotta returned to New York, she received notice that *The Jury of Fate* had been postponed indefinitely. At thirty-two, she was once more an unemployed actress, and her prospects were dimmer than they had been a year ago. She suspected that she had burned her bridges with the Shuberts. The letter she'd written had been a gamble that she'd lost. She was now dependent on Chamberlain Brown to find her roles with independent producers outside the Shubert organization. She put on the pressure, and in mid-February, Brown called with the good news that George M. Cohan wanted to know if she would like to be considered for the lead in a new play he was producing, a straight play.

It sounded too good to be true, and Carlotta was wary. "George M. Cohan and there's no singing or dancing?"

"No, and the play is by Augustus Thomas. You can't get any more legitimate than that."

This was an impressive name, an almost certain ticket to success. "What is the play?" she asked.

"It's called *Nemesis*. It's a detective play. The gimmick is the criminal's use of fingerprints to implicate someone else. You play Marcia Kallan, a high-society lady who is having an amorous affair with a sculptor. Your husband finds out and hatches a plan to destroy you and your lover by stabbing you and leaving the sculptor's fingerprints on the murder weapon. It's a Thomas kind of play—it hinges on the problems with use of fingerprints to convict murderers and the technical details of faking the fingerprints."

"What sort of woman is Marcia?"

"Oh, not a vamp, if that's what you're worried about. She's a smart, beautiful, young woman who is married to a boring, much older man, and she gets seduced by the sculptor's promise of a romantic life in Paris. She has some good scenes with her friends as well as the sculptor."

Carlotta read for Cohan twice and had to wait while he auditioned several other actresses, but in the end, she won the part. It was to be her first starring role on Broadway, and she worked very hard. In Carlotta's view, the tryout weeks in Philadelphia could not have gone better. Hailing the play as one of Thomas's best, the *Philadelphia Inquirer* said, "Not in years has such a perfect ensemble been observable in the American theatre." Carlotta herself was singled out for her "finesse and distinction." On the last night in Philadelphia, there were five curtain calls. Carlotta nearly floated to her dressing room carrying a large bouquet of red roses presented by a gentleman who told her he had seen the play three times. This, she thought, was the play she had been waiting for.

Waiting in her dressing room was George M. Cohan. He looked as if he wished he were elsewhere. She affected not to notice his discomfort and hoped there weren't going to be big changes made at this point.

"Did you see the show?" she asked, turning her beaming face to him. "I think we've finally smoothed out those rough spots in Act Two. John is really brilliant at staging these things."

"Yes," he said. "You've all done a great job. But I'm afraid I have some bad news for you, Miss Monterey. You won't be going to New York with the show."

The twinge of doubt she had felt when she saw his face became a wave of panic that rose from her stomach to her throat. "I don't understand," she said, doing her best to control her voice. "The reviews have been so positive. The audiences have been wonderful. They gave me and Emmett a second curtain call by ourselves tonight. What's wrong with my performance?"

His voice grew hearty, false. "Your performance is fine," he said. "No one faults your performance. We just think we need to go another way for the play to make it in New York. It's kind of a specialty play, and we need a star to put it over. You and Emmett are great. People love you in it, but neither one of you has the star power to bring 'em in before the show gets a reputation. You understand that."

Carlotta did not respond.

"Well," he went on, even more heartily than before, "we managed to get Olive Tell, who was such a hit in *Civilian Clothes* last year. We'd had her in mind before, and she just got free."

Carlotta looked at him. "Olive Tell."

"I know she's known more as a comic actress, but we think she'll bring a light touch to this part that will help to put the show over."

"But the show is a success. Everyone says it depends on its unusually good ensemble cast. Why would you throw it all off balance like that?"

Cohan shifted in his chair. "Look, Miss Monterey. I know you're upset about this. Anybody would be. But I can't argue with you about the show. This is the way we've decided to go, and I'm sorry that means that you won't be coming to New York."

"I see," she said, controlling her voice with a great effort. "I think you're making a big mistake, Mr. Cohan."

Cohan stood up and smiled. "I hope not," he said, "but it wouldn't be the first." He held out his hand and she shook it.

Of all Carlotta's recent setbacks in the theater, this was the worst. She felt that Marcia Kallan was her part. The one that was to bring her not only the attention but the respect of the theater world. It was proof at last that she was a serious actress and a leading lady. And she had just lost it because this little mick wanted to give a part to a chit of a movie actress he was screwing, or hoped to. She had been in the position of the replacing actress before, but never of the replaced. She had always thought the resentment of the companies was uncalled for. Now she knew what the other actors thought of her. She hated the theater, loathed it. If she had not put so much of her effort, so much of herself, into her quest to be recognized, if the alternative had not been worse, she would be done with it right then and there. But she had a year, one year in New York, and she was seized with a renewed determination to make the most of it. This was it, no holds barred, sink or swim. Whatever it took, she resolved, she would make her way in New York. She knew a lot more about how to do that now than she had five years ago.

Part of the strategy Carlotta planned for the rest of the year was to make and exploit all the theatrical connections she could, so when Merle Maddern asked her to come along to a theatrical benefit at the Players Club, she did not make an excuse to avoid a large social gathering filled with strangers, as she might have before. If there was anywhere she could meet and talk to new producers, it would be the Players Club. When she appeared, it was in her most becoming afternoon outfit, a bottle-green Schiaparelli dress and matching coat that had taken a large bite out of her salary from *The Dauntless Three*, an expense she had not mentioned to Mel. There were several important producers at the event, among many other theater people and patrons of the arts. She presented her most engaging persona to the ones she met—sophisticated but warm and good-humored, with an approachable, down-to-earth "California" quality that made her exotic beauty all the more captivating to the beholder.

Halfway through the evening, Carlotta noticed that someone was watching her from across the room. He was a small, trim man with a neat mustache and dark hair who looked to be in his fifties. A number of people engaged him in conversation, in which he joined politely, but he seemed always to have her in view somehow. This in itself was not unnerving. Carlotta was used to being stared at. But there seemed something different about this man, so calm and self-possessed, and yet so intent. When Merle came up, Carlotta shot a little glance toward him and said, "Who is that man? He's been staring at me all night."

Merle looked around the room and turned back to her. "You mean that little man over in the corner? That's James Speyer. If he's really staring at you, you're a lucky girl. He's richer than God."

"Truly?" Carlotta took another swift glance.

"Yes, he's Speyer of Speyer and Company, the international bankers. They're as big as J. P. Morgan. He's a philanthropist, gives a lot to the arts. His wife just died a month or so ago. She was even more charitable than he is. She started the free animal hospital and the workhorse parade before the war, and the Irene club for working girls. She was always holding events for the

Actors Fund that Minnie was involved in. I'm surprised you never heard of them."

Carlotta looked across the room again and nearly caught the man's eye as he looked away. "It does ring a bell now," she said. "Why don't you introduce him to me."

Merle laughed. "Oh, I don't know James Speyer. Just know of him. But he seems so interested in you that if we made our way across the room, I have a feeling introduction would not be necessary."

Fifteen minutes later, the two actresses were chatting with James Speyer as if they were all old friends. Five minutes after that, Merle excused herself, saying she should find her cousin. Carlotta decided to be direct. "Have we met before, Mr. Speyer? You seemed to be looking in my direction earlier."

"No," he said, equally direct. "I just appreciate a beautiful woman."

"Why, thank you," she said. "There are a good many beautiful women here this evening."

He smiled. "But you're the most beautiful," he said, "so you merit my attention."

"Thank you again, kind sir," she said, looking at him through her long eyelashes.

At that point someone came up and began talking about Players Club business, so Carlotta thought it a good time to make her exit. She expected that she would see Mr. Speyer again, and she was not disappointed. She had told him nothing about her living arrangements, but two dozen red roses arrived at her apartment the next day with a note saying that he remembered she had said she enjoyed opera and inviting her to join him in his box the following Thursday to see *Oberon*. She was delighted. It had been a while since she had had this kind of attention, and he was a very rich man.

Carlotta knew she looked dazzling when she appeared in Speyer's box at the Met on Thursday. She wore a flattering white *décolleté* evening dress that was not Paul Poirot but easily could have been, and all the Moffat family jewels she had managed to hold onto. Speyer was enchanted. Carlotta had not actually seen *Oberon* before, but since she was well-acquainted with *A Midsummer Night's Dream* and trained enough in opera to discuss the finer points of the performances, she was able to make some intelligent comments during the intermissions, which endeared her further to Speyer. After the performance, he didn't take her to supper at Delmonico's, as most men his age would have, or to one of the new nightclubs to dance, as a younger man might have, but instead took her to a quietly elegant restaurant where a string quartet played Viennese waltzes and none of fashionable New York was on display.

"I hope you enjoy this place," he said. "I like it because it's quiet enough for conversation and I'm partial to the Viennese music and German food."

"It's charming," said Carlotta, looking around. "I'm so glad we'll have a chance to talk." And talk they did. About the opera and Shakespeare, and the theater and the arts in general. Speyer was an avid theater-goer and knew more about the season than Carlotta did, but he was more interested in talking about dramatic literature than the theater gossip that Carlotta was usually called on to supply. She had not had such an animated literary discussion since the Academy days, and she enjoyed it. She was conscious that her enjoyment brought a glow to her cheeks and a sparkle to her eyes that made her look younger and more beautiful.

Observing Carlotta, James Speyer thought her a rare combination of remarkable beauty and stimulating company. Although he had been devoted to Ellin, his late wife and partner in philanthropy, he considered himself something of a connoisseur of women, and he had not met many like this. Speyer was a cultivated man, a collector and patron of the arts. Although he had been born in New York, he was brought up in

Frankfurt, where the family banking business was based, and had been placed in banks in London and Paris to complete his financial education before he returned to New York to join his father at Speyer & Company. Since the bank specialized in marketing U. S. bonds abroad and foreign securities in the U. S., Speyer had traveled regularly throughout his life, often spending several months at a time in Frankfurt, London, Amsterdam, Paris, and Berlin, and traveling throughout Europe. Multilingual, he eagerly soaked up all the culture he could in these various countries. Both his Fifth Avenue mansion and his estate in Westchester County were filled with art he had collected abroad, and he did what he could to encourage the arts in New York. He was delighted to be able to have such a stimulating conversation with a beautiful actress.

Carlotta wished her dinner partner were a little taller and a little younger, but otherwise, she thought him the perfect companion. When he brought her to her door, she said she couldn't remember when she had had more delightful evening. Speyer felt the same way, and their evenings at the opera soon became a weekly engagement. Over the spring months, their social relationship deepened into a real friendship. He told her about the unexpected devastation he had felt when Ellin died after years of illness, and he thanked her often for helping to fill the emotional void she had left. Carlotta played the part of ministering angel impeccably. At first, she was just doing her best to perform his ideal vision of her, but as she got to know him, she felt a true affection and admiration for him. To her he was always the cultivated gentleman, wonderfully generous and attentive, open to confidences and free with advice and material help. Eventually Carlotta trusted him enough to confide her deep disappointment in her career and her fear that she would be trapped in Oakland if she didn't find the right role to make her a star soon. She told him that her dream was to do great plays, by playwrights like Shakespeare and Schiller, where her talent would be challenged and grow. He began to assume a protective role toward her that was part avuncular, part romantic. She referred all her dilemmas to him, whether they were professional, financial, or personal.

Chapter 30

In May of 1921, Carlotta took a role in a piece of summer fluff called *Zizi*. She had no interest in the play but needed to earn some money and to have some kind of a part in order to report back to Oakland that she was working. The show opened in Atlantic City and moved on to Washington. Sam Harris, the producer, was free with advance publicity, which focused on Carlotta's beauty, highlighted by an alluring photograph, nude from the shoulders up, by Marcia Stein in the "artgravure" section of the *Washington Post*. Carlotta was becoming well known in Washington, where several of her performances had been applauded although they had not been seen in New York. She got favorable reviews, but the response to the play was not enthusiastic, and Harris decided to close the show in Washington.

When Carlotta returned to New York at the end of May, she unloaded her frustration and depression on James Speyer, who had become her most intimate confidant. The intensity of his response surprised her.

"Carlotta, my dear one," he said, "why do you continue to waste yourself on these roles, for these ingrate producers who don't understand the gift you are giving them? You must stop lending yourself to this tripe and accept only challenging roles in good plays that will give you the opportunity to practice your art."

Her dark eyes regarded him sadly through her lashes. "But I don't have the luxury of waiting, James. I have to pay the bills. And you know I'm under pressure from Oakland to come back if I'm not pursuing my career."

He looked at her keenly, his shrewdness momentarily overcoming his affection. "Carlotta," he said, "tell me truthfully. Do you intend to remain married to Melvin Chapman after you've achieved success in the theater? Would you stay in your marriage if you had another way of supporting yourself?"

Despite her attempt to maintain a worldly composure, she blushed as she met his look. "I'm very fond of Mel," she said. "He's done a good deal for me, and I'm grateful for it. But I don't see a future for us, no."

He nodded. "In fact, you would be doing him a favor if you put an end to this and let him get on with his life."

He held up his hand as she started to respond. "Now, just please remain quiet and listen to me for a few minutes," he said. "I have something to suggest to you." He folded his hands on the table, his soft grey eyes regarding her calmly. "Carlotta, you know that I am well-acquainted with the theater, and I fancy that I am a good judge of talent. You are very talented, my dear. I do not want to see your talent and youth wasted on these bad roles and frivolous plays. I want to take away the need for money as a motivating factor in your career and allow it to be replaced with what I know is your deep desire to create great art. I would like to settle an amount of money on you which will remove your financial worries. Call it an artistic trust. The money will be out of my hands once the arrangement is made. I hope that we will always remain intimate friends, of course. Beyond that, what you decide to do with your personal life will be your own business."

Carlotta looked at him. "Do you mean you would support me whether I acted or not?"

He smiled. "I'm sure we can arrange to make the trust sufficient for your needs. But, of course, I would hope that the luxury of financial independence would allow you to pursue the truly artistic opportunities in the theater, even if they are not financially rewarding."

"But James," she said. "This is so generous. I'm not sure how to broach this without being crude, but in such arrangements the man usually expects a certain quid pro quo for his generosity."

He laughed. "Not too crude at all," he said. "I will be honest with you, my dear. I would like nothing better than to have our intimate friendship become even more intimate. But this is not a condition of the arrangement. I'm sixty years old, more than thirty years older than you, I expect. I was never a handsome man at the best of times, and what's more, I'm shorter than you," he smiled. "I don't expect that there's a great physical attraction. And I want nothing of the mercenary in our relationship with each other. There are plenty of pretty women who can be bought with a diamond broach or an emerald necklace. I know that you are not one of those women, and it is one of the many things that endear you to me. You see, I may look like an old French *roué*, but at heart I am a German romantic. I am very fond of you, Carlotta. For many reasons, I don't plan ever to marry again. That is all the more reason why I place the utmost value on our friendship. Your sympathy, your candor, your intelligent response are things that I hope to be able to rely on in the future always. I assure you that the financial arrangement I propose will have nothing to do with our friendship. Once the money is settled, we will say no more about it. It will be yours to spend as you see fit."

Carlotta looked at him with tears in her eyes. "But this is too much," she said. "It's as if my fairy godmother suddenly appeared and handed me my future."

"Godfather," he said, smiling. "*Patenonkel.*"

"Or just Papa. You are like the dearest, kindest, most generous Papa one could imagine."

He screwed up his face. "Not Papa," I hope. "I would like something a little less paternal sounding, if you please. *Pate* would be better."

She smiled the warmest, most genuine smile she had smiled in years. "*Pate*, then," she said, "but in my heart, you will always be dearer than my own Papa. But I am going to do something to earn this money. I will serve as your interior decorator."

He laughed. The outmoded décor of his Fifth Avenue mansion had been a running joke between them since Carlotta had first visited it. He and Ellin had decorated the house together at the turn of the century. He was very fond of it because it represented the happiest time in his marriage, but he knew that it was looking tired and out of date, especially when viewed through Carlotta's eyes. "Very well," he said. "It is a bargain. When I return from Europe, you will assist me in redecorating."

In the weeks before he left for his annual trip to Europe, James arranged the trust he had planned for Carlotta. They also made several visits to an exclusive and discrete hotel in Gramercy Park. Carlotta was more than happy to have their friendship take this romantic turn. With the surge of gratitude for James's securing an independent future for her came an increasing warmth in her affection for him. She also felt that sharing what he gallantly called "her favors" with him helped to even the balance sheet of their relationship. His gratitude was of a different order than hers, but it was palpable, and their physical intimacy brought his feeling for her to a greater intensity. She knew that she did not have nearly the power over him that she had enjoyed over Mel Chapman, but she did feel a shift in the dynamic of their relationship.

She was surprised to find that he was a more than satisfactory lover. James Speyer was a worldly man, with a great fund of curiosity and a great capacity for the appreciation of life's pleasures. He had married late and been a devoted, but not necessarily a faithful, husband, especially during the last years of Ellin's illness. Over the years, he had had a great deal of experience with women, and this, combined with his natural sensitivity, made him an inventive and attentive partner. Carlotta found herself enjoying the sex as sex much more than she had expected to.

When James left for Europe at the end of June, Carlotta found that she missed him terribly. Apart from the romantic side of their relationship, he was her most trusted companion, her confidant and advisor. When she felt a rising tide of panic over something, she could usually calm herself by repeating that Papa would solve it. Papa would make everything right again. During the summer, she wrote to him often, and he responded fondly and helpfully. Her friend Merle Maddern, who was in New York playing the wise older woman in Rachel Crothers's flapper play, *Nice People*, was curious about Carlotta's relationship with Speyer. "I hear you've been out and about with our millionaire friend," she said when they met for lunch one day. "That meeting at the Players seems to have worked out well."

Carlotta managed to appear nonchalant. "Oh, he's a dear," she said. "You know, he really cares about the theater. He takes me to the opera and the high-brow openings. And he's a real cosmopolitan. The conversation is delightful."

"Well, as long as the conversation is delightful," Merle grinned. "I suppose you aren't wasting your time."

In early July, Carlotta wrote a carefully worded letter to Mel, telling him not to expect her in Oakland. When he wrote back urging her to come, at least for a visit, since she had no theatrical engagement for the summer, she told him that it was important for her to be in New York. He responded with uncharacteristic insistence that, if she wasn't in a summer show, there was no reason to hang around New York because there were no prospects at that time of year. There was nothing she could say. He knew enough about the theater that she couldn't put him off except with a complicated lie. Instead, she acted on her impulse to just get it over with. She wrote to him that she wished to separate from him and live permanently in New York. She told him he could do as he saw fit to formalize the separation legally. As she expected, she received a telegram three days later, saying that he would be arriving in New York in four days.

Mel's visit was an emotionally wrenching time. At first, he thought Carlotta was just reacting to his new tougher stance and told her that nothing had really changed in their agreement and he was only anxious to have her back. When she insisted that the agreement was no longer enough for her and she wanted her freedom, he used every argument he could think of to persuade her not to take such a reckless course. On his third day in New York, exhausted from all the emotional talk, they sat in the small sitting room of her apartment. It had the feeling of a final showdown. In the end, it came down to two questions. What would she do for an income when she had no engagements, and how could she abandon Cynthia? For Mel had no intention of allowing Cynthia to come to New York. Carlotta could not tell Mel that in her heart of hearts, she felt that she was being freed from Cynthia, not abandoning her. In Oakland, Cynthia was loved and more than well cared for. Carlotta rarely thought of her and felt no anxiety about leaving her to Nellie and Mel and Oto and Mel Sr. The income question she refused to go into, saying that she had been offered a long-term contract with a very good guaranteed salary.

Mel was bitter. "So now that you finally have what you want, you don't need your family anymore, and you just cut us loose," he said. "You were just using me all this time."

Carlotta's anger rose. She refused to take the blame. "You got plenty out of it. You said it was everything you wanted. And if it's true that I was using you, I would think you would be happy to be free of me."

Mel's pale face flushed, his upper lip curled in an ugly sneer, and he spoke in a caustic tone that Carlotta had never heard from him before. "Maybe I am," he said. "Maybe much more than I have ever let myself think. And don't think I believe that 'guaranteed salary' crap. It's not like you've been any great success lately. You're in no position to demand something like that. I know you've found yourself a sugar daddy to pay the bills. And I'm warning you, Carlotta. If you go down that road, you can't come back."

Carlotta flushed a deep red and jumped to her feet. "You know nothing about me," she cried, "and I'm through pretending that we have a marriage. I don't want anything to do with you. I want a divorce."

At the sound of the word, Mel's face registered surprise. His body seemed to deflate like a punctured balloon. He looked at the floor. Then he looked at her. "It's what I expected, really," he said, more quietly. "You're right that we don't have a marriage. I've known that for a long time. There's no point in a separation. You're already a divorcée, so it's not as if your social position were involved, and mine in San Francisco can only improve by being divorced from an actress. If a divorce is what you want, I can arrange it easily enough. There are only two questions, alimony and Cynthia."

"I don't want any alimony, and Cynthia can stay just where she is."

"It's a question of custody.'

"It makes no sense for me to have custody. You can have custody—as long as I can visit her, of course."

"I will give you unlimited visitation rights if you will just come to see her sometimes. The child needs you," he said. "I hope you'll remember that." He stood up. "I'm going now," he said. "Send me the name of a lawyer."

"All right," she said. She put out her hand. "No hard feelings."

He shook his head. "I'm sorry. I can't say that." And he left the apartment. It would be many months before she saw him again.

When James Speyer had left for Europe at the end of June, Carlotta had surprised herself by how sad she was to see him go. When her first check from Speyer & Company arrived on July first, she had been overwhelmed by his generosity. Her first feeling was of gratitude. Her second was of liberation. At thirty-two, after all these years of struggling, she had a substantial, secure income, and she could do what she liked with it. She was freed from begging for acting roles that were beneath her, from grabby actors and leering producers and casting couches, from the grubby desperation of the agent's waiting room, and from the theater itself. No need to endure the stifling dressing rooms and merciless footlights of hot summer theaters, the dirty trains, the bad food, the ugly, stuffy hotel rooms. Not to mention the humiliating roles in bad plays and pretending to everyone in and out of the theater that she was happy with her career.

Carlotta decided to take the summer off and not even think about the theater. She talked Merle, who had finished the successful run of *Nice People* at the end of June, into renting a cottage on Long Island for the rest of the summer. For six weeks, they enjoyed acting like the well-to-do "civilians" around them, playing tennis, taking golf lessons, spending whole days at the beach, and accepting dinner invitations from people who were excited to entertain actresses from the Broadway theater.

Occasionally they went into New York and shopped. Carlotta was putting together a new wardrobe and a new look for the twenties. She was careful not to make her hem lines too short, for she had been manipulating them cleverly for years, along with carefully designed handmade shoes, to mask her short legs and wide feet. She knew several designers who were adept at compensating for these flaws, and they were delighted to make clothes for her that harmonized with the new Jazz Age fashions without looking cheap or flapperish. Her signature was a plunging neckline and a dramatic white collar or lapel, contrasting a dark, often black silk dress or jacket that set off her exotic beauty.

Merle marveled at the money and energy Carlotta spent on her appearance and was privately grateful that she herself had never been a beauty. At thirty-three, Merle was satisfied with being a character actress. She reflected that, after all, she had a much steadier career in the theater than Carlotta ever would.

Chapter 31

When James Speyer came back from Europe in October, he was pleased to find that not only did Carlotta not have an engagement for the new season, she wasn't even looking for one. While he was in Europe, he had come to terms with his bereavement amid the many distractions and new experiences that he always sought while traveling. But now that he was back in New York, the absence of Ellin was making itself felt again. Instead of a joyous homecoming and many days of wonderful talk about what had happened in Europe and New York over the last three months, he returned to a house that was empty and silent, a constant reminder of the loss of his dearest companion. It was a great comfort to have Carlotta available to him, whether as a sympathetic listener and dinner partner or as a beautiful woman to have on his arm at the theater or on public occasions.

With her new wardrobe to show off, Carlotta was happy to play the part, and she played it well. At first, she loved being a lady of leisure with nothing to do but dress for the evening. It was the first time in her life that she had all the money she wanted to spend on clothes and shoes, and the admiring looks she got more than compensated for the time she took on her appearance. When she didn't have to think about performing, she found that she really enjoyed the opera and the theater, and she took great pleasure in meeting the society ladies on their own ground when she accompanied James to large dinner parties or social events. Having done her time with the British aristocracy, she could handle the most snobbish grande dames of New York society with impunity. She generally looked around the room and determined that she was the most beautiful and the most stylish woman there, and certainly the most well-spoken. She only needed the beaming look on James's face to affirm her belief.

As fall passed into winter, Carlotta grew bored with the empty days, and to fill them, she proposed to make good on her promise to decorate the Speyer mansion. She was surprised to find that James was agreeable to the idea, even enthusiastic. He told her he was ready to move on from that period in his life, happy as it had been, but he said they would redecorate only the downstairs rooms. The private apartments upstairs would stay as they were.

Carlotta plunged into the project with relish. Since James Speyer had great confidence in his own taste and far more informed ideas about art than she had, she took his direction on aesthetic matters, and found she was learning a good deal in the process. But when it came to the actual execution of the ideas, which did not interest James particularly, she had a free hand and enjoyed herself immensely. She found that she had absorbed a lot more of her mother's business during her summers in Oakland than she had been aware of. She was comfortable with contractors and drapers and furniture dealers, and she could communicate with the plasterer and the painter and wallpaper hanger on their own terms. She unconsciously took on Nellie's manner, and, once they got over her looks, the workmen accepted her as the boss. James laughed when he came home one day to find her standing in the middle of the library, superintending a gang of five strapping young men as they boxed up the books and carried them to the basement. He thought all this very amusing, but he had to admit that Carlotta produced results. Everything was done to suit her standards, or it was done over.

The redecoration project was useful in several ways. It gave Carlotta a reason to be a fixture in the Speyer mansion, so that soon, no one, not even the servants, took much notice when she was there from breakfast through dinner, or even stayed overnight. The new situation gave a more domestic feeling to her relationship with Speyer. It was just natural for them now to be in each other's company. When they went out together, Speyer now introduced Carlotta as his interior decorator. Since it seemed that everyone in the 1920s was either buying a new house or renovating an old one, the conversation would immediately turn to houses and furniture and color schemes, and Carlotta was consulted and deferred to as an expert rather than treated as Speyer's accessory.

As the project drew to a close in the late fall, Carlotta began to feel a familiar restlessness and boredom. She had what most of her contemporaries in the theater dreamed of, a wealthy admirer of whom she was fond and who squired her to the most exclusive restaurants and events on the social register. Having plenty of money, beautiful clothes, and the freedom to do what she liked with her time were the side benefits. But they were not enough. She was not Peggy Hopkins, driven to accumulating expensive and beautiful things, seemingly compelled to drain each man she captured of all his money and move on to the next. When she had no work to do, Carlotta could fill her days with shopping and other expensive leisure activity, but as the fall faded into winter, her life began to have an aimlessness about it that was dangerously reminiscent of the days with Jack Moffat. It was not that she missed the theater. Now that she was freed from it, she could easily admit that there was a great deal she loathed about the theater. But while she was pursuing acting roles, she had a career and a goal. She was acutely aware that this life was not that goal.

It was on Thanksgiving that Carlotta's feeling of vague restlessness coalesced into unhappiness. Although Nellie had told her she would be welcome in the house on Santa Clara Avenue, and that Mel Jr. was in fact hoping she would come to see her daughter, she did not go to Oakland. It was too soon. Everyone there would be angry with her, including Nellie, who did not know about James Speyer, and thought she had done a foolish thing in separating from Mel. James Speyer was spending the long weekend at his niece's estate in Mount Kisco. Merle Maddern was away on tour. Carlotta was not really surprised that she was not invited to any of the festivities that the theater folk held to stave away loneliness on holidays. She had already dropped out of the theater scene as far as her friends and acquaintances were concerned. Theater friendships were such present tense sorts of things. A group of people spent every day in each other's company for a month or six months or a year, and then they might not see each other again for years. It was part of the life. And then there was so much competition. There were very few true friendships in the theater.

On Thanksgiving Day, Carlotta was determined not to sit in her apartment feeling sorry for herself. She dressed in her new fur-trimmed coat and walked across Central Park toward the Plaza Hotel on Fifth Avenue. It was a cold, cloudy day. There were not many people in the park, just a few families out for a walk and three couples sitting alone on benches, oblivious to the cold. Carlotta entered the Plaza and went to the Palm Court, where she could have a festive afternoon tea. She had the *maître d'hotel* seat her in a little alcove she was fond of, a secluded spot with a little table where she could see the whole room but was screened by the greenery from the view of the other patrons. There were several families in the room, and the well-behaved little girls made her a little nostalgic for family life. She wondered what Cynthia looked like now. It had been several months since Nellie had sent her a photograph. In the end, the tea was dispiriting rather than cheering. She finished and left more quickly than she had planned.

It was dark when she came out of the Plaza. She walked along Sixtieth Street to Central Park West rather than going through the park by herself. The street was empty. As she walked, she reflected that she had never felt so alone. Not solitary, a condition that she liked and often craved, but alone in the world. At this moment in her life, there was nowhere that she belonged. She existed on the margins—of her family's life, of James Speyer's life, of the theatrical world, of society. It suddenly struck her that she had become her mother. The thought was shocking. Most of her adult life had been dedicated to resisting Nellie's fate. She had been determined not to be the unacknowledged woman. Carlotta was to have an identity, recognized by all, whether as a great actress or as a celebrated society beauty. But she knew very well that James Speyer would never marry her, and without that, she would never be accepted into society. Could she really have given up the theater, her only chance to make her mark, so easily? She was beautiful now, and would be for another eight years or so, but with all the care in the world, it would be hard to keep that up after forty. Then what would she be? If she was lucky, she would be just like Nellie, only on a larger scale, the independently financed companion to a wealthy man. It took her the rest of the long, gloomy evening to fully digest this perception and its implications, but at the end of it she had a plan.

On Friday, Carlotta spoke with Chamberlain Brown, letting him know that she was ready to return to the theater. She told him that she was determined to maintain a worldly, sophisticated image and needed to be selective about her roles—no more Lakatoolas or Luanas. To her surprise, he was delighted that she had called. There was a new play by Cosmo Hamilton, the writer of plays like *Scandal* and *An Exchange of Wives*, which addressed modern issues around sex and marriage in a way that just skirted impropriety and was very popular with audiences. *Danger*, the new one, addressed the topical subject of the loveless marriage. The producer was desperate to find someone to play the socially ambitious Englishwoman who marries a man for his money and then refuses him her sexual favors, knowing that English law would not allow him to divorce her without an embarrassing disclosure of the unconsummated marriage in court. In despair, the husband attempts suicide and is saved by his sympathetic young secretary, who becomes "a wife in the highest sense of the word, without the sanction of the church." The part presented a challenge. The character was not without her sympathetic elements, but it would be up to the actress to convey them to an audience that would not be on her side. After she read the script over the weekend, Carlotta thought the part had possibilities. She agreed to take it.

When James Speyer returned from Mount Kisco, he was a little dismayed to hear from Carlotta that she was going back to the theater. "I just can't sit idle," she told him. "And deep down I still have the ambition to be a great actress. The only way I can get there is by acting. But don't worry. I won't take any parts that would make you embarrassed to be seen with me."

During rehearsals, the producer decided that Carlotta would not draw enough sympathy from the audience, and he replaced her with a more endearing actress. Carlotta's hopes for a play to occupy her during the holidays were dashed. She had Christmas Eve with Speyer before he left to spend Hanukkah with his niece's family, and his gift of a luxurious fur coat did a great deal to brighten her outlook, but the feeling that had arisen at Thanksgiving did not leave her. She was determined that 1922 would be the year she got a role that made her name in the theater.

She took the first role that was offered her, that of a Russian peasant named Olga in a new play by Earl Carroll that was to be the inaugural production in the new Earl Carroll Theatre, directed and produced by Earl Carroll. She thought Mr. Carroll could have used a second eye on his play *Bavu*, which was an old-fashioned melodrama set against the modern background of the Russian Revolution. Critics complained that they didn't get to see the up-to-date technical capabilities of the theater in action because the play and the production were both in the style of the 1890s. The critic Alexander Woollcott counted a few old standby tricks from nineteenth-century melodrama, including missing signet rings, interchanged passports, interchanged bags of gold, signals flashed from the attic window, mysterious sliding panels, violent stage sword play, and bits of Poe's "Cask of Amontillado." It was Carlotta who was the victim of "The Cask of Amontillado." In attempting to seal up the aristocratic hero of the play in a wall, her revolutionary Turkish lover, Bavu, inadvertently sealed her up instead, "a pitiful fate for one so comely," wrote one reviewer. The theater got much better reviews than the play, and Carlotta was soon out of a job.

By early February, Carlotta was feeling a little desperate. She was overjoyed when Arthur Hopkins, whom she had known affectionately as "Hoppy" since he had produced *Be Calm, Camilla*, offered her a part in a new play about Voltaire. Hopkins had been building quite a resume as a Broadway producer who stood for high-quality literary drama against the Broadway show shops like the Shubert Brothers and the Theatrical Syndicate. He had suc-ceeded in producing Ibsen and Shakespeare as well as Zoë Akins, Eugene O'Neill, and some contemporary European playwrights. Carlotta was offered the role of Mlle. Clairon, an eighteenth-century actress who performed in the *Comédie Française*. She felt comfortable with this role, which allowed her to draw on her Paris experience, and she had a gorgeous wardrobe.

The play *Voltaire* was something else again. It was an effort by two college students who looked like flappers but spoke earnestly of their literary aim of writing a play against intolerance. The play's plot was curiously old-fashioned and melodramatic because, as the young authors explained, they had learned how to write a play from reading books on the subject, books which focused on the plot construction of the nineteenth-century "well-made-play." Treated as a curiosity by the critics, *Voltaire* ran for only sixteen performances. Carlotta's beauty was universally acknowledged, of course, but her acting was not so acclaimed. As the reviewer for the *New York Sun* put it, "Carlotta Monterey tried very hard to act and succeeded."

James Speyer, for one, was delighted with Carlotta's appearance in *Voltaire*. She looked so stunning in her makeup and costume, a dark green velvet jacket and voluminous light green silk skirt, that he commissioned Abram Poole to paint a large portrait of her in character. He urged her to take only parts that would place her in such a flattering and distinguished light. Carlotta tried to explain that she did not have that luxury, and she would not until she had made a hit in something as a leading lady, but he found it hard to believe that the producers of Broadway couldn't see what he saw.

After the failure of *Voltaire*, Hoppy again came to the rescue, this time with an offer for Carlotta to take over the part of the spoiled rich girl, Mildred Douglas, the leading female role in Eugene O'Neill's controversial play, *The Hairy Ape*. As a career move, this was a great opportunity. The young O'Neill was just emerging as the most respected playwright in New York, America's best hope to write a truly great play. He had set the Broadway theater world on its head with *The Emperor Jones*, an avant-garde expressionist play with a black actor in the lead, *Anna Christie*, his second Pulitzer Prize winner, and now another expressionist play that was stirring up talk of censorship for its rough language and its treatment of radical politics. When this play opened on Broadway, it would certainly garner a lot of attention. The problem was that the Provincetown Players, the amateur group that produced O'Neill's avant-garde plays, had been performing *The Hairy Ape* at their theatre in Greenwich Village for a month with their lead actress Mary Blair in the part of Mildred Douglas. Once again, Carlotta would be joining a cast that was already formed, and one that had a much tighter bond than most because these actors had been together in the Players for five or six years. With a sigh, she resigned herself to once again being the unpopular member of the company and signed on.

Although Mildred had the key line of the play, when she called the steamship stoker Yank a "filthy beast" and set in motion the frenzied journey of self-discovery that led to his death, her part was not a large one, and she learned it quickly. She thought things were going well at her first rehearsal when Hoppy brought a young man up to her where she sat at the side of the stage and introduced him as Eugene O'Neill. Carlotta was surprised at O'Neill's appearance. From what she had heard of his living and drinking habits, she had expected a scruffy Greenwich Village bohemian, but in front of her stood a slim young man dressed in a well-tailored dark suit. As she looked up at him through her long lashes, she saw that he had dark, wavy hair, a handsome face with a clipped mustache, and deep brown eyes almost as dark as hers. In her characteristic gesture, she extended her hand gracefully and said, "How do you do, Mr. O'Neill? I'm very pleased to meet you at last."

O'Neill ignored her hand, and, his eyes fixed on a spot over her head, mumbled, "How do you do?"

Quick to cover social awkwardness, Hoppy jumped in with a voluble speech about how much he and Gene admired her acting and how happy they were to have her with them. O'Neill stood there looking at the ground until the end of it and then wandered off to talk to the men who were hanging the lights. Carlotta thought she had never seen anything so rude. She told Hoppy, "His looks aren't as bohemian as I expected, but his manners certainly are."

He laughed. "Don't take it personally," he said. "That's just his way. I spend half my time covering his social gaffs."

As predicted, *The Hairy Ape* was a controversial hit. The New York censors targeted its language, and many theater and culture critics weighed in, supporting the play. Its avant-garde treatment of social and economic oppression came in for a great deal of discussion in newspapers and magazines, and Louis Wolheim's performance as Yank was considered a masterpiece. Carlotta's beauty received its usual attention, but the circumstances of her addition to the cast, well known in the theater world, colored the reception of her acting. Some reviewers went so far as to say that she was adequate to the role, but no better than Mary Blair, who was, as one critic put it, "in every way sufficient."

Carlotta never succeeded in cracking the tight bond of the Provincetown Players cast. To the others she was an interloper who had supplanted their friend Mary for the worst of reasons in their view, Broadway's commercialism. But the play was a hit in the more sophisticated literary and cultural circles, and even James Speyer found nothing objectionable in her part, so she stayed with it through the summer.

Chapter 32

On the first Sunday in May of 1922, Carlotta was invited to a party at the studio of the fashion photographer Nickolas Muray. She thought twice about going because Muray's studio was on Macdougal Street, in the heart of Greenwich Village, practically next door to the Provincetown Playhouse. Because of her distaste for bohemians, Carlotta did not often venture south of Fourteenth Street, and she expected this party to be full of scruffy men and unfashionably dressed women getting quickly drunk and arguing at the top of their voices about politics, painting, and poetry. This was definitely not her set. But Muray was quickly emerging as a photographer who was important to know, especially for someone whose fame depended on her image on magazine covers. Besides, her friend Gerald Kelley had particularly asked her to come. So she went along with several of the *Hairy Ape* cast members, who had become major celebrities in the Village, down to Macdougal Street, the site of their first triumph.

The party was well advanced when they arrived. Carlotta surveyed the crowd. As she had expected, it was dominated by Village types, men in soft collars and loose ties and jackets that needed a good brushing and pressing, women in that long, loose, uncorseted look that had been daring in 1912, Greenwich Village bohemian in 1917, and just old-fashioned and dumpy in the 1920s. Carlotta had dressed much more simply for the evening than she would have for a mid-town party, but even her simple black silk frock, with its plunging neckline framed by a dramatic white pleated lapel, made her feel a little over-dressed. She was relieved when Gerald Kelley came up to her with a delighted smile on his face.

"I'm so happy you were able to come, Carlotta," he said. "There is someone I'd like you to meet."

Carlotta was a little leery of his enthusiasm. "Who?" she asked.

"Ralph Barton," he said, his smile broadening. "I really think you two would get on together."

Carlotta knew very well who Ralph Barton was. His chic caricatures and illustrations for *Harper's Bazar*, *Judge*, and *Vanity Fair* were recognizable to anyone who kept up with the New York social scene. A few months earlier, he had scored a sensation with the intermission curtain for the fashionable Russian revue, *La Chauve-Souris*. Asked to do some caricatures of performers for the curtain, he had decided to draw the audience instead, and he spent two months painting caricatures of 135 New York celebrities, many of whom were in the opening-night audience. The souvenir program for the revue contained a key to all the figures. It was said that nobody went to the lobby during intermission because everyone was too busy discussing the curtain. This had sealed Barton's reputation as the premiere caricaturist in the country at a time when caricature was a staple element in fashionable magazines, and everyone in New York was dying to be drawn by him. Carlotta smiled up at Kelley. "All right, Gerald, if you think we should meet."

Carlotta had never seen Barton, but she had heard him spoken of as a dandy. He traveled back and forth between Paris and New York so often that he was known as "The Commuter," and he was said to affect a French fastidiousness about his appearance. She was expecting a rather pretentious, fussy man. When Gerald brought Ralph Barton up to her, she was pleasantly surprised. The young man who stood smiling before her was indeed impeccably dressed, and he stood out against the Village background as starkly as she did, but his manner was relaxed and gracious. "I thought the two people who win the prize for best-dressed and most attractive people here should meet each other," said Gerald with a big smile.

"I'm afraid that Miss Monterey has no competitors on either score," said Barton, "but I'm pleased to be in her company." He was a small man, only an inch or two taller than Carlotta. His light brown hair was parted fashionably in the middle and combed straight back. His features were not strikingly handsome in the way that Lou Tellegen's were, but his smiling face had a pleasant, harmonious appearance. His dark blue eyes were the most striking thing about him. When he looked at her, he exuded an intense vitality. "You flatter me, Mr. Barton," she said, "but looking around I must say that I don't see much competition for either of us." They all three laughed and plunged immediately into animated conversation about the theater. Both Gerald and Barton had seen *The Hairy Ape* and were full of compliments for Carlotta's performance as well as questions about the play's meaning and Eugene O'Neill's ideas, which she could only answer at third hand as they had been explained to her.

At some point, Gerald drifted away, and Barton steered Carlotta toward a relatively quiet corner of the room. She was surprised at his familiarity with her career on the Broadway stage. An avid theater-goer, he had seen *Bavu* and *Voltaire*, and even remembered her in *The "Ruined" Lady* and *A Sleepless Night*. "Of course, this is all just to keep my hand in while I look for the play that will give me the great role I have always longed for," said Carlotta. "There is so much in the theater that is not worth your time, but unfortunately you have to do some of it if you are to have a career at all."

Barton nodded sympathetically. When his eyes fixed on hers, she felt that he had no other interest in the world than what she was saying. "It's the same thing in the visual arts," he said. "I make more money with all this commercial art than I know what to do with, and the commissions keep pouring in so that I don't have time to do anything else. What I would really like to do is take six months off and just paint. Believe it or not, my heroes are Rubens and Michelangelo. But if I did that, I'd be terrified the whole time by the thought that I would never get another commission, and I wouldn't be able to paint at all. So instead, I take on too many commissions and work like a maniac to meet the deadlines."

Soon Barton suggested that they leave the party for a quieter place, and they wandered up towards Union Square until they found a cab. They went as far as Times Square, where they stopped into a coffee shop that was serving breakfast at 2:00 a.m. The conversation went on without a break. They went on from the theater and painting and their aspirations to talking about Europe. Barton was something of an expert on post-war Paris, having sailed back and forth even during the war and chronicled the changes in the city for magazines several times. Carlotta told him that she had had a great love for dear old Paris since she had gone to finishing school there and had visited the city often with her first husband who was British, but since the war she had been a little afraid to go and find it so changed. She was surprised to hear that Barton was from Kansas City. She told him that her father was a member of the Danish aristocracy who had gone to California to conduct some experiments after studying horticulture all over the world, that he had met her mother, the daughter of Swiss *émigrés*, there, and Carlotta had been born amid the orchards. They talked a good deal about the shock of encountering New York from west of the Mississippi.

With the dawn, they started walking up a nearly deserted Seventh Avenue toward Central Park, and the talk took a more intimate turn. They found that they both were in their second unhappy marriage and both had young daughters. Carlotta expressed sympathy with Ralph's anguish at the thought of leaving his little daughter Diana, just one year old, if his marriage should break up. He also had a twelve-year-old daughter, Natalie, from his first marriage, whom he doted on. He told Carlotta about his adventure of going to Kansas City and "kidnaping" her from her grandmothers when she was just six years old, so he could take her to New York and bring her up himself. Carlotta told him how hard it was to leave Cynthia in Oakland with her grandmother, although she knew it was for the best given the demands of her career and the need to spend so much time on the road.

Before they knew it, they had reached the park, and they laughed when they found that they lived just five blocks from each other on its west side, he on Sixty-Eighth Street and she on Sixty-Third. "It's very convenient for walking you home," he said. "Just like Kansas City."

During the next few weeks, Ralph Barton traveled those five blocks compulsively. He besieged Carlotta with daily flowers, twice-daily notes, and visits as often as she would permit. He took her to lunch on the days she had no matinee, and he showed up at the theater and either took her to supper or took her home at night. Carlotta had never been so close to an artist before. Although compliments on her beauty were a way of life for her, she had never known anyone who considered it in such detail. After an early visit, he wrote that he couldn't work because he was so upset that he could not visualize her nose satisfactorily. He had concentrated entirely on her eyebrows the day before. For her part, Carlotta was amazed at how carried away she was by Ralph Barton. Although she had known handsomer men, Ralph was the sexiest one of them. It was a combination of his own intense vitality, the deep interest in those dark blue eyes of his when he looked at her, and the passion for her that he made no effort to disguise.

It was not very long before they were lovers. Carlotta felt that the expression "head over heels" finally had meaning for her. She wanted to be always in Ralph's company. She found the sex the most exciting and most satisfying she had ever had. Ralph was unpredictable in everything, and never more than in bed, where his years of experience with many women on both sides of the ocean had given him a seemingly inexhaustible store of tricks.

But the most important thing was his almost obsessive passion for her. He literally could not get enough of her, nor she realized, could she get enough of him.

In June, Ralph moved out of the Sixty-Eighth Street apartment he shared with his wife and daughter and into his own on Fifty-First Street. The summer was a mad whirl for Carlotta as she was swept into Ralph Barton's world while she continued to do eight shows a week in *The Hairy Ape*. It was also her introduction to Ralph's erratic work schedule. He would feel that he needed money and accept piles of commissions. Then he would be unable to work because he felt paralyzed by the pressure of so many commitments. He would distract himself with friends and parties and amusements until the magazines and publishers were clamoring for the work, and then in a burst of activity, he would work for three or four or five days straight, almost without sleep, and, turning out an astounding number of drawings, finish everything. Then he would collapse with exhaustion and be unable to work at all. Then the cycle would begin again.

Ralph had complained to Carlotta that his commercial work left him no time to pursue the serious art he hoped to do. She could see why. Once he was in his own apartment, Carlotta set about organizing his life to get rid of the self-imposed pressure and make it possible for him to work on something besides commercial commissions. She hired Mary Jefferson, a sympathetic cook and housekeeper who tolerated the artistic lifestyle. Along with Mary, Carlotta planned their meals, and she saw to it that Ralph ate regularly, whatever he did in the evening. They got into the habit of dining at six-thirty so that Carlotta could be at the theater in time to go on at 8:30. She insisted that they dress for dinner. She told Ralph it was a habit she had acquired while married to her aristocratic first husband. As he usually went to the theater or to a party after dinner, Ralph didn't mind this, and it gave a sense of order to the day.

When *The Hairy Ape* closed in July, Carlotta was free to devote all her time and energy to Ralph. Having seen to his home, she turned her attention to his business dealings, which she perceived to be the heart of his problems. She found that he kept only a sketchy record of his commissions and deadlines, which left him not knowing when anything was due and what he needed to work on next. His system was to work on the project he was getting the most pressure to deliver. When the pressure came from several sources, he went on one of his work binges, with terrible consequences for his health and disposition. She also found that he kept no business calendar and that his business correspondence was hit or miss. Whether he answered a business letter or not depended on the general state of his mind and his interest in the project or demand that was being made. He had an enormous income for a commercial artist, but he alternately felt overwhelmed by the amount of money that came in and worried about having enough to pay for things like Natalie's tuition, which could be covered by a single drawing for *Vanity Fair* or *Harper's Bazar*.

With her usual knack for organization, Carlotta took hold of Ralph's business mess and put it in order. She made a record of his commissions and a calendar of deadlines, which enabled him to see what he had to do rather than wait to be overwhelmed. She took over his business correspondence, acting as both secretary and agent, and encouraged him to exercise more judgment about what work to accept and what to turn down. She kept a ledger of his accounts, drawing on the business knowledge she had accumulated while working for her mother. She could show him clearly what was coming in and what was going out at any given time, reassuring him that he had plenty of income. And, with the knowledge of investing that she was getting from James Speyer, she urged him to invest his capital rather than leaving it in the bank.

Ralph never knew about James Speyer. Carlotta ascribed her independent income to a bequest from a mythically wealthy Aunt Sophie Tharsing. She told Speyer about Ralph, of course, as she told him about everything. She praised Ralph's talent and bemoaned the fact that he was wasting it on so much commercial art that could never be anything but ephemeral. Her hope, she said, was to free him from mundane concerns in order to unleash the real art that it was in him to create. Speyer smiled affectionately and encouraged her. "If you see this in him, by all means, you should encourage it," he said. "You were born to be a muse. Let us hope that he is worthy of you." He had seen Ralph Barton's work, but had not seen signs of greatness in it. He did not expect this liaison to last very long.

Ralph was amazed at the sense of relief he felt now that Carlotta was ordering his life. He slept better and ate better. The headaches he had been having in the last few years were all but gone. "All I do is draw pictures," he told his friends. "Carlotta sees to all the rest." In October, his wife Anne filed for divorce. He arranged to have his daughter Natalie, who had been spending the summer with her grandmothers in Kansas City, remain there for the fall term, and left for his annual trip to Europe. Carlotta had been offered the lead role in *The Star Sapphire*, a murder mystery the playwright had yet to complete. She liked the part and had no money worries, so she decided to wait out the fall season until it opened.

In September, Carlotta was temporarily unsettled when she was replaced by the Swedish actress Martha Hedman in *The Star Sapphire*. But when Ralph returned, she plunged into decorating the new apartment at 28 West Forty-Seventh Street where they were to live together. For Carlotta, the decorating project was critical. She felt that she was creating a set where their unique partnership was to be performed. Not only was theirs a great, passionate love, it was a union of artists. As Ralph described it in Nietzschean terms, it was the perfect combination of the wild

Dionysian artistic temperament in Ralph and the Apollonian spirit of clarity and order in Carlotta. The apartment showcased Ralph's art, with one wall given over to a select gallery of his pictures above a low bookcase. At the center of the top row were a self-portrait of Ralph and his caricature of a swanlike Carlotta. In a nod to twenties minimalism, the apartment's floor was painted black and covered with a few carefully chosen rugs. The furniture all had clean, functional lines, the one note of luxury being some silk upholstery.

Chapter 33

When they moved into the new apartment, Carlotta and Ralph let it be known that they had married quietly, and they presented themselves to the world as Mr. and Mrs. Ralph Barton. They had not really been able to marry because Ralph's divorce was dragging on in the courts, but they wanted nothing more than a settled domestic life in the home that Carlotta had created for them. Aside from some petty gossip, no one questioned whether they were married or not.

Natalie came back from Kansas City in January of 1923 and was enrolled in the exclusive Warrenton School as a weekly boarder, spending her weekends in the apartment, where she slept on the living room couch. Ralph had wanted an apartment that had a bedroom for Natalie, but Carlotta had convinced him that they'd found the perfect apartment for them. It was even across the street from Ralph's favorite daytime haunt, the Gotham Book Mart, a good omen. She argued that it would be silly to give up the apartment for the extra room when Natalie was home only for weekends and school vacations. Natalie took the situation in stride. Her thirteen years had seen such a multiplicity of apartments, houses, hotels, and dormitories that she had no real attachment to any particular place and could adapt to just about anything in the way of living arrangements.

In February, Carlotta got a role that she thought might at last be the one she had been looking for. She was cast as Maria Lorenz, the lead female role in a play with the misleading title *Ladies for Sale*. Although its plot was contrived, she thought Porter Browne's play painted an eloquent picture of life in post-war Austria, and especially of her character's plight. The action hinged on a plan by some New York business magnates to enlist an important potential partner, Livingston Craig, in a big merger by offering him a beautiful Austrian aristocrat (Carlotta) as bait. Carlotta thought the second act, set in the Cabaret Hohenlohe in

Vienna, was a powerful expression of the defeated nation, impoverished in every way, and the dire straits to which even its wealthiest citizens had fallen.

In her first reading of the script, Carlotta saw that it would take a great deal of artistry to represent the pride and grace and moral probity that were central to Maria's character against the absolute pragmatism into which she was forced by the desperation of her situation. Maria accepted the offer to join the shady business scheme in exchange for a new life in the United States, but she reserved a cyanide pill, saved from the war, to take in case she was not able to avoid "immorality" with Livingston Craig. The scene in which Maria convinced Craig to refrain from taking her as part of the bargain was a rare chance for an actress to show what she could do. With the new confidence in her artistic and personal power that Carlotta's relationship with Ralph had given her, she found her way to depths of feeling that she had never expressed onstage before. In the unusually long tryout period, her performance gained in depth and confidence as the show moved to Buffalo, Rochester, Syracuse, Baltimore, Washington, and Pittsburgh.

After both play and performers were welcomed warmly by audiences and critics, Carlotta was crushed when *Ladies for Sale* closed in Pittsburgh for want of a theater in New York. There were so many new productions in 1923 that competition for theaters was fierce, and the young producers could not get a booking. They decided to close rather than to continue on the road. More than ever, Carlotta loathed the limitations of the theater and the commercial forces that drove its every aspect. No matter how great an effort she made to create something lasting and important in the art of acting, she seemed doomed to be always thwarted by circumstances.

When Carlotta returned to New York, it was with determination to help Ralph break free of commercial constraints and produce the genuine art that he aspired to in painting and writing. What she found made her see how difficult that project was going to be. In the month that she had been on the road, Ralph had written to her constantly, almost daily, and she thought his state of mind was good. He seemed cheerful and busy, and often referred to work that had been commissioned or that he was completing. He did not tell her that he had reverted completely to his old way of doing things. He kept track of nothing, and the systems she had set up to make order in his business life had fallen apart. When she opened the door to the apartment, she found him in the living room, hunched over his drawing board, unshaven and looking as though he had not bathed or changed his shirt in days. Piles of drawings were strewn about the floor so that she had to be careful to avoid stepping on them. As she stood in the middle of the room, Ralph turned to her and stared, blinked twice, and then sprang up and embraced her. "Carlotta!" he said. "My angel. You're here!"

"Ralph! What happened?" was all she could say.

He looked around the room. "I know it looks a little chaotic," he said, "but I seem to have gotten behind on my commissions, and I decided to just dig in and turn them out."

"You look terrible," she said. "When is the last time you slept?"

He laughed. "What day is it?" he asked.

"Have you eaten?"

He looked around vaguely. "Oh yes. Mary brings me food and makes me eat it."

Carlotta was taking off her hat and coat. "I'm just going to talk to Mary for a minute," she said, "and then we'll see what we can do with all this."

In a quick report from Mary, Carlotta found that Ralph had been at it for about thirty-six hours straight. Mary didn't know whether he had slept, and she'd had to stand over him while he ate. When she came back to the living room, Carlotta found Ralph frantically trying to pick up all the drawings and put them in some kind of order. She took them from him firmly and said, "Sit down, Ralph. You're exhausted. We'll sort these out together, and then you can get some rest."

Going through the drawings one by one, Ralph was able to tell her which of what turned out to be six different commissions each one was for. Once they had them sorted, he told her what order to put them in, and before too long they had six neat piles of drawings laid out. "Now," she said. "I want to you to take a relaxing hot bath while I sort out the business side of all this."

Turning to the avalanche of papers on the desk, she set herself to organizing things. In the next few hours, she sorted the correspondence and, as Ralph's secretary, wrote appropriate letters to accompany each of the piles of drawings. She packaged them up and brought all but one parcel, illustrations for George Jean Nathan's articles in *Judge* that were due that day, to the post office. She hailed a cab and delivered the *Judge* illustrations personally. When she got home, Ralph was in the living room, clean and shaved and in a somewhat better state, but still agitated and pacing up and down. For the next hour, he talked nonstop and very fast, trying to explain what had happened. It seemed he simply hadn't been able to work after she had left and had socialized compulsively, going out every night and not coming home until the wee hours. Then four days ago, he had gotten several phone calls wanting to know where the drawings were. This had precipitated his frenzied binge of work. "I hate this, Carlotta," he said. "I can't stand to go back to that crazy way of living. I need you to keep me on track. But I did get everything done," he said with a wry grin.

"Well," she said, "that's fine if you want to kill yourself in the process. We'll have a nice quiet dinner here, and then you have to get some rest."

During dinner Ralph seemed to wind down a little. He even asked Carlotta for details about the show and expressed sympathy for what had happened. Afterwards, they made rather frenzied love and Carlotta, exhausted from the day, fell asleep. Ralph did not. When Carlotta awakened in the early hours of the morning, she found him pacing the living room again. "I just can't seem to rest," he said.

She took his hand. "I think you need to get out of the apartment and out of New York for a little while," she said. "Why don't you go down to Atlantic City for a couple of days? You love the Ritz down there, and the place is empty now. It will give you a chance to collect your thoughts."

"But it's Friday, isn't it? Natalie will be coming this afternoon."

"Natalie and I will be fine on our own. It's time you had a little holiday."

Carlotta saw Ralph off on an early train, and then she set about putting his business life in order, updating the schedule and ledger, making calls to magazines to confirm that the illustrations had arrived, reading and responding to correspondence about future commissions. When Natalie arrived, she told her Ralph had been called away for a weekend visit related to business. "We'll just have to entertain ourselves," she said. "What do you say to a matinee tomorrow? Maybe we can work in a little shopping afterwards." Natalie was thrilled to be going to the theater with her glamorous stepmother, and Carlotta felt with satisfaction that all was now well in her domain. She took it upon herself to write to Ralph's mother in Kansas City, explaining that Ralph had broken down under his workload and urging her to send him only encouragement and cheerful thoughts.

Having seen how fragile Ralph's balance was, Carlotta made no effort to pursue a theater role that would take her out of town for the rest of the year. In July, she was in a musical revue called *Fashions of 1924*. She enjoyed wearing elegant clothes and looking beautiful while she performed an easy singing role, but the thirty-two cast members made for overcrowded and stifling conditions backstage, and she was glad the show ran for only ten days.

While she and Ralph spent two weeks on Long Island afterwards, she used their time together to work on the issue of Natalie, who was spending the summer with her relatives in Kansas City. Without saying that she didn't want the girl in the apartment, she made a point of discussing her future, reminding Ralph that his daughter would soon be a young lady. She said she had noticed that Natalie was picking up the values of the wealthy girls at the Warrenton School and hardly knew the difference between fifty cents and fifty dollars. Her own education at St. Gertrude's had been much more thorough and intellectual than the instruction Natalie seemed to be getting at this expensive school, she said, and she wondered if it wouldn't be better to send her to a convent in Kansas City for high school. She suggested that Ralph's financial situation would be vastly improved if Natalie could live in Kansas City with her grandmother or Ralph's niece, Bee, with whom she was very close. Having done her homework, Carlotta was able to mention that she had heard Notre Dame de Sion was a very good school run by a French religious order who would give Natalie the training in manners and etiquette that she was not receiving in New York, as well as vastly improving her French, a subject that was close to Ralph's heart. In a couple of years, she thought they could send her to a finishing school in Paris where she would encounter the cultural opportunities she would miss in Kansas City.

Ralph took all of this in with growing concern. For the last seven years, Natalie had been the most precious thing in his life. He had, after all, brought her up since she was six, when he had spirited her away from Kansas City to be with him. Carlotta always treated her well, and Natalie adored her, but he was aware without her saying so that she found the girl in the way when she was in the apartment. Her ideal of their relationship, of two intense artistic temperaments working toward a realization of their potential, did not include a thirteen-year-old girl chattering away about the week's events at school and sleeping in the living room on Friday and Saturday nights. Since Carlotta had taken over his finances, Ralph maintained an even vaguer idea of how much money he had coming in or going out, but she implied that the Warrenton School was a big expense, along with the child maintenance he was paying Anne for little Diana.

Ralph foresaw problems ahead for both Carlotta and Natalie if things continued on as they were. And he agreed with Carlotta about the Warrenton School. Natalie was absorbing attitudes and values that had nothing to do with the reality of her life. She was always happy in Kansas City and loved her relatives there. She was already spending the summers with them. He thought it was a practical plan for her to go to school there. But he knew very well that his mother, the erstwhile duenna of "Christian Metaphysics," a version of Christian Science, would balk at sending her granddaughter to be educated in a convent. In the end, he wrote to his niece Bee, who was near his age and a close friend since childhood, and asked if Natalie could live with her while she attended Notre Dame de Sion. Bee immediately wrote back that she would be delighted to have her young cousin stay on through the school year, and it was easily arranged. Ralph was relieved, but when the fall came, the apartment felt empty and joyless to him. He missed Natalie.

As the social season revved up, Ralph was glad of the distraction. There was no need for him and Carlotta to seek out social invitations. The publishers he worked with, Alfred A. Knopf and Horace Liveright, were both lavish party-givers, and Liveright was known in this period of Prohibition for his generously equipped bar. The fashionable magazines Ralph contributed to were always holding some reception or other, and Carlotta's circle of theatrical acquaintances was greatly enlarged by Ralph's from the art and literary worlds.

Carlotta did not like large parties. Her perennial shyness tended to surface when she was surrounded by a crowd of people, especially when they were witty members of the Algonquin roundtable she couldn't keep up with or artists who liked to talk philosophically about aesthetics. When she was at a large party, she took refuge in her acting skills, playing the role of a stylish sophisticate who took in the intellectual conversation with an amused tolerance, but did not enter into it. It worked for the most part, but after a few meetings, the literary people tended to ignore her.

Most of the time, Ralph felt as Carlotta did, and, relying on their small apartment for explanation, when they entertained, they held small dinner parties with conversation or perhaps a little performance or party games with the guests afterwards. Ralph's closest friend at the time was Charlie Chaplin, who spent many hours in the Barton apartment when he was in New York. He would come for lunch and stay for the day, often indulging Ralph in his favorite hobby of creating amateur movies. Their closest friends as a couple were Fania Marinoff and Carl Van Vechten. Fania was a Russian-born actress Carlotta had known since 1915, when they had been introduced by Lou Tellegen. They had clicked immediately and spent time together whenever the unpredictable currents of the theater world brought them in close proximity. In the fall of 1923, Fania was in New York performing in a hit play by Gilbert Emery called *Tarnish*. Since Carl's sexual preference was for men, Fania's marriage to Carl was one of social convenience, but it was also a deep friendship and productive artistic union. Carl was a polymath in the creative arts. From a family of bankers in Iowa, he had first made his mark in New York as a dance critic, but had moved on to music, theater and art criticism, and had published two novels, most recently the best-selling *Blind Bow-Boy*, a satirical take on the New York social scene that had prompted a great deal of moral opprobrium and made Carl famous.

In the fall of 1923, Carl and Ralph struck up a close friendship that surprised both of them. The artistic temperaments that had made them both oddballs in their Middle Western home towns gave them a shared perspective both on the past and on their present lives in New York, and their relationships with beautiful, volatile actresses gave them a lot of common experience. The Van Vechtens were enthusiastic socializers. Carl took great joy in mixing the different worlds from which he drew his many friends, so that the New York literati met Harlem, Greenwich Village, and Broadway in their large apartment on Fifty-Fifth Street. It was a stimulating world, one that Ralph, unlike Carlotta, was much drawn to. When he was in the mood for socializing, Ralph was one of those guests who would stay to the end and then suggest adjourning to a club or speakeasy. Carlotta would have gone home hours before. She reminded him constantly that such late hours were bad for his work and health, but although alcohol was not his problem, he was like a binge drinker when he was in one of these moods. Once he started on this compulsive socializing, Carlotta just did her best to keep him together and doing some work until the phase was over.

During the fall, Carlotta was intensely focused on helping Ralph fulfill his often-voiced aspiration to free himself from the restrictions of commercial art and realize his ambition of wedding his caricatures to satirical writing. She told him he could be America's Voltaire, but more effective than Voltaire because he could satirize his targets in images as well as words. With her encouragement, throughout the fall, Ralph worked on a book of light verse illustrated with his own drawings. *Science in Rhyme without Reason* included verses about subjects like meteorology, psychology, zoology, and the Theory of Relativity as well as a series of humorous biographies of famous scientists, each in a single couplet. It was a clever book, turning to account Ralph's wide reading and intellectual curiosity in fields no one would suspect him of knowing anything about. His friends expressed their admiration, but the book was dismissed by critics as a trifle, which was disturbing to Ralph and Carlotta. Ralph had expected readers to see the seriousness beneath the humor, but they failed to see the book's underlying theme, the pervasive influence of science in modern life, and treated it as a series of party tricks by a well-known cartoonist. As 1923 drew to a close, Ralph was feeling deflated and depressed.

Chapter 34

Beginning in November of 1923, Carlotta had been occupied with a new play adapted from the French and produced by the "Bishop of Broadway," David Belasco. It proved to be the most successful she had been in since *Be Calm, Camilla* and *A Sleepless Night*. In *The Other Rose*, she was cast in the familiar role of an exotic adventuress, this time a Spanish beauty. It was a thin play, and familiar stuff to Carlotta. The play was not well reviewed, but the young, engaging lead actress, Fay Bainter, made a real connection with audiences as Rose Coe, and after tryouts, it ran on Broadway through March of 1924.

While either on the road or playing eight shows a week in New York, Carlotta had much less time to concentrate on Ralph. He had become used to having her in the apartment, managing everything so smoothly with Mary Jefferson that he hardly knew the housekeeping was taking place, tending to his business and all his little needs and whims as he worked, and then dressing beautifully to go out or just for dinner with him. To keep her attention on him, he took to making little demands or complaining about the way she had arranged his schedule or the housekeeping or the state of his clothes. She was irritated that he no longer seemed grateful for all she did to order his life so he could attend to his work. He seemed oblivious to the great effort that went into making things easy for him. She began to respond sharply or sarcastically to his demands and complaints, which led to quarrels during which neither one of them voiced what was really bothering them, leading to further frustration and further quarrels.

They began to think their problem was that the apartment was too small. They were in each other's way too much and needed more space for Ralph's work, for Carlotta's ever-expanding wardrobe, and for entertaining. After *The Other Rose* closed, they took a lease on a bigger, more luxurious apartment on East

Fortieth Street. Ralph liked the fact that it had more room to display his art collection along with his own work. Carlotta liked the fact that it had bigger rooms and more space to decorate. She made sure that Ralph's work was strategically displayed along with favorite items from his book and art collections. But they had hardly moved into the apartment in the middle of June when Ralph began to complain about the noise from the traffic, seven floors below. The noise made it impossible for him to sleep or work, he said, and they would have to move.

It was a particularly difficult time for Carlotta because she was deep into rehearsals for a new play, *The Sable Coat*, a melodrama that centered on the theft of the Czarina's priceless jewels and fur coat after the Russian Revolution. Carlotta played another glamor-ous villain, part of an international gang of crooks. The play was to begin tryouts in Atlantic City on the fifth of July. She told Ralph she could not possibly find and decorate a new apartment while this was going on. He insisted he could not possibly stay on in this apartment another day. While Carlotta was in Atlantic City, Ralph had their belongings moved several times to different vacant apartments in the building, each on a higher floor than the last, trying without success to escape the sound of traffic. When the play closed out of town two weeks later, Carlotta returned to find Ralph in a frantic condition. They spent the rest of the summer looking for a house to buy or a lot to build on outside of Manhattan, but they found nothing that pleased them.

The solution Ralph came up with was to rent a studio in the Hotel des Artistes, on West Sixty-Seventh Street near Central Park, where his fellow artist and old friend from his first days in New York, Neysa McMein, had her studio. Ralph's instinctive solution was to retreat to the hotel and Neysa's soothing friendship whenever he became frantic with New York living. Carlotta couldn't see a better one, so they moved Ralph's art materials and their essential belongings to the studio. Part of

Ralph's anxiety was caused by the sixty-five drawings he was commissioned to produce in a few weeks' time. The noisy apartment had been one of a series of things that he insisted had kept him from working. In the new studio, he hoped to get down to drawing, but he was irritable and brusque with Carlotta, deliberately starting quarrels that she found herself unable to resist escalating.

Perhaps it was the atmosphere of the Hotel des Artistes, Carlotta reflected, but she felt her emotions often rising beyond her control when she was dealing with unreasonable words or behavior from Ralph. She had often gone to rehearsals or the theater seething with anger, which dissipated as she became engrossed in her work. When she was not involved in a play, her anger festered as she brooded about Ralph's behavior and his failure to acknowledge all that she did for him. It broke out finally in screaming fights like those of the old days with Jack Moffat. They always made up, usually with passionate sex to follow, and Carlotta wondered if this were just the inevitable consequence of a union of two volatile artistic temperaments, but she wished she could control the situation.

In September, Carlotta decided it was better for her to be out of the apartment working rather than hanging around waiting for Ralph to set her off. When George Broadhurst offered her a role in a play that he had co-authored, she accepted, even though the part was yet another exotic beauty who tempts the hero away from the heroine. *The Red Falcon* was an old-fashioned costume melo-drama set in sixteenth-century Sicily. In a complicated plot involving nuns and marauding bandits, she played a passionate young woman who was in love with a priest but engaged to his best friend. She thought it was a bad play and took the role only because Broadhurst owned the New York theater where it was to be produced, practically guaranteeing a short tryout period and a Broadway run. It did run at the Broadhurst, but only for fifteen performances. The reviews were merciless. The critic from the

Herald-Tribune wrote that "the clothing of the play is beautiful and so is Miss Monterey who wears most of it." By the end of October 1924, Carlotta was again out of a job.

After the show was over, Carlotta and Ralph began a serious search for a new apartment. They found one at 68 East Sixty-First Street, in a much quieter neighborhood than Fortieth Street, and near Central Park, which they both loved. They were still paying rent on both the Forty-Seventh street and the Fortieth Street apartments, but Ralph said the expense was worth it for the peace and quiet. Once again, Carlotta set herself to decorating. By this time, they had a kind of formula, with books, *objets d'art*, and drawings on display in simple modern rooms with Chinese touches like the ornamented lacquer screen that hid Ralph's drawing desk and materials in the living room. Although this was a large apartment, he still preferred working there to being off in a separate room. Once they had settled in, Ralph bought a car and hired a chauffeur. He told friends and relatives that it was important for business reasons for him to make a good appearance, and he had no intention of driving in New York. As profligate as he had been with money in the last year, Carlotta knew that he could well afford it. He was receiving twelve hundred dollars for a single drawing from the magazines at a time when working people were making forty or fifty dollars a week—and he turned out a lot of drawings.

In November, the venerable actor and producer Henry Miller cast Carlotta in an adaptation from the French called *The Man in Evening Clothes*. She played the Countess Germaine De Lussange, whose husband becomes convinced that she doesn't love him and goes off on a spree, spending his fortune on other women until he is reduced to bankruptcy and, by French law, left with a single suit of clothes. He chooses evening dress, so he can continue to receive invitations to dine out. Germaine meets him at dinner one evening, and they reconcile. The critics panned the play, although the Bartons' friend Alexander Woollcott described "the lovely and capable Carlotta Monterey" in the *New York Sun* as looking like "an animated Botticelli fresco."

The December issue of *Vanity Fair* had a full-page photograph of Carlotta and Ralph by Nickolas Muray with the caption, "Mr. and Mrs. Ralph Barton, American Artists, One of the Drawn, One of the Spoken Line. . . . a distinguished couple in the artistic circles of New York." It was a confirmation of Carlotta's ideal for them, in one of the most influential New York publications, but it rang hollow for her. The time between her birthday on December twenty-eighth and New Year's day was always a time of taking stock. On this birthday, she was thirty-six years old. She passed in theatrical circles for thirty, and on stage she could get away with playing a young woman in her early twenties, as she had in *The Red Falcon*, but she was fast approaching the age when her beauty could no longer carry her. She knew she did not have the skills or the talent to play character parts the way Merle Maddern and Fania Marinoff did, and she wasn't sure she would ever want to. She had gotten into the theater to become a leading lady, and it was becoming clearer with each month that the part she had awaited for ten years, the part that would bring her the fame and esteem of a Helen Hayes or an Ethel Barrymore, was not going to arrive. She was very tired of it all. But to give it up and become a silent junior partner in Ralph Barton, Inc.? Was it something to devote her life to, especially as an unsung collaborator? "Who am I if I'm not Carlotta Monterey?" she thought. Hazel Tharsing? She wasn't even Mrs. Ralph Barton. And remembering the tempestuous fall of 1923, she had no desire to go back to being without work of her own.

In early January, Effie Shannon, a good-natured older actress Carlotta had become friendly with when they were in *The Other Rose*, called to find out if she would like a part in a movie she was in. They were just about to start filming the new Richard Barthelmess movie *Soul Fire* at a studio on Forty-Eighth Street, and the actress who was to play the part of Princess Rhea had pulled out. Effie told Carlotta she could play the part in her sleep. It was the beautiful and mercenary fiancée of a young composer who drops him when he turns from writing popular jazz music to composing the symphony he has dreamed of writing, telling him she won't waste herself on "an empty-headed fool chasing phantoms." A few years earlier, Carlotta would have dismissed this opportunity because it was a movie and another typecast role. But she knew from listening to Charlie Chaplin and seeing a lot of movies with Ralph that the standards for making them had improved immensely just in the six years since she had made *The Cost*. There was a real art to film acting now, and many of the background shots and technical effects were better than those in the most technically adept productions of David Belasco. It would be no detriment to her career to be in a movie. More and more actors were going back and forth between motion pictures and the stage. "It will be fun to be on the set together," said Effie. "You can't beat the working conditions. There's no travel. You work during the day and sleep in your own bed every night. And you don't have to learn any lines."

"Well, why the hell not?" said Carlotta.

"That's the girl," said Effie. "Now things happen fast in the movie business. They want you to come down this afternoon at three o'clock for a test, 318 East Forty-eighth Street. I'm sure it will go well, so I'll see you on the set tomorrow."

Carlotta laughed. "All right," she said. "See you soon, Effie. And thanks. This will be a change from the rut I've been in, whatever else happens."

Two days later, Carlotta was on Forty-Eighth street, deeply involved in making *Soul Fire*. Ralph was delighted that she was making a movie. Every night, he wanted to know the details of what they had filmed that day and all about the camera set-ups and lighting. The director, John Robertson, did not like extra people on the set, but Ralph was so eager to see the filming that

Carlotta used her charms to get him to let Ralph come to watch the filming one day. He stayed from beginning to end, getting as close as he could without annoying Robertson. He engaged all the filmmakers in conversation when there was a break, from Robertson and the cinematographer to the cameramen and grips. Carlotta had thought Ralph might draw a caricature of Barthelmess or the female lead, Bessie Love, but he didn't have time for the actors. "You're so lucky to be part of this every day," he said to her on the way home. "You should do nothing but films from now on." The movie was a success. Carlotta was happy with her performance, and when the film was released in early May, she was singled out for praise by the *New York Times* critic, who called her "sinuously effective" as Princess Rhea.

Chapter 35

While Carlotta was making *Soul Fire*, the work schedule was helpful for her home life. During the day, she wasn't in the apartment, and Ralph could draw all day in the living room without their getting in each other's way. Since she was not dashing off to the theater in the evenings, Ralph didn't go out as much looking for company, and they didn't have to rush through their six-thirty dinner. They often stayed in the apartment for the evening, reading, listening to the gramophone or Ralph's player piano, and talking. But by the middle of February, when Carlotta finished filming, Ralph was showing ominous signs of restlessness. As she was catching up with the business details, Carlotta found that he was falling behind schedule. When she started spending a good part of her day in the apartment, she realized that he was not drawing very much and would seize on any pretext to go out on an errand, often not returning for hours. Before long, this extended to the evening, and he would stay out so late, often coming home with the dawn, that he slept most of the day away. When he was at home, he was irritable and uncommunicative, except for a familiar string of complaints about New York and the impossibility of working in the city. He insisted they would have to move if he was going to get any work done.

All of this was familiar to Carlotta, but this time, instead of talking about moving across Central Park, he started saying they should move to Paris. It was the only civilized city, he insisted. They could live a calm, productive life there. He said they should buy a house and move all their belongings to France, returning to New York only for a few weeks at a time, as tourists. It would be good for them to be settled in Paris when Natalie came there for school next year. At first, Carlotta thought it was a crazy idea, but as she thought about it, she agreed that Paris would be a better place for Ralph's work at the moment. He needed to break from the frenetic all-night drinking life that had been spawned by Prohibition. His interests and social habits in Paris were much calmer and more intellectual than they were in New York. And a change of scene was always good for his work. She was not too concerned about the effect the move would have on her career. She knew very well it would not be permanent, given Ralph's volatile personality. It would be expensive, but if he was working steadily, they would have no trouble paying for it. She was ready to be free of New York for a while herself.

"If you really mean this," she said to Ralph, "there's one detail we need to take care of. If I'm going to pull up stakes and become an expatriate, I want to be really married."

"All right," he said. "I'd forgotten that we weren't."

As they began making plans to go to Paris, Ralph pulled quickly out of the doldrums and not only finished the commissions he owed but started a backlog for his regular magazine features so there would be no break in his contributions during their travel. He also took on a new commission for *Harper's Bazar* that turned out to be one of the most important of his career. Anita Loos, a young writer he knew through the Algonquin circle and whom he had caricatured a few times, had written a piece as a kind of joke for H. L. Mencken about a seemingly stupid but worldly-wise young flapper named Lorelei Lee, who managed to fleece a series of besotted middle-aged businessmen by taking them shopping and sweetly demanding presents.

She had sold it to the magazine, which agreed to a story in a series of six installments, to be called "Gentlemen Always Prefer Blondes." Ralph was engaged to do six illustrations for each of the six installments. After turning in the first one, both Anita Loos and the Bartons sailed for Paris, where a good part of the story was to be set. But before they left, Ralph and Carlotta slipped down to Elkton, Maryland, a little border town that capitalized on the state's lax marriage laws to run a profitable wedding business. On the seventeenth of March 1925, Hazel N. T. Chapman was married to Ralph Barton. There were no guests. When they boarded the *Minnetonka* for Europe a week later, they were in truth Mr. and Mrs. Ralph Barton. The Paris trip was their honeymoon.

They arrived in London on April sixth and found it so dull and gloomy that they escaped to Paris as soon as Carlotta was able to visit the makers of her favorite hand-made shoes and place her order for the next season. They were soon settled in a rented apartment on the rue Scribe, across from the *Palais Garnier*, the Paris opera house. That spring was the best part of their life together. Ralph simultaneously relaxed and came to life in the city he loved best in the world, and Carlotta was happy to have him recognize her expertise in French living. They spent the days in museums and galleries. In the evening, they dressed to the hilt and enjoyed being looked at while they dined and went to the theater or a cabaret. They made several trips to the suburban countryside, ostensibly to look for a house to buy, but Carlotta was sure by then that it was only a caprice of Ralph's, and he was much happier living a transient life in the City of Lights.

Ralph worked faithfully on the Loos illustrations as Anita sent the manuscript installments to him and he contributed a number of drawings and caricatures to other magazines, especially the newly minted *New Yorker*, of which he was one of the founders. Carlotta visited the designers she loved and replenished her ever-growing wardrobe. She found it hard to keep up with the fashions changing so fast in the twenties, and most of her income from the Speyer trust was going for clothes and shoes. Ralph never inquired about the prices of things or the state of her finances. It was enough for him that she looked beautiful and stylish.

The middle of May brought an end to the idyll. Seemingly overnight, the tourists started to arrive en masse. The city seemed to be engulfed in vulgar Americans. Museums, cafes, and restaurants became crowded. They found themselves in social situations with people they would never see in New York. Ralph lost his inspiration and started to mumble that they might as well be in New York, since Paris was ruined by Americans. Carlotta saw that it was time to go if Paris wasn't to turn into a disaster. On the twenty-seventh, they sailed from Le Havre on the *Paris*.

When they arrived in New York on the sixth of June, they heard from the Van Vechtens that *Soul Fire* had been released in New York with great fanfare. Richard Barthelmess and Bessie Love had been on hand at the Strand Theater, along with a symphony orchestra to play the ambitious score. They showed Carlotta the review in the *Times* with its praise for her performance. "You're a movie star now," said Carl.

"Well, hardly," said Carlotta. But she thought she would be glad to take on another movie role.

The summer of 1925 was busy. The Anita Loos story, which ran from March through August, was such a hit that *Harpers Bazar* had increased its readership four-fold, and plans were afoot with Boni and Liveright to publish it as a book with Ralph's illustrations in the fall. They spent a lot of time in Anita's company that summer. It was not company Carlotta enjoyed. Like most of the people in the Algonquin set, Anita paid no attention to Carlotta. She considered her one of the decorative objects in Ralph's apartment, a wife who needn't be taken seriously. When she was around, Carlotta might as well not have been in the room as far as either Anita or Ralph was concerned. He loved the quick repartee of the "smart set," laced with literary references and inside jokes that Carlotta often didn't get. She had a hearty, earthy sense of humor, and she enjoyed a good joke, but the snide, ironic viewpoint of these people did not strike her as funny. She tended to be quiet in their company unless directly spoken to, and they did not speak to her often.

One night, after they had been at a party with the literary set, Carlotta complained to Ralph that he had paid no attention to her, left her in a corner by herself or with some bore while he flirted with other women. She felt that he no longer saw her, not only when attractive women were in the room, but when he was with men who interested him. She had always felt jealous of Charlie Chaplin, but now she began to have these feelings about New York friends, even Carl Van Vechten, who often went to the theater with Ralph, and took him who knew where afterwards, leaving her in the apartment alone. She confronted Ralph, complaining that he did not appreciate all she did for him, that he no longer complimented her or gave her little notes or gifts. She felt invisible in their apartment, like somebody's wife.

"Well isn't that what you wanted to be, Mrs. Barton?" he asked flatly. He rarely answered her complaints directly, which only infuriated her more. As the rage grew within her, she could not control her tirades. His response to them was silence, after which he usually left the apartment. By the time he came back, she was feeling drained and remorseful for her attack, and she apologized, usually leading to a passionate reconciliation. 1925 was turning into 1923 all over again.

At the end of the summer, Monta Bell, a protégé of Charlie Chaplin's, offered Carlotta a small part in his new movie, *The King on Main Street*. She jumped at it, even though it was yet another adventuress who gets her just deserts. With stars like Bessie Love and Adolphe Menjou, the movie was bound to be widely viewed, and she was delighted to get out of the apartment. Ralph's friendship with Charlie gave him credibility with Monta Bell. He visited the set more than once, taking it all in and asking all sorts of technical questions. Carlotta thought he might really be happy if the next phase of his career was in the movies.

Carlotta's scene in the movie, on location in Cony Island, took only a few days to shoot in September. As the social season revved up, the dynamics of her relationship with Ralph grew worse. The Loos book, now called *Gentlemen Prefer Blondes*, was scheduled to be released soon, and Horace Liveright was concentrating his efforts on making a big splash with it. Since Horace loved nothing more than a good party, he was keeping Ralph and Anita busy on the social circuit. Ralph was staying out all night, drinking too much and working very little. In the apartment, he was either silent or irritable, ignoring Carlotta or finding fault with everything she did. His failure to appreciate, or even acknowledge all she did for him bothered her more and more. Their life was a series of explosions and passionate reconciliations. Carlotta found herself threatening to leave Ralph when she was roused to anger.

One evening in September, they had the Van Vechtens to dinner, and Carl stayed on after Fania had left to go to the theater. When they sat down in the living room with some fine brandy Carl had brought, Ralph struck an urbane pose and said, "Carl, I wonder if we could get your opinion on something. Carlotta and I are finding it more and more difficult to get along, and we're wondering whether we should separate."

Carlotta felt the blood rush to her face. Ralph had never expressed this wish to her in so many words, and she was upset at having their marital difficulties aired in this way. But with an effort, she controlled her anger and said nothing. She trusted Carl's loyalty. He was certainly aware of their troubles, and she thought it might be good to hear his objective view of them.

Carl was reluctant. "I don't know," he said. "I realize that I am a champion gossip, but when it comes down to it, who among us can really understand the intimate relationship of a couple who are in love? You are in love, aren't you?"

Ralph looked at the floor. "I don't know," he said. "Are we, Carlotta? You seem to spend a good deal of time screaming at me."

"Because you make me furious," she said. "You pay no attention to me. You aren't grateful for everything I do for you. You only mention it to complain about something. When anyone else is around, you ignore me."

The argument escalated from there, with Carlotta responding more and more stridently to Ralph's shrewdly calculated remarks.

Carl sat and watched them, occasionally asking a question or offering a short remark, but, a dedicated novelist, he was too fascinated by the dynamics of the two people in front of him to really intervene. The passion rose, Ralph goading and Carlotta responding, until Ralph finally got up from his chair, went over to Carlotta, pulled her to her feet and looked directly into her eyes. "Enough," he said. "We know we love each other. I want you to show it, now." As they began frantically to undress each other, Carl knew that he was meant to see this. It had been Ralph's intention all along, perhaps a test of Carlotta. In any case, there was no doubt about their sexual desire for each other, and they both liked to be looked at. They put on quite a performance, which Carl later recorded in his daybook, not that he was likely to forget it. After it was over, he drank the rest of his brandy and left. There was nothing else to say.

There were more incidents like this throughout the fall, and Ralph began to play with fire, flirting openly with other women and reviving his reputation for promiscuity, something he knew Carlotta would not abide. One afternoon in November, Carlotta came home unexpectedly to find Ralph in bed with Ruth Goldbeck, the young widow of the painter Walter Goldbeck. This was a woman Carlotta particularly detested, a society girl from Rhinebeck-on-the-Hudson, New York who was a close friend of Anita Loos's. Carlotta was sure Ralph had insulted her on purpose by bringing this person to their bedroom and that he expected her to find them. Whether he had intended it or not, it was the last straw for Carlotta. She left the apartment and checked into the Madison Hotel at Fifty-Eighth and Madison. When she called Mary Jefferson the next day to ask her to pack some of her things and send them over to the hotel, Mary said she might as well come over and choose what she wanted herself. Mr. Barton was at the Hotel des Artistes.

Since adultery was still the only grounds for divorce in New York, Carlotta's lawyer arranged with Ralph to have a private detective come to his studio and "catch" him with a woman. This happened on January second. Two days later, Carlotta wrote to Ralph, detailing the things she wanted him to send her from the apartment. Stricken with remorse, Ralph wrote to Carlotta and asked her to consider a reconciliation. He talked mutual friends into interceding for him. But having once taken the step, Carlotta was finished with this marriage. She realized that she had been miserable or seething with anger for most of the last year, and she knew that reconciling with Ralph would just start the whole cycle over again, with higher emotional stakes. That was how Ralph played the game. It was just not worth it to her anymore. She might be distraught now, but she knew she would recover. On March tenth, Carlotta filed for divorce on the grounds of adultery, requesting no alimony. In one last shot at her, Ralph filed a reply, contending that Carlotta's jealousy of his daughter Natalie was the cause of their marital difficulties. Both charges were true in their way.

Chapter 36

After the break from Ralph, Carlotta set about beginning a new life. She was surprised by the supportive response when she wrote to Nellie in January. Mel had remarried and moved out of the Santa Clara Avenue house, but Cynthia remained with her grandparents. Nellie was the strongest parent figure Cyndy knew, and the nine-year-old had not wanted to move from the house that had always been her home to live with her stepmother and stepbrother. Caring for her granddaughter also gave a socially acceptable reason for Nellie to remain in the house with Mel Sr. They all had asked Mel to let her stay. Nellie saw to it that Cyndy wrote her mother little letters regularly. And now that Carlotta was in the movies, Cyndy was very interested in her mother's career.

Carlotta thought about a visit to California but decided in the end that it was better to recuperate from her break-up in New York. She saw a good deal of James Speyer as well as her friends Merle Maddern and Fania Marinoff, who were both in the city. She reflected that her life was more than Ralph Barton. She had sacrificed a great deal and subordinated her career to helping him fulfill what he said were his artistic aspirations, only to feel that she'd been deluded. If Ralph had ever had real aspirations, he had left them behind long ago. Now he was interested only in the quick commercial success that came from doing drawings that were easy for him. He could turn out a devastating caricature without turning a hair, and once he had an image of the characters in something like *Gentlemen Prefer Blondes*, illustrations were effortless for him. He would never give up the easy success and the big money from these drawings to devote himself to hard striving after an artistic ideal. Carlotta determined that she would not make this mistake again. When she got involved with a man in the future, he would be someone who was worthy of her devotion, a serious and proven artist who had the makings of a genius. Only then would she consider the sacrifice worthwhile.

In March of 1926, Carlotta was with James Speyer at a benefit for the Actors Guild when Bess Marbury took her off into an alcove for a private chat. Carlotta was a little surprised because she had never had dealings with Bess, but she was happy enough to talk with her. As a young woman from a prominent New York family, Elisabeth Marbury had practically invented the profession of theatrical agent. Back in the 1880s, she had become the agent for the writer Frances Hodgson Burnett, author of the wildly popular *Little Lord Fauntleroy*. Traveling to Europe, she had made use of her success and social status to connect with the literary establishment in England and France, securing clients like Oscar Wilde and George Bernard Shaw. She was the agent for some of the most successful American playwrights of the twentieth century and had joined with other agents to form the American Play Company, a successful producing organization that stood its own against the Shubert and Frohman theater trusts.

Aside from her business acumen, Bess had stood against Victorian conventions by living in a well-known lesbian relationship with Elsie de Wolfe, a former actress who had become a pioneer in the profession of interior decorating. They had lived together for twenty years, during which Elsie de Wolfe, with the leaders of New York society as her clients, had been a major force in transforming New York's Fifth Avenue mansions from Victorian trophy houses, paneled or wallpapered in dark hues and crammed full of heavy furniture and draperies, to beautiful houses inspired by seventeenth-century French design that were meant to be lived in comfortably, with walls painted in light colors, and furniture upholstered in stripes or prints.

De Wolfe liked to say that she had opened the doors and windows of American houses and "let the sunshine in." She had transformed Bess Marbury's Sutton Place townhouse by essentially turning it around to give the main rooms access to the garden and the view of the East River and using those facing the street for service rooms. She was something of a heroine to Carlotta, who had adapted her ideas in decorating James Speyer's house and her own apartments.

Once she had Carlotta seated next to her stout form on a small sofa, Bess got right to the point. "I saw that you've filed for divorce," she said. "It looks as though we're in the same boat, Carlotta."

At first Carlotta had no idea what she was talking about, but then she remembered that a week before her divorce was announced, she had seen the coverage of Elsie de Wolfe's marriage to Sir Charles Mendl, a British diplomat in Paris. "Yes," she said, "I read that Elsie de Wolfe made her home with you when she was in New York. You will miss her."

"Carlotta," Bess said, looking at her in her direct way. "I'm glad to have run into you here. I've been thinking of contacting you. Why don't you come and stay with me on Sutton Place for a while? I've always thought you were a lovely person whom I would like to know better. We're both theater people who are used to a certain standard of society. I think we would be good company for each other while we're adjusting to things."

This was completely unexpected. "But that's so kind of you, Miss Marbury," Carlotta said.

"Bess."

"Bess, then." Carlotta looked at the elderly lady and smiled. "Well, I don't see why not. I'm still living at the Madison Hotel. It would be lovely to spend some time with you at Sutton Place."

"Good," said Bess, giving her hand a squeeze. "It's settled, then. I'll have the car call around for you. Today is Thursday. Shall we say Saturday, at 2:00?"

"That would be fine," said Carlotta.

"I'll see you then" said Bess. Then, her business concluded, she got to her feet with the aid of Carlotta and her cane.

"Well," thought Carlotta. "One adventure closes and another one opens." She went off to find James Speyer, who was not too happy to hear that Carlotta was moving in with Bess Marbury.

"This won't be good for your reputation," he said.

"I can't imagine it could do much damage," she said. "Bess is so old." Immediately, she thought that this was not the thing to say to Speyer, who was sixty-four. "She must be well into her seventies, and she seems older than her years. The opposite of you," she said, smiling.

A little chuckle escaped him. "Very kind of you," he said.

Carlotta was surprised at the state of things on Sutton Place. As she had expected, the house was beautiful, with no expense spared in the architecture or the detail of the decoration. But it was not well-kept. The meals were often not ready on time. Her bedroom was not attended to during breakfast, but was often left until late in the morning, when she would have to either stay out of the maid's way or leave the room while she cleaned it. Paying close attention to the housekeeping, she noticed that the entrance hall was sometimes dirty, and there were actually cobwebs in the library. The beautiful white woodwork and the curtains were badly in need of cleaning. One day when there were no guests and they were chatting over their tea in the drawing room, Carlotta picked up a little figurine from a side table and, holding it out to admire said, "Goodness, it's covered with dust. She flicked it with her handkerchief and put it back on the table. "You know, Bess," she said. "I don't think you are getting the best from your servants."

Bess laughed. "No, I'm sure I'm not," she said. "I'm hopeless with servants. I've always left everything about the house to Elsie, and when she's away, the mice will play, I suppose. Now that she might not be coming back at all, I don't know what I'll do."

"I'd be happy to help," said Carlotta. "I'm actually a bit bored since I don't have any real work to do right now, and I have a lot of experience with household staffs. My first husband's family live in castles in England and Scotland."

Bess laughed. "Well, this is no castle," she said. "But it is a beautiful house when it's taken care of. If you think you can whip these people into shape, I wish you'd have a go at it."

"All right," said Carlotta. "If you will tell the staff that I'll be taking charge of them, I would be happy to help."

Carlotta was actually very good at running a household. Long ago, she had learned from Nellie how a house should be cleaned and how American workers should be managed. From Jack's mother and sister, she had learned many of the flourishes of gracious living. She had never been able to afford most of these things, but Bess Marbury could. Carlotta happily took charge, being careful not to alienate the staff by being demanding or imperious at the beginning. She gained their confidence as she would the supporting players in a theater company, with the general attitude that they were all in this together and the house was their production. She used her usual arsenal of compliments and little attentions, gaining their loyalty and putting them on their mettle to produce the best results in whatever their jobs were, from polishing the car or cleaning the bathrooms to cooking impressive meals for guests. Before long, the house was running as smoothly as the Bartons' apartment had.

Bess did not notice the individual things that had made the change, but she appreciated the result. In early May, as they sat together in the breakfast room, she asked Carlotta if she would come with her to her summer house, Mount Vernon, at Belgrade Lakes, Maine. "I hope you can work the same magic up there that you have here. That place can really use it."

"I don't know," said Carlotta. "It's so kind of you to invite me, Bess, but Maine seems so isolated."

"Oh, but it's a beautiful place, and we have our artistic community there," she said. "Florence Reed and Malcom Williams are good friends, and there are several other theater people nearby. Richard Madden tells me his prize client Eugene O'Neill is going to be there with his family this summer."

Carlotta raised her head at this. Eugene O'Neill. She remembered how he had insulted her by his indifference on the set of *The Hairy Ape*. He was a handsome young man who was fast getting the reputation of America's greatest playwright. This was the sort of man she was determined to associate with now. "Well, you certainly make it sound more interesting," she said. "But I really shouldn't trespass on your hospitality any more than I have."

"Don't be silly," said Bess. "I think of you as the dearest of friends now." She reached across the table and gave her hand a squeeze.

"As I do you." Carlotta returned the squeeze. "But people will start to talk, if they haven't already."

Bess tossed her head. "People will talk regardless. What do we care? I know you don't make love to women, and I'm seventy years old, but that's no reason why I shouldn't have a beautiful woman join me on vacation."

Carlotta laughed. "I suppose not," she said.

On the outside, the house on Long Pond resembled the rustic Maine camp that Carlotta had envisioned, only it was much bigger. The house was set back on a broad lawn that led to the water. In a rambling, cedar-shingled addition to the main structure, Bess had built a guest wing with eight bedrooms and eight baths. The property had an old barn and a new boathouse. To get around, there was a speedboat as well as the car. The story was the inside. Inspired by the many antiques that had come with the house when Bess bought it, Elsie de Wolfe had created a beautiful interior. The sense of history embodied in the American antiques was framed by a light, modern, and comfortable decorating scheme. Supplied with every new appliance available, the kitchen was a wonder.

Carlotta soon found that the staff from the New York house was delighted to be in Maine, where their accommodations were more generous than in the city and the working conditions were more relaxed. She added to them a couple of local young women who did the wash and heavy cleaning and helped out when Bess was entertaining. She found it an invigorating challenge to open the house and spruce things up. By early July, Mount Vernon was running as smoothly as the Sutton Place townhouse, and, unless they were planning a big dinner party, Carlotta was free to spend her days as she liked after giving directions to the cook and the maids in the morning.

On an intensely bright, sunny day in the middle of July, Carlotta went with Bess to see Florence Reed and Malcolm Williams over on Great Pond. For her visits with Florence Reed, who had enjoyed a big success as Mother Goddam in *The Shanghai Gesture* that season, Carlotta paid particular attention to her appearance. On this day, the deep vee of her white frock emphasized her long, graceful neck as well as her breasts, and her famous profile was framed by the short brim of a pretty, cherry-red straw cloche, which had been dyed to match her hand-made shoes. When she got out of the car and looked toward the pond shimmering in the intense sunlight, she just made out Eugene O'Neill coming up the path from the water in his bathing suit, his lean, muscular figure tanned very dark and his handsome face looking positively chiseled in the sunlight.

"You go ahead," she said to Bess. "I'll be right along. I just want to take in the beauty of the pond before I go inside."

With a glance, Bess saw what Carlotta was eager to take in, but she just smiled and waved her hand. When Carlotta reached O'Neill on the path, she could see that he had been looking at her as she came toward him. She extended her hand, cocking her head and looking up at him through her long lashes. She knew the sunlight was at the perfect angle to emphasize the framing of her lovely face. "Hello," she said. "Do you remember me?"

There was nothing for O'Neill to do but take the proffered hand. A little flustered, he said, "Of course I remember you, Carlotta. It hasn't been that long since the *Ape*."

She smiled. "No, but you've done so much since. I know how it is when you get busy in the theater. You go from cast to cast, and your fellow workers become instant intimates, while the ones from the last show are forgotten. Then it's out of sight, out of mind until the next time you meet on stage."

O'Neill nodded. "I know what you mean. I'm certainly discovering that since I've been doing Broadway shows. It was different at the Provincetown. We were so much one big, squabbling family that we couldn't forget each other if we wanted to."

They had started strolling toward the house. Given the disaster of their last meeting, Carlotta was surprised at the immediate rapport that grew up between them. After being greeted by their hostess, they sat side by side in a corner, O'Neill still in his bathing suit, and talked together for the rest of the afternoon, only joining in the general conversation when one of them was addressed directly. In the car on the way home, Bess remarked that she had never seen Eugene O'Neill so at ease in a social gathering.

That night over dinner, Florence Reed and her husband were discussing the day. They too thought that O'Neill had been unusually sociable. They were used to his sitting silently unless he was alone with Malcolm or swimming the side-stroke alongside Florence as she paddled her canoe. Then he would talk a blue streak. "Did you see what was going on?" Malcolm asked.

"What do you mean?"

"Carlotta seems to have left a scarf behind."

"Well, we can have Annie return it to her when she goes out in the morning to shop."

"No need. She'll be back to claim it tomorrow at two-thirty when Gene comes up to the house after his swim."

And she was. This time it was only O'Neill and the Williamses in the room, so the talk had to be general, but when O'Neill walked Carlotta out to the car, he asked if she would like to come and swim with him. "I swim every day," he said. "I usually swim from my house across the pond to here and stop to talk to Malcolm for a while before I swim back."

Carlotta looked up at him and smiled. "Oh, I could never swim that far," she said. "I never learned to swim properly."

"Well, why don't you come by our camp on Friday," he said. "You can swim a little, and then we can canoe or something. Come around 2:00. Agnes will be glad to have you for tea afterwards."

From their conversations, Carlotta already knew that O'Neill's routine was to get up early and work until lunch time, then go for a long swim and work some more or read in the late afternoon. In inviting her, he was giving up his cherished exercise and his afternoon's work. She smiled at him. "All right," she said. "But I'm warning you, I'm no swimmer."

Chapter 37

When Carlotta stepped into the O'Neill living room, she was appalled at what she saw. The house was nice enough, a rather large Maine vacation house covered with cedar shakes. A beautiful fieldstone fireplace dominated the living room. But the place was chaotic. The first thing that assaulted her was the smell of the baby diapers, not very well washed, that were hanging in a corner of the living room. Children in wet bathing suits trooped loudly through the room while Carlotta was chatting with Agnes, and their towels and toys and fishing gear seemed to be everywhere. Agnes, a pretty but rather disheveled woman with striking blue eyes, must have noticed her reaction, despite her attempts to conceal it. "I hope you'll excuse the vacation mess," she said. "It's bedlam here with all the children. This is Oona," she said, picking up a toddler who had been pulling at her skirt. "And that is Shane." She pointed to a little boy about six years old who sat on the floor trying to untangle a fishing line. "My daughter Barbara is also with us this summer, and Gene's son, Eugene Jr. So it's quite a full house."

Carlotta was much relieved when Eugene appeared and quietly suggested that she change into her bathing suit. "Is everyone going in?" Carlotta asked, a bit reluctantly. She was torn because she wanted to put on her suit, actually a boy's knitted suit with a white top and dark shorts, quite daring with its low neck and lack of a modest overskirt and calculated to reveal her curves. But she did not like the water. She had been terrified of it ever since her father had pitched her into the Feather River at age three, insisting it was the best way to learn to swim. In her teens, she had learned to do a respectable side stroke, but she still hated to put her face in the water. Knowing how important swimming was to O'Neill, she didn't want him to see how poor she was at it so soon.

"I'm afraid Oona has a bad cold," said Agnes, "so she and I are staying out of the water for now. Barbara and Gene Jr. are off somewhere. You two should just go ahead and have your swim, and then we can have some tea afterward." Agnes had caught the glowing look that Carlotta had given Gene, taking it for the usual actress's attempt to ingratiate herself with the Great Playwright. Before yesterday, she had never heard him mention Carlotta Monterey except to disparage her acting, so it didn't bother her to send them off together and give herself some time to tend to things in the house.

After its awkward start, the afternoon proved to be everything Carlotta could have hoped for. They swam around in the shallow water near the shore for a while, but once O'Neill saw her limitations, he suggested that they take the canoe out. They paddled to a sandy spot O'Neill knew and dragged the canoe up, lying in the sun and talking for half an hour before they started back to the house. During all these activities, Carlotta knew that however badly she performed, she looked good doing it. Afterwards, when they came in for tea, she made a point of talking to Agnes and to Shane and the teenaged Eugene Jr., who basked in the attention from this glamorous actress.

During the rest of the summer, Gene and Carlotta met often at different houses, and they usually found a way to talk together by canoeing or going for a walk. Much as they tried to disguise it, their growing intimacy was evident to Bess, who was quite fond of Agnes. She warned Carlotta that she was playing with fire. "O'Neill might seem like a domestic cat around here," she said, "but, trust me, he's as wild as ever. He cleans up his act when he's writing, but when something sets him off, he'll be off on a binge, and it's always Agnes who goes and drags him out of the gutter and gets him on his feet again. You should take my advice and keep your distance."

It was far too late for that. At first, Carlotta had intended just to flirt with him, perhaps draw him into a little romance, to show that she could. But as he talked and talked to her during these summer afternoons, he revealed his unhappy childhood, permeated with the feeling of being unmoored and unloved, his adolescence when he lost faith in everything but his older brother's cynical teaching that life was a game that was fixed against you, his desperate hope to find something different by shipping out to sea, and his downward spiral into drunkenness and despair in the slums of New York, ending in a failed suicide attempt and then a year in a tuberculosis sanatorium. It was his writing that had saved him, he told her. Finding that was finding something sacred again, something worth going on for. He had cut down his drinking so that he was able to abstain while he was writing, only going on an occasional binge after he finished a play. The plays were everything. He could stand being sober, he could stand anything, as long as he was able to write.

During these bouts of revelation, Carlotta felt that she had found the genuine, dedicated artist she had been searching for, the genius she could nurture and inspire to create great things. She reflected that Gene had no idea how much he was being held back by the circumstances of his life, by the noise and chaos around him. Agnes's slapdash housekeeping and the constant presence of loud, demanding children was the worst thing for his work. She thought about the things she would do to create a quiet home for him, a place where everything was done to smooth the way for his writing. She had done a lot of this for Ralph, but he lacked the fundamental thing for creating great art, an artistic soul. Eugene O'Neill had that all right, and she began to feel that it was her destiny to serve his genius.

In the fall, Carlotta resolved to put some distance between her and Bess. When they returned to New York in October, she rented a small but elegant apartment on East Sixty-Seventh Street, near the park. O'Neill was in town, staying at the Harvard Club while he attended rehearsals for the new production of *Beyond the Horizon*, due to open in November. Agnes and the children were at the O'Neills' house in Ridgefield, Connecticut. Carlotta invited Gene for tea one Tuesday afternoon following the rehearsal, with not very satisfactory results. He came into her apartment, took off his coat and hat, sat himself down in a chair, and began talking about the rehearsal and everything they were doing to ruin his play. Carlotta understood this shoptalk perfectly, and she made the right expressions of sympathy and interest as she served him his tea, but he seemed hardly to notice. After an hour or so, he got up and left, barely thanking her for the tea. It was a different O'Neill than she had known in Maine, more like the man she had met during *The Hairy Ape* in 1922. She stood looking at the door after he had left. "Well, that's that," she said.

The next Tuesday, Gene phoned to ask if she would have lunch with him on Thursday. "There's a decent restaurant at the Hotel Wentworth," he said. "I've moved in there. There's more room, and it's near the theater." So Carlotta took a cab down to Forty-Sixth Street and had lunch with the great Eugene O'Neill in the heart of the theater district. They got some stares, which Gene seemed not to notice, but this was a much more pleasant meeting than the last one had been. He talked quietly, asked her opinion on some things, and even apologized for being "distracted" the last time they met. As he put her into a cab, he kissed her on the cheek and thanked her for the day. She wrote him a note, thanking him and telling him that the luncheon had meant a good deal to her. On Saturday, she received a letter from him, saying he had tried to phone and suggesting that they get together soon, perhaps for a walk along Riverside Drive. Carlotta was charmed that he was so obviously trying to recreate their Maine meetings.

In the early days of November, they met for lunch or for an afternoon walk whenever O'Neill could take time from a rehearsal. After lunch at the Wentworth one day, Carlotta decided that the time had come to move things along. She went to the ladies room and bit a nail, making a ragged tear where she pulled it off. At the table, she told O'Neill she had broken it, and asked for a nail file. O'Neill patted his pockets and said, "I'm afraid I don't have one on me."

"Perhaps you have one upstairs?" said Carlotta.

"I think I have one in my toilet kit," he said.

"Well let's just run up and look," she said. "I really need to fix this."

When they got to his room, O'Neill took the situation quite literally, looking through all the drawers until he located the canvas bag that passed for his toilet case. Carlotta observed a beat-up suitcase on the floor, and in the drawers, a couple of shirts, a pair of pajamas missing some buttons, three suits of rather shabby underwear, and three pairs of socks, one of which had a big hole in the toe. Clearly Gene's clothes were not Agnes's first priority. After he had located the file and she had used it, she calmly took off her hat and coat and sat in the room's only chair. "This is cozy," she said. "Let's sit and talk a while."

Gene did not need a further invitation. Lightly placing his finger under her chin, he tilted her face up to his. "You don't know how long I have been waiting to do this," he said as he leaned over and kissed her. They spent the rest of the afternoon in his room. Carlotta took pleasure in his lean, muscular body and found that, for such a self-absorbed man, he proved a sensitive lover. The next day, she went to Abercrombie and Fitch and bought six shirts, six pairs of socks, six suits of underwear, and a fitted leather toilet case. She had the package sent to him along with a note that read, "Here's to something new!" She was a little nervous after she'd sent it, thinking that she had gone too far, and he might take it as too great a liberty, but she was happy to find he was pleased with the gift. "You certainly know what I need," he wrote.

The next two weeks were a delight for Carlotta. Not only had she caught the biggest literary fish on Broadway, but she found him a surprisingly satisfactory lover. He lavished attention on her, coming to see her or writing every day, and he even sent her flowers. On his last evening in New York, they had spent a long time talking about their future, coming back again and again to Carlotta's assurance that "everything will come out as we wish it." Gene said that he would tell Agnes about his love for Carlotta when he returned to Bermuda. "We have a firm understanding," he said, "if one of us should fall in love with someone else, the other will set them free, no strings attached." Carlotta doubted that a woman who had three children and only her income from writing magazine romances would stick to this agreement, but she was elated that Gene would take such a step for her.

When Gene sailed for Bermuda on the twenty-seventh of November, Carlotta felt unsettled and bereft, to a degree she had never expected. Although he addressed her as "Dearest" and "Dear One," the letter he wrote from the ship was disappointing. He took refuge in corny dialect from *The Hairy Ape* rather than expressing his love directly, although he did say that his longing for her was a kind of hell. Over the next few weeks, Carlotta poured out what she found to be her increasingly desperate unhappiness in letters to him. She wrote three to his one and felt that his became more distant and offhand with each passing week. He had indeed told Agnes about her, but she began to wonder whether his declaration hadn't been more to get Agnes's attention than to secure his freedom. He told Carlotta that he loved both of them, and while he kept writing of his longing to see her, and he sent her a box of roses as big as a coffin for Christmas, he made no more allusions to the idea of leaving Agnes. By the end of December, he was apologizing for letting so much time lapse before he answered her most recent letters. In February, after letting three weeks go by, he said that he had been so taken up with writing *Strange Interlude* that he had not had a chance to write to her. His letters became more and more about his work, with just a perfunctory expression of love at the end.

Feeling him slip away, Carlotta was shattered. She had put so much hope into this relationship—had felt, as she phrased it, faith in her heart and dreams in her head, for the first time since the early days with Ralph. She became depressed and anxious. She took morphine for the insomnia she developed, which made her restless as it wore off. As she always did when she felt despair creeping up on her, she turned to James Speyer for comfort, spending more time with him than she had in years. He was always interested in her life. One evening toward the end of February, when they were having supper at the Viennese restaurant after the opera, he looked at her kindly and asked, "What is the matter, Carlotta? You are so pale, and you have been restive all evening."

She looked across the table with tears in her eyes. "I have had a romance, and it has all gone wrong," she said. After telling him the story, she said, "It's been such a disappointment to me. I thought he was at last the great artist whose genius I could nurture, but I think he's lost interest."

Speyer observed Carlotta. She clearly had been suffering. There were dark rings under her beautiful eyes. Her famously luminous skin looked dull and washed out. And he had never seen her so helplessly emotional as when she told him about this love affair. He knew she was an emotional woman, but she was a good enough actress to keep the intensity of her feelings from showing when she wanted to. He was quite aware that the feeling she had for him was only a sort of grateful affection. He flattered himself that he pleased her in bed, as she did him, but there was no passion on her side. He thought that, at its height, her feeling for Barton had been an infatuation, or more accurately, a response to the intensity of Barton's apparent infatuation. Her response to O'Neill seemed to be of a different order.

"I've seen for the last few weeks that you are uncharacteristically anxious and depressed," he said. "It is painful to me to see you suffer. What you need is distraction from this. Why not come with me to Europe this summer?"

Carlotta looked at him. "But how could we travel together?" she asked. "It would be all over the newspapers."

"We can be discreet. It would not be the first time I have taken a holiday with a lady," he said with a smile. "We can sail on different ships, and once we're in Europe, as long as we have separate suites in fairly large hotels, no one will pay any attention."

Carlotta smiled. "Oh, it's a wonderful idea. Where would we go?"

"I would like to show you my beloved Germany," he said, enthusiasm lighting his grey eyes. "I think it would do you good to take the cure at Baden-Baden."

"The cure?" She had visions of hospital gowns and doses of strange medicines.

"Don't worry," he laughed. "It is a mineral spa, quite delightful, and there are all sorts of entertainments for diversion. We might also go to Marienbad. I have the usual business in Paris and Berlin and some other cities. You can travel with me or stay in one place if you choose to."

"I would love to go," she said, her image of a dreary summer in New York or a trip to California fading from view. "Thank you so very much, dear James. You always know how to banish my blue devils of despair."

The planning for the trip took up a good deal of time and attention during the spring, buoying Carlotta's spirits. She and Speyer spent so much time together that they began to be noticed by the gossip columnists. This seemed not to bother him, so Carlotta ignored it, except to write to California that Speyer was a dear friend, thirty years older than she, and there was nothing to the rumors that they were a couple. To O'Neill in Bermuda she wrote that she would be sailing for Europe alone in the middle of June. He wrote back that he was very sorry he wouldn't be seeing her until the fall, when he came for the rehearsals of *Strange Interlude*.

As Speyer had predicted, the trip restored Carlotta's health and self-confidence. She enjoyed the cure, which amounted to a daily bath in the mineral spa, followed by a massage. The town of Baden-Baden, a resort for the wealthy of Europe, had the best of everything when it came to dining and amusements. They went every night to a concert or the opera or theater. For casual relaxation, there was a casino, and they spent a good deal of time just sitting in cafes and watching the stylish parade pass by. Carlotta went with James to Frankfurt, Berlin, and Amsterdam, cities she had never visited before, as well as to Marienbad for another week of the cure. To see these cities in the style of cultivated luxury with which James Speyer did everything was a treat she was not likely to have again.

Chapter 38

Carlotta arrived back in New York on the ninth of September 1927 feeling fit and pampered and beautiful. She had thought little about Eugene O'Neill since her voyage to Paris in June. At that time, it had seemed that her last hope for a meaningful artistic life was fading away. Now the future seemed open to her. On the voyage home, she had thought about going back to acting in films or trying her hand at writing. She certainly knew a good deal about plays and how they worked in the theater, and she had always liked to write about people.

As soon as she opened the door to her apartment, she saw an envelope with the small, distinctive handwriting that she immediately recognized on top of the mail in the basket where her cleaning woman had been collecting it. O'Neill's letter, dated August 30, described the desolation of New York when she was not there and asked her to please have lunch with him at the Wentworth on September 10. Immediately, all of Carlotta's carefully won composure was gone. He sounded ardent. She was excited at the thought of seeing him. But she was not eager to be drawn back into all of that. In the end, she could not resist the opportunity to see the state he was in and to bowl him over with her new Paris clothes, her healthy, youthful look, and her composure, which she was sure she could simulate if she didn't feel it.

The lunch was a surprise in many ways. O'Neill was genuinely delighted to see her. He could not stop telling her how beautiful she looked. In what was obviously a carefully planned speech, he explained to her what had happened in Bermuda, with the writing of *Strange Interlude* claiming his mind and the chaos of the household, major renovations adding to the usual disorder, deadening his soul. He explained that, while he had thought of her endlessly, a kind of paralysis had crept over him. His despair at finding a way to make "everything come out as we wish it," kept him from writing to her. Now that he was in New York, alone, he said, he was amazed that he hadn't seen the way before him in a clear light. It was Carlotta he loved. He could not imagine a future without her.

Carlotta wondered how much of his certainty and ardor had to do with the fact that Agnes had not come to New York with him, and she was right in front of him, looking radiant. Nevertheless, she forgave him for the lapse in letter writing. They had a quiet lunch, talking of Carlotta's trip and of the state of *Strange Interlude*, but she could feel the tension rising between them right up until they refused dessert or coffee and rose to leave the dining room. She felt Gene's hand on her back, confident, possessive, steering her toward the elevator. "If you have a minute," he said, "I have something to show you upstairs."

When they reached his room, he said nothing, but started gently unbuttoning the front of her dress, kissing her mouth, her neck, her breasts. "How many times have I dreamed of this," he said. "Your skin is matchless. It is divine. I could live off it alone."

He undressed her slowly and deliberately, and they made love luxuriously. There was no hesitation in his manner. He held nothing back. Carlotta thought later that she had never felt such ecstasy, such spiritual exultation, as she had felt that afternoon. She now knew what the word transcendent meant. She thought theirs was a deep, spiritual connection that she would always feel, no matter what else happened with this mad genius of hers.

The next day, Carlotta called James Speyer at his office and asked him to take her to lunch. When he saw her walk into the restaurant, he knew that something momentous had happened to her.

"What is it, my dear one?" he asked after they were seated. "You are simply glowing."

She smiled at him with no effort to conceal her happiness. "O'Neill," she said. "He's come back, and he is in love with me."

Speyer had suspected as much. He had made something of a study of O'Neill since the episode the previous spring, wondering what it was that had so shaken Carlotta. O'Neill was a handsome man, certainly, and, he noted with a certain chagrin, still in his thirties. If she was looking for a great theater artist, she could probably do no better. O'Neill was considered the next best hope for a truly distinguished American playwright. Speyer had seen most of his plays, and he had taken the time to read the ones he hadn't seen. He thought O'Neill very accomplished for a writer his age, although the talk of greatness was still a matter of potential. In Speyer's view, *Beyond the Horizon*, which had started all the talk in 1920, was a conventionally romantic, although well-constructed play. The excitement with which it had been received was more reflective of the state of the American theatre than of the play. *Anna Christie* was an original character study, but O'Neill had failed to push through on its tragic implications, taking refuge in melodrama which was, once again, conventional.

Speyer found O'Neill's experimental, expressionistic plays more interesting. *The Emperor Jones*, which he had seen in New York, was an extraordinary experience. It drew the audience helplessly into the primal state of fear being enacted on stage. *The Hairy Ape*, despite O'Neill's denials, was certainly influenced by Georg Kaiser's *Von morgens bis mitternachts*. It was less original than *Emperor Jones*, but again penetrated to a primal human experience, profound alienation from one's own kind. Speyer thought *Desire Under the Elms* old-fashioned theater with its New England dialect and its melodramatic trappings, but its unblinking revelation of jealousy, greed, and what Freud would call Oedipal feelings, was worthy of the Greeks. The esthetic ambition of O'Neill's most recent play, *The Great God Brown*, with its Nietzschean underpinnings and its experimental use of masks in performance, exceeded the playwright's grasp, but the ambition itself was remarkable. At any rate, he was certainly more original than any other playwright working in America, and there was clearly some kind of genius in the way he laid bare the most primal of human emotions and forced the audience to feel them.

Speyer thought O'Neill had the potential to create plays unlike any others, plays that would reveal essential things about humanity. But he was also a cruel and remorseless truth-teller. This would be a challenging combination in a lover, although certainly an interesting one. He suspected that the intensity of O'Neill's emotions would match Carlotta's. In some ways, this could make for an extraordinary experience for her. In others, it would surely make her miserable. But there was no doubt that O'Neill could offer what she said she wanted, a true artistic talent that could be nurtured, perhaps into genius.

"Do you think that pursuing this romance will make you happy?" he asked.

"I don't know," she said. "But I don't seem to have a choice."

"Well, then, you must pursue it," he said with a gentle smile. "But try to keep your eyes open."

The next six weeks was the happiest time of Carlotta's life. Gene came home to her every night after rehearsals. In the city, they did many of the things they had done the previous year, but to them, the world seemed altered. Every walk in the park was freighted with meaning. When Speyer invited the two of them to dinner at his house on Fifth Avenue, Carlotta explained to Gene that he was one of her oldest friends in New York and had taken a kindly avuncular interest in her life and career. If O'Neill had suspicions about this relationship, he did not reveal them, and he found Speyer such an engaging companion that he dismissed any jealous thoughts.

Speyer spoke to O'Neill out of a deep knowledge of the drama, and especially of O'Neill's plays, that the playwright had rarely encountered outside the theater. Having seen several of the plays in translation in Europe as well as the productions in New York, Speyer kept placing O'Neill's work in the context of great European dramatists like Strindberg and Ibsen as well as esteemed contemporaries. They also spoke of O'Neill's deep philosophical affinity for Nietzsche and of his skepticism about Freud.

"If you want to see what I really think of Freud's ideas," he said, "wait until you see *Strange Interlude*. There are no holds barred in this one."

"I would like to escort Carlotta to the premiere, if I may," Speyer said, smiling.

"Of course, James," she said. "I will look forward to your commentary at the dinner break."

"And I'll look forward to hearing it from Carlotta," said O'Neill.

Speyer was reassured by his meeting with O'Neill. The playwright was much more engaging than he had expected, having heard and read so much about his dark, self-absorbed and brooding nature and his lack of social graces. He had been simple and modest in affect, responsive in conversation. Of course, it helped that the conversation had all been about him and his work, which was clearly his overwhelming interest. But he did seem to be very much in love with Carlotta, and she with him. If Carlotta wanted to make a career of nurturing a great talent, this was certainly her opportunity. From what she had told him about the domestic chaos that kept O'Neill from concentrating on work, he knew that Carlotta could do a great deal to improve things. It was what she was best at. James Speyer told Carlotta that she had made the right choice. O'Neill was a genuine artist. With her inspiration and help, he would someday write a great play.

In late October, Gene had to return to Bermuda, and this time, he wrote the kind of love letters that Carlotta had dreamed of, addressing her as Dearest Shadow Eyes, declaring all that was left of him was a great empty ache for her, and saying he counted the days and hours until he was in her arms. He wrote nearly every day. His friend Kenneth Macgowan brought her huge bouquets of roses O'Neill had commissioned him to buy.

The joy of their reunion when Gene returned on the fifteenth of November was something neither had ever experienced. During the next month, they only grew closer. Carlotta took such a deep interest in every detail of the *Strange Interlude* production that Gene managed to bring her to the closed rehearsals a couple of times, so she could give him her advice. Nina Leeds was the role that Carlotta had dreamed of during her whole career in the theater. Using his experimental technique of having the characters speak their thoughts in asides that served as a stream-of-consciousness commentary on the dialogue, O'Neill dramatized a psychologically complicated woman in all the facets of her relationships with men—with her father-figures, her lover, her husband, and her son. She was the center of the action in a nine-act play that would run for five hours in the theater, so long that it began at five-fifteen and included a dinner break, ending at eleven. Before its opening, *Strange Interlude* was already the talk of New York. A year earlier, Carlotta would have been consumed with jealousy of the celebrated Lynn Fontanne, who had the role. But now she was observing the rehearsals with the playwright and giving him notes on Fontanne's performance, suggesting ways the director could improve some of the scenes. And O'Neill was listening carefully to her.

As the *Strange Interlude* rehearsals went on, Carlotta and Gene were also planning their escape from New York. They knew it was only a matter of time until their relationship was discovered, and they became the focus of gossip-mongering reporters and photographers. For Gene, being hounded by the press in this way was a circle of hell to be avoided at all costs. Carlotta was determined to become Mrs. Eugene O'Neill and to assume the social position of devoted wife and muse of the Great American

Playwright. It was vital that she appear before the public with him only after their marriage. They decided to go to Europe as soon as possible after the premiere, traveling separately, and each booked passage for Southampton on the *Berengaria*, departing just ten days after *Strange Interlude* was to open. Their plan was to spend a short time in London and then go on to France, finding a house or a small chateau in a remote region where they could live quietly until Gene's divorce came through and they could marry. Anxious to be out of New York, Gene was enthusiastic about the trip. He talked about extending it eventually, perhaps going as far as China, which he had always wanted to see.

After writing to Agnes in the middle of December to pack up and send his manuscripts to New York because he thought someone wanted to buy them, Gene wrote her a letter in which he offered her, as a Christmas present, her "absolute liberty," essentially declaring their marriage over. Agnes cabled that she understood what he was saying and promptly came to New York, moving into the Hotel Wentworth where he was staying. The ostensible reason was to come to an agreement on the terms for their separation or divorce, but Agnes was really interested in a reconciliation. Carlotta was devastated. When she talked to Gene about it, she could feel the old panic rising, her hard-won composure leaving her. "She can't *be* here!" she cried desperately, "You have to get her out of here!"

Taken aback by a side of Carlotta he had never seen before, Gene insisted there was nothing he could do to get Agnes out of the hotel. They had to hammer out the terms of the divorce somehow, and she had a right to be there. Before they knew it, the argument had escalated beyond control. Carlotta was wildly accusing Gene of bringing Agnes to New York on purpose in order to get rid of her. Gene was yelling at her to stop behaving like a hysterical woman and see the reality of the situation. Finally, Carlotta left, telling him to write to her if he ever decided what he really wanted.

The estrangement between Carlotta and Gene did not affect his relationship with Agnes. It quickly became clear to her that there was no way to save their marriage, and she concentrated on getting the best terms she could. In mid-January, when they had come to a temporary agreement with the help of the family attorney, Agnes went back to Bermuda. With Agnes out of the picture, Carlotta was able to see how irrational her fears had been. She admitted as much to Gene. As a token of her apology and his forgiveness, she bought him an overcoat lined with fur, a luxurious item that he never would buy for himself. He loved the coat, not only for what it stood for but for the grand gesture itself. "You are queenly," he said to Carlotta.

When *Strange Interlude* opened on the thirtieth of January, Eugene O'Neill avoided the theater, as was his custom, awaiting news of the play's reception with an old friend in his hotel suite. Carlotta went to the opening on the arm of James Speyer. During the dinner break, they phoned the good news of the enthusiastic audience reception to the playwright. The newspaper reviews were beyond anything even O'Neill had imagined. "A great play," said the *Post*, "a rich and wise and beautiful and original and profound and immensely moving play." "The most important event in the present era of the American theater," said the *World*. "A venture magnificent, and a milestone to cleave the skyline of the future," said the *Sun*. On the next day, the lines for tickets stretched around the block. *Strange Interlude* was that almost inconceivable com-bination, a great work of literature and a smash hit on Broadway.

In the ten days after the opening of *Strange Interlude*, Gene put out a press release that said he was leaving for a vacation in Del Monte, California, a little play on Carlotta's name, and that he planned to be on hand for the American premiere of *Lazarus Laughed* in Pasadena.

Carlotta sublet her apartment and packed up her life. She put most of her belongings into the set of Louis Vuitton trunks she had bought for her trip with James Speyer. Since most of her belongings were her vast collection of clothes and shoes, it wasn't hard. The few household items she wanted to save went into storage. After sending her luggage ahead to the ship, on the morning of February tenth, she took a taxi from Sixty-Seventh Street down to the pier. In the cab, it occurred to her that the sum total of all the hard work and determination and struggle of her thirty-nine years was contained in those exorbitantly over-priced French boxes. She suddenly felt alone in the world. She had not seen her daughter or her mother in more than two years. She vowed that she would make it up to Cyndy and be a mother to her when she got back from Europe, but even as she made it, she knew it was a futile promise. She was nothing to Cyndy but an occasional letter or gift in the mail. The girl hardly knew her. And if the deepest truth be told, Nellie was glad to have her daughter out of the way. Carlotta was leaving the comfort of James Speyer and her life in New York for Eugene O'Neill and the promise of a brilliant future. He was a stranger really, despite her mad passion for him. Of all the chances she had taken in her life, she thought, this was the riskiest.

When Carlotta opened the door to her stateroom, the first thing she saw was a glorious bouquet of flowers in shades of red, tastefully luxurious. Immediately, the anxiety she had been feeling began to ease. In the midst of his own emotional turmoil, Gene had made an extravagant and thoughtful gesture to assure her of his love. She opened the card. "Remember," it said, "you will always be treasured in New York. James."

Epilogue

Mrs. Eugene O'Neill

On a summer afternoon in 1956, Carlotta Monterey O'Neill sat in her suite at the Hotel Lowell on Sixty-Third Street in New York, waiting for a visit from three young men. They were from an obscure Off-Broadway theatre, Circle in the Square, which had just done a surprise hit revival of Eugene O'Neill's *The Iceman Cometh*, a play the Theatre Guild had all but killed with its botched production in 1946. The young men, director José Quintero and producers Ted Mann and Lee Connell, didn't know about the gift Carlotta was planning to bestow on them. It was O'Neill's masterpiece, *Long Day's Journey Into Night*. The play had so far been produced only in Sweden, in translation. The decision to produce it on Broadway was controversial, to say the least, since O'Neill had left directions with his publisher that it was not to be published until twenty-five years after his death and was never to be produced.

Carlotta felt justified in what she was about to do. Gene had been so concerned, back in 1940, that the play would damage his reputation or his children's lives. But what did it matter now? Gene was dead. Eugene Jr. was dead as well. Craving attention to the last, he had slashed his wrist and ankle in the bathtub, imitating a Roman Emperor like the classics professor he was, and left a note next to an empty whiskey bottle, "Never let it be said of O'Neill that he failed to empty a bottle. Ave atque vale." Shane was a hopeless drug addict who couldn't be harmed by the revelation that the same was true of his grandmother. And Oona, for whom she and Gene had both had such hopes when, in her early teens, she'd visited them in their beloved California home and was so bright and well-mannered and lovely. Oona had been the worst disappointment. Gene never forgave her for trading on the O'Neill name for publicity, and then at eighteen, marrying Charlie Chaplin, of all people, without so much as informing her father and stepmother beforehand. It had been Carlotta's idea to cut Shane and Oona out of the will, so she would have sole control of the plays as well as the money, and Gene had agreed with her. He knew she would make better decisions than those two ever would. And she was convinced that the best thing to do now, for O'Neill, for his waning reputation, and for her own good, was to have *Long Day's Journey Into Night* produced.

Carlotta reflected that she had been there from the beginning with this play, "written in tears and blood," as Gene had written in his inscription to her. She had listened to him day after day as he raked up the painful memories from the past and shaped them into scenes. She had typed the first draft, working with a magnifying glass to decipher his miniscule handwriting, the only way he could write once the tremor had begun to affect his hands. The play was hers as much as his, and it was good. It was the best thing ever written by America's greatest playwright. She was convinced the production would wake up the theater to a true appreciation of O'Neill. More productions and revivals of his other work would follow, and there would be royalties. She admitted frankly to herself that she needed the money. The income her trust fund brought in had been enough for a comfortable, even lavish life in the 1920s, but now she had to watch her expenses. The royalties from a hit play would give her peace of mind about the future, something she had certainly earned after twenty-six years as Mrs. Eugene O'Neill.

As she sat in the little parlor of her two-room hotel suite, waiting for the young men, Carlotta's mind wandered back over those years, and her grand plan to serve the great artist. What had it meant, really? Gene had often called her his "mother, wife, mistress, friend." Add to that architect, building contractor, decorator, secretary, nurse, and, at times, cook, gardener, and maid. How she had tried to make a real home for them, where he would have the perfect conditions for his writing and they could live a peaceful and happy life together. During the "exile" in France before his divorce was final, when they were flush with royalties from *Strange Interlude*, she had modernized the chateau at Le Plessis and put in a pool, so he could have his daily swim.

With French servants, she had run their home as well as any of the Moffat relatives had run their English castles and manor houses. Thinking back, it might have been their happiest time, when they were passionately in love with each other, and they weren't bothered by anyone else except the few visitors they invited to stay with them.

Things had become difficult when they'd returned to New York. The Park Avenue apartment was impossible. There were too many associations from the past for both of them, too many New York people they didn't want to meet. Carlotta had meant for them to come from Europe with fresh identities. She had fitted Gene out with English tailoring and hand-made shoes in order to leave all semblance of the bohemian Greenwich Village writer and marathon binge drinker behind. In 1931, he looked the part of a distinguished man of letters and, with their quiet country life at Le Plessis, had almost conquered his drinking.

For herself, she had fashioned Mrs. Eugene O'Neill as O'Neill's muse and an elegantly refined lady, the chatelaine of a perfectly run household. She wanted to be the hostess of exclusive evenings with carefully chosen guests. The main problem in New York was that the past was always intruding itself in the form of Gene's old friends and drinking buddies from the Village, and even the Bowery, as well as less than desirable connections that both of them had in the theater and some alarming eruptions from the past. It hadn't helped that Ralph Barton had shot himself two days after their return to New York, leaving a suicide note that called Carlotta his "beautiful lost angel, the only woman I ever loved" and said that she was "the only person who could have saved me had I been savable." She sighed. Something in her had felt vindicated at having Ralph say this, but she also knew this breach of their privacy was Ralph's revenge on Gene for being a more acclaimed artist than he was. He knew the publicity would be exactly what they most dreaded. The next day, poor Gene had had to face a press conference, already scheduled by the Theatre Guild to publicize *Mourning Becomes Electra*. It was a horrible ordeal. Only natural then that their revulsion from New York would leave them susceptible to the charms of Sea Island, Georgia. They had decided to move there in the course of a two-week November vacation.

The house in Sea Island had been Carlotta's first, and in some ways, grandest creation. It was to be their final home, their retreat from the world, the perfect setting for Gene as he did his greatest work. It had a pristine white sand beach where he could swim in the ocean every day of the year. The beautiful twenty-room house that Carlotta designed had cost a fortune—$100,000 in 1932, in the depths of the Depression—and had taken the lion's share of Gene's *Strange Interlude* earnings. They came up with the little play on their names, Casa Genotta, to honor their creative life together.

The building reflected Carlotta's unique taste. It was like an English manor house built in a Southwest style, with its tiled roofs and floors and architectural details meant to keep the building cool in the stifling Georgia heat, but also high-arched windows and heavily beamed ceilings in the downstairs rooms, which were furnished like an English country house. She did a mental tour of the house and found she still remembered every carefully considered detail of every room. She could look out every window and see the view. She knew the way the light fell at every time of day in every season. She remembered how she had acquired every piece of furniture. Gene had loved his study, a spartan room that was shaped like a ship captain's cabin, furnished with just book shelves, two chairs and a simple desk. The house had a central courtyard with a beautiful garden and a fountain. Carlotta had relished every minute of creating it—the hours of talk with Gene planning their perfect home, the meetings with the architect, the months of construction. She had handled it all, and she had succeeded in realizing her vision.

The finished house was beautiful. But they hadn't reckoned on the climate. In those pre-air-conditioning days, they couldn't live there in the summer, when they both were reduced to a trance-like lethargy, dripping with perspiration if they tried to move. Throughout the year, the salt air and the humidity made for a constant battle with the mold and mildew. The curtains went limp. The bed sheets were clammy. Gene suffered from chronic health problems and could not work. Carlotta grew heartily sick of the humidity, the punishing heat, and the ocean. By 1936, it was clear that they couldn't live in Sea Island. They sold the house at a $25,000 loss and moved to the West Coast. Carlotta thought wistfully that the best thing they had salvaged from the years in Georgia was the devoted Herbert Freeman, who had stayed on with them even after she'd had to fire his incompetent wife. It was a godsend that he agreed to move West with them.

She passed over the short, disastrous stay in Seattle, which Gene had spent mostly in the hospital after nearly dying of peritonitis poisoning. Rainy, grey, and humid, Seattle in January just seemed like a cooler version of Sea Island. It was Carlotta who decided they should move to the San Francisco area. Now that they were in the West, she felt a strong desire to be on familiar ground. But she knew she would have to plan carefully. For one thing, she was wary of being too close to her family. She had given careful attention to shaping Gene's understanding of her background. He had met Nellie and Cyndy, but Carlotta had been careful to control the circumstances. In New York, she kept them busy with shopping and the theater and restaurants so there was no time for long conversations with Gene. When Cyndy visited them in Sea Island, Carlotta packed her off every day with Freeman to drive her around and show her the scenery. In the evening, they listened to music from Gene's record collection and went to bed early. After a few days of this, Cyndy got so bored that she begged Nellie to let her come home early from her visit. When, at sixteen, she married Augustus Barnett, Cyndy became his problem for a couple of years. They moved to San Diego, and Carlotta no longer felt the need to play the concerned mother to a teenaged daughter.

In general, Carlotta had given Gene to understand that her family had a higher social standing and more money than it had. She had been playing that role since her years in England, and it was habitual by the twenties. What's more, it was what gave her power in the marriage, something that, after three disasters, she knew she needed. With Gene, she was the urbane and well-born sophisticate who was there to tutor her rough-edged Irish American husband in elegant living. Nellie understood what her daughter was doing, and did her best to keep up the pretense, but she could not fool an observant person for long.

After finally making a success of his last farm, Chris Tharsing had retired and moved to Marin County to raise his five children with his third wife. He had died in 1932, and Carlotta had never met her half-siblings, so she no longer had to worry that Gene might discover that her father was a blunt immigrant fruit farmer rather than a highly educated experimental horticulturalist from an aristocratic Danish family. But in Oakland, there were all the Gotchett and Shay relatives, and of course, her aunt Sophie Tharsing, who was supposed to be the source of her generous income. Gene would never believe that for a minute if he met her.

She decided they should create an estate in the hills east of Oakland. The climate would be perfect for them. The air was dry, and the rain was confined to the winter months. It never got too hot or too cold, and if they had a heated pool, Gene could swim every day. They rented a house on the eastern outskirts of Berkeley and began to look for land. Their Golden West arrived in the form of a 158-acre parcel in the Las Trampas hills with a view of Mount Diablo, an isolated rural spot at the top of a winding road that had been part of a ranch.

Carlotta smiled as she thought of the day they had found it. It was a good thing they had the $40,000 from Gene's Nobel Prize to work with, because the house Carlotta created there cost more than $100,000. They called it Tao House, which stood for "the right way of life," and was built, like an ancient Chinese house, around a central courtyard. Carlotta took credit for the unique fusion of Chinese motifs and California ranch style architecture. It had long, low brick wings with tiled roofs surrounding the courtyard. Inside, she decorated with a simplicity that she thought was true to the house as a setting for the life of artistic creation, but also fashionable. White brick walls, dark blue ceilings and mostly tiled floors set the stage for a few pieces of very good furniture. Bookcases were the main adornment. Gene's study was another small sanctuary like a ship's cabin, dominated by a writing desk and books. The house was constructed according to principles she had observed during their trip to China back in 1928, and to take advantage of the best views of Mount Diablo.

Carlotta leaned back and sighed, smelling the sweet air and feeling the California sun. How they had both loved Tao House in the first few years. At the top of their hill, with a secure gate limiting access to the property, she had been able to control their little fiefdom completely. Only the invited were admitted, and she was careful about the invitations. Of course, she had to have her mother from time to time, but she was careful to be there when Nellie was talking to Gene and to steer the conversation away from any uncomfortable topics. Cyndy came with her new husband Roy after she moved back to Oakland, and she even helped to type some of Gene's manuscripts, but Carlotta kept the rest of the relatives and local friends from the past away. Frank and Celia Shay had told Nellie that they would love to visit Hazel and meet Eugene O'Neill. Frank thought he would have a real affinity with O'Neill since they had both been to sea when they were young. But Carlotta let it be known that Mr. O'Neill was not to be disturbed while he was at work on a play. And he did work a lot. Not only did he write *Long Day's Journey Into Night*, *The Iceman Cometh*, and *A Moon for the Misbegotten* at Tao House, but much of a cycle of nine plays that he had envisioned as his great masterpiece.

But then had come the War, and the impossibility of holding onto servants. The household staff of four in addition to Freeman dwindled to a series of very unsatisfactory arrangements. Both Freeman, who had been functioning as a butler, and Carlotta were reduced to doing the upkeep of the house and grounds, and there even were periods when Carlotta had to do the cooking. Gene had insisted on keeping chickens, which had been his pets when he was a boy. This turned out to be not a bad idea with wartime rationing, but it fell to Carlotta and Freeman to take care of them. She smiled. It was funny now to think back on herself in an apron, feeding the chickens, but it hadn't been funny then.

It was in the late thirties that Gene's illness had really begun to show, that cursed degenerative brain disease that was always misdiagnosed as Parkinson's, so he received all the wrong treatment for it. The tremor in his hands made it harder and harder for him to write, which made him more and more frustrated and irritable. With all the work, she was irritable herself, and their California version of gracious country-house life dwindled to seemingly endless work and a dreary wartime domestic scene of sniping back and forth and quarreling. When he was unable to write, Gene became obsessed with the war news. He sat night after night listening to the radio, ever more depressed over the state of the world. Carlotta was too tired and depressed herself to do anything about it. They quarreled over things large and small, and both were often ill. When Freeman left to join the Marines, Carlotta felt as though the whole burden of the house had descended on her.

Finally, in 1944, they conceded the inevitable and sold Tao House, moving into the Huntington Hotel on Nob Hill, where they stayed for a year, feeling pent up and irritable as they waited out the war. Then it was back to New York for the premiere of *The Iceman Cometh*. Carlotta knew it was a mistake to stay in the city afterwards. And to make matters worse, O'Neill insisted on renting the haunted penthouse apartment of the recently deceased playwright Edward Sheldon, a grand eminence of Broadway who had lain paralyzed there for twenty years, presiding over an adoring group of acolytes that included Helen Hayes, Katharine Cornell, and John Barrymore. Carlotta thought O'Neill had ideas of becoming the next Ned Sheldon, a notion that chilled her to the bone.

The apartment was too accessible, both to Broadway and to Greenwich Village. Odd types from O'Neill's old days were always turning up looking for a handout, or just sprawling in the living room as if it were a Village bar. As Carlotta had expected, O'Neill was soon drinking heavily again. And in the small world that was the Broadway theater, he was hearing details of her wilder days with Ralph Barton, her early days in the theater, and worse, her relationship with James Speyer.

Dear Papa, as she always thought of James, had died in 1941, leaving her trust fund intact. She knew O'Neill had suspected for a long time that its source was not Aunt Sophie Tharsing, who had died in 1937. Her mother had told her that, when Carlotta was away, O'Neill had come to see her and insisted her nurse companion leave the room while they talked. He had interrogated her about the details of Carlotta's early life, including the source of the money. Nellie said she thought she hadn't given anything away, but Gene could be intimidating, and she didn't have her wits about her as she had when she was younger. Whether it was Nellie or someone in New York, Gene had put two and two together and accused Carlotta of carrying on an affair with James Speyer, before and during their marriage. She denied it, but he returned to this theme whenever he drank, and with her quick temper, escalating fights were inevitable. O'Neill was a mean drunk. Finally, he hit her, and she left. She would have come back eventually, she was sure, if he hadn't fallen and broken his arm.

It was then that his phalanx of friends got involved, interfering in their business. It was what she thought of as the New York conspirators—the Theatre Guild people and that main-chancer Bennett Cerf, who had come to see them in Sea Island when O'Neill's old publisher went bankrupt and talked him into signing with his new venture, Random House. O'Neill signed, a real prize for Cerf, on the condition that that weasel of an editor, Saxe Commins, would come with him. Carlotta hated those two like no one else because they had pretended to be her friends as well as O'Neill's when all they wanted was to get him away from her and in their control. She knew they had tried to talk him into leaving her then, but they hadn't succeeded. O'Neill came back to her, and she took him back on the condition that they get out of New York. They'd moved to the Ritz Carlton in Boston and begun looking for a house.

That was how they ended up in the "cottage" on Point O' Rocks Lane in Marblehead, Massachusetts, her final attempt to make a home for them. It was to be their refuge, a kind of East Coast Tao House, only with the ocean rather than the mountains for company. Gene had always loved the ocean, and he believed that he might be able to write again if he could live close to it, as he had during his early days in Provincetown. The cottage they found was at land's end, actually anchored to the rocks. In a big storm, waves would wash up over the windows. It ended up costing them $85,000 to buy and renovate the small house, which was nothing compared to the earlier ones, but Carlotta made O'Neill's seacoast home the way he wanted it, and he didn't seem to mind taking James Speyer's money to do it.

Carlotta had very quickly come to loathe the Marblehead house. There was not much to show for their money, which had mostly gone into structural reinforcement. Since she'd always been afraid of the water, she did not care for the ocean view, and the sight and sound of the crashing waves in a storm terrified her with the thought that the house would be swept into the ocean. Since they had no driver and no car, they were more isolated there than ever before. They had to call the village taxi to come and get them when they wanted to go anywhere. The neighbors on either side kept to themselves, and the only people she had to talk to for weeks on end were the cook and the maid, the doctor, the postman, and dear Earle, the decorator who had become a personal friend, and would come up from Boston to visit with them for an hour when he could.

Despite his hopes, O'Neill was not able to write, in fact never wrote again after they left California. He read a little and listened to his records, but mostly he sat staring morosely at the ocean. They were both miserable. They quarreled often, and they were both constantly being treated for this or that illness. Since they both had trouble sleeping, they had started taking bromine sedatives regularly. She only learned how dangerous that was when it was too late.

That horrible night. Much as she hated to think of it, it still rushed back on her, an insistent haze of memory. They had been fighting, and O'Neill stormed out of the house without a coat or his cane, tripped on a rock, broke his leg, and lay in the snow. He said later that he had called to her and she'd come to the door and taunted him, refusing to help, but she didn't remember that. She did remember Dr. Mayo arriving, but whether she had called him, or he'd come on his regular house call, she didn't know. He put O'Neill into an ambulance and told her she was in no condition to come with them. She remembered his telling her to stay there and rest. He would call her from the hospital once they knew what state Gene was in. She took a bromine sedative, thinking it would calm her nerves. All she remembered after that was the over-whelming compulsion to get to the hospital. Later, they told her the village policeman had found her wandering along the shore road, thinking she could hail a cab to take her to her husband. They put her in the hospital too and found out that she was suffering from acute bromide poisoning, which was causing her mental and emotional distress. She would never forgive O'Neill for signing a petition to have her committed to a mental hospital. The two horrid months she spent in that place was a time she simply refused to recall.

She knew it was the conspirators who had put him up to it, but still she had never forgiven him. Lawrence Langner from the Theatre Guild and that weasel Saxe Commins had come to Salem and talked O'Neill into going back to New York. They kept him in the hospital there for months, trying to persuade him to leave her, but it didn't work. He always came back to her, and she took him back. When he was well enough, he took a train to Boston to meet her, accompanied by just a nurse.

After they went to live in that little suite in the Shelton Hotel where he could sit watching the boats on the Charles River all day, they never went back to Marblehead, thank God. So that was where O'Neill had died. After all her efforts to make them a perfect home, they had spent their last two years in that cramped little space, with only dear Jean, his nurse and her only confidante, for company.

O'Neill had finally accepted the fact that he would never work again. One day he had told her he was worried that someone would try to produce the unfinished plays in his cycle. He insisted that all the drafts be destroyed. And so they sat all one winter afternoon in front of the fireplace as she tore up the pages, hundreds and hundreds of them, and put them in the flames.

Long Day's Journey Into Night, on deposit at Random House, was finished, he said, and was one of his best plays. He would allow it to be published twenty-five years after his death. She knew he had written that to Cerf, and that it was never to be produced. But he had made her, not Cerf, not Commins, his literary executrix. *Long Day's Journey Into Night* was her property. What's more, she really felt it was their joint creation, the baby they never had. She had suffered the tears and blood as much as he had.

Carlotta had made up her mind. She had wrested the manuscript from Cerf, who had no legal right to it. She would give it to Yale to publish. And she would give it to these three young men to produce. After seeing their *Iceman Cometh*, she knew they had the talent, the understanding, the appreciation of O'Neill's genius, to bring *Long Day's Journey Into Night* to life. It would be the right thing to do, her gift to the world.

Coda

Long Day's Journey Into Night premiered in New York on November 7, 1956 and ran for 390 performances, winning Eugene O'Neill his fourth Pulitzer Prize. It has since been revived five times on Broadway and taken its place in the repertoire of classic plays throughout the world. Many consider it the greatest play written by an American.

Author's Note

Becoming Carlotta is a work of fact-based historical fiction. Public events such as births, marriages, deaths, employment, education, and Carlotta's theatrical career are all a matter of record. The newspaper stories and reviews are real. With the exception of Lili Forbes, Mrs. Graham, Clarisse Huntington, Mabel Glenn and Jane Baird, who are what Henry James would call *ficelles*, characters invented to serve as confidantes for Carlotta, and a few characters who had to be invented for particular scenes, like Dickie Coats, Tom Miller, Jimmy Potter, and Peter Stone, everyone who acts a significant part in this narrative was a real person. Private incidents are mostly invented, sometimes drawing upon family interviews, memoirs, letters, and biographies. Likewise, characterizations are informed by these sources, but they are to a large degree a matter of imagined construction. Conversations and personal letters are all imagined, as are the characters' thoughts. In short, this narrative is a mix of public fact and private fiction. It is not a biography, but a biographical novel, the imagined inner narrative of a life, built upon a base of facts. The act of writing it was an attempt to understand who Hazel Tharsing was, and what it meant for her to become Carlotta Monterey.

Chronology: Hazel Tharsing/ Carlotta Monterey

28 December 1888 Hazel Nielsen Tharsing born in Yuba City, California to Nellie Gotchett Tharsing and Christian Nielsen Tharsing

1893 after bout with malaria, goes to live with aunt and uncle, Mary and John Shay, at 1430 Sixteenth Street, Oakland, California

1895–1900 attends Cole Elementary School in Oakland and Miss Boardman's elocution school

1900–1905 boarding student at St Gertrude's Academy, Rio Vista, California

June 1905 after graduation from St. Gertrude's Academy, lives with mother at Audubon Apartments, 928 Ellis Street, San Francisco; attends Paul Gerson School of Acting and appears in a farce, "The Arabian Nights"

22 February 1906 leaves San Francisco for New York and London

1906–1908 studies singing and acting at Sir Herbert Beerbohm Tree's Academy of Dramatic Arts (later the Royal Academy of Dramatic Art) 62 Gower Street, Bloomsbury, London; lives at 69 Torrington Square, London while taking classes at the Academy

1907 is named Miss California in national beauty contest sponsored by the San Francisco *Call* and other newspapers; 5 May, with travel paid for by the *Call*, arrives in New York from London and goes on to Chicago with mother for beauty pageant finals

1908–1910 boarding student at the *Pensionnat de Mme. Yeatman* in Neuilly-sur-Seine in Paris

1910 returns to London, lives at 27 Welbeck Street, Mayfair

31 March 1911 marries John Moffat in Grace Church, New

York

August 1912 arrives back in New York after visiting Moffat family in Scotland and England

April 1914 files for divorce from John Moffat in Oakland; final notice of summons to John Moffat appears in the *Oakland Tribune* July 1914; Hazel Moffat is listed as "Widow" in 1914 Oakland City Directory

15 March 1915 after assuming stage name of Carlotta Monterey, opens in first Broadway role, as Lucy Gallon in *Taking Chances* with Sarah Bernhardt's leading man, Lou Tellegen; play runs for 85 performances

September 1915–February 1916 stars as Luana in U. S. touring company of *The Bird of Paradise*; tour includes Cleveland, Colorado Springs, Salt Lake City, Sacramento, San Francisco, Los Angeles, San Jose, Portland, Anaconda, Duluth, Kalamazoo, Peoria, Wilkes-Barre, Providence

12 October 1916 marries Melvin Canfield Chapman Jr in Oakland

20 August 1917 birth of daughter, Cynthia Jane Chapman in Oakland

18 June 1918 opens in a minor role in *All Night Long*, which plays in Philadelphia, Asbury Park, and Long Branch; moves to a furnished apartment in the Bronx

9 September 1918 opens as Adelina Bonfanti in *Mr. Barnum*, which runs for 24 performances on Broadway

31 October 1918 opens as Celia Brooke in *Be Calm, Camilla*, which runs for 84 performances on Broadway

1918 signs five-year contract with the Chamberlain and Lyman Brown theatrical agency

18 February 1919 opens as Ilma Harper in *A Sleepless Night* with Peggy Hopkins; play runs for 71 performances on Broadway

30 October 1919 is announced for lead in a new play, "Esther," by Wendell Phillips Dodge; production does not

materialize

1919 plays Pauline Gardiner in the movie *The Cost* (Paramount /Artcraft), based on the David Graham Phillips novel; plans for Carlotta to star in a play by Owen Davis produced by the Shubert brothers fall through; in December, is engaged for "Esther" but plans fall through

1920 lives at 63 W 63rd street, New York; 14 January is announced for lead in "The Trickstress" to be produced by the Shuberts, but play does not materialize;

19 January 1920 opens in vamp role of Olive Gresham in *The "Ruined" Lady*, which runs for 33 performances on Broadway

March 1920 operation Carlotta describes as "emergency appendectomy" in Oakland financed by Lee Shubert

17 May 1920 opens in vamp role of Amy Cary in musical *Page Mr. Cupid* in Brooklyn, also plays in Philadelphia, but closes on the road

5 July 1920 opens as Lakatoola in *The Sacred Bath* in Atlantic City, New Jersey; plays in Long Branch and Buffalo before closing

8 November 1920 replaces Betty Murray as Elaine Gordon in *The Dauntless Three* in Washington; play is announced to open as *The Spider* on 22 November in New York, but closes out of town

14 March 1921 plays lead role of Marcia Kallan in *Nemesis* tryout, but is dropped by George M. Cohan before reaching Broadway

17 May 1921 plays lead role of Geraldine in *Zizi* in Washington, but play closes before reaching Broadway

December 1921 is announced for a role in *Danger*, but is not in the opening night cast

1921 probably after his wife's death in February 1921, Carlotta becomes involved with wealthy New York banker James J. Speyer; he settles an annual income of approximately

$14,000 on her, which continues after his death in 1941

25 February 1922 plays Olga in *Bavu*, which runs for 25 performances on Broadway

21 March 1922 plays Mlle. Clairon in *Voltaire*, which runs for 16 performances on Broadway

17 April 1922 replaces Mary Blair as Mildred Douglas in Eugene O'Neill's *The Hairy Ape* when it moves to Broadway; play runs until 1 July

7 May 1922 meets artist Ralph Barton at a party in Greenwich Village

19 August 1922 is cast for role in "The Star Sapphire," which never materializes

February 1923 plays leading role of Maria Lorenz in *Sold* (*Ladies for Sale*) in Rochester, Syracuse, Baltimore, Washington, and Pittsburgh, where it closes

18 July 1923 opens in *Fashions of 1924*, which runs for 13 perfor-mances on Broadway

September 1923 moves with Ralph Barton to 28 West 47th Street, where they live as a married couple

20 December 1923 opens as Rose Helen Trot in *The Other Rose*, which runs for 84 performances on Broadway

July 1924 plays "a lady devoid of morals" in *The Sable Coat*, Atlantic City

7 October 1924 plays Clarina Prioni in *The Red Falcon*, which runs for 16 performances on Broadway

5 December 1924 plays Germaine in *The Man in Evening Clothes*, which runs for 11 performances on Broadway, her final Broadway role

17 March 1925 marries Ralph Barton in Elkton, Maryland

6 April 1925 arrives with Barton in London, en route to Paris

31 May 1925 the movie *Soul Fire* (First National Pictures/ Inspiration), in which Carlotta plays the Russian Princess Rhea, is released

06 June 1925 arrives in New York from Le Havre after Paris

trip

25 October 1925 *The King on Main Street* (Paramount/ Famous Players/ Lasky), in which Carlotta plays Mrs. Nash, is released

16 February 1926 files for divorce from Ralph Barton; Interlocutory decree is granted on "evidence" of staged adultery committed at Hotel des Artistes

June 1926 becomes involved in a close relationship with Elisabeth Marbury, partner of Eugene O'Neill's agent, Richard Madden; takes over her Sutton Place household and brings order; vacations with Marbury at her summer home in Belgrade Lakes, Kennebec, Maine, where she becomes involved with O'Neill

1926 moves alone to 20 East 67th Street in New York

19 June 1927 leaves for Paris en route to Baden-Baden and other European destinations with James Speyer

9 September 1927 arrives in New York from Europe

Fall 1927 renews love affair with Eugene O'Neill when he comes to New York for the production of *Strange Interlude*

17 February 1928 arrives in Southampton, England with O'Neill; after visiting London and Paris, they settle temporarily in Guéthary, France, and take an extended trip to China

June 1929 moves with O'Neill to the renovated Château Le Plessis in St. Antoine-du-Rocher, near Tours, France

22 July 1929 marries Eugene O'Neill in Paris

17 May 1931 O'Neills arrive in New York and rent a house on Long Island, then move to 1095 Park Avenue

19 May 1931 suicide of Ralph Barton, who leaves a note calling Carlotta his "beautiful lost angel, the only woman I ever loved"

November 1931 O'Neills visit Sea Island, Georgia and decide to build a house there; Carlotta supervises the building of Casa Genotta, finished in June 1932 at a cost of $100,000

January 1932 introduces mother and daughter to O'Neill

1 November 1932 father Chris Tharsing dies in California

November 1936 O'Neills move to Seattle

1937 after selling Casa Genotta at a $25,000 loss, supervises building of new home, Tao House in Danville, California

31 October 1941 death of James Speyer in New York

February 1944 O'Neills sell Tao House at a $40,000 loss and move to Huntington Hotel in San Francisco

October 1945 O'Neills move to New York, staying at the Hotel Barclay until they move into penthouse apartment at 35 East 84th Street

13 February 1946 death of mother Nellie Tharsing in California

January 1948 leaves O'Neill; they are reconciled in March

April 1948 O'Neills move to Boston; Carlotta supervises renovation of house on Point O'Rocks Lane in Marblehead Neck at a cost of $85,000

6 February 1951 after a fight during which O'Neill falls in the snow and breaks his leg, Carlotta is hospitalized as a psychiatric patient with bromide poisoning; O'Neill signs petition alleging that Carlotta is insane and incapable on 23 March; she is released from hospital on 29 March; O'Neill withdraws petition on 23 April

17 May 1951 O'Neills move into the Shelton Hotel on the Charles River in Boston

27 November 1953 death of Eugene O'Neill in Boston

7 November 1956 Broadway premiere of O'Neill's *Long Day's Journey Into Night* under Carlotta's auspices; play runs for 390 performances on Broadway

1956–1968 lives alone at the Hotel Lowell and later the Carlton House in New York

1968 after showing increasing signs of dementia, is admitted to the psychiatric war of St. Luke's Hospital in New York and later transferred to De Witt Nursing Home in New York

July 1970 is transferred to Valley Nursing Home in Westwood,

New Jersey

18 November 1970 dies from arteriosclerotic coronary thrombosis in Westwood

28 November 1970 Carlotta's ashes interred next to O'Neill at Forest Hills Cemetery in Boston

Acknowledgements

I would not have thought of writing this book without the body of facts about Carlotta Monterey and her life that have been amassed by the major biographers of Eugene O'Neill—Louis Sheaffer, Arthur and Barbara Gelb, Robert Dowling and Stephen Black—as well as many scholars of American drama and theater in general and Eugene O'Neill in particular. Margaret Ranald's article, "When They Weren't Playing O'Neill: The Antithetical Career of Carlotta Monterey," has been an indispensable guide to my own research, as has the work of William Davies King, Madeline C. Smith and Richard Eaton. Bruce Kellner's biography of Ralph Barton, *The Last Dandy*, and Donald Gallop's memoir, *Pigeons on the Granite,* have both provided valuable information and insights. Mark Girouard's *Life in the English Country House: A Social and Architectural History* has been a tremendous help in understanding the day-to-day life of the Hay and Moffat families.

My own understanding of Carlotta Monterey is deeply indebted to the letters, diaries, and other material in the Eugene O'Neill Collection of the Beinecke Rare Book and Manuscript Library at Yale, a collection that Carlotta herself began. Louis Sheaffer's excellent notes on his interviews with Carlotta's family and friends, which are in the Sheaffer–O'Neill Collection of the Charles E. Shain Library at Connecticut College, were an invaluable resource for understanding her life in Oakland and later. I'm also indebted to the Huntington Library for copies of the letters from Carlotta to her friend Gene Frances McComas, to the University of Miami Libraries for a copy of the script of *Taking Chances*, to the Mount Holyoke College Library for a copy of John Moffat's novel, *Ray Farley,* and to the Library of Congress for copies of Carlotta's letters to Joseph Wood Krutch. I am also indebted to New York Public Library for the Performing Arts and the University of Connecticut Libraries, whose many historical databases of newspapers and other publications made it possible to research Carlotta's life and theatrical career in detail. The numerous resources available through Ancestry.com were crucial in helping to determine the facts about Carlotta and her family. The cover photo appeared in the San Francisco *Call* in 1907.

My deepest gratitude goes to three very astute readers, Rich Murphy, Laurie Porter, and Pat Murphy, whose insights and advice have been invaluable as I've written and revised Carlotta's story, and, as always, to my husband, George Monteiro, who has been with this project every step of the way.

About the Author

Brenda Murphy is the author of twenty books about American drama and theater, including studies of Eugene O'Neill, Tennessee Williams, Arthur Miller, and American Women Playwrights. *After the Voyage: An Irish American Story* (2016) was her first work of fact-based historical fiction. She taught for more than thirty years at The University of Connecticut and St. Lawrence University, and lives with her husband in Connecticut.